Clouds over BOWLAND

Rosemary Sturge

For my husband, Theo, who upholds me in so many ways...
and to the memory of my friend, Christine Eccleshall, who died
before she got to read it.

ISBN (B format paperback): 978-1-914578-12-0

ISBN (hardback): 978-1-914578-14-4

ISBN (e-book): 978-1-914578-13-7

This is a work of fiction. Names, characters, places and incidents are the product of
the author's imagination, or are used fictitiously. Any resemblance to actual persons,
living or dead, is entirely coincidental.

Cover design by Charlotte Mouncey

Printed and bound in Great Britain by Clays Ltd, Elcograf SpA

Published by Cadence Timepiece, an imprint of Cadence Publishing

www.cadencepublishing.com

Characters

Hugh Armstrong, land agent to Sir John Hathersage
Sir John Hathersage, mill owner and would-be country squire
Lady Lavinia, his wife
James Carr, Sir John's coachman
Elspeth Muir, Hugh's grandmother
Katie, her maid

At Rush Ghyll Farm

Wilfred Hutton, farmer
Lydia, his wife
Their children in age order:
Young Wilf, son
Susannah and Dorcas, twin daughters
Jonathan, son
George, son, currently missing
Isaac, son, away at school
Betsey, daughter

At Lane End farm

Samuel Braithwaite, farmer
Martha, his wife
Nathaniel, their eldest son
Other children: Henry, Joseph, and several others

At High Bield Farm

Matthew Trawden, farmer
Bartholomew (Batty), his brother

At Quernstones Farm

Daniel Jackson, farmer
Philip and Timothy, his sons
Gabriel Waller, drystone wall expert, a distant relative

Staff and inmates of Lancaster Castle (prison)

Mr John Higgins, governor
Jabez Hartley, warder
Luke Johnson, warder
French prisoners of war (not all of them actually French)
Debtors, British, too numerous to mention.

Prologue

Netherdale, Forest of Bowland, Lancashire

January 1814

Their hope had been to find their small flock beneath the drifted snow, huddled together, keeping one another warm and alive, in the lee of an ancient drystone wall. Icy pellets of snow from the distant Arctic whipped across the two men's faces, sharp as the bite of a tawse. They were barely visible, even to one another, bundled up in heavy greatcoats, their heads wrapped in layers of sacking, the winter standby of farmers and shepherds. Bent nearly double against the howling wind, one man prodded ahead with his crook into the drifting snow. The other carried a spade.

'Wall's 'ere somewhere!' the man with the spade mouthed. His words went bowling away over the grey-white fellside in the murky afternoon. His companion nodded without replying and continued to prod.

Then his crook hit something solid.

''Tis the wall, surely,' he said, 'got to be hereabouts.' He staggered closer. The snow had piled up deeper against it, although the land beyond sloped away.

'Aye, but where along 'un?' mumbled the other man. 'Where'd they be?'

'Summat's here,' the first replied, 'under t'wall. Soft like.'

His companion grunted, accepting this without comment. They dropped crook and spade and began scooping at the snow with cowhide-mittened hands.

'A dead un, like as not.'

'Aye.'

They were expecting this. In this bitter cold, the hardiest sheep, even Swaledales and Herdwicks, bred to it, could founder.

A rotting corpse it was. Not a sheep though.

He had been there a while. His britches and coat had perished, as had his features when they scraped away sufficient snow to see. Difficult to tell his age, even, or what manner of man he might have been.

'Seen 'un before?'

'Never. Stranger in these parts.'

'Aye.'

'Can't do owt. Not in this.'

'Reckon he'll keep. Report it, like, when t' weather breaks?'

'T' yon young agent, Mister Hugh Armstrong?'

'Aye. He'd do. Good as any.'

Chapter One

Hugh Armstrong

Early days of April 1814

'Those who are about to die salute you.'

Goodness knows why those words rushed into my mind as I found myself nose to nose with the man with the pistol. My classical education ended abruptly when my father was declared bankrupt by a court in Edinburgh back in 1791. Here I was in lonely Netherdale, fortunate I'd supposed, to be agent to Sir John Hathersage, Lancashire mill owner and would-be country squire. The last thing I had expected was to be shot dead by a Frenchman.

Two Frenchmen. Even as the first man rammed the muzzle of his weapon up against my ribs, a second fellow emerged from behind a rock, flapping his hands. It took me a moment to realise that he was trying to discourage his companion from actually shooting me.

'Non, non!' he cried, holding out a hand and pointing to his palm with the other, 'Gif monies! Not shoot.'

'Money, *non*,' I mimed. My arms were shaking, though I tried to disguise this. I dragged out the pockets of my coat and tipped the contents of my satchel onto the ground, hoping to demonstrate that I spoke nothing but the truth.

That had them bamboozled. The first man turned to his comrade in consternation. Their yellow shirts and patched britches were torn and dirty. It was common knowledge that such clothing was issued to prisoners of war.

The last time I was down in Lancaster, calling for instructions at my employer's townhouse on Castle Hill, I'd glimpsed a bedraggled band of them being unloaded from a cart. I hadn't thought much about it at the time, but passing down the street, I'd overheard someone say, 'Them's Frenchies, being took up ter Scotland.' Why, I now found myself wondering, if these are two of Boney's finest, haven't we yet won this wretched war? Also, what were they doing here in Bowland? *In Netherdale,* of all remote places!

Meanwhile, I posed a problem that they can't have foreseen – that a warmly-dressed fellow on a brisk spring morning might not carry money. I shrugged again, spreading my arms, letting them see my withered left hand. 'No money,' I said, speaking slowly and clearly. I've never learned a word of French beyond 'oui' and 'non.' I spread my arms wider and gestured around us, drawing their attention to our remote surroundings.

The smaller man, the unarmed one, now poked with his booted toe at the contents of my satchel, which lay strewn on the ground. He settled on my luncheon, bread and cheese tied in a linen napkin. My notebook, pencils, pocketknife, map, folding measuring stick, ball of twine, and tool for extracting stones from Polly's hooves, he ignored.

'Can eat?' he demanded, doubtfully examining the unwrapped bread.

'Oui, bread, and cheese,' I said. 'Also, beer.' I indicated the corked bottle.

'Bien. We take.' He grabbed them, nodded to his comrade, and to my astonishment, they immediately set off, running away down the lane without a backwards glance.

'I wonder where they think they're going?' I asked out loud but resisted the temptation to yell, 'Oi! France is that way!'

From higher up the dale, they would have been able to see Morecambe Bay and the Irish Sea. Possibly, they imagined this to be the North Sea coast. Possibly, they didn't care.

I did call, 'Set foot in Lancaster and they'll lock you in the black hole!' A man feels better when he speaks his enemy's doom, senseless as this might seem when the enemy is no longer close enough to hear it.

I'd come upon them, and hence they upon me, in the lowest part of the dale, on the banks of the Nether beck, which purled and chattered close by, quite unconcerned by human dilemmas. After the cruellest of winters, the sides of the dale were greening. Sheep cropped, lambs bleated. A sub-committee of rooks argued in a grove of pine trees which grew on top of a rocky outcrop.

There was no visible human habitation in this part of the dale. I knew, but hoped the Frenchmen did not, that Rush Ghyll and High Bield farms lay higher up, hidden from here by the folds of the Bowland fells.

Regretting my luncheon, I scooped up my scattered belongings and walked as far as the little hump-backed bridge over the river. There, I sat down on its rough stone parapet. My breath, to my annoyance, was still coming in gasps, and my left arm shook violently, defying my attempts to hold it still. 'Stop it!' I hissed, hugging the arm across my chest. My bane.

My grandmother and her friends had shaken their heads over it. 'A difficult time she had, poor Effie,' they used to say of my mother, 'but it's the lad's left arm, praise the Guid Lord, so he'll no' suffer tae much.' Little did they know what a bairn can suffer.

Little, I thought bitterly, did the 'Guid Lord' care. I was jeered at by school fellows, and my older brothers called me a coward because I could not fight back. My left arm was near useless, and shook uncontrollably at the smallest upset.

Perhaps those rogues had escaped from a party headed for north of the border. Grandma had written to me of a new and commodious prison being built in Perth – did she say? – to house prisoners of this never-ending war. The government was intent on dispersing them as far from the English Channel as could be managed.

A pied wagtail, bright of eye, landed on the opposite parapet and began to walk up and down, his tail jerking energetically, head swivelling from side to side as he seemed to study me. That forced a smile from me. I breathed deeply and felt calmer.

Today, I hadn't shown my fear. Those men hadn't shot me. Yet, whenever an upset occurred, I felt again like that terrified child cowering beneath the kitchen table as my father rampaged through the house, lashing out at anyone who stood in his way.

I was no longer in Scotland, and my father was in prison in Dundee. I had left all that behind forever. I had work here in Lancashire. I had responsibilities.

'So, what should I do first?' I asked the bird. 'I'll need to report this to someone. There could be more of these fellows, escaped from some troop of prisoners and hiding out up here in the braes – *fells*. Do I go first to my employer, Sir John? Or to warn his tenants?'

With no advice to give, the wagtail flew off. The Nether Beck gushed and gurgled through clumps of reeds. A pair of white chested dippers plunged beneath its waters and re-emerged further downstream.

I must, of course, inform Sir John Hathersage, but before I went stravaiging down into Lancaster, seven miles away, surely it would be prudent to know if there were other escaped prisoners hereabouts. I needed to be able to assure him that his tenants were safe, on the lookout and primed to inform me of anything untoward.

Rush Ghyll and High Bield. I would walk up to those farms. Warn them. Ask if they had seen any strangers hanging about. Nesting in their barns, or stealing food from kitchens or dairies. Having a plan of action further soothed my spirits, but it meant a stiff climb.

'Oh, well,' I said aloud, 'best foot forward. Bother ye, Polly!'

Polly, my elderly fell pony, had caught her foot in a rabbit hole the previous week and strained her left foreleg, but now I rather suspected the old girl of malingering. I couldn't entirely blame her for feigning lameness. All through the cold of winter, she'd been mewed up in her stable. With the thaw, she had the freedom of the paddock at home and was able to munch on sweet new grass. Until my encounter with the prisoners, I hadn't thought I'd need her. I'd been bound only a short distance up the dale to inspect the place where the riverbank had been undercut by the rushing force of meltwater. That must now wait at least until the morrow.

As I shouldered my satchel and set off tramping up the rough track to Rush Ghyll, sunbeams fell across my shoulders, the first real warmth I'd felt in months.

I'd taken up my post the previous November, before one of the harshest winters in many a year had set in. It had been as severe here in Lancashire as any I'd known in Fife. Those seven miles down into Lancaster had been impassable. No, not quite impassable – a small band of the older farm lads had made it on two occasions, with sledge and spade, bringing back vital supplies to this remote dale. They had brought a letter from my grandmother, telling me that my father still languished in gaol.

Scotland, too, had suffered severe weather, which had delayed his trial.

I'd sent letters with the same boys to Sir John, dreading that he might consider I should have taken to a sledge myself, but his replies seemed only concerned that I should collect his rents as soon as possible.

'You won't have any trouble with my tenants in a general way,' he'd assured me, when I first took up my position, 'on account of they're all Quakers.'

I must have looked surprised. (We do not, so far as I know, have any of that persuasion in Fife.) Sir John had laughed and said, 'a stern, joyless sect to my mind, but they're good farmers, and they're honest to a fault.'

I made no comment. What others chose to believe was their business as long as they do not expect me to share it. Religion and I fell out a long time ago.

The friend who had recommended me for the post had warned me that the dates of quarter days in England differ from those in Scotland. So, when no money was offered to me at the end of November, I knew to wait until December 25th.

However, by this time, the whole dale was snowed in. Thus, I didn't expect anything until after the thaw, but, towards dusk on the first day of the new year, one of the sledge lads, face muffled in scarves and wearing several coats, arrived at my door with four money bags – rent for the farms in the district leased from Sir John Hathersage. With them, he handed over a box of provisions, which some kind soul had realised that I might need.

I'd greeted the lad heartily, having seen no other human being for over a week. 'My first footer – and bringing me coin too, which presages good fortune for the year ahead!'

The laddie stared at me blankly. First footing, I was to discover, is a custom not much honoured on this side of the border.

By the next quarter day, at the end of March, the snow was retreating up the fellsides. The same lad returned astride a rough-coated pony. This time, he dropped the money bags at the gate as soon as he saw me. Then he rode off with a wave of his hand, but never a word.

Words here were a problem – in a way I hadn't anticipated. My Lowland Scots speech seemed as alien to these people as their Lancashire dialect was to me.

I'd had much to learn, almost a new language, I reflected, as I trudged up the track towards Rush Ghyll.

'A dale is a glen. A beck is a burn. A fell is a brae, and a lile 'un's a bairn,' I chanted under my breath.

Whit rubbish! said the voice of the poet in my head. Why, I asked myself, could Robbie Burns compose so sweetly at the plough tail or on his morning walk, when all I seemed able to summon up was doggerel?

Chapter Two

Hugh

Rush Ghyll farm was set over and beyond a steep rise in the ground. Just below it, the fellside was split by a deep, narrow ghyll, a miniature gorge, from which it took its name. After winter snow and rain, this struggled to contain a roaring torrent, but today in the spring sunshine, the water trickled over the rocks, amidst the first grey-blue leaves of the new season's water mint.

The farmhouse itself stood in a shallow green hollow, which gave it some shelter from the winds. These blow equally in from the Irish Sea and the Atlantic beyond, or come roaring through the Trough from the East. The Trough of Bowland, should you happen to be unfamiliar with this region, is a pass running through the Pennine hills. It creates an easy transfer (in good weather) for drovers and merchants transporting their animals and goods from Lancashire into Yorkshire or vice versa. Cattle thieves and poachers too, of course, but happily, I had found these less common here than up beyond the border.

I paused to catch my breath and look back. How lovely this glen, this *dale* looked, now spring was finally here. The fellside showed the new tendrils of bracken, and the silver glint of the becks. It was quite comparable to the Ochil hills. I was still trying to convince my grandmother, Fife-born and bred like me, of this.

She kept to her belief that Lancashire was entirely covered in cotton mills. 'Whit is there for an agent tae do there?'

There were no towering cotton mills in Bowland, just small villages, hamlets, and isolated farms. I had described all this in a letter, but Grandma made no reference to it in her reply.

Now, Rush Ghyll farm was before me. The farmhouses here were of no particular beauty, square and solid, built of gritstone and slate, their windows small and set deep against the weather. The dip in the ground before this one formed a natural 'garth' as the local parlance has it, and this was surrounded by a drystone wall. Several orphaned lambs gambolled within this sheltered spot, and the grass was starred with primroses and small wild daffodils. A lovely sight.

To one side of the farmhouse stood the barn, the cow byre, and pens for livestock, as well as a gig, several carts, a plough, a stack of hurdles, and all the bits and pieces that any farm, anywhere under the sun, has to store. Everything here was neat and in its place.

On the other side of the house, two women and a small girl were busy spreading out the results of their washday on roughly tamed bushes.

I walked past, pretending I hadn't seen them. My employer had introduced me briefly to Wilfred Hutton, the farmer, but I'd never met his womenfolk. The notion of meeting them for the first time, surrounded by their freshly laundered shifts and underbodices, made me acutely uncomfortable. I veered towards the farmyard, hoping to find Hutton.

To reach this, I had to pass a small outbuilding, open to the morning air. I could hear the clanking of a bucket and a voice within. So, I paused, hand on the doorframe, to peer into the gloomy interior.

As my eyes adjusted to the darkness, I saw somebody dressed in a dirty old coat, far too large, fiercely bound in place with knotted rope. It took me a moment to realise this was a young woman holding a weakly looking calf. She dipped her hand into a bucket of milk and allowed the animal to suck from her fingers.

'Yes?' She turned her head to stare at me with wide grey eyes. She looked like a youthful witch; her hair so carelessly tied that several locks had drifted over her face.

'Err, good morning, Miss. Hugh Armstrong, Sir John Hathersage's agent. Could you tell me where I might find the farmer?' I didn't know how better to frame this request, being unsure whether she was a farm servant or a daughter of the house.

'Papa's round in the yard,' she replied, her voice colourless, 'they're fixing the cart.'

That was it. No salutation, no further explanation. She turned her attention back to the calf. Mildly affronted, I walked away, thinking the witch had beautiful eyes if nothing else to recommend her.

Skirting the barn, I entered the farmyard, where I found two men and a black and white collie. The younger man was fixing a wheel to a four-person dogcart whilst the older one and the dog looked on gravely. They all three turned their heads as I entered their line of sight.

'Good morning!' I recognised the older man now as Farmer Hutton.

Wilfred Hutton nodded pleasantly enough, but he didn't bow. The lad fixing the cartwheel half stood, holding the wheel in place. His expression was strained, as any man's might be, when he fears he'll be forced to drop everything and have to start his task over.

Farmer Hutton made no move to shake my hand. I wasn't sure whether to offer it. Sir John, a bluff and hearty fellow, shook his tenants by the hand whether they wished it or not. Wilfred Hutton, however, was a Quaker. I had a vague notion that they disdained this form of greeting. The lad resembled him to a high degree and was presumably his son.

'Good morrow to thee,' Wilfred Hutton said. 'How may we be of service on this fine spring morning?'

'It-it's not so much that I require your service, b-but I have had an unpleasant encounter, and would wish to warn you and your family.'

Wilf Hutton's grizzled eyebrows lifted, 'Then let us go indoors and let me hear this warning.'

He nodded to the lad to continue in his work, and we left the yard for a side door to the farmhouse. I had learned that this was common throughout the North. Farming families, always conscious of the state of their boots, made more use of it than the ceremonial front entrance. The dog, which had risen to its feet, must have decided this was no business of his, yawned widely and sat down again.

Wilfred Hutton led me down a narrow passage and into what was, to me, a most enviable room with a sturdy desk and two up-right chairs. My eyes fastened on the bookshelves lining two sides of it, stuffed with a goodly number of books and pamphlets. A window showed a view of the farmyard so that he could keep his eye on anyone working there. This must be his office, where he conducted business, paid his bills, and interviewed farm visitors such as myself. I made an inward vow to create such a 'snug' for myself at Low Bield, the rather bleak cottage my employer had assigned to me.

'Take a seat, lad,' said the farmer. I briefly wondered whether I ought to insist on '*Sir*.' As his agent, I needed to be respected by Sir John Hathersage's tenants, but I doubted if he was being deliberately insolent, so I obeyed.

'I haven't spoken to anyone about this yet,' I began, 'as it happened less than half an hour ago. The fact of the matter is, I was held at gunpoint by a couple of rogues. I believe they must be escaped French prisoners of war.'

Farmer Hutton made no exclamation of surprise. He reminded me, suddenly, of the wagtail I'd encountered at the bridge, watching me, his head cocked, his eyes intent.

I continued. 'Obviously, I must inform the authorities, and Sir John Hathersage, of course, as soon as possible. But my first concern was to warn you and your family, and also the people up at High Bield. You've none of you seen any such fellows hanging about? You've discovered nothing missing around the farm? Or any sign of people sleeping rough in your outbuildings?'

'Thee's had a nasty experience,' Farmer Hutton said. 'It'll have shook thee up. These men didn't fire the pistol, I take it?'

'No, and I have no idea whether it contained bullets or not,' I admitted, 'but I didn't care to take the chance.'

'Wise of thee,' approved the man before me. '*I've* seen nought of any such, and I'm sure my wife and children would have spoken to me of it if anything had gone missing. But tha can ask them.'

The inner door creaked open, and a small girl peeped into the room.

'Yes, Betsey?'

'Papa?' said this moppet – I judged she was about eight or nine years of age. She had tightly braided pigtails and was gazing at me with her father's bright grey eyes. 'Mama says, if thee pleases, is the visitor to eat with us?' 'Someone new!' her expression said.

Farmer Hutton turned to me, 'We take our midday broth about now. 'Would thee care to join us?'

I remembered my stolen bread and cheese. 'I'd be pleased to meet your wife and your sons and daughters,' I said. 'It could be that they have noticed something of these men I was telling you about.'

We followed little Betsey as she skipped ahead of us to the farm kitchen. This was a square, low-beamed room with a window looking out over the upper slopes of the dale. Bacon flitches and bunches of dried mint, lavender, and sage hung from the beams, and I had to duck my head to avoid them. (I'm a tall fellow in comparison to these short, sturdy dales folk.)

'My wife, Lydia.' My host nodded to a small woman with streaks of silver through her dark hair. She stood at the end of the scrubbed wooden table, stirring a ladle around a pan of steaming broth, plain white bowls piled up in front of her.

'This is Hugh Armstrong, Hathersage's agent,' Wilfred Hutton said, awarding neither me nor Sir John an honorific. His wife nodded and smiled, but didn't bob a curtsey as I might have expected.

The young fellow I'd seen mending the cart was wiping his hands on a rough towel. Another lad of perhaps fourteen years was waiting his turn. I thought I recognised him as the youth who had twice collected the rents for the four farms in the dale and brought them to me. Before I could make up my mind on this point, however, two young women, the daughters of the house, appeared and took their places at the table. One was the girl I had seen feeding the calf. She had shed the filthy coat, tidied her dark hair into a neat knot at the nape of her neck and added a plain white cap. She'd missed a streak of dirt on one side of her face. I hoped she'd washed her hands.

It was the other girl who took my breath away. She was a beauty. Her brown hair, plaited into a coronet around her head, possessed highlights of copper. Her pale grey gown showed off her slender shape.

'My daughters,' said my host. 'Betsey, thee has already met. To thy left is Dorcas, and to thy right, Susannah.' I turned and made a small bow to each of the young women. Dorcas did not react. Susannah smiled at me. 'The lads are Wilf, my eldest, and Jonathan. Shall we be seated and give thanks to the Lord for what we are about to receive?'

We sat. The girls on either side of me folded their hands in their laps and bowed their heads. I did likewise, expecting that the older Wilf, the paterfamilias, would intone some prayer. However, apart from the stately ticking of a clock on the wall, silence prevailed.

'Of course,' thought I, 'I am amongst Quakers, and of the silent persuasion. I wonder how long this praying lasts.'

It seemed like a long time. I was no friend to Religion. My father practised as a minister before the old hypocrite suffered his great and terrible fall from grace. I'd eaten little in the way of breakfast, and the prisoners had stolen my lunch. If my thoughts could be called a prayer, it was that this period of silence would soon end and my stomach would hold its peace.

Chapter Three

Hugh

At last, Wilfred Hutton raised his head, and the family turned to look expectantly at Lydia, who, wielding a deft ladle, began to serve the broth. The two older girls rose and made themselves busy passing bowls and placing plates of fresh-cut bread and butter before us. All the crockery was plain white, solid, and unadorned, but the food was plentiful. Dorcas gave her father a part-cut round of cheese on a wooden platter, and he carved thick slices.

The broth was delicious, and all the more so because my portion was handed to me, with an entrancing smile, by the delightful Susannah. Young Wilf passed me bread, and Dorcas took a knife and laid a slice of cheese on my plate without touching it. Her hands appeared to be clean, for which I was grateful.

'What did thee pray about?' a small voice demanded from across the table, and the eager eyes of little Betsey pinned mine. Without, fortunately, waiting for an answer, she went on, '*I* prayed that we shall have a fine First Day in four weeks for Susannah's wedding,' she said, 'Although Mama says it must be as the Lord wills. But I do so hope He will allow it, because Sukie's gown is *so* beautiful, and Mama and Dorcas and I are to have new gowns too! It would be sad to have them spoiled by the rain, does thee not think? Oh, and I asked the Lord to make thy poor hand better,' she added, nodding towards my twisted left hand with which I was attempting to steady the bowl of broth.

Various members of the family clucked and shushed Betsey, and her father shook his head at her. 'Now, Betsey, thou must not speak disrespectfully to our guest. Still thy busy tongue and eat thy broth. Let our friend eat in peace, for he has had a disquieting experience which he will tell us about presently.' This pronouncement quieted the child but caused all the other members of the family to turn towards me.

Crushing my sense of disappointment that beauteous Susannah was already promised to another, I said, 'About an hour ago, I was down by the burn – I mean the beck – close to the bridge, when I was set upon by two men in ragged yellow clothing. One of them had a pistol, the muzzle of which he pressed to my chest. I believe, from the way they spoke – or attempted to speak – that they must be escaped prisoners. Frenchmen.'

Before I could say more, the irrepressible Betsey exclaimed, 'Did they steal thy money? Had they fought with our George?'

'Betsey!' scolded her mother, 'thee *must* learn to guard thy tongue, indeed thee must.'

'No, they didn't steal my money because I had none,' I said. 'All I had was my luncheon tied in a cloth. They took that. Why do you think your George might have fought them?'

There was an in-drawing of breath around the table. Betsey seemed to understand that now she really had said something she should not have, and hung her head.

An uncomfortable silence now prevailed. Somehow, I seemed to have offended in responding to the child. Unable to say anything to ease the situation, I concentrated on swallowing the excellent broth. These people might live plainly, as I had heard the Quakers did, all of them dressed in sombre shades, but they didn't stint themselves of good food.

Wilfred Hutton steered us out of the morass by asking his family, as I had hoped he would, whether any of them had seen any sign of strangers about the farm. Everyone shook their heads.

'Tha thinks them Frenchies?' asked Young Wilf, who had been silent until now. 'Could be off the Duke's land, happen? Put to work, like?'

Everyone's eyes, including mine, now fastened on Young Wilf. He blushed and stammered, 'Happen not, but folk were speaking of it, when Ah were down in t' market last fifth day.'

'On Buccleuch's land?' prompted his father.

'So t'was being said. Does tha think it could be?' Young Wilf asked me.

'I hadn't thought of that, but you might be right,' I said.

He had made a useful point. Large sections of the old royal hunting Forest of Bowland belong either to the Crown or His Grace the Duke of Buccleuch, and what those worthies choose to do on their land is not for mere mortals like me (or Sir John Hathersage, for that matter) to question. The Huttons' scorn to speak of the Duke by his title would certainly have caused that nobleman considerable offence. However, the family were feeding me, and feeding me lavishly. I didn't feel it was up to me to correct them.

'Why, what would such men be doing there?' Lydia Hutton enquired; her ladle poised to dish out second helpings.

'Work gangs?' mused Wilfred Hutton, 'that could be. As our Friend John Ford said at last Quarterly Meeting, is it not better that prisoners should be given useful work than be held in overcrowded cells with no occupation? Even Dukes, I fancy, would not be averse to free labour if they could get it.'

'But Papa, what could they do?' Dorcas, my hitherto silent neighbour, suddenly asked.

'Clear ditches, clear grazing land of rocks, or walling, likely.'

'Would they know how, Papa? Frenchmen?'

'Happen they can learn,' said her brother.

'It would seem the two I encountered didn't care to,' I said, 'and had escaped, probably hoping to find a ship to take them somewhere. America perhaps.' I'd now had time to think about this. My attackers might have had a more reasoned plan for their escape – and a better sense of geography – than I'd credited them with.

'Martinique, Guadeloupe, French West Indies,' suggested Wilf Hutton the elder. 'They might well try for that. Ships for the Indies still trade out of Lancaster, even though *that* trade, God be praised, has ceased at last. Although there are some,' and here he looked around sternly at his own family, 'who fail to see the harm. Even amongst those who sit amongst us on the benches on First Day. Cotton. Sugar. All produced by enslaved negro people, and bought and sold for profit in Lancaster by people who should know better.'

He might live on an isolated farm, but Wilfred Hutton was well informed. I should have guessed that from his book-lined study. He might not be worldly himself, but worldly events did not pass him by.

I'd been horrified to learn that my employer's father had made his money from the transportation of African slaves. True, Sir John no longer plied that evil trade, but he wouldn't have his cotton mill in Preston, or be building a fine new house at the foot of the dale, or employing me as his agent, but for the profits his father had accrued. Would I have stayed, much as I needed a wage, if I'd discovered his son to be a slaver still? I hoped not.

Made uncomfortable by these thoughts, I turned to Susannah and said, 'Ma'am, may I facilitate you on your forthcoming nuptials? Am I to understand that the happy day will be quite soon?'

Polite, correct, but meaningless. As the words left my mouth, I realised how ridiculous I sounded amongst these plain speakers.

Susannah, however, received them with a sunny smile, 'on the second First Day in Fifth Month at our Meeting,' she said, 'I thank thee for thy kind wishes.'

Rapid mental calculation told me that Fifth Month must be the one we ordinary folk call May. 'Do I know the fortunate fellow?'

She seemed somewhat confused by this, but her mother answered, dryly, 'Nathaniel Braithwaite from Lane End. Thee will know the farm.'

I did indeed. A large one, situated at the foot of the dale, and more prosperous than this. Susannah, I thought, was doing well for herself, and with her charming face and manners, who could wonder at it?

'Are you looking forward to having your own kitchen and dairy? Your own household to manage? I couldn't bring myself to attempt this 'theeing' and 'thouing,' although here 'you' felt awkward too.

Susannah blushed prettily. 'Oh, as to that, I suppose I will help where I can, but Martha Braithwaite, Nathaniel's mother, is still very hale, and Nat spends more time at the silk mill now than on the farm. His father and brothers can manage without him. He is looking about for a house for us in Lancaster.'

'And how will you like living in town?' I asked, masking my surprise. I wondered what Sir John would think of these social aspirations. Farmers' sons buying their way into mill ownership? Whatever next! But a silk mill explained Susannah's wedding gown. Nathaniel Braithwaite sounded an ambitious young fellow, confident of success. How I envied him.

'I think I shall like it very well,' said artless Susannah. 'I liked it when Dorcas and I attended the Friends School, and boarded with Rachel and Eliza Stout.'

Dorcas pulled a face. Her memories of town life – or school life – were evidently less happy.

'Although tha was no scholar,' chuckled Susannah's father. 'Dorcas got more from her schooling than ever thee did. I wasted my guineas there. Thee will have to study henceforth, to keep thy household accounts, Sukie.'

Susannah primmed her pretty lips at this and said, 'Oh, Nat knows how I detest arithmetic, so I daresay he will help me if I get into a muddle – or Mama and Dorcas will come visiting now and then and put me straight.'

There was gentle, affectionate laughter around the table. It appeared that Susannah, though as lovely and fragrant as Mr Wordsworth's 'violet by a mossy stone,' was not clever. Ah well, I thought. One cannot have everything. Would it be enough to have that lovely face smiling at one across the breakfast table, whilst knowing that the local tradesmen might be cheating one, right, left and centre? It seemed, for Nathaniel, it would.

It was Lydia Hutton who brought the conversation back to my morning's misadventure. 'So, what will thee do about these Frenchmen?' she asked. I sensed that she hadn't appreciated my complimenting Susannah. Did she fear I would make the girl vain? Or unsettle a lass on the brink of matrimony?

Full of broth, fresh-baked bread, and homemade cheese, my ruffled feelings eased, and I was ready to be magnanimous. If it had not been for the pistol, I might have been inclined to forget the whole incident.

'I'll write to Sir John. He will be the best person to raise the matter with the other landowners. What I cannot understand is how they came to be in this dale. It comes from no great place and leads to none.'

Around the table, heads were shaken. No one had suggestions to make.

'I'll walk up to High Bield this afternoon,' I said, 'in case they've seen anyone hanging about there.'

'If tha thinks it worthwhile,' said Wilfred Hutton. 'They're a strange pair, the Trawden brothers. Maybe they would take note of strangers about their place, or maybe not.'

The meal over, there was another, shorter, period of silent thanksgiving. Then, somewhat to my surprise, it was Lydia Hutton who doffed her apron and offered to show me 'the short way' up the hill to High Bield. 'The girls will clear the meal,' she said. 'I've been back and forth between the washtub and the range all morning, and I find myself in need of a breath of air.'

Was there something she was loath to tell me in front of her husband and children? I wondered what it could be.

Chapter Four

Hugh

We walked, side by side, through the orchard, where plump hens pecked beneath the budding apple trees, amongst straggling leaves of snowdrops now faded and gone. I tried to thank her for the box of provisions which I now realised she'd sent to me back in January, but she waved this away.

'These Frenchmen with their pistol? How long, Hugh Armstrong, does thee think these men have been on the loose in Bowland? Days? Weeks? Months?'

I answered that I did not know. 'Months, I'd very much doubt, Ma'am. The weather has been so severe throughout the winter that they could hardly have survived. They were poorly clad.'

'Then it cannot be them, God be thanked. I was fearful, for a moment, when thee spoke of them, that they might have killed George, but I see my thought was foolish. Thee heard Betsey speak of her brother, George. He has been gone since Tenth Month – October, as thou wouldst call it.

'I gathered he is no longer at home?'

'He disappeared.' She clutched at the top rail of the wicket gate that led out onto the moor. 'My husband and young Wilf believe he may have taken the King's shilling and gone for a soldier, but we don't *know*.' Then she continued, 'He was restless, dissatisfied with his life of late. He told Young Wilf once he was minded to enlist and go and quarrel with Frenchmen, who could not be worse than his brother. I thought it was just childish irritation – that he'd said it to anger Wilf, who'd set him a task he disliked. I could not believe he would really do such a thing.' She paused, breathing hard in her distress, her knuckles white against the greying wood of the gate, as she gazed out over the rising moor beyond. 'It's against our beliefs, thee must understand, to engage in any fightings or outward strivings.'

I nodded. This much I did know.

'Thee goes about the Trough, Hugh Armstrong,' she went on, turning to look me in the eye, 'and meets with all sorts – farmers, travellers, drovers, packmen. Does thee know – has thee heard – have there been any youths pressed for the navy in these dales? Or taken for the army by the recruiting sergeants?'

'I haven't heard of any such,' I said, 'and you are well known to be a Quaker family. They could not *legally* press your son for either the army or the navy. Quakers and Catholics are acknowledged to be exempt.'

She nodded. 'But mistakes are sometimes made?'

'I suppose that *could* happen. Someone told me there *is* a recruiting sergeant for the Lancashire Regiment of Foot based at the Militiaman Inn in Lancaster. Has your husband enquired there?'

'Yes, but the man denied he'd ever set eyes on George. Wilfred didn't think he was being untruthful.'

It occurred to me that there must also be naval men on the lookout for youths to press around Lancaster docks. Had George strayed down there?

Evidently, Lydia had thought of this herself. 'George never came back to us from Yorkshire, so he surely never went on down into Lancaster. Perhaps he really has volunteered, taken the King's shilling, as they say.' She sighed.

'He'd been over into Yorkshire?' I prompted.

'Yes, he should have been on his way back, coming through the Trough by the second week of Tenth Month. However, none of the families we know between here and Gisburn, on the Yorkshire side, have seen him.'

'I see. He went through the Trough into Yorkshire on some business for his father?'

I was imagining a youth driving a small flock of sheep, or going to fetch a couple of heifers, Wilfred Hutton might have bought in Slaidburn livestock market. But it seemed this was not the case.

'No, he went with his brother, Isaac, to take him to school. Isaac is twelve years old. George is fifteen now. We thought it a good opportunity for him to show what a sensible lad he could be, taking charge of his little brother. An adventure for them both.

'You felt you could trust him?'

'They were not to make the whole journey alone. At least two other families we know were taking their children to the school. George and Isaac were to meet up with them and walk together. As we know they did. After he saw his brother settled, George was to return with them as far as Newton-in-Bowland.'

'But he didn't?'

'They say not. He set out with them as far as Leeds, where they all stayed at an ale house – Wilfred had given George funds to pay his way – but when the others rose in the morning, he was gone. They never saw him again. Robert Topham, who farms by Newton, told us he thought George might have slept poorly because the inn was filled with noisy revellers. Perhaps he rose early and set out to explore the town. They expected to meet up with him along the way, but never did. Robert told Wilfred he thought the lad must have hitched a ride on a cart, and so got too far ahead for them to catch up.'

'*Leeds*? Where is this school? They *walked* from here to beyond Leeds?'

'Yes, to Ackworth Friends' School,' she replied calmly. 'It's close by Pontefract. Perhaps you wouldn't know that place? My husband calculated it's about one hundred and sixty miles from here. That would be four or five days' walking if the weather stayed fair. A fine adventure for the two of them. It was not as if they were travelling alone. Other families and their youngsters were with them. On the return journey, the parents were with George until he left them at Leeds.'

I knew these hill farmers were hardy folk, but I was still amazed by the idea that a twelve-year-old and a fifteen-year-old had walked one hundred and sixty miles, and the older one had almost immediately set out to do the journey in reverse.

'And your younger boy is safe at the school?'

'Thanks be to God,' she said. 'Wilfred wrote to the superintendent. He told us he had questioned Isaac, asking if his brother had said anything to him, which gave the impression that he planned not to return, but Isaac said no. The superintendent reported that Isaac is well settled and they have high hopes for him.'

I could now think of a myriad of things which might have befallen George, the most likely being that some Recruiting Officer had laid hands on him as he walked alone through the streets of Leeds, a town where he would be a stranger. Would the boy have been believed there if he said he was a Quaker and exempt? I thought it unlikely.

I had seen accounts in the newspapers of angry skirmishes in the streets in some of the mill towns on *this* side of the Pennines. Men and youths had been bundled into carts to be taken off to serve in the army in the Peninsula. In vain did they protest that they were serving their country by producing cloth for army officers' shirts. Once the army got hold of them, they were destined to be cannon fodder. This might well have been what happened to George Hutton.

'The Friends' Day School in Lancaster is good in its way,' she told me. 'We sent the others there for as long as seemed necessary for them to pick up reading, writing, and reckoning – but the Friends' School at Ackworth has gained a reputation for teaching all branches of these new sciences, which our Isaac very much wanted to study. So, we decided to send him, despite the expense,' she sighed. 'I would have loved to have given Dorcas a similar chance, but we just couldn't see our way to it.'

What I'd seen of Dorcas hadn't suggested that she aspired to be what my brothers would have called a 'blue stocking'. Her mother might never have heard this disparaging term used of learned women who had their noses perpetually in books.

Lydia Hutton must have sensed my surprise, because she told me, 'We *Quakers*, as thee calls us, believe in equality for men and women. But alas, girls do marry and have children, and so it is difficult to justify a lengthy education, for even the cleverest girl.'

'Ma'am,' I said, as she loosened her hold on the wicket gate and swung it open for me to pass through, 'I'm sorry not to be able to give you any comfortable news of your boy. I'll certainly keep my eyes and ears open as I go about the district. If I hear anything of use, I'll be sure to let you know.'

Chapter Five

Hugh

High Bield was the highest situated and most remote farm in the dale. My own dwelling, down in the valley, was named Low Bield and sometimes confused with it. As I climbed, the land grew bleaker, and both the soil and the sheep that grazed over it, thinner. However, these sheep were Swaledales, bred for their meat as well as their wool. Many had lambs at foot, and even after such a hard winter, their condition was probably better than their bedraggled fleeces suggested.

The sun still shone, but clouds were rolling in from the Irish Sea. At this height, the views over the lower dale and out to the ocean caught my breath, but a sharp wind plucked at my hat, sending it bowling away. After chasing it amongst the thorn bushes, I was discouraged from pausing to admire the scene further. Here and there, patches of the limestone pavement had broken through the turf, and amongst these 'clints and grikes', a few bright pink flowers bloomed. Tiny bird's eye primroses, rare blossoms. I gazed on them in admiration, but poetic inspiration? Alas, none was granted to me.

Then, a shout from above made me raise my head. High Bield farmhouse squatted on an open slope, where it must be scoured by every wind that blew. Similar in construction to Rush Ghyll, it nevertheless seemed less welcoming even than the cramped cottage that served as my home.

'Bield' is a common enough name in Scotland too, and can mean a dwelling, or just a group of farm buildings where animals are kept. I think my grandmother, on being told my address, imagined me being forced to dwell in some half-ruined shelter for sheep and cattle. Just what she would expect of the English, in fact.

No trees or bushes thrived at High Bield. Unlike Rush Ghyll, there was no walled garth, orchard, or drying ground. Instead, around it were humped untidy piles of useless or broken farm gear.

Growing closer, I heard a man's voice crying out in anger and alarm, and then, to my dismay, the sound of a shotgun being discharged rattled across the moor.

Cursing myself for a fool – who but one of these rushes towards the sound of gunfire when he knows himself to be unarmed and part-cripple to boot? – I hurried over the rough patch of grazing land and up a short slope to where I could see the front of the farmhouse. Before me on the ground, a man clutched at his leg, two sheepdogs crouched beside him, yowling at the sky. There were more distant howls from someone running away over the brow of the next hill.

I squatted at the injured one's side. 'What happened, man?'

'Nothing,' he grunted. ''Tis only buckshot. I'd a dispute with our Batty.'

'Batty?'

'Me brother. Our Batty. Bartholomew, that is, t' give 'im 'is Sabbath Day name.'

'Your brother shot you?' I asked, aghast.

'Nae, man, nae. 'Twas an accident,' He sat up, commanding the dogs, 'Stop that! Belt up, won't yer!' The dogs ceased their noise and licked their chops. The howls from the man in the distance had lessened too.

'But you're injured!'

'Nae, told tha, 'tis only shot pellets. Couple o' pellets in me leg. I'll dig 'em out in a tick. Dogs don't like me and Batty argufying. Happen they don't know which side to tek.' He hauled himself to his feet, apparently unconcerned. 'Tha'd be t' new agent? Mister Hugh Armstrong? Matthew Trawden at tha service. What can ah do for tha?'

'I came about the Frenchmen – some escaped prisoners – in case you might have seen them hereabouts?'

'Ain't seen a soul save our Batty, and too much o' he! Never seen a Frenchman in me life that I knows of. How many? What did them look like?'

'There were two of them. They wore the uniforms they're issued with as prisoners of the war, yellow in colour but dirty and ragged. One of them had a pistol.'

Matthew Trawden appeared to consider the matter. His dogs followed his gaze across the moor. 'Ain't seen any such.' He shook his head slowly from side to side, and then something seemed to occur to him. 'T'country's at war with France just now, am I right?'

We, meaning the British nation, had been at war with France for nigh on twenty years, on and off. Farmer Trawden seemed to have only just discovered this.

'Yes, and we have taken many prisoners,' I replied, trying to hide my exasperation, 'and it appears some may have escaped and be roaming in these fells.'

'Never seen none.' A sudden thought appeared to strike Matthew. 'Ah, but there was that fellow though. Me and Batty found un under a snowdrift. Back was it January or maybe February.' He spoke as if it were an everyday occurrence.

'You mean a *corpse*?'

'That's right. Us meant ter tell tha, but the weather's bin that foul, and just now we've bin busy wi' lambing. Slipped me mind. What should us do with un? Will Sir John 'Athersage want un taken some place?'

'What *did* you do with it? This corpse? I assume it was a man?' I was gabbling, so many unanswered questions were now churning inside my skull. 'Did you have reason to think he was a Frenchman?'

'Dint do nothin' with un. Snows were three-foot deep back then. Us were digging sheep out at the time. Ah sent Batty t' pack snow over un and put stones on top. Keep foxes and bird's o' prey off un. Meant to let tha know once the thaw set in a lile bit. Couldn't say if he were a Frenchman. He were dressed ordinary like.'

My first thought was *this is outrageous*. Leaving the man here for months, telling nobody. But then, was it? In the depths of such a harsh winter, how could they have got word to me? And busy myself once the thaw set in, supervising the clearing of collapsed riverbanks, a broken plank bridge, fallen trees, and a flooded building site, I had not found time to visit the Trawden's farm.

I took a deep breath. 'He's still on your land, beneath a pile of stones?'

'Happen so,' replied the phlegmatic Matthew Trawden, 'If foxes ain't had un.'

'You could show it to me.' Though I didn't relish it, I supposed it my duty to look. 'I shall have to acquaint Sir John with the circumstances.

Matthew glanced down at his injured leg. A small amount of blood was now seeping through his thick felt gaiters. He hobbled forward a few steps and picked up the abandoned shotgun in his left hand. Then he put the fingers of his right in his mouth and whistled, a blast so shrill that they probably heard it down in Lancaster. It made my ears ring, and several curlews and a ring ousel rose from the ground in a panic and wheeled away over the fellside. The dogs, which had risen when Matthew did, seemed to recognise that the whistle was not for them, and sat down again.

'Come back, Batty, yer daft bastard!' he roared, 'T'agent's here and he wants t' see t' dead un!'

It was some minutes before Bartholomew Trawden reappeared atop a low ridge, presumably because his brother now had possession of the shotgun.

'Tek Mister Armstrong ter see t' corpse!' Matthew roared.

Batty stood his ground, and it was I who trudged across the rough ground to join him.

'Where is this dead man?' I demanded, 'Is it far off?'

Batty gazed at me, his jaw slack. Then he turned on his heel and began to stride away, so that I had no option but to follow.

I stumbled over tussocks in his wake for two hundred yards or so towards a drystone wall. These are a feature of this northern landscape, snaking away over hill and dale, marking ancient boundaries, and serving to keep livestock where they are meant to be.

This one, like many in the district, had been damaged by the weight of snow. It had crumbled at various points along its length, and the top stones lay scattered on both sides. Batty Trawden, without a word, led me to a larger pile of these and pointed.

I gulped. If these two lunatic brothers were not playing some strange practical joke on me, I was being invited to view a man three or four months dead. Remembering Lydia Hutton's troubled face, I put up a hasty prayer to a God in whom I did not believe, that this would not turn out to be her missing son.

We removed some of the stones, revealing the man's face and the top half of his body.

He was far too advanced in years to be George Hutton – perhaps fifty or so. He had a thick, bristling beard and light brown hair receding at his temples. He was of a stocky build, judging by the breadth of his shoulders, and was close to six feet in height. I told Batty to cover him up again. I would send a team of men to fetch him away as soon as I had made contact with Sir John. I interpreted Batty's grunt as agreement. He might, I decided, be dumb, and his understanding seemed limited, but he wasn't deaf.

We covered the body again and added a few extra stones for luck – or, luck wasn't a possibility for this poor fellow anymore – to keep him safe from predators.

The day had clouded over. I felt a few large spots of rain on my face as we tramped, in silence, back to the farmhouse where it was speckling the lintels and doorposts. Matthew had disappeared indoors, but the two dogs were curled around one another on the threshold. One raised his head and snarled as we approached. I wasn't sure whether it was for my benefit or Batty's. I took a couple of steps back.

'Bartholomew, will you tell your brother what I said? I will send people to take the body away as soon as I hear from Sir John.'

It appeared he could speak because he said, 'Aye, Ah'll do that.'

I set off back down the fellside. Should I write to my employer? Or would it be better if I went down into Lancaster to tell him this news to his face?

Sir John had suffered several setbacks to his grand plans for the manor house and country estate at Dalefoot. Careless workmanship, Autumn gales, followed by the harsh winter weather, had already caused disaster and delay. The finding of an unknown corpse on his property, albeit on a distant boundary, would only increase his displeasure. Unless someone could identify the body, I assumed its discovery must necessitate investigation by magistrates.

As the rain stopped, I quickened my pace, debating whether or not I should saddle Polly and ride to Lancaster. If she decided to go lame on me again, I'd have to leave her at some farm along the way. That might mean paying the farmer to stable her and walking the rest of the way.

Even if we reached town without mishap, it seemed unlikely that Sir John would offer me a bed for the night, so unless I bespoke a bed at one of the inns – at more expense – I would need to return to Netherdale, probably after dark, and stumbling over rough tracks in pitch darkness was neither wise nor sensible. Although my legs are as sturdy as anybody's, my weak left arm makes the upper part of my body unstable, and I topple over more easily than other men do.

Rush Ghyll farmhouse came into view once more. Now I had a new problem. Should I call and tell the Huttons what had been discovered on High Bield's land? I wouldn't want Lydia Hutton to hear of it and fear that this was her missing son. Yet to call and explain would take time, and from the height of the sun, winking at me from amongst those hurrying clouds, I knew the day was wearing on.

Deep in thought, I squeezed with more haste than caution through a stile onto the Huttons' land and nearly fell over Dorcas Hutton. She was just inside the field, seated splay-legged on the ground, intent on disentangling a long trailing briar from the fleece of a yearling sheep. She was wearing the dirty old coat over her dress once more, but had now managed to get oil and dirt from the fleece all over her hands and face. The hogget, distressed, kept lunging away from her, although the briar was still stuck fast, and the girl, to my astonishment, was swearing at it.

'Damn thee! Stand still, damn thee!' she muttered, 'I'm trying to help thee, damned fool of a creature!'

'Goodness! I had no idea a Quaker girl would even know such indelicate language.' As soon as the words escaped my lips, I regretted how priggish they sounded. As though I didn't on occasion use a few expletives myself, but I hadn't expected it from a member of that family.

The girl's face turned a fiery red, 'Thee was not meant to hear,' she growled. 'When God made sheep, I believe he did so that we might be sorely tried.'

Chapter Six

Dorcas Hutton – Her Journal

4th Day, 2nd Week, 4th Month

After the upsets and unexpected events of this day so far, I have set myself down in this sunny corner of the field, my presence here hidden by the curve of the wall. Various kindly Quakers have advised me to write a journal. It should be a record of my spiritual progress, they tell me. What I write here is to be between myself and God, to be shown to none. I hope it never will be. I know Mama and Susannah will not pry, but I take care not to leave it anywhere where my brothers might find it. What I write here does <u>not</u>, I'm afraid, demonstrate any spiritual advances. However, I find it is a source of both solace and amusement to me. Here, I can take my pencil from the pocket of Papa's old coat and record all I truly think and feel.

Today, I never felt such a fool in my life. To be caught by that young agent with my skirts rucked up above the hem of my chemise – and swearing. And with my most disgusting pair of stockings on display, full of the clumsiest darns – and tangling, as I was, with a dirty sheep. Dorcas Hutton, thou art a disgrace. He must have been shocked beyond anything. Such a polite fellow, with such a charming Scottish lilt to his speech.

I suppose Hugh Armstrong thinks we are a primitive lot here in Netherdale. Quakers, religious zealots, he must think. Still saying 'thee' and 'thou' as though we still live in times gone by. Oh, the pained look on his face during our silent Worship before our midday meal. It was unfortunate that we gave him that chair with the unsteady leg. I would have offered to exchange, but Papa wouldn't have liked me to interrupt the Worship. He had such an expression of anguish all through it, poor fellow. And when Betsey asked him what he prayed about, he looked so taken aback. I don't know how I stopped myself from bursting into laughter.

And naturally, just now, he had a look of disgust over the business with the sheep, but whether it was for the swearing or for indecently displaying my legs, or both, I couldn't tell.

Later, in the outhouse

I did not apologise. Any person who has ever wrestled with a sheep would know I was trying the only remedy. A sheep will give thee no help, poor beast, not knowing why this human creature is determined to free it. But if the strong briar thorns tangle deep into its fleece and are dragged behind the animal, they will come to tear at the skin and cause infection. I cannot bear to see animals suffer. My brothers have laughed at me countless times for what they call 'my o'er tender heart.'

It was George who taught me to swear. I'm sure he knew many more bad words besides 'damn', but he wouldn't tell me. He learned them from going amongst the other farmers at the beast market, and he'd mutter them under his breath whenever our Wilf told him what to do. He never did so around Papa, naturally.

I do give thanks that Hugh Armstrong told me about the dead man at High Bield, and told me to tell Mama that whoever he may be, he is <u>not</u> my brother. Mama frets, as I told him, although the rest of us believe George has come to no harm and will turn up in his own good time. I pray it may indeed be so.

Chapter Seven

Hugh

Some girls would have turned pale, fainted even, at the thought of a rotting corpse. When I told Dorcas Hutton about it and asked her to assure her mother that whoever this man was, he was not her brother, she had merely shrugged, saying, 'Mama worries, but the rest of us don't suppose any harm has come to George. Unless he has enlisted as he threatened, but I don't believe he ever would. He is too fond of his own skin to go for a soldier. Perhaps someone offered him work of some kind where he doesn't have to bend his back or get his hands dirty.'

This grubby, grumpy girl rather shocked me.

'I had thought all Quaker families lived in love and peace?'

'It's Mama and Papa's intention that we should, but that state is easier sought after than achieved.' She saw I was about to hasten away. 'Oh, there is no need for thee to go to Lancaster with this news, because John Hathersage is here at his new house. I saw his carriage turning into the dale as I came across the fields.'

She turned her attention back to the sheep, tugging once more at the entangled bramble skein, and exposing more of her snagged and dirty stockings (and I have to admit, her trim ankles) than was seemly.

She really was a strange creature, not at all the kind of young woman I cared to know better. I thanked her, then dismissed her from my thoughts as I hurried on downhill. If Sir John were at Dalefoot House, he would want me on hand to give him an update on the work. My one comfort was that he would be distracted from the lack of progress by what I had to say about the dead body at High Bield. You'll find it hard to credit, but my encounter with the Frenchmen earlier in the day I'd almost forgotten.

Supervising the building work at Dalefoot was not something I felt qualified to do, nor, though I dared not say so, did I think Sir John should expect it of me. I was a land agent, for goodness's sake! I am neither an architect nor a clerk to the works. The architect, however, was in Preston and seemed disinclined to travel, even now that the roads were clear. I was available on the spot, and through February and March, had not been overworked. No doubt it was Sir John's opinion that I could better earn my keep by badgering the builders, in addition to my other duties.

As I neared the house, he stumped into view, his pouchy face aflame, clearly annoyed. 'Armstrong!' he hailed me, 'what's this I hear of escaped French prisoners? I've just met with the eldest Braithwaite lad, Nathaniel, driving the Hutton lass over to Lane End to take tea with his mother. She's told him you went calling at Rush Ghyll to warn them all. *I've* heard nothing of this! What's going on, man? Why did you not send for me at once?'

Oh, thank you, sweet Susannah! The beauty had tattled the tale all over the district before I'd had the chance to inform Sir John.

'Sir!' I gasped, out of breath from my downhill rush, 'I was... just about to set out for Lancaster... to acquaint you with this. But there's more, I'm afraid – a dead body found on High Bield's land.'

At these words, Sir John's face blanched from red to white, and his bulging eyes started from their sockets. 'A body! At High

Bield? By Heaven, Armstrong, what's been going on? Escaped prisoners, dead men? This is too bad! Too bad, I say! Dereliction of duty, Armstrong! Surely you should have discovered this before now and kept me informed?'

I thought for a moment that he meant to dismiss me on the spot – and then where would I go? I had come away from Scotland to escape from family troubles that were not of my making. I needed employment, and to lose this man's goodwill would be a disaster.

'I dislike standing about discussing this kind of thing,' he said, gazing around as though there was a crowd of folk listening, although the only other person close by was James Carr, his coachman, who stood, blank-faced, at the horse's head. 'We must go indoors, man, and you can report to me in private.'

Due to the lackadaisical efforts of the builders, there was little of Dalefoot that could be described as 'indoors', but we made our way into the roofless shell. It had once been a small, pleasant old manor house, built in the days of the Merry Monarch, Charles Stuart the Second. Sir John was in the process of enlarging it – notice that I do not say 'improving'. He was adding an extra wing, which would double its size. The new roof, which would one day cover the whole, had not yet been started.

Inside, Sir John planted his stout body on one of the stone bench seats and folded his hands on the head of his cane. I stood before him, like an errant schoolboy.

'Well, Armstrong, tell me the worst!' he growled.

I summarised the day's events. 'I don't think, Sir, that the two are connected. The Trawden brothers found their dead man in January or February, buried under the snow. I'm no expert on the deterioration of corpses following death, but I imagine,' I gulped, recalling what I had seen, 'that the man might have died even earlier, perhaps caught in those first heavy snows in December.'

'Could he be another Frenchman?'

'Sir, that I cannot say. The two miscreants who held me up this morning were dressed in the yellow clothing they issue to prisoners of war, but not this man.'

Sir John waved this away. 'Not connected then, Armstrong, that's obvious,' he pronounced, as though I had suggested they were. 'One is sorely tempted to ask the Trawdens to bury this dead fellow and keep quiet about it. No? No, that won't do, word is bound to get about.' He thumped his cane on the stone-flagged floor.

'I'd better send someone to help you fetch him away. Nasty job,' he added thoughtfully, 'but the Lancaster authorities will want to have a look. See if someone can put a name to him. As for these escaped prisoners, if they were making for the docks as you suggest, I daresay they've been apprehended by now. Forget about 'em. No harm done.'

He rose, ready to depart, and led the way back out into the lane.

No harm done? This whole day had been one of agitation to my spirits, but as I was a mere employee, my well-being was of no interest to Sir John Hathersage. 'A man's a man for all that. His toil's obscure an' a' that.' I wondered what the Bard of Scotland would have made of discovering a corpse rather than a rosebud on his early walk?

I noted too that *I* was to be sent men to help *me* fetch this corpse away. I could hear my grandmother's voice in my head. *Man up, Hughie, you mun learn tae tak these things in your stride, laddie!*

'Yes.' My employer tapped the palm of his hand with the head of his pearl-handled cane, seeming delighted to have solved our problems. 'I shall tell the magistrates to send a couple of constables up here tomorrow to look that dead fellow over. *Someone* must know who he was, but if they can't put a name to him... Well, be he gentleman or guttersnipe, they must plant him in the churchyard down in the village. On my way back, I'll call in and have them have a grave dug ready – and the parish coffin and a shroud to hand.'

The corpse was to have the most basic of burials, 'on the parish', not, you will note, at Sir John's expense. The coffin would be trundled to the graveside and the corpse, in a rough sackcloth shroud, rolled out into a hastily dug pit, so that the coffin could be used again.

At this point, my eyes met those of James Carr, the groom, still patiently waiting at the horse's head. He rolled his eyes heavenwards, and his mouth twitched in a sly grin. I'd the devil's own job not to grin back. Working for Sir John Hathersage was frequently exasperating, but it had its humorous moments. Suppose this dead stranger *was* a gentleman, I found myself wondering, and his relatives came looking for him? Was he to be buried in haste and dug up at leisure?

However, Sir John held the purse strings, and he would proceed as he wished. Neither of us would dare question his decisions if we wanted to eat or keep roofs over our heads. And praise be, he hadn't today uttered a single word about the lack of progress on the house.

He signalled to Carr to turn the carriage. 'I'll call in at the parsonage and prepare them,' he said as he hauled himself aboard. 'I trust all this can be dealt with expediently... and Armstrong?' He shook a finger at me. 'Understand me, no gossip!'

I bowed briefly as he bowled away.

Swallowing my dissatisfaction and thinking to 'improve each shining hour', as my grandmother always said, I did a quick survey of the delayed building works. Three weeks must have passed since I had last done this. Sir John had been deflected by other news today, but soon, perhaps as soon as tomorrow, he would remember my missing progress report.

I walked through the husk of the house. There was no sign of workmen. However, to my surprise, considerable progress had been made on the rooms in the new wing of the building. As I've said, they were little more than a shell and still roofless, but the dividing walls and doorways were in place. There were new window embrasures in the chamber at the end of this wing overlooking the lower dale. The view was framed by oaks and sycamores, on which leaf buds were now unfurling. I had not yet met Lady Hathersage, but felt certain she would be pleased with her new withdrawing room once it was complete. Now that the weather had improved, surely it could not be long.

I might as well confess here that I knew little or nothing about house building. Questioned about gates, fences, field walls, ditches, drainage, and coppices, coverts, deer runs, grouse moors, and fire breaks, I had answers ready to my tongue – or if not, a shelf full of treatises on estate management back at my lodging.

And my inquisitor would also have been correct if they suspected I had a second shelf given over to other matters – to volumes of poetry in the main – and it is to that shelf that my hand and eye most often strayed. The sheets of paper that lay scattered over my desk were not all maps, field plans, or estimates for digging drainage channels. Some were my own attempts at poetry.

There, I've said it: I, Hugh Armstrong, aspired to be a poet. To one day see my poems in print. If some future reader should come across my work, I hoped he or she would be kind. We writers are sensitive souls.

I came down from Fife in November to take up my post here. By mid-December, the dales were buried beneath several feet of snow. How should I then have filled my days? It was impossible for me to be inspecting boundaries, calling in workmen to coppice woodland, or to rebuild broken walls and repair gates. A long, dark winter had set in. So, what better than to use the time to take up my pen? Knowing that once spring came, I might be too busy to write a line. A man makes these fine resolutions!

Two nights back, looking over the lines I had written some weeks ago, I accepted my progress had so far been anything but glorious. Rabbie Burns might sleep easy in the churchyard at Dumfries. Mr William Wordsworth and his fellow versifiers might stroll beside their lakes and beneath their trees and have no fear that Hugh Armstrong was about to out-rhyme them.

My eye fell on two lines I'd scribbled as the snows retreated during the previous month, and the first buds appeared in the hedgerows:

Now are the hedgerows sprung anew,
Now doth the breeze the blackthorn blossom blow...

Yes, I know. Dire. Derivative. It didn't even rhyme. Now did the poet seize that sheet of paper and tear it into strips to make spills to light the fire.

Chapter Eight

Dorcas' Journal

Later, in the byre by lantern light

(Mama thinks I am seeing to the sickly calf.)

What a strange thing for the Trawdens to find a dead man on their land beneath the snow. How like them, though, not to take the trouble to tell anyone until now. Mama says they're eccentric, that they have lived too much on their own since their old father died. They've become strange and distant. I believe she worries sometimes that I may turn out like that.

Whoever could have wandered up so high and died there? High Bield is so remote. There's no metalled road to it, only a track across the moor. Perhaps he, whoever he was, was lost in a snowstorm. But even so, to wander so far from any road or dwellings?

Perhaps I am a little overexcited by all this. I should try, I know, to control these sensations, but so little occurs here in Netherdale that is out of the ordinary. Then today, two extraordinary things have happened. No three, the third being the dead man.

First, we had the visit from Hathersage's agent. I had seen him around in the dale, of course, poking into ditches and eying the broken bank above the beck that runs alongside the fell road.

I'd noticed his withered hand and arm, and the worried frown he seems to have forever on his brow, although otherwise he is a well-set-up young fellow. Is it not natural enough to be curious about any new face? My brothers would tease me without mercy if they thought I had developed a partiality for him.

His visit was the first extraordinary thing that happened, and the second was the news he brought of the escaped French prisoners. None of us had seen any such men, but it was certainly something new to talk about at table. A change from scrapie, foot rot, and how many weeks until we shear. And, of course, Sukie's wedding. I love my sister. Truly, Lord Jesus, I do. I'm happy for her that she is to marry Nathaniel Braithwaite, to whom I know she will be a most excellent wife. I just don't want to hear another word about her trousseau, her gown, or the house Nat is to hire for them in Lancaster. Even Mama, who is usually such a high-minded woman, seems entranced by all these tiresome details.

Am I jealous? I know Mama thinks so, although she has never upbraided me with it. She understands, which makes me feel worse. She knows that I wouldn't have wanted Nathaniel, even if he'd offered for me. Nat Braithwaite and I would not suit at all! One or both of us would have ended our days in the Retreat, the new Friends' mental asylum in York. He is so worthy, so self-satisfied, so sure of his place in the world. And so very, very dull.

Yet, I would love to see this silk mill in which he is now a partner. I'd be curious to see the spinning sheds and the looms, never having been in such a place. I would like to find out how it is run, what skills are required, and what the hours are for the workers – whether they are paid fairly for the tasks they have to perform. But nobody thinks a woman, even a Quaker woman, could or should involve herself in such matters.

Sukie has a tender heart, so I suppose she would speak up if she saw children there who were too young to be working in the mill, or if there were any cruel practices. I hope she would. She might plead with Nat and his partners to start a little school for them. Perhaps I should suggest it, offer myself as the schoolmistress.

No, that I cannot do. I made one attempt to become a teacher, but it ended in humiliation and failure.

Mama knows how I suffered from that disappointment and tries her best to comfort me and show me ways to find contentment with my lot. 'The Lord will find thee a new way, Dorcas,' she says, 'I'm sure He hath need of thee, and the way will open.'

So far, it hasn't. I think the Lord Jesus has forgotten me, out here on the moors, under the wide spring skies, amongst the sheep and lambs. They say He spoke of lambs, of lost sheep. Perhaps one day I will feel the hook of His crook about my neck, and He will pull me from the midst of the flock to the place where He judges I am needed. Oh, please, may it be soon!

Mama will have more need of me once Susannah is wed, although I cannot sew and darn as neatly as she does, nor have I such a light hand with pastry. However, though I am short and slight of build, I am wiry. I have strong arms to lift a full wash tub and beat carpets. I can lift down a heavy bacon flitch, or turn a mattress, or hold fast to feed a struggling orphaned lambkin. Papa and Mama will be glad of me, at least for a time. Until my brothers take wives.

Wilf, my oldest brother, I believe, has his eye on Mary Stout, Rachel and Eliza's niece, daughter of their brother, Jacob, who farms at Over Kellet. Wilf began to notice her, I think, at Monthly Meeting in Lancaster last year, and he makes sure to speak to her whenever they're in company. She is a pretty girl. Young yet, only sixteen and a giggler, but she sews, knits, crochets, and tats to a perfection that even Sukie can barely match. The gown she had on, last time I saw her, had the neck of its bodice in-filled with tatting so fine I would have supposed it was bobbin lace. That little show of finery caused a few pursed lips amongst the old Quakers! But in a year or two, if Wilf and Mary are minded to marry, I'm sure neither her parents nor mine will make any objection.

Next morning, early

Once the sheep was freed and the long bramble skein broken up and tossed high into the bushes, I was free of farm tasks. Free to curl up in a sheltered corner between two walls come together, and write in this journal. And read the book that had been burning a hole in the pocket of this old coat of Papa's all day.

It isn't the kind of book I would find in Papa's work room. Papa always allows us to take whatever books we want from there, and indeed, some of them are interesting. I've consumed all the writings he has on the education of the poorer classes and the conditions of slaves in America and the West Indies, but he and Mama would, I think, be quite shocked if they knew I was reading fictional tales.

Perhaps they would be even more shocked if they knew who gave this book to me. It was Eliza Stout – such a dear, gentle old Quaker lady! It's our secret, hers, and mine. Not even her sister, stern-faced Rachel, knows.

It is entitled 'Pride and Prejudice' – by a gentlewoman, the cover assures me – not that I care for <u>that</u>.

Eliza slipped it to me during the refreshment break at Quarterly Meeting, murmuring to me that she was a little worried at first that the tale might be <u>too frivolous</u>. Eliza has provided the book with a slipcover of plain grey buckram in order to disguise it from her sister and anyone else who might disapprove. It is not so much that Mama would be angry, more that she would be saddened that I should be chasing after artificial excitements. Be that as it may, I cannot resist. I shall put my journal away now and read just the first chapter.

Chapter Nine

Hugh

Next morning, Sir John sent me two ruffians equipped with peat spades and a cart to carry the dead man down from High Bield, and this they had done with dispatch. Once the stones were removed, they had simply slid the long blades of these spades under the corpse. Then, at a signal to one another, they heaved it, in one practised movement, onto a spread of tarred canvas in the bed of their cart. Nothing had been required of me beyond going with them to show them where to find the corpse. Even that proved unnecessary as Batty Trawden, fairly gibbering with excitement, had run ahead of us to show them the spot.

I had told my pony that I considered her period of convalescence to be over, and ridden her up to High Bield. She showed no sign of lameness. Indeed, she followed the cart down to the village at a rattling pace, as though as interested in the outcome as I was. Although it could have been the presence of the nag who pulled the death cart that intrigued her. He was a rough-coated pi-bald with a wall eye, untroubled by the presence of the corpse on his wagon. I guessed that rubbish collection, scavenging, and the retrieval of the occasional body from the byways and ditches of Lancaster constituted the daily round for himself and his owners. He was certainly gelded, however, so if Polly's interest was romantic, she was destined to suffer a disappointment.

We arrived at the church. I tethered her at the inn across the way, where she could see her hero but not progress the friendship, and made my way to the newly dug grave.

This had been prepared to a couple of feet. Apparently, we were not really burying him at all, merely storing him underground until he was identified. The Minister, the Reverend Mr Chorley, his church warden, and his grave digger were eager to assure us that the soil underneath had been loosened so that it could be speedily made deeper. The coroner for the district could not be present today, as he was 'suffering mightily with the gout.' Instead, Sir John was accompanied by a thin man in dun coloured clothing, a mustard wool scarf, and a wide-brimmed hat. This was the fellow who was to scrutinise the corpse in the hope of giving him a name.

I was surprised to find that my employer had braved this unpleasant occasion himself. However, he stayed with the parson and the churchwarden, well back amongst the tombstones. The grave digger had no such qualms and hovered close.

'Ah, Armstrong,' said Sir John, 'this is Mister Augustus Fenwick, a detective.' He lowered his voice. 'He happened to be in the neighbourhood, staying at the Golden Lion, and looking for a missing man, *a Frenchman*, an officer, supposedly,' he now dropped to a whisper, 'who has broken his parole. Naturally, when I discovered *that,* I sent a message suggesting he came here and looked at our corpse.'

'You're the one that saw this fellow?' Augustus Fenwick asked me, 'but could give 'im no cog-no-men?'

Cognomen? 'No, no,' I replied. 'Until yesterday I'd never seen him before.'

I would not have thought the dead man French. It had passed through my mind when I first saw him that he was the sort of fellow I had often seen rolling through Kirkcaldy on a Saturday night with a whisky jar protruding from his pocket.

'Ah, that's disappointing,' said this gloomy Augustus, 'so he hasn't been spotted creepin' about in this vicinity?'

Sir John burst in, assuring the detective that if the man had been seen anywhere in the district, someone would have told him. 'Most of the people hereabouts are my tenants, and honest men,' he said. Augustus Fenwick looked as doubtful as I felt. The gravedigger, shifty of eye, looked as though he was doubting himself.

By no means was everybody Sir John's tenants, nor had they any reason for excessive loyalty. Sir John was 'new money' to them. Worse still, he was an 'incomer', and would be seen as such for the next twenty years.

'Wherry well, then,' said Fenwick, 'let's 'ave a look.' The gravedigger whipped the shroud cloth away. Silence fell.

Sir John gulped, clutching a handkerchief to his lips. Even the gravedigger sucked hard on his blackened stumps of teeth.

Fenwick seemed disinterested in examining any more of the man than his head and shoulders. Myself, seeing the corpse a second time, I noticed a blackened scar on his brow under the hairline. What did I know of what death might do? After four or five months, this could be just part of the process of decomposition.

Fenwick touched his own brow, looked round at us, and said, 'Old head wound. Been a fighter, I'd hazard, in his younger days.'

This felt all too likely. His nose had a pronounced lump on the bridge.

'Well?' demanded Sir John.

'Could be,' Augustus Fenwick replied, slowly. 'Don't bury 'im too deep. Might need to have 'im up again.'

Then he signalled that the grave cloth could be replaced.

'You think this man was a French *spy*?' asked Sir John, forgetting the presence of the church officials and throwing caution to the moorland breezes.

The detective shook his head. 'As I say, don't bury 'im too deep. Have to confer wiv' colleagues. London men,' he added, 'which are familiar wiv' the current situation regarding foreign incursions.'

Augustus Fenwick's use of words intrigued me. By his speech, he was not from an educated background, but he had picked up some rarefied vocabulary – *cognomen, colleagues, vicinity, foreign incursions* – a whole lexicon to describe suspicious people and actions. Sir John had described him as a detective. I doubted, despite what sounded like a Cockney accent, that he was one of the famous Bow Street Runners.

Fenwick, like Armstrong, I knew to be a name from the borders of England and Scotland. I found myself wondering, was his accent feigned? Was he, in fact, the counterpart of the corpse we might have just been examining – an *English* spy-catcher? The government in London probably employed such men to watch the ports and follow up sightings of foreigners whose presence could not be accounted for.

'Drop 'im in, cover 'im up,' Fenwick told the gravedigger, and abruptly turned his back on the scene. Sir John and I, perforce, followed him as far as the churchyard gate. The Reverend Chorley hurried over the graves after us, urging us to go with him and partake of refreshments. His good lady was expecting us at the parsonage.

A genteel party with this parson's wife held no attractions for me. However, before I could even open my mouth to excuse myself, Sir John turned to me and said, 'Armstrong, I won't be too long here – just politeness, you know – I'll see you back at Dalefoot.'

So that was me told. I was his employee. No tea drinking on his shilling, whether I wanted to or not. I crossed to the inn, unhitched Polly and rode away.

Chapter Ten

Hugh

At Dalefoot, I found a gang of builders, for once, at work. Their foreman hurriedly appeared, having heard Polly's hooves on the slabbed forecourt.

'Ah, 'tis only you,' he said, unimpressed. 'Isn't old 'Athersage coming?'

What to do with these disrespectful fellows? '*Sir John Hathersage* is coming,' I said, dismounting. 'Just now he's been delayed by the Minister and his wife, but he'll be here shortly. And he'll certainly want to see progress.'

'Minister? Dost tha mean *Parson* Chorley? No Ministers down 'ere lad. You're not in t' wild Ighlands now.' He consulted a surprisingly elegant pocket watch, which he kept in the bosom of his grubby waistcoat. 'Another hour then, afore he gets here. Madam Chorley can whittle on fer England,' he waved a hand. 'We're affixing roof beams and battens. Do yer want ter see these roof slates? They've come down fr'm Ennerdale. Decent quality, not too many broke on t' journey.'

He led me around to the rear of the building, where cut slates now lay neatly piled, ready for the new roof. These, I was certain, had *not* been here when I called yesterday. Yet surely, they couldn't have been brought down overnight from the quarries of Ennerdale, eighty miles north of here. It was Sir John, not I, thank goodness, who had been responsible for engaging these men. I had a growing suspicion that they were rogues, although as yet I had no means of proving it.

From the time I took up my post, the work had seemed to me to proceed in fits and starts. When I hire men to cut back bracken or repair walls and gates, severe weather apart, I accept no delays. This last winter had been an unduly harsh one, and I had understood that these men could then do nothing, but why this prevarication? Yesterday, there had been no sign that they were about to start work on the roof. Today, beams were going up, and the slates were here. They must somehow have heard of Sir John's intended visit today and made haste to be ready for him. It had been a stroke of luck for them that he hadn't then gone through the house yesterday and seen their paltry efforts.

As I have mentioned so many times that I am in danger of becoming tedious, house building is not my trade. Everything about this project made me uneasy. I was resentful that Sir John expected me to supervise these rascals, and worried he would shuffle blame onto me if things went horribly wrong. It would be my word against theirs, and I was by no means sure that my employer entirely trusted me. A friend of my grandfather's had recommended me, but being an honest man, I could imagine him saying something like, 'Hugh's family background is a difficult one, but he's a good lad and deserves a chance.' If Sir John should ever discover my father's current whereabouts, I feared my chance would be at an end.

I recalled a recent letter from my grandmother.

You're a Woesome Wullie, Hughie! Always fearing the worst. Why should Sir John Hathersage put the blame on you when 'twas himself who em-

ployed these varmints? Ye should tell him so! If he turns you off, he's a fool, but I'm thinking he won't. You're a good laddie and a hard worker, and praise the Lord, you've no taint of your father.

I didn't go tae the court tae see him brought before the judge, but I heard he raised a mighty rumpus, blaming his so-called friends for his own ill deeds. The lawyers could nae hear themselves speak, so they took him back to the gaol.

I suppose he'll be sentenced in a wee while. I'm fearing 'twill be the rope to disgrace us all, but at least we'll be free of him at last.

I hoped no one here would ever hear of it. Having one's father hanged for his dishonesty was not something any man would want his employer to know. Grandmother might believe that Sir John would keep me on, or if not, that my abilities would soon win me alternative employment, but then she had always sat tight on Grandfather's siller, and had less need than I to consider where her next meal would be coming from. Thinking these things, I had almost forgotten the foreman.

'What is your name?' I should have asked him months ago.

'Barker Tatham,' he replied. 'My mother were a Barker. The eldest oft times teks his mother's family name in these parts. No Macdoodledums hereabouts.' As a descendant of borderers, I was already familiar with this custom. I suspected it would be useless to explain to Barker Tatham that not all Scottish names begin with Mac.

Now, he indicated with pride the rising beams being hauled aloft on ropes by two of his men. Not knowing if this was being done as it should be, I was scratching my head for a suitable comment when we were interrupted by the clatter of hooves.

'That's never 'imself,' exclaimed the foreman.

Indeed, it wasn't. A fat, rough-coated fell pony, ridden bare-backed and astride by little Betsey Hutton, her skirts and pigtails flying, clattered into the courtyard.

The pony lurched to a grateful halt, snorting and blowing, and Betsey, after gasping for breath herself for a few moments, addressed me. 'Hugh Armstrong... Mama said to tell thee... a man came... just now... and threatened Papa, and knocked him down!'

'Just now? When just now?' I found myself babbling idiotically. 'Did he hurt your papa?'

'Yes, he did!' Her little face screwed up in fierce disapproval. 'Papa spoke peaceably to him, but he knocked him down with the iron doorstop, and it made his head to bleed ab–abundantly. Mama and I were in the larder when we heard the man shouting. Mama made me hide behind the door until he was gone. She is tending to Papa's hurts, and she told me to ride and find thee.'

'Certainly, I'll come,' I said, 'but was there no one at home but you and your mother?'

Betsey appeared to consider this carefully before answering. How well I remembered my grandmother urging me to think before I let words come tumbling forth.

'Susannah was persuaded to stay overnight with Nathaniel's family at Lane End, and I think Nat has taken her to view a house in Lancaster where they might live when they are married. Wilf and Jonathan have taken the flock up over the moor,' she said, solemnly counting off the family on her fingers. 'Mama said they'd been gone an hour, and she didn't know the direction they were taking. They'd likely be too far away for me to catch them. She said it would be best to ride for thee, because thee would surely be in the village today to see the poor dead man from Trawdens' laid to rest, but then – as I rode down the track – I saw thy pony was here at Dalefoot, so I stopped.'

'And Dorcas?' I unhitched Polly and swung myself up into the saddle. 'Where is she?'

Betsy shrugged, 'Don't know. We never know where Dorcas is gone. She never tells us.'

Chapter Eleven

Hugh

Wilfred Hutton was not too much hurt. We found him seated in his study, his head bound up in clean strips of sheeting, through which blood still leaked a little as head wounds are inclined to do. His wife stood by, urging him to drink a willow bark potion. 'Or thee will have a great headache, else, Wilf,' she insisted.

'What happened, Farmer Hutton?' I asked.

He smiled weakly. 'That I cannot rightly tell thee. A man came bursting in here and shouted at me in some foreign tongue. He, I suppose growing exasperated at my lack of understanding, hurled yonder doorstop at my head, and down I went! I knew no more until I came to and found my wife and child bending over me.'

'What manner of man was he?' I asked., 'Was he a respectable fellow? Or a ruffian?'

'Again, I cannot rightly tell thee. He was dressed in a heavy greatcoat despite the day being mild. He was well-barbered, and to judge from the number of words he spoke, although I understood none of them, he may have been a man of some learning.'

'I can only think,' I said, 'that he has something to do with the body found buried at High Bield. The news of a corpse being found there has got about. A number of people in the village seemed to know of it, although I told no one except yourselves.'

'*We* have not spoken of it to any,' exclaimed Lydia. 'I thank thee for that message, Hugh Armstrong. Otherwise, I would have been troubled.'

I bowed, accepting her thanks, but at the same time thinking, 'That is not entirely the case. *You* may not have spoken to anyone, but your daughter Susannah and her swain didn't keep still tongues.' For aught I knew, they had told several others besides Sir John.

I spoke my next thought aloud. '*This* man may be a comrade of the dead man. He has heard he's been found and came wanting to know more. Somehow, he knows that the body was on one of the farms here in Netherdale, but he doesn't know which one. He may not be aware that High Bield is yet higher up the fell. He may not even know that the body has been removed.' I turned to Lydia Hutton, 'You must have come quickly when you heard the commotion. Were you in time to see which way the stranger went?'

'No, I was too busy attending to my husband.' She considered for a moment. 'I had the impression he ran down the fell, rather than up, though I cannot be sure. The only one of my children who was by me was Betsey, so I sent her to find thee.'

'As she did, most promptly,' I said. Young Betsey beamed and hugged herself with pleasure, while I asked myself why this had become a matter for me to deal with. Had I become some kind of constable, charged with keeping order in Netherdale?

'We are sorry to trouble thee,' Wilfred spoke with his eyes closed. His head must have been aching abominably. 'But my wife did not know what to do. Our ways are peaceful. We have always upheld the law, and never needed the law to uphold us.'

I had seen this for myself, and Sir John had informed me there had never been any reason to employ a constable or any guardian of the law nearer than Lancaster. However, these good people were gazing at me anxiously, apparently expecting me to take charge. To my relief, I remembered Augustus Fenwick.

'Sir John brought a detective up to the village with him today. He was down in the churchyard earlier, to see if he could put a name to the dead man.'

I paused, undecided what more I could or should say to them. The presence of foreign spies and counterspies in these peaceful dales seemed so utterly ridiculous.

'Papa? Maybe he didn't come about the *dead* person?' said little Betsey suddenly, her small nose screwed up in consideration. 'Maybe he was an important soldier. Or a man from the prison. Could he have come looking for those two wicked men who frightened thee, Hugh Armstrong, with their gun? And stole thy luncheon.'

We all gaped at the child in astonishment. Was this not actually a more probable explanation? The corpse at High Bield had lain dead for months. Although a friend or comrade might only just have heard of its discovery, why would he rush here and draw attention to himself by attacking a peaceable farmer? Could he instead have been a prison official or a marshal from another part of the country, seeking escapees?

It had taken me weeks to fully attune myself to the speech of these Pennine farmers. Men from Glasgow, from parts of Wales, and Cornishmen, if one has not grown up amongst them, can be nigh impossible to understand. Edinburgh folk insist that we speak strangely in Fife. Yet Wilfred Hutton was an intelligent and patient man who would have listened attentively. Surely, he would have made out *some* words of English had there been any.

'My daughter here may have the truth of it,' he said, touching his head and wincing. 'Soon we must think of sending thee and thy clever little head to school, Betsey. Thy mother and I had intended the Friends' School in Lancaster for thee, but perhaps we should think of thee following Isaac to Ackworth in a year or two.'

There was a creak behind us. Dorcas Hutton stood for a moment on the threshold, scowling. Then, without a word, she turned and strode away, slamming the door behind her.

Lydia Hutton shook her head, smiling at me a little tremulously, 'Poor Dorcas. She feels it very much, but when she was Betsey's age, things were not going well with the farm. We'd had two or three bad years. A contagion amongst the cattle one year, and a wet winter the next. We lost many of our sheep to foot rot and bloat. We simply could not afford to send her away to school.'

'And when Dorcas wanted to be a teacher at Lancaster Friends' School,' piped up Betsey, 'they said she could, but then they gave back word. Wasn't that unkind?'

Her mother made shushing sounds, and Wilfred Hutton, holding his head between his hands, said, quite harshly, 'Hush, Betsey. Thee must not repeat things thee was not meant to overhear.'

Embarrassed at witnessing family discord, I said that since I knew I was leaving Wilfred well cared for, I would now go down to Dalefoot House and seek the advice of Sir John and Augustus Fenwick, the detective.

As I gathered up my hat, Wilfred Hutton said, 'One thing I recall about this man. He wore a very thick greatcoat and large, heavy boots which turned over at the top. I remember thinking they looked like seaboots.'

A heavy coat and seaboots? Who on this earth could this man be?

I strode out to collect Polly. Barker Tatham was probably correct to predict that Sir John would be delayed by Parson Chorley and his wife. Nevertheless, it would be foolish to rely on it and keep him waiting.

Polly was more or less where I'd left her, however, now with her reins thrust over a gatepost. As I approached, I saw she had company. Dorcas Hutton leaned against her stout side, stroking her nose. Polly was munching on something.

'My pony hasn't been eating something she shouldn't?' I said. In my haste to see what had happened to Wilfred Hutton, I'd relied on Polly's laziness to remain where I'd left her. I hadn't stopped to consider what damage she might do to Lydia's Hutton's flower bed.

Dorcas turned a strained face to me. I thought she might have been crying, but she squinched her eyes, ducked her head, and said, accusingly, 'Did thee know daffodils are poisonous to horses?'

Her tone caught me on the raw. I did know it, but again, I hadn't stopped to think when I dashed into the farmhouse. Fortunately for me, it appeared Polly knew it too.

'I'm sorry,' I said, 'I was in such a hurry to see what had happened to your father.'

'And now thee knows he is not likely to die, so thee will hurry away again.'

With this thrust, she unhooked Polly's reins and handed them to me.

I thanked her, abashed, mounted, and rode off down the fell-side. What a strange, fierce young woman she was! She must be at least eighteen years old. Was this not old enough to understand why her parents had been unable to send her to this school they thought so much of? I attempted to push the tiresome girl from my thoughts, but the whole encounter had unsettled me.

Would Sir John have already arrived at Dalefoot and be wondering why I had deserted the place?

As it happened, we arrived simultaneously. Augustus Fenwick was with him, riding a knock-kneed bay mare.

'Where have you been?' Sir John demanded. 'I expected to find you here well before me.'

'I *was* here before, Sir.' I replied, sliding from the saddle, 'but I was called away to Rush Ghyll. Someone has attacked Wilfred Hutton. His wife sent for me. He is not too severely injured, but naturally they were alarmed.'

'Someone attacked Hutton! Truly? I cannot imagine such a thing!'

'A complete stranger, Sir,' I told him, 'An unknown man, dressed in a heavy topcoat and boots like those worn by seamen. He marched into the farmhouse, shouted demands at Hutton in a language he couldn't understand. He then threw a doorstop at Hutton's head, knocking him senseless, and dashed out. Neither Hutton nor his wife has any notion who he was. She was too preoccupied to be sure which way the intruder went.'

Sir John turned to Augustus Fenwick, who pulled on his bottom lip and shrugged his bony shoulders. 'I suppose this farmer fellow is ignorant of the French tongue. Would he recognise it when he heard it spoken?'

'He *didn't* recognise it. I don't know whether he has ever had the occasion to hear French spoken. This is a remote spot.'

Sir John was shaking his head, frowning, and tapping the side of his boot with the tip of his cane. 'Wilf Hutton has a pack of grown children. Did none of them see this man? Try to stop him?'

'Apparently not. The two lads had gone over the fell with some sheep. One of the daughters came for me.'

'The sulky one, I suppose,' said Sir John. 'Head in a book, she probably took no notice of the rumpus until her mother called her.'

I opened my mouth to say 'No, it was Betsey,' but thought better of it. Sulky wasn't the precise word I would choose for Dorcas. Difficult – angry, perhaps. To my surprise, I found I wanted to defend her – despite her irritating manners. Had I not, so many times, had my own dreams frustrated? And been accused of having 'ma heid in a book' when my presence was required?

Chapter Twelve

Dorcas' Journal

5th Day, 2nd Week, 4th Month

I am writing this in the barn. There is enough hay still to conceal the corner which has been my retreat in times of trouble ever since I was small. Soon it will be too dark to write, so I must scribble down my thoughts while I can. And hope, with God's assistance, to find my better nature.

I was furious when I heard Papa say that Betsey shall go to Ackworth School. That was very <u>wrong</u> of me. I am ashamed of my bad temper. Poor Papa was injured, and he and Mama must have been very frightened. If I had only been there and not in the upper meadow reading, I might have stopped the man, or at least taken note of where he went.

I am ashamed too that I let Hugh Armstrong see my bad humour. I should not have suggested that he had neglected his pony, leaving her where she might eat poisonous plants.

I know well that if things had gone better with the farm when I was the age Betsey is now, both Papa and Mama would have championed my desire for learning.

There was nothing wrong with the education I received at the Friends' School at Lancaster. We were taught to read, write, and reckon, and fitted for whatever our teachers and our parents believed we needed for our future lives. It was just that I longed for more.

Most of us would be returning to our parents' farms. We girls are expected to help there in the house and the dairy until we marry. Therefore, budgeting and needlework skills were much encouraged. A few girls were to be apprenticed in the town as shop assistants or maidservants. I remember wondering what that would be like, and envying Hannah Reeves, whose widowed mother apprenticed her to a milliner. That caused quite a stir of disapproval amongst the older Friends. She told us she thought she would like the work. I was sure she would, being so deft with her needle. How jealous Susannah and I were that she would be creating hats and bonnets. Not only plain Quaker bonnets, but pretty ones trimmed with lace and silk flowers for fashionable ladies.

Fortunate Hannah – or so we thought – we later heard that her pretty bonnets caught the eye of a rich man's son who got her with child and then abandoned her. Poor Hannah. The old Quakers shook their heads, saying that was where the vanity of dress was <u>bound</u> to lead.

I'm not very skilled at needlework, so would not have made a successful milliner, but I did yearn for something other than going home to the farm.

I longed then for knowledge, for scientific facts. I wanted to understand the weather, plants, the diseases of cattle and sheep, and how best to treat them, but I knew it could not be.

Papa understood how I felt, and he spoke with the School Superintendent about me. Then they offered me the chance to stay on at the school as a pupil teacher. I knew it was an honour, and I determined, with God's help, to do my best to meet their expectations. Although even then I wondered whether I would be able to control the younger children and make them mind me.

Mama is calling me to set the table.

Chapter Thirteen

Hugh

'I'd best go and interview this Farmer Hutton,' said Augustus Fenwick without enthusiasm.

'I've told you all he and his wife were able to recall,' I said, irritated.

'No doubt, but after the first shock of the attack, victims often remember something further, some detail that at the time seemed irrelevant or of no importance.' He gave me a look that said, 'I'm the detective here. You mind your business, young fellow, and I'll mind mine.'

As he mounted his knock-kneed nag and trotted away up the fell track. I became aware of Barker Tatham lurking in the doorway. I gestured to my employer that we should inspect the house.

'You will see considerable progress.' I said, hoping Sir John would assume it had been at my urging.

We viewed the newly installed roof beams. Tatham took us outside again to see the slates and explained their superior qualities to Sir John. All he got by way of reward was a series of grunts, and then, 'The weather seems set fair for now, Tatham, but as we well know, that could change. When I come next, I expect to see the roof completed and the windows fitted into their places. Lady Hathersage doesn't care for the house I hired in Lancaster.

She claims it is poky. She wishes to take possession of her new home as soon as possible.'

Once outside again, and free of Tatham, he said, 'I shouldn't have employed that gang. They did well enough at the mill, but they were up against competition in Preston. There are plenty of other men there who'd have liked the work. They think they can take their ease here, and I'll still be forced to pay them. I suppose they disregard most of what you tell 'em?'

Honesty, as always, must be my best policy. 'They do,' I admitted. 'They must sense that I know little about the business. Building drystone walls is not the same thing as building a house.' It sounded feeble to my own ears.

To my relief, Sir John shrugged and said, 'A man cannot be master of every trade. I suppose *I* must come out here oftener and kick those fellows up the backside. I need *you* to pay attention to that landslip on the upper fell road. I suppose you haven't done anything about it yet?'

It felt like weeks rather than a meagre forty-eight hours since he had given the order to deal with that.

'Not yet,' I admitted. 'I was on my way up there yesterday morning before I encountered the escaped prisoners. And to-day, of course, what with burying the corpse and the trouble at Rush Ghyll—'

'Two wasted days, then,' said Sir John, 'and too late to summon men up there now. Be sure to get it underway to-morrow, Armstrong.'

'Yes, Sir, I will.'

He looked Polly over critically as we went to untie our mounts. 'This creature of yours is not much of a nag, a bit long in the tooth. You ought to look around you for something better. She'll founder on you one of these days.'

Whether she understood this or not, Polly chose this moment to blow mucus all over my coat sleeve.

'Have a word with young Nathaniel Braithwaite. He was telling me he's got a nice fell pony he hasn't much use for. He bought it for his bride, but apparently, she doesn't care to go on horseback.'

'I might have a word with him then.' I gave Polly a dirty look as I pulled out my handkerchief to wipe my sleeve. I doubted I could afford a replacement, but Polly wasn't to know that.

I parted from Sir John. Evening was fast approaching. The sun was spreading a carpet of gold over the Irish Sea. The Isle of Man was a faint smudge on the horizon. In the village below us, the church bell tolled.

As Polly and I plodded homeward, I recited one of my poems.

> *Evening draws on, as shadows cloak the fell,*
> *O'er woods and dwellings sounds the evening bell,*
> *And now within their stalls, all tired creatures*
> *drink,*
> *Into distant waters, the golden sun must sink.*

She blew softly, as though to say, 'not one of your best, but not one of your worst.' Perhaps she liked the line about weary creatures drinking. On reflection, I didn't. Clumsy. It would have to go.

The trouble with composing on horseback is that the verse inevitably acquires a jog-jogging rhythm. Rabbie Burns, our Scottish Bard and my hero, almost always set his verses to music, to traditional songs he had heard from his Ayrshire childhood, which dictated not only the rhythm but the tone of the piece, be it merry or melancholy. Unfortunately, he had already made use of the best tunes, and I am not particularly musical.

I had heard that William Wordsworth walked a good deal, 'on high o'er hill and dale,' as he himself had written. Did he match his pace to his lines?

'I'll be walking up to that collapsed riverbank tomorrow,' I told my pony, 'and I'll see if I can improve that line as I go.' It amused me to pretend Polly understood me, a habit I had formed that winter when there had been no one else around. 'So, after today's busyness, you can take your ease once again.'

Low Bield, my isolated cottage, lay in a dip, its stone walls dimly visible in what we Scots call the gloaming. A bird chirped, a sheep bleated in the distance, calling home her lamb.

We turned down the short slope. The cottage was overshadowed, not only by the fell which rose sharply behind it, but by overhanging evergreens. We were in almost total darkness.

'*The ploughman homeward plods his weary way... and leaves the world to darkness and to me,*' I recited. (Unfortunately, this wasn't one of my own compositions, but it seemed appropriate. My thanks to you, Mr Grey.)

Polly drew to an abrupt halt before the opening that led around the cottage to her stable.

'No, you daft animal, keep going!' I pressed my heels into her sides. 'You've done enough today, auld lass, to deserve a rub down and your feed.'

She stood stock still, only her ears twitching.

I slid down from the saddle and took the reins over her head, meaning to lead her to her stall in the stone-built outhouse in which I stabled her, but she resisted.

What could be worrying her? I slackened the reins and listened.

Now I heard it. Rustling, as though a creature of some size was moving through the surrounding bushes. My nostrils caught the sharp smell of crushed vegetation. Some large animal, I thought – perhaps a fox or a deer. Whatever this was, it was pushing, barging its way through. It was making enough noise for a stray bullock, but there were none grazing in this part of the dale. Then, the rustlings ceased, and I caught, very faintly, the sound of footsteps above me on the lane. Human footsteps. I thought of the man in seaboots.

It was disquieting, but whoever he was, he had gone.

If he had broken into the cottage to rob me, he must have been sorely disappointed. What I had was of little value to anyone but myself. No more than a few pence in a purse on the mantelshelf. A couple of changes of under-linen, three shirts (one in sore need of mending). Books, yes, I have plenty of books, volumes about land use, drainage, and all aspects of upland cultivation. And books of poetry. Other men's verses. Should I ever take up thievery, it would be these that would tempt me. But there cannot be many such fools as myself.

I led Polly round to her stable. Now the trespasser was gone, she came willingly. Passing behind the house, I could see no sign that windows had been broken or forced. Perhaps I had arrived home in time to discourage the loiterer before he discovered that I rarely locked my door.

It seemed to me that I should be grateful to Polly for the warning. I rubbed her down vigorously, gave her water, a generous bunch of hay, and as a reward, a shrivelled carrot. Not one for showing gratitude, she lurched across her stall to get at these treats, shoving me out of her way with her rump.

I barred the stable door and managed to roll a heavy stone up against it with my one useful hand. No one would be able to move that without some effort and consequent noise. It had never before occurred to me that somebody might want to steal Polly. As Sir John had pointed out, as a piece of horseflesh, she was anything but a prize. However, she would be transportation for someone who had none.

There was no other human habitation within a quarter of a mile of my cottage. Through the long winter past, I had often been lonesome but never fearful. But these were unusual times. Those escaped Frenchmen with the pistol, and the fellow who had attacked Wilf Hutton, could still be hanging about the dale, looking for something besides my pony.

I made my way across the rough garden patch to the back door of the cottage. I slept in the nearest room, and if someone attempted to break into either house or stable, surely, I would hear them. But if, thwarted by my return this first time, they did succeed in breaking in, what would I, a half-cripple, do? I had no sword, no pistol, no weapon of any kind.

I remembered my grandmother's words. 'If a thief comes in the nicht, Hughie, Ah wad push a lighted candle in tae his maw!' I smiled. I didn't doubt for a moment that had the occasion arisen, she would have done so.

A lighted candle it would have to be. I had a store of tallow candles in the kitchen drawer. This must be my line of defence. Perhaps, having heard me talking to myself, the thief might believe I had someone else staying here with me.

Summoning my courage, I thrust open the back door and went inside. All was silent. I went straight to the room I had decided to call my study. It was a poor, bare place, plaster peeling from its walls, but here I had placed a table, a candlestick, and set out my writing materials. My books were in neat piles against the wall. My purse lay on the mantel shelf above the empty grate. In it were such coins as I possessed. Nothing had been disturbed. I went through the rest of the house. No sign of the prowler.

A man's rational self tells him all is well, but the irrational self remains a prey to the jitters.

I shut the wooden shutters to the lower rooms. They were anything but lightproof, but I wanted the candlelight to be visible, signalling that the place was occupied.

Others might have prayed for protection, but it was many a long year since I'd believed in prayer. God had never protected my brothers and me from my father's drunken rages. Instead, I sat late in my study, achieving little, meddling with those last two lines of verse. Seeking one rhyme or another, I eventually dozed. I awoke yelping in pain. Hot wax had dripped onto the cuff of my coat, burning a small hole and causing me to wake as it touched my skin.

Groggy, half awake, and cursing myself for being too cowardly to have gone to bed, I quenched the drooping candle and opened the shutters. The sky over the Eastern Fells was stained with the first golden glow of dawn. It promised to be a fine day. Last night's fears, and even yesterday's earlier alarms, now seemed completely absurd.

'You're a shargie wean, Hugh Armstrong,' I thought, 'a poor wee mannie,' just as your father and brothers always said. Then I thought of my elder brother Dougie, killed by a cannonball at the battle of Talavera. Of Neil, my other brother, who had struggled home from Portugal, with an injured foot and sick of mind, still unable to do more than sit by the fire all day; given to sleeping terrors, and screaming the whole household awake at nights. Braver, both, than I. But how had this served them? About my father, I refused to think at all.

Chapter Fourteen

Dorcas' Journal

6th Day, 2nd Week of 4th Month

Papa isn't, Our Lord be thanked, too much hurt. He looks rather grand in his turban of bandages, just as I imagine a Turkish Sultan. Wilf, Jonathan, and I teased him over the evening meal. Mama shook her head at us for our levity, but said several times how relieved she was that his hurts were no worse. I said how sorry I was that I had not returned from my mission to rescue a sheep and her lamb from a thicket in time to at least catch sight of the villain before he ran off. Mama sent me a sharp glance, as though she knew I was being deceitful. Susannah would have asked, but she has stayed the night at Lane End Farm and knows nothing of Papa's mishap yet.

Last night, once supper was cleared and Mama and I had washed the dishes, I slipped outside again. No one would miss me. Papa and Wilf were discussing how soon they might begin docking the lambs' tails against fly strike. Mama was knitting stockings to send to Isaac, away at school, stopping every so often to rescue Betsey, who was struggling to knit a scarf for her doll, and dropping a stitch on every row.

It was a fine night, cool but promising a spell of fair weather. Wrapped in my shawl, I walked down the meadow, my eyes adjusting to the darkness.

There were night creatures about, and of course, they heard my feet moving through the grass long before I heard them. A long-eared hare bounded across my path. A late blackbird called in alarm. Mice and shrews rustled in the long grasses at the field's edge.

Sounds travel further at night. I laid my hands on the wall at the foot of our meadow, and stood looking up at the stars, firstly those over Morecambe Bay, and then those above the fells behind our farm.

I was looking towards the trough road when I sensed something immediately below me, moving through long-neglected bushes and saplings – something larger than a sheep. My eyes had adjusted to the darkness, and I could make out the varying shades of black and grey. Below our meadow, the ground falls away sharply, so I was standing almost on top of the roof of the Low Bield stable. I could hear his horse pulling hay from the rack.

Whoever, or whatever this was, was moving across the parcel of land behind Hugh Armstrong's cottage.

My eyes soon found the moving shadow. It was a man, bent double, trying to move by stealth. Not Hugh Armstrong, surely, for why would he do such a thing? Could this be the man who had attacked Papa?

I froze, but he wasn't looking up, fully focused on his stealthy passage through the bushes. Then he stepped into the lane and disappeared. His footsteps sped up, then died away. He could have been a poacher from the village, after a hen or a rabbit. I don't think Hugh Armstrong keeps either, so he must have been disappointed. I would have liked to warn Hugh, but he would think it strange if I turned up on his doorstep, and what would I say? The man was gone.

Chapter Fifteen

Hugh

Next morning, I turned Polly out to graze before I had my oatmeal. The coming of dawn had restored me to my senses. Although Polly didn't move fast, she was a canny wee beastie, and as I knew to my cost, devilish difficult to catch. If anyone was planning to steal my pony from her paddock, good luck to them!

I set out on foot for the high lane. There, the March floods had eaten away at the bank above the beck and undercut the roadway that ran above it. Although it was early, the sun was already warming the fellside, and the sharp scent of the unfurling bracken shoots was in my nostrils as I tramped. Last evening's terrors now seemed completely idiotic. Why hadn't I called out to whoever it was who had been hanging about the cottage? Perhaps he had only been some tramping fellow, looking for a barn or a stable to sleep in.

The damage to the riverbank was much as I'd been told. I would need a team of men to clear the stream of rocks and boulders which the spring torrent had brought down from higher up the fell. We would also need to pack the undercut section with a barrier of stones to prevent the rest of the road above from collapsing. This track was one used mainly by drovers to take sheep and cattle to higher grazing grounds, or over into the next dale. However, though used infrequently, it was useful. Sir John was right to want to keep it serviceable.

An agent like myself must calculate to a nicety the number of hours a task will take, the additional materials needed, and the number of men he should summon to do the work, assuming they can be spared from their normal employment.

This ought not to have presented a problem, as Sir John had made clear to his tenants when he bought the estate that they must release men to work for me wherever and whenever I wanted them. In the midst of heavy snowfall, every farm except High Bield had willingly volunteered men and lads to dig out the lanes and go for urgent food supplies. However, this time, I was asking after the thaw – for people to pull men away from work on their own farms. Two days' labour, perhaps three, for three or four men by my calculation, for which, since the repairing of the collapsed bank was as much for their benefit as Sir John's, there would be no payment. It would be a test of my authority – how quickly and readily my summons was complied with.

There *should* be no problem. (*Worriting again, Hughie!*) Lambing was over, and oats, and such vegetable crops as were grown here were already planted out. The weather, though fine, continued cool, and the hay crop, which covered most of the lower slopes of the fells, would not be ready for cutting before the end of next month.

I tapped my pencil against my teeth, considering. How much warning should I give? As Sir John had remarked, the weather just now seemed set to stay fair for at least a day or two. Would the day after tomorrow be time enough for hired men or sturdy sons to be called back from ploughing, ditching, or coppicing, or on whatever tasks they were already embarked?

Most of the necessary stones for the fill could be removed from the beck itself. There were plenty of them, half-blocking the flow where the flood had helpfully dropped them.

I was sitting on one of the larger boulders, my notebook in hand, sketching the kind of barrier I thought would be needed to support the undercut, when I heard the scrape of footsteps on the track. I looked up.

Standing before me was Susannah's betrothed.

'Good day to thee,' said Nathaniel Braithwaite. My first thought was that he was dressed as though he was going to his wedding this very day. His coat was of the best grey superfine, his britches cut by a tailor who knew his work, his broad-brimmed Quaker hat adding inches to his height. His polished boots shone, and his stock, though of plain linen, was a starched poem. What on earth, dressed thus, was he doing up here?

He flushed slightly and said, 'We were to drive into Lancaster to look at a house I'm minded to take – to see, does Sukie like it. But then we got word this morning that her father had been attacked. Nothing would do but I must drive her back home – she's been staying with us at Lane End – to see how he was. I've left her at Rush Ghyll for an hour to satisfy herself that all's well. We can go down to Lancaster on the morrow if needs be, but I thought – Dorcas said she'd seen thee walking up this way – I thought I would like to ask *thee* about what's been happening.'

'I doubt if I can tell you much more than you will have already heard,' I said, blinking. I had seen him around with his father and brothers, but always in worn and patched britches and coat, better suited to herding cows or shovelling snow drifts. His sudden appearance, dressed, despite the muted colours, as a fashionable beau, astonished me. Surely an elegant Quaker was a contradiction in terms.

Of course, I recalled, Nathaniel was buying his way into mill ownership and would need to create a prosperous appearance. He was a slender young fellow, Susannah's beloved, taller than most of the dale's menfolk, with a fresh complexion and clear blue eyes.

I'm sure he was weighing me up at the same time that I was studying him. 'Susannah told me,' he said, 'about those men who attacked thee, then we heard the Trawdens had found a body on their land. Now, Wilfred Hutton has been struck down by a stranger. Nobody seems to know why these things have been happening.' His tone suggested that I should have ridden round to each family in Netherdale and explained what was going on.

I might well have done, had I had the least idea myself!

'What can all this be about, Hugh Armstrong?' he went on, 'and what does thee suppose Hathersage will do about it?'

Definitely accusing. Disapproving. Jealous perhaps. Could the lovely Susannah have spoken of me too warmly? I hugged that pleasant thought to my bosom.

'I know no more than you do, Nathaniel,' I said, 'I wish I did. Sir John is employing a detective, a man named Augustus Fenwick.' I realised, as I said this, that it was not strictly true. Sir John had *involved* Fenwick, who was already in the area, supposedly in search of a wanted man. Some arm of His Majesty's Government must keep the fellow in funds.

'This man, Fenwick,' I said, 'will very likely call to question your family, to hear if any of you have any information about strangers. Or anything unusual you, your parents or your brothers may have seen.'

If Fenwick proved to his satisfaction that this was the man he sought, he would also look for any associates in the locality. I didn't imagine for a moment that the Braithwaites at Lane End Farm had anything whatsoever to do with it, but some mischievous wee de'il in me hoped to aggravate this overly earnest young man.

'I thank thee. I'll tell my father the matter is being looked into,' Nathaniel said, solemn as a tombstone. 'I'm sure my parents and my brothers have seen nothing untoward.' He nodded towards the broken bank. 'Dorcas Hutton tells me thee is looking to repair this landslip?'

Did she now? And how did Dorcas know that? I had, as yet, spoken of it to no one other than Sir John. She must have been out and about this morning as I set out up the fell. Perhaps she had been looking for a sheep that had strayed, or checking on a calf, and knowing about the land slip, had guessed that this was my destination. There was nothing secret about my errand, but I found myself slightly uncomfortable with the notion that I was being watched. Or should I be flattered that someone was interested in my movements?

'Yes, I'll be calling out some men to help.' I said, gesturing to my notebook. 'Maybe some of your brothers can be spared? My idea is to build a wall of stone up against the bank to support it. Perhaps double thickness to give strength, with a base of large boulders. Most of the stones we can take from the burn...I mean the beck. I don't consider we would need to cart any up from below.'

'Happen not. I mean, I *suppose* not. I'm sure my father will send people up to help thee.'

I hid a smile. This fellow was setting himself up to speak like a gentleman. Soon he would be rounding those flat north country 'a's, and saying 'you' instead of 'thee' and 'thou'.

'I hear you are leaving the farm for the mill? How do your father and brothers feel about that?'

'We are in unity on the matter,' he told me, deadly serious. 'I felt it was right for me to do this, and if I can make a success of it, our whole family will benefit.'

Yes, I thought, and if all goes as you hope, there will be a pleasant town house furnished with little town-wrought luxuries that the farm could never provide, and with the beauteous Susannah, queen of this domain, pouring tea for callers in a charming parlour. In my head, I recalled what I had heard an acquaintance say, 'Ah, the Quakers! They set out to do good, you know – and they do very well!'

Yes, Nathaniel Braithwaite, I felt sure, meant to do very well indeed.

'I wish you every success,' I said, hoping success wouldn't find him in too much of a hurry. Envy, pure envy, on my part. I had no real reason to dislike Nathaniel Braithwaite. He was undoubtedly a good, sound, if overly serious-minded young man, kindly disposed to his fellow men and women. He was a polite fellow, too. I could see he had observed my weak arm and shrivelled hand, but he'd not mentioned them.

'I must go,' he said. 'Susannah will have had time to reassure herself that her father is not seriously hurt.' He pulled a plain but handsome watch from his waistcoat pocket. 'There is still time to drive into Lancaster. Are there any errands we could do for thee there?'

Surprised, and a little ashamed of my unkind thoughts, I assured him there were none. As he disappeared from sight, I thought that I should have asked him to check at the staging post if any letters were being held for me. I had heard nothing from Grandma for some weeks.

Chapter Sixteen

Hugh

Three days later, we commenced our reinforcement of the river-bank. Wilfred Hutton had sent me Young Wilf and Jonathan. This was generous of him since he must still have been feeling the effects of the attack upon himself. Two of Nathaniel's brothers, Joseph and Henry, and an older Kelsall cousin whose name I never learned, also came, apparently quite willingly, from Lane End. To my surprise, Batty Trawden also joined us. Such was his excitable nature that there was an ever-present danger that he'd drop the stones he was carrying on someone else's foot. The other lads tolerated him with surprising good humour, but I grumbled to myself that we'd have done better without him.

The Braithwaite brothers had brought a message from Daniel Jackson, who farmed Quernstones, the fourth farm in the dale. He was suffering from quinsy, but was pleased to spare me a hired hand, a man named Gabriel Waller. Seven men.

They all listened in polite silence while I outlined what was needed. Then they turned as one man to Gabriel Waller.

I should have guessed from his name. He must be the many-times-grandson of men who had, over many centuries, built the walls that snaked away over these fells as far as the eye could see. Apparently, he'd shored up many a fallen riverbank, too.

'Does thee think it can be done, Gabe?' asked young Wilf Hutton.

'Aye,' responded this individual. ''Appen t' lad's' (meaning me) 'got the right of it, but we mun 'step' it. Match stones so they lock one another in place where we can. Tha mun choose them as 'll fit together to stop 'em slipping. Dost tha see? Biggest 'uns at t' base, and lean 't' wall into t' undercut careful like. Use small stones behind the big 'uns 'to reduce the strength o' flood water so it don't leech more o' the soil from the bank.'

My workers hung on every word, although my own head was buzzing, trying to follow his manner of speech. He was worse than a Frenchman! Yet heads around me were nodding. What he was saying was undoubtedly sound sense.

'An' then,' said Gabriel Waller, with only a brief, questioning glance in my direction, 'it'd be best t' build out a leg into t' stream, a letter J as they calls it, wi' biggest boulders. That'll push water away from this bank towards t' middle of the flow. That way, when the flood waters do come down, they'll stay in t' middle o' the stream.'

This was certainly something (if I was understanding Gabriel correctly) that was worth trying. We would cause the stream to change course slightly, so that the main force of the torrent in times of flood would travel down the centre of the stream bed, and not pound relentlessly against this bank.

So we did. Or rather, they did. A man like myself, who has only one useful hand, could only watch and encourage. Stone was piled upon stone, and boulders were hauled together and set in a curve out into the stream bed to deflect the current away from the newly reinforced bank. I was supposedly the man in charge, but I might as well have sat down, taken my copy of Mr Wordsworth's latest verses from my pocket, and left them to proceed. No one said anything. I saw no sly glances in my direction, but still I felt a useless lummox.

Before I could sink too deeply into dejection, however, there was an excited shout from Batty Trawden on top of the bank. We had visitors. Lydia Hutton and her daughter, Dorcas, were walking up the lane.

They were carrying great baskets of provisions. I hadn't thought what my workers were going to eat. I'd assumed that, like me, they would fill their pockets with a hunk of bread and a slice of cheese, and drink, when they needed to, from the stream.

Clearly, I had misjudged how things were done here. Without a word, the young men assembled around the two women and bowed their heads.

'We give thee thanks, Oh, Lord, for this our daily bread, and we thank thee for thy many blessings, and thy care for each one of us as we go about our appointed tasks this day,' proclaimed Lydia Hutton, and the men and boys muttered, 'Amen.'

Only Gabriel Waller and I removed our hats. Quakers, I later learned, consider that the Lord is uninterested in hats, and they give 'hat honour' to no one. Except sometimes God.

'I'm inclined t' Methodism, meself,' muttered Gabe at my side, 'and I don't hold wi' women doing the praying and preaching.' He cast darkling looks in Lydia's direction, but if she noticed, she gave no sign of it. This gathering of young men seemed to find it quite normal that she should be the one to pray over their meal. When she finished, they arranged themselves in groups on the ground, while Dorcas moved amongst them, inviting them to take bread, cheese, and corked flasks of small beer from the baskets.

I thought Dorcas looked better today, her hair tidier, and she had washed her face. Instead of the filthy old coat, she was wearing a russet cloak and bonnet which suited her olive complexion.

Perhaps, I thought, she looks for a husband amongst these young farmers. However, I could detect none of the flirtatious smiles and giggles I had seen so often when a young woman found herself surrounded by young men (although seldom when around me). Presently, she came to us. Gabriel had brought his own repast and declined, but I didn't want to appear rude, so I took some food from Dorcas.

'Did your sister like the house Nathaniel took her to see?' I asked, hoping she wasn't offended that I had taken only a small portion.

She frowned. 'I believe she liked it well enough, but the day did not go well because Nathaniel developed a fever, and Susannah had to take the reins and drive them home.'

'Lot o' that going around,' contributed Gabriel Waller. 'Spring fever, I reckon. She didn't tip 'em into t' ditch then?' He chuckled, nudging me in the ribs with his elbow, 'When a woman teks the reins, I say watch out!'

For all his expertise with walls and riverbanks, I could take a dislike to Gabriel.

'Oh, Zebedee is a steady animal,' Dorcas replied, gravely. 'Susannah managed him well enough, and he knows his way home.'

'I hope Nathaniel's illness is not of a serious nature?' I said, hoping to discourage Gabe, or at any rate make it clear that I didn't share his opinions. Or enjoy being dug in the ribs.

'I think not,' said Dorcas. 'His mother didn't seem alarmed, and as thee can see, his brothers felt no qualms at leaving him for the work here.'

With this, she walked away.

'A girl who says only what she must,' I murmured, shaking my head.

'Aye,' agreed Gabe, and blow me if he didn't dig me in the ribs again. 'A good sign in a woman, that.'

I stood, to move away, frowning. Lydia Hutton and her daughter were gathering up the remains of the meal, and the prisoners were getting to their feet and stretching, when we heard a shout and rapid hoof beats coming up the track.

'Armstrong, the Master sez come quick!' It was James Carr, Sir John's groom, riding bareback astride his master's carriage horse, the long driving reins doubled in a clumsy bundle over his arm.

He slid down and took a moment to catch his breath. 'Him an' the detective fella has caught yon spy. Mebbe the same fella as knocked Wilf Hutton out of his senses? Will yer come? Here, yer can tek the hoss. I'll walk back down.'

It was a command I couldn't refuse. Yet, scrambling onto the horse's back, I wondered why they needed me. *I* had never set eyes on this spy. Would it not have been of more use to show him to Wilf Hutton? Or to Lydia, who had at least caught a glimpse of him? *If* this was the same man.

The horse, however, seemed to think he had his own orders, which were to get back to Dalefoot as quickly as he could. He swung away down the track at a smart pace, with me clinging on by my knees and lower legs, my good hand entangled in both his mane and the long driving reins. I hung on, in acute danger of being thrown over his head, as we forged off downhill. Only sheer determination not to slide off ignominiously in front of an interested audience kept me on the wretched animal's back.

When I arrived at Dalefoot I could not immediately find Sir John and his tame detective. The carriage, however, was there, the shafts resting on the ground, so they could not be far away.

I slid down from wilful Incitatus and went indoors, noting as I did the lack of Barker Tatham and his merry band. Evidently, it was too much to expect these builders to be present on a daily basis.

I found Sir John, Augustus Fenwick, and their captive in what would one day be Lady Hathersage's drawing room. I'd expected to find the supposed spy bound and gagged, or at the very least cowering before his captors, but this was not the case. The man was seated in one of the window embrasures, head cocked, hands on his knees, apparently completely at his ease. He was a stocky personage with sparse gingery hair, clad, as Wilfred Hutton had described, in a heavy overcoat and a huge pair of boots, their loose tops turned back at the knee.

'This is the rogue!' pronounced Sir John, shaking his stick at him. 'Fenwick spotted him on the road and ordered him to come along with us. We took him and showed him to Wilfred Hutton, and he recognised him!' Sir John was mightily pleased with himself.

Why then was I needed?

'We cannot make anything of his discourse,' Augustus Fenwick explained. 'Armstrong, you said you knew the French lingo when you heard it spoken, so maybe you can make something of what he says?'

'I do recognise French when it is spoken as *being* the French tongue,' I said, 'but that doesn't mean I can understand it.' As I looked the man in the eye, I saw a cheerful twinkle. I believed the wretch understood us.

I held his gaze. After a moment, he seemed to come to a decision and grinned widely, displaying his quite appalling tobacco-stained teeth.

'Francais, non,' he said, 'Américain.'

The three of us gaped at one another.

'American,' gasped Sir John, 'but don't Americans speak English? I'm sure they do, unless they happen to be Red Indian braves, or African slaves?'

'There are some French settlers along the Eastern seaboard, around Louisiana,' said Augustus Fenwick.

The French-speaking seaman – if he was a seaman – hearing the word Louisiana, nodded vigorously, and then spat on the floor. 'Napoleon,' he growled. 'No good!'

'Ah, he doesn't like Napoleon,' said Sir John, nodding sagely as though he now understood everything. Augustus Fenwick and I looked at each other in mutual bewilderment.

Why was this man here? A French-speaking American could hardly arrive in Netherdale by accident. And, whoever he was, why had he attacked Wilfred Hutton?

'The Parson,' I asked, tentatively, 'the Reverend Mr Chorley. Might he own a French phrase book, or know of someone in the district who does?'

Chapter Seventeen

Hugh

'A good thought, I'll go to him,' said Sir John. 'Carr can drive me there in a jiffy.' Catching my eye, he corrected himself. '*Quickly* – as my carriage is here, and the Reverend Chorley knows me well. I'm certain he'll be more than happy to lend me such a book if he has one.'

I wasn't sure if Carr had arrived back yet, but he must have fairly scampered down the fell road after me, because we soon heard the carriage rumble away.

This left Augustus Fenwick and me to guard the prisoner, although he showed no sign of running off, but sat smiling on his window seat, apparently waiting for us to entertain him.

At our previous meeting, Augustus had shown himself to be a man of many words, but he seemed, surprisingly, to be stuck for any suited to this occasion.

So, I tried. 'Louisiana? You? Ship? England?'

Our prisoner thought about this for a few moments and then nodded vigorously. 'Lan-cus-tair.'

'Lancaster?'

'Oui.' He grinned, exposing his horrid teeth once again. So, he had sailed to our local port, but in what ship, and whether he was the master of it, or merely a common sailor, and how he had found our dale, eight or nine miles inland, and why, it seemed he could not, or would not, tell us.

'Man,' I pointed the way Sir John had gone, 'get book.' I mimed opening and closing it. 'French.'

Our captive heaved a sigh and said something that sounded like 'Jay fam,' and rubbed his belly.

'I think he's hungry,' said Augustus. Then he added, 'So am I, come to that. Sir John was going to drop me so I could bespeak a bite in the village, but then we spied this fellow lurking in a ditch along the road. I jumped down and collared him, and came on here.' He took a pocket watch from his waistcoat and studied it, adding gloomily, 'I suppose that parson's wife will offer Sir John refreshments. Nothing but them tiddly bites at Madam Chorley's, but she takes her time over the serving of 'em. We could have quite a wait.'

The hunks of bread and cheese in my coat pocket weren't enough to offer to both men. Perversely, I was more inclined to give it to the Américain. His cheerful demeanour made it hard for me to think of him as a great villain. I must not forget what he had done to Wilfred Hutton.

'I suppose we might as well be seated,' said Augustus, walking towards the second stone bench and slumping down on it.

'We might,' I agreed, 'since your prisoner shows no signs of escaping, as he easily could – there is no glass in these windows. I suppose he believes *we* may have information about the man or men he is seeking. So, rather than running away, he intends to wait to discover what it is.'

Augustus snorted. 'If I had been on foot when we came across him, I would have gone on by, but then doubled back and followed him, to see where he went. He could easily have got away when Carr and I took hold of him, but he didn't seem bothered.

Kept grinning when we stowed him in the carriage, as though he was pleased to get a ride.

'He's looking for someone in this district, and urgently. We may be sure of that. By my reckoning, he's here to make contact with someone, but as yet, he hasn't found them. He's either a spy or he's being paid to give or receive information. Which amounts to the same thing.'

The man beamed steadily at us. I still thought he understood more of the English tongue than he would admit.

I held his gaze and pointed to my chest. 'Name, Hugh Armstrong,' I said, and gestured that I expected a reply. He frowned, puzzled. I repeated my name, once again pointing to my chest. His frown deepened, and he shook his head.

I turned to Augustus Fenwick. 'You must know this better than I. In this present war, are there many Americans who have chosen to fight for the French?'

'Hundreds of 'em,' he grumbled. Some don't believe their War of Independence is over. Others go for this 'Liberté, Egalité, Fraternité' stuff in a big way, so they've weighed in on the French side. They say there's shiploads of 'em been captured and incarcerated. I heard they've even got a gang of 'em helping to build the new prison on Dartmoor.'

'But our friend here,' I nodded towards him, 'seems not to care for Napoleon Bonaparte.'

'Ah!' Augustus widened his eyes and raised a finger in the air as though a great light had dawned, '*That'll* be because of the Louisiana Purchase. That and the fact that Boney has made himself Emperor, which displeased those who thought all men should be equal.'

Our nameless French seafarer was nodding vehemently. He understood and agreed with our assessment. It was I who was now at sea.

'But what *is*, or was, this Louisiana Purchase? I've heard of it, but what did it consist of?'

Augustus lowered his voice. '*Boney* sold a great parcel of American soil to the government of the United States. Land that France had staked a claim to. But those American rascals offered him a deal of money for it. The money he needed for his wars in Europe. So, he sold it. And not just the State of Louisiana on the Eastern seaboard, but thousands and thousands of miles of good land beyond there, empty of anything but tribes of pesky Indians! The President and his senators were well pleased with their bargain.'

I whistled. 'The French settlers must surely have felt betrayed?'

A snort from the prisoner told me I was right.

'Then,' I asked, 'how is it that there are French-speaking Americans fighting against Great Britain now?'

Augustus shrugged. 'Some are sailing ships for the United States' navy. There's mercantile shipping too, of course. Transporting goods back and forth between the Americas and the Continent. Piracy, as others see it.'

'And so, we capture their ships and imprison the crews?'

'Not just Americans,' said Augustus, 'Dutchmen, Danes, Norwegians too. They all swear blind they're not in the pay of the French, that they didn't know when they signed on that they'd be supporting Boney's war effort. Some of 'em get ransomed by the ship owners, some are left to rot in prison for a year or two. *You* must know, Armstrong, that the gaols are bursting at the seams with all kinds of filthy foreigners.'

He gave me a look that made me uneasy, as if he knew *I* might have some special knowledge of prisons. He had what I supposed a Cockney accent, but Fenwick, like Armstrong, was a name from the Scottish border. He might still have relatives on either side of it. Was it possible he had heard something about my father's disgrace?

I made an effort to steady my voice. 'A relative wrote to tell me they've built a great new prison in Perth to house prisoners of war, as far from the English Channel as possible. So they cannot escape, steal small boats, and row themselves back to France.'

'Costing the government a fortune, no doubt,' grumbled Fenwick. 'And we'll all be taxed to pay for it. Although I suppose it's work for your compatriots, building these places and guarding the inmates.'

Maybe he knew nothing of my family's troubles. Was he actually a Londoner who thought the whole Scottish nation came under the heading of 'filthy foreigners', along with Norwegians, Danes, and Dutchmen? I was wondering how to steer our conversation into less turbulent waters when we heard footsteps and voices, and Sir John Hathersage burst into the room.

He was accompanied by the Reverend Chorley, his wife, Wilfred Hutton, his head still swathed in bandaging, *his* wife Lydia, and their daughter Dorcas.

Dorcas had something in her hands.

'It's been quite a conundrum,' declared Sir John, 'to find a book of the French language. The Chorleys had none. I thought we might have to go into Lancaster and consult with some schoolmaster, but then we met with Mistress Hutton and her daughter, and it seems that Miss Dorcas owns a French phrase book, and here we are.' He glanced around the room, but did not immediately spot the Frenchman.

'Gah! You haven't let the rogue escape?'

Augustus indicated our captive.

'Has he told you his name and what he's doing here?'

'Not a word, Sir John,' I said. 'All we know is that he is from Louisiana, he maintains that he speaks only French, he has no favourable opinion of Bonaparte, and he's hungry.'

Sir John waved this away.

Come, Miss Hutton,' he said to Dorcas, 'Let us hear what you have in this phrase book of yours.'

Chapter Eighteen

Dorcas' Journal

2nd Day, 3rd Week of 4th Month

(I am writing this in bed, Susannah still being away. I hope Mama will not see the light from my candle burning on the night shelf.)

They were waiting for me at Dalefoot, in a bare, half-finished room. I untied the strings of my cloak, shrugged it from my shoulders, and passed it to Mama. Then I stepped forward, phrase book in hand. The room seemed full of people, although, to my relief, most of them were hidden from my sight by the brim of my bonnet. I looked straight ahead at the prisoner, who was seated on a stone bench. This surely could not be so different from reading out a passage from the Bible, or from the writings of one of our Quaker forbears. I have never minded reading aloud, although it always sets poor Sukie atremble.

Determined that my quaking knees should not betray me, I opened the phrase book at a place I had marked with my finger on the drive from Rush Ghyll. Then I planted my feet and took a deep breath.

'Bonjour, Monsieur,' I declaimed. 'Je m'appelle Dorcas Hutton. Comment vous appellez-vous, s'il vous plâit?'

Realising I was speaking to him, the man rose to his feet and gave me a mocking bow. Whether I had spoken the words correctly to a French ear, I cannot judge. However, it must have been approximately right, since he blinked, grinned, and then shook his head.

'Mais non, ma petite,' he replied. He was laughing at me. At all of us, I suppose.

'Non?' I demanded, in my sternest tone. Sometimes this had worked when I stood in front of a class at Friends' School. Unfortunately, sometimes, indeed too often, the children had paid me no attention at all. 'Non, Monsieur?'

'Non,' the man said, beaming from ear to ear now. I had the impression that everything about the situation struck him as amusing – the crowd of onlookers, mouths agape, the only one to attempt his language, a young, plainly dressed Quaker girl. He had no intention of giving the information he must have known we wanted.

I read out several more phrases, but all the Américain did was laugh, bow, and kiss his hand to me.

I didn't want to give up, but I could see no help for it. I turned to our landlord, John Hathersage, and said, 'I'm sorry. I think he knows very well what I ask, but he doesn't wish to answer.'

'Well, I'll grant you have tried,' he said, 'so now we'll take him to the authorities and have him incarcerated until the wretch changes his tune.'

I would have liked to explain this to the captive. I riffled urgently through my phrase book, but could find no way of saying, 'These men will take you to prison. It will be horrid there, and you would be better advised to tell them what they want to know.'

Then the detective, together with John Hathersage's manservant, James Carr, stepped forward to take hold of the man's arms. He thrust them away. Everyone tensed. I think we were all convinced that he would attempt to jump out of the window and run away. Instead, to my astonishment, he walked up to me, seized my hand, and planted a kiss on it! The first time I have ever received a public salute from an unknown man. What was I to make of that?

'Ma belle! Très charmante,' he murmured, laughing, as Fenwick and Carr hustled him out of the room.

As he passed, he dragged back for a moment to look at Papa's bandaged skull, shook his own ginger head, and murmured something I couldn't hear. Papa, who is always charitable, said later that he thought it *may* have been an apology.

Everyone then streamed outside to see the prisoner bundled into the carriage. I followed slowly, disappointed at my failure, although I didn't see what else I could have done. If *only* I had been able to study the French language properly.

Augustus Fenwick bound the man's hands behind his back with a narrow coil of rope. I suppose a detective must keep such things in his pocket in case of need. He and James Carr manhandled the Américain into the carriage, although he made little resistance. Sir John Hathersage followed, flourishing his cane to let the man know it would be useless to attack him during the journey. James Carr, mightily pleased with himself, jumped up onto the perch. Then they drove off, leaving everyone standing in the road staring after them.

'What will happen to the rogue?' the parson's wife asked as the carriage disappeared round the bend in the road. 'Surely they'll hang him.'

'I shouldn't think so, m'dear,' said Parson Chorley, 'since he's bound to claim to be a prisoner of war. I daresay they'll find someone who has a much better knowledge of French than the

Hutton chit. Someone who'll be able to question him effective-ly.'

Chapter Nineteen

Hugh

Dorcas Hutton remained standing in the doorway, watching the carriage until it disappeared from sight. I attempted to thank her. I thought someone ought to.

'I wish I'd had more time to search through this book,' she replied, biting on her lower lip. 'Unfortunately, this is intended for persons who travel to France and wish to book a bed in a hostelry, or admonish a dishonest tradesman. Apart from asking him his name and where he comes from, most of the phrases I found in it were quite unsuitable.'

'You have studied French?'

She shrugged. 'I've tried a little on my own, but even if I'd made more progress, I doubt if that man would have answered me. And if he had,' she sighed, 'I may not have been able to make anything of his replies.'

With this, she walked away to join her mother and father, who were setting out to walk back to Rush Ghyll.

I had been sorry about the Chorleys' slighting comments. Now I felt somewhat slighted myself. Dorcas Hutton was a difficult creature, no doubt about that.

I had intended to ask after her father. How was his head wound healing? And about Susannah and her betrothed. Had Dorcas heard how Nathaniel was? Was he recovering, and was

Susannah remaining at Lane End Farm to help nurse him? The common phrases of polite discourse. One might as well try to converse with a standing stone in the middle of a field.

Ah, well, the day was too far advanced to return to the work site up on the fell. The sun was now low enough in the sky to tinge the clouds above the Trough with salmon pink and gold. Milking time. Which would, I realised now, have called all the labourers home an hour ago.

The task of reinforcing the riverbank was most likely finished anyway under Gabriel Waller's expert tutelage.

This left me to close such doors as had so far been hung at Dalefoot and set out along the lane for my own home. I could see Lydia and Dorcas Hutton turning up the track to Rush Ghyll. Dorcas was hugging her phrase book to her bosom.

Wilfred had dropped behind. He now turned, a hand shading his eyes, to look back along the dale, following the progress of Sir John's carriage on its way to Lancaster. Seeing me, though, he waved and began to walk back down the fellside. I quickened my pace, and we met at the foot of the track.

'That French fellow,' he said, 'will Sir John tell thee how it goes with him?'

'He may, but if not, I will try to find out what becomes of him, and let you know.'

Wilfred nodded, 'They'll imprison him in the Castle. I'm hearing that conditions are bad there. *Inhumane.* Joseph Dockray and John Ford spoke to us on this matter at our last Quarterly Meeting.'

I didn't say anything to this, being ignorant of prison conditions generally myself, and never, for private reasons, having been inclined to enquire. A portion of Grandma's most recent letter flashed across my inner eye.

...Your father is still awaiting sentence. They say now he'll likely escape the rope, but may be transported.

Your brother Neil and I have been twice to visit him. Would ye believe, he would not see us! The gaoler would have let us in (once I had given him the price of a drink), but he himself denied us. Sent word we were no to come bothering him, an innocent misused man! He that has cheated so many, ruined so many, and caused those who defied him to go in fear of their lives!

Well, what could we do but leave him in that terrible, stinking place? However, on the second occasion, as we left to journey home, Neil hobbling along with his injured foot, the gaoler hailed us back to the gate with a message.

The man did his best to recite your father's words, but what was meant was a puzzle. It seems he has written a will, and we, meaning Neil and I, since we insist on coming to pester him, are to expect nothing by it but the house (which I believe we already own!) But 'the cripple,' he said, meaning you, for he has not set eyes on Neil since he came back from the war, 'since he, at least, has taken himself off, and not stayed around to gloat over my suffering. I have sent him a small package to remember me by.' (I'd imagine it's his watch.) Naturally, we

121

*asked the gaoler to repeat this over again, but I'd
advise you not to get your hopes up, Hughie.*

'Seems we should be looking into the state of the prisons,'
Wilfred was saying now. He stood staring out over the moorland,
bruises showing below his bandaged brow. 'We got them to listen
about the slaves. I myself wrote to Prime Minister Pitt once a
week. Happen we should try to get this Robert Jenkinson fellow
to listen about conditions in the prisons.' He meant the Earl of
Liverpool.

He seemed utterly serious. He had written to the Prime Minister once a week. Did he genuinely imagine that the great politi-
cian actually read his words? It struck me as the greatest affron-
tery that these Quakers thought our rulers might change course
at their urging, but then, even if it changed nothing, perhaps they
felt better for having their say.

By 'we', he must mean his fellow Quakers. Like everyone who
ever scanned a news sheet, I suppose, I had read that the Quakers,
Nonconformists, and other English worthies of the Dissenting
sort had campaigned hard against the transporting of slaves from
Africa to the West Indies and the Americas. I hoped he wasn't
attempting to include me in this new crusade. My relationship
with Sir John Hathersage wasn't such that I dared involve myself
in such things lest it get back to him.

Wilfred Hutton and I parted with a polite nod on my part, but
nothing more.

I arrived at Low Bield to find Polly at the gate, nickering
expectantly. I told myself the animal was pleased to see me, but
knew in my heart she was just hoping for a carrot. I thought of
fair Susannah tending her pompous ass of a swain, and sighed.
Would there ever be a smiling fair one at my door to welcome me

home? A man living in a damp cottage, with a pile of discarded attempts at poetry, and just three shirts – one needing mending? I doubted it.

Chapter Twenty

Hugh

We heard nothing more of the captured Américain for the better part of two weeks. Life in Netherdale continued in its familiar courses. No one held me up or pointed a gun at me. No one else reported wild men accosting them with iron doorstops.

Nathaniel Braithwaite still had some fever but was thought to be mending. It had been agreed to postpone the wedding for a few weeks while he recovered. I'd discovered that the Quakers organised their weddings as they pleased. Needing no licence or clergyman, the couple made their vows before the congregation, or as they would say, 'the Meeting', and those present acted as witnesses, the couple's proof that the ceremony had taken place. We did almost the same in Scotland, although so haphazard were our Scottish arrangements that it was doubtful that every couple obtained much in the way of proof.

After a day or two of heavy showers, I walked up to the place where we had repaired the landslip and found it holding well. As I helped a pair of adventurous lambkins out of a ditch, I considered how soon it would be reasonable to summon another work gang for a stretch of dilapidated walling along the main road out of the dale.

Early one fair May morning, I set forth towards Dalefoot, determined, if I found them, to tackle Barker Tatham and his rascally crew.

They were not only there when I arrived but were setting out their tools and materials to begin putting slates on the roof. Which rather 'spiked my guns', as my soldier brothers might have said, and made redundant most of the blistering speech I had prepared to chivvy them along. When I had been barely a quarter of an hour inspecting their progress, who should ride up on his big roan gelding, but Sir John Hathersage himself.

'They've placed that Frenchie fellow in a cell on his own,' he told me. 'Seem to think putting him in solitary confinement may loosen his tongue.'

My personal opinion was that it little mattered whether the man's tongue was loosened, since it was unlikely anyone would be found who could understand what he said, but this I kept to myself. Hesitantly, I said, 'Sir John, is it possible that the two escaped prisoners who held me at pistol point were also some of these Américains?' We had all of us assumed he was here in search of the man buried on the Trawdens' land, but perhaps he was trying to meet up with those fellows?'

As I spoke, my conscience prodded me sharply in the ribs. It reminded me that little Betsey Hutton had first pointed this out, but I decided this need not be mentioned.

'That's not for us to worry about!' grunted Sir John. 'Certainly, any such escapees should be rounded up. I have said my piece to the authorities and intend to leave such matters to them. Although I must say I thought we'd heard the last of these pesky fellows from the other side of the Atlantic since that disgraceful treaty of '83. Our government gave in far too easily on that, far too easily.' He jabbed the air in front of him. 'And now I hear that this monster Bonaparte is to be exiled rather than hanged. I'm sure we all thought that battle he lost at Leipzig back in October would put a stop to his pretensions, but no. *We* should have been at Leipzig, not left it to those Austrians, Prussians, *Russians*, and other European riff-raff. He should have been imprisoned, but our Generals left that to those others. Exile to Elba! Pah! And they say King George is mad. So, we are to be ruled, if *ruled* is the word for it, by the Prince Regent. What sort of example is *one like that* setting our young men? Wine, women, and gambling at cards! The whole country's gone to Hades!'

I said nothing to this sudden outpouring. Who was this 'we' he spoke of, who should have been at Leipzig? Not himself, of course. Young men like my brothers, who, seeing no chance of advancement at home, had gone willingly enough to serve under Wellington on the Peninsula. Or those snatched from the streets by recruiting sergeants. They all made cannon fodder.

Sir John was glancing at me expectantly, but before he could question my silence, there was a yell and a sharp scraping noise as a ladder slid from the roof, bringing down a flurry of slates. The workman standing below scrambled out of the way, but one of the falling tiles had cut his scalp. A stream of blood poured down the man's face, dripping into his eyes and mouth. A gory sight.

Sir John Hathersage, that fiery fire-side Major-General, gulped, moaned, and slithered into a dead faint at my feet.

'Eh! Now what?' demanded Barker Tatham, who had come charging forth at the sound of the crash.

'*Is he dead*?' He peered down at Sir John, looking as though he might faint himself, probably at the thought that a dead employer would not pay. Others of the builder's crew now emerged and stood about, staring at the apparent carnage.

There was a short silence, followed by a good deal of throat clearing. It seemed they were expecting me to take charge. I seized the arm of the injured roofer to stop him stepping on Sir John's motionless form.

'Whoa, hold still, fellow,' I commanded, 'One of you lads, take him to the pump and clean him up! He isn't badly hurt. It's just cuts to his forehead where the skin is stretched tight. That kind of wound bleeds freely.'

All three workmen went with him, preferring not to be around if and when the owner of Dalefoot regained consciousness. I said to Tatham, 'Get one of them to fetch a bowl or a jug of water. We need to revive Sir John.'

Barker Tatham inched forward again and stared down at the prostrate mill owner, 'Tha's *sure* he's not dead?'

Since the mound of Sir John's stomach was visibly rising and falling, I was able to reassure him.

'Don't know as we 'as any jugs or bowls,' he said, doubtfully.

'Anything that will hold water!' I snapped, exasperated. '*Water* to bring him round!'

'We might 'ave a bucket?'

'Then go and fill it!'

However, as he turned to go in search of it, hoof beats and the rattle of wheels in the lane made us both look round. Sir John's carriage came to a halt at the gate. James Carr jumped down, pulled down the steps and opened the carriage door.

Tatham and I watched in surprise as a large female posterior appeared in the doorway. A lady swathed in many ruffles and flounces, and wearing a viridian pelisse trimmed with white fur, took a step backwards. She was a big woman, and her flowing garments made her bigger, so that she completely filled the doorway. Nevertheless, the descent was going well until her poke bonnet caught on the upper edge of the carriage door. This headgear sported a face-framing brim before, and an upstanding high crown behind. Two huge dyed green ostrich feathers waved above it. It seemed the lady could not complete her downward climb without strangling herself with her own bonnet strings.

James Carr stood mesmerised on the spot, his mouth open wide enough to swallow a passing crow. I advanced to offer assistance. 'Madam, I fear your hat is caught,' I said. 'Perhaps, if I steady your arm, you could untie the strings and remove it?'

Her head turned, and small twinkling eyes half-buried in a fleshy face, met mine.

'Better make meself decent first off, lad,' she said with a chuckle, and began tugging at the bodice of her gown. During her struggle to exit the carriage, it had slipped to reveal a good deal more of the lady's ample bosom than she intended. It was this, I now realised, that had struck the manservant dumb. There was nothing for it but to avert my eyes while she hitched up her gown and untied the bonnet strings. Then she removed her hat, placed her hand on my shoulder and stepped onto the ground.

'Lady Hathersage, your servant,' I said, bowing. I should probably have said, 'your humble servant,' but something about the plain speakers of Netherdale had rubbed off on me.

'Ah, you must be Johnny's new land agent,' she replied amiably, replacing the bonnet, but leaving the strings dangling. 'I was away on a visit to my cousins in Manchester, and missed meeting you when you first came.' Then her eyes strayed to her husband, who was coming round, waving his arms, and attempting to turn over. He looked, for all the world, like a large beetle stranded on its back.

She trotted over to him 'Whatever's happened to tha, Johnny?'

'Lavinia! What the devil? What are you doing here?'

'I've come to see my new house,' she replied. I've waited long enough to see it. You went off early on the hoss, or we could have travelled comfortably together in the carriage. What are you doing down there like a stranded whale, old lad?'

'Blood!' my employer gasped, 'Oh, Lavvy, you *know* I can't stand the sight of blood.'

Chapter Twenty-One

Hugh

'Why, who's been bleeding?'

'One of the... workmen. There was an accident.' Sir John quavered. 'Oh, it was horrible, *horrible*, Lavvy! Is he dead?'

This last question was addressed to me.

'No, Sir. All will be well once they've cleaned him up. Just a few cuts to his scalp, Ma'am,' I assured Lady Hathersage.

'Ah, all's well then,' she said. 'Do get up, Johnny, and show me about the place. I *am* going to live here after all. I want to see what I'm getting. I suppose there's no one hereabouts that could brew up a dish of tea for us?'

She turned to me once more. 'You look a handy young fellow,' she said. 'Could you boil some water? Here,' she produced a package from her reticule, 'I brought enough for a dish of bohea. Johnny, tha'll feel much better with a hot drink in tha belly. Tha knows tha will!'

I was beginning to like this woman. I liked the twinkle in her eye, the way her speech slipped back to the way she must have spoken as a girl, before Sir John inherited his fortune and made her Lady Hathersage. I approved of the way in which she looked at things. No one but Grandma had ever asked me to make tea, but I agreed at once. The workmen kept a fire burning in the yard behind the house. Very likely, they had a tea kettle I could use.

'Perhaps Sir John should go inside and sit down, Ma'am?' I suggested, 'while I boil the water and find some err... suitable receptacles.'

'Cups, tha means?' said the lady. 'Oh, I supposed there'd be none up here and packed 'em. James, look to the hamper!'

Sir John had by this time managed to struggle to his feet. His lady took him firmly by the arm and led him indoors. Carr followed with the hamper. As he passed, he tipped me a wink.

There was precious little comfort to be had within the bare walls and glassless window frames of the manor, through which a brisk spring breeze blew unhindered. However, by the time I returned with a pannikin of boiled water, Sir John and his wife had established themselves on the stone window seat in what would one day (soon, I sincerely hoped) be the parlour. Sir John was still mopping his brow with a great linen handkerchief, while her Ladyship laid a dainty lace-edged tablecloth beside her on the stone and added three delicate China cups.

'There now,' she said, producing a teapot and a stoppered jar of milk from the basket, '*Now* we shall have a brew. Then we'll all feel ready for anything.' Sir John, still mopping and sighing, didn't appear convinced, but she was not to be discouraged.

She proceeded to fill the cups. Beaming, she offered one to me. I was touched by this, although there being no chair, table, or indeed any piece of furniture to rest it on, I realised to my dismay that I would be forced to stand to drink it. No easy matter for a man with only one good arm and hand.

I need not have fretted, however, because our genteel tea drinking was not to be. From outside, we heard two angry voices, one of them James Carr's, soon to be drowned out by the bleating of many sheep. And in they rushed, a herd of twenty or so, ewes and half-grown lambs, trotting and skittering through the empty rooms until they found us.

Behind them came young Jonathan Hutton and James Carr, both shouting at the woolly invaders to 'git on out of it!'

I don't know if you have ever been surrounded by a flock of sheep. If so, you will know that their woollen coats after a long winter are nearly as solid as their bony bodies beneath. Pushing against your legs and thighs, they can have you capsized in an instant and trampled upon. I hastily backed myself against the nearest wall. The teacup I held up before me like a flag of surrender. I knew I must look ridiculous, but I hoped my employer and his wife were too busy worrying about themselves to pay attention to me.

Being seated, they were not in any danger to their persons, but Sir John bellowed, 'What the devil!' and Lady Hathersage shrieked and dropped her cup, which smashed on the stone sill. The room echoed with bleats and baas and shouting from Sir John and James Carr, while Jonathan Hutton, red in the face and gasping for breath, poor laddie, tried to use his crook to turn the invaders back the way they had come.

The flock would have none of it. The leading ewe – there is always one – fixed me with a wicked yellow eye and then plunged out of the next window. Over the sill she went, with the rest of the flock, ewes and lambs, streaming after her, leaping over it and down onto the sloping field below. Away they flowed, across land farmed by the Braithwaite family. After them, but not before he had (I thought) caught the eye of each of us, leapt Rush Ghyll's sheepdog, Rags. If a dog can be said to have a pained expression, his declared, '*This* was none of my doing!'

'Sorry, laddie,' I said to Jonathan. 'You've lost them!'

'Happen tha'll have to go and ask Sam Braithwaite to give 'em back!' panted James Carr, but there was a glint in his eye. I was beginning to understand that James enjoyed any kind of mischance, provided it could not be blamed on him.

'Get yourself out of my house, boy!' roared Sir John. 'I shall have words with your father, indeed I shall. If you can't control a flock, he shouldn't trust you with them.'

Jonathan, I saw, was in tears. With mumbled apologies, he turned and fled from the room. Now that the sheep had gone, we could see the deposits they had left liberally sprinkled over the floor.

'Carr, could you hail one of the builders and ask him to come with a broom?' I suggested.

'Well, I do declare!' Lavinia Hathersage was breathing heavily, bosom and chins wobbling, but eyes still twinkling, 'I said, did I not, that once we'd had a refreshing cup of tea, we would be ready for anything. Of course, I never expected something of *this* nature.' She looked at the state of the floor, kicked up the hem of her gown to examine her modish satin half boots, and said, 'I hope James can find a broom. I wouldn't want to walk through that lot. Whatever can have made those sheep come in here?'

While I hesitated to reply, Sir John grunted.

'That was one of Wilfred Hutton's boys,' he finally said. 'I'd have expected better. Hutton trains them up well as a general rule.'

I held my peace. My guess was that Jonathan Hutton, herding his flock a little carelessly, had crowded them against the glossy paintwork of the Hathersage carriage. James Carr, responsible for keeping it in prime condition, had intervened, shouting and waving his arms. This then caused the flock to panic and rush in through the open front door.

'I hope that poor boy will catch them again,' said Lady H.

'I'm sure he will, Ma'am,' I said. 'They've struck across the fields onto the Braithwaites' land. Samuel Braithwaite's walls and fences are in good order, and the dog will keep them together. Jonathan will find them safe enough. It's possible he is on his way to Lane End to have the lambs' tails docked. They were planning to do that in the course of the week.'

'Yes, yes, no harm done in the long run,' opined Sir John. 'The oldest Braithwaite boy is set to marry that boy's sister. I shan't make a fuss with Wilfred Hutton. Let the boy worry that I might. He'll be more careful another time.'

'Didn't you tell me the wedding is delayed?' Lady Lavvy demanded.

'So I'm told, said Sir John, 'The lad picked up some kind of fever, though I can't think how he should. I understand he's on the mend though, so the wedding won't be put off many more weeks.'

'I heard she's a very pretty girl,' began Lady Hathersage, stopping when one of Barker Tatham's minions appeared with broom and shovel.

'Looks don't count with *them*,' said her husband, ignoring the in-comer. 'Dressed so plainly, all their women look homely. It's 'Is she walking in the Light?' Whatever *that* means! Or 'Can she turn her hand to baking and rearing sickly lambs?"

Nonsense, I thought. Susannah Hutton would still be a beauty dressed in sackcloth and ashes. But I held my tongue.

'I'm sure that's very sensible,' said his wife, comfortably. 'I mean, that's what must be needed on a farm, surely.' She ran her hand over the soft, rich fabric of her own gown where it fell smoothly over her plump thighs. The man with the broom gave her a sideways glance.

''Tis mortal damp in these mills,' he suddenly remarked, 'and allus dust in the air. Happen tha can catch a fever thereabouts.'

Sir John's face turned the colour of a fresh-dug swede at this uncalled-for interjection from a mere labourer, but Lady Lavinia was eager for information from whoever could provide it.

'Oh, do you think so?'

'T'is sure,' the man replied. 'They keep them weaving sheds warm and damp, Missus. Cotton or silk, both. Keeps the thread pliable, see?' With cotton, it's them *speckles*, from the fibres that comes afloating in the air and gets swallowed down on t' men's chests. Can mek a man powerful sickly. I don't know as 'tis the same wi' silk, but they say it's dusty, so I reckon so.'

'That poor young man! I do hope he recovers in time to marry his sweetheart,' declared Lady Hathersage. She dabbed her eyes with a corner of her handkerchief.

'Oh, for sure he will,' said Sir John. I could tell he wanted to turn the conversation rather than have his wife indulging in idle chatter with this low fellow wielding a broom.

'Do you think you will like living here, your Ladyship? Once the house is finished?' I asked, thinking to help him out.

'Oh, I'm certain I shall,' she replied. 'Once it is truly finished, and furnished throughout. It's hard to tell how it will look when it's so bare and empty. I've been looking at samples of wallpaper,' she announced. 'This new printed paper to line the walls is very expensive, you know, but I've seen some lovely designs – flowers, and suchlike. They assure me it's quite the fashion, and Johnny here did say I might have what I liked. You *did*, Johnny, now don't go forgetting your word! It's all printed with blocks on paper rolls. Then they apply flour paste to the back of the roll and hang it on the wall. And there it stays. I'm sure it will look quite exquisite here.' She looked around the empty room, evidently seeing these glories in her mind's eye. 'When it's all finished, and we're settled, we must have an open day, my love – and invite all our friends. Do you suppose our farmers and their wives would like to see it?'

Thinking of the whitewashed simplicity of the Hutton and Braithwaite farmhouses, I doubted Lydia Hutton or Martha Braithwaite would care for such things, but I didn't want to pour cold water on Lady Lavinia's scheme to welcome her neighbours to her new home.

'Oh, they'll all come for a look, see,' said her husband. 'Bound to. Human curiosity.'

Chapter Twenty-Two

Dorcas' Journal

2nd Day, 5th Week of 4th Month

The wedding will be two First Days hence. How relieved I will be when it is over, and Nat and Sukie are gone on their wedding journey to Westmorland. They are to stay in a hotel close to Lake Windermere. The lakes and the mountains are said to be very like Switzerland, and the hotel claims to arrange pleasant jaunts and expeditions. Very grand. Mama and Papa did not quite like the idea, thinking it not in keeping with our Testimony to Simplicity, but Nathaniel prevailed.

I am writing on the kitchen table today. Everyone has gone to Lane End. Papa and the boys are to help with the sheep. Mama and Sukie are to talk with Martha Braithwaite about the last-minute arrangements. I cannot imagine what more needs to be arranged.

The wedding breakfast is to be at Lane End as it is nearer for everyone coming from Lancaster and through the Trough, and the access for carriages will be easier. Mama was a little put out, as it is the custom for the bride's family to host the breakfast, but she tried not to let her disappointment show. She says she quite understands that some of the elderly Friends won't want to climb up the rough track to Rush Ghyll. Of course, she is already planning to bake up a storm to add to the feast. Is Mama competitive? Oh, Dorcas, how could you think such a thing of your dear mother!

My dress and Betsey's are finished. Sukie, bless her, helped me a great deal with mine. I think it becomes me better than I expected. Nathaniel gave us a bolt of dark green silk from the mill. It had a long flaw in the lower edge of the weave and would otherwise have been discarded. Happily, we were able to find enough unblemished cloth for both dresses.

Mama agrees it suits my sallow complexion, but was a little unsure about the colour. I reminded her that Margaret Fell of Swarthmore Hall, one of our revered founders, disliked the fashion among Quakers to wear nothing but grey and black, and urged us to wear the colours found in nature – browns, greens and russets.

Betsey's dress is only just long enough. I'm sure she has grown quite an inch while the wedding was put off.

Hugh Armstrong called to see Papa two days ago. I saw them talking in the yard, but he didn't come indoors – perhaps fearing we would subject him to another dose of Silent Worship! He told Papa that the Américain remains imprisoned in Lancaster jail, and no one has been able to get a word out of him, although they feed him only bread and gruel. Hugh has heard nothing of the two soldiers who held him at gunpoint. Some think they may have made it to the docks under the cover of darkness and found a ship to take them off. Or they may still be hiding out somewhere around Morecambe Bay.

Papa is somewhat exercised about the Américain. He has received letters from acquaintances who attended our Yearly Meeting Gathering in London. A good deal was said about the bad conditions in the prisons all over Britain, and not just those housing prisoners of the French War. It seems Friends are particularly concerned about the conditions for <u>women</u>. Many, they say, have their little children with them, since there is no one to care for them. I should like to visit Lancaster Castle and see for myself whether the same is true there, but I am unlikely to be given the opportunity.

Chapter Twenty-Three

Hugh

The lambs' tails had been docked and each flock treated for maggot and foot rot. Sir John's tenants hoped the sheep would flourish and that the clip this year would be a good one. My assistance was not much needed. I had been made to feel in the way at times. The Netherdale farmers had long learned to be self-sufficient. The man who owned the land before Sir John Hathersage hadn't taken much interest in the farms hereabouts, having a much larger estate across Morecambe Bay. Apparently, he had required little of his agent other than that he ride over the sands whenever he could, to collect the rents.

Nathaniel Braithwaite, much recovered from his fever, though still clucked over by his mother, was as little wanted as I. We spent an hour together, leaning on the gate, watching the farmers at work. He told me a house had been found for Susannah and himself in Lancaster, although neither of them had seen it. 'I *think* we will be happy there,' he said. 'It would be a great shame to have all the business of packing up and moving to another place. However, Sukie is a very amenable girl, and I'm certain she will do her best to make our home a place of peace and refreshment.'

What a bag of wind he is! How can that lovely lass bear to listen to him prosing on? I thought, quite unfairly.

Then, to my surprise – and shame – he invited me to their wedding!

The building work at Dalefoot House had taken a great leap forward, and Sir John and his lady would soon be moving in. The house was full of painters, carpenters, and men with pattern books of fabrics for sofas and chairs. Lady Lavinia drove up in her carriage twice a week to tell them how little she liked what they'd done. I had decided my presence was unnecessary now that the major building work was complete. However, Lady Lavvy (as she urged me to call her, saying everyone did, although I would never dare to her face) insisted she valued my opinion, and would send for me to say what I thought – or rather have me agree with her against the advice of visiting tradesmen.

This could be inconvenient. On one occasion, I had to heave myself out of a ditch and walk half a mile (slapping my thighs as I went to remove mud from my work britches) simply to confirm what the lady had already decided about fabric for the drawing room chairs.

Sir John, however, was happy that I had taken his lady's fancy, excusing him from what he admitted were 'tiresome domesticities'. And, as I've never been sure of my employer's temper or his approval, I did my best to humour his wife.

Lambing was over, but 'haytiming' would start in a month or so, requiring the efforts of every man, woman, and child. Meanwhile, the wall along from Lane End farm needed to be rebuilt. If we didn't do it now, there would be no time before the autumn. Meanwhile, it would be necessary to rig up some temporary fencing for Sam Braithwaite's field lest his animals stray.

I had resolved that I would get the new wall built without any interference from Gabriel Waller. However, having assessed the job and found the footings of the original to be more decayed than I had thought, I gave in. This required an expert. I swallowed my pride and went to see Daniel Jackson at Quernstones to ask if he knew Gabriel's whereabouts.

Jackson was the Netherdale farmer I knew least well. His farm appeared tidy, his stock well cared for, and he always paid his rent on time. I'd had no reason to have more than a passing acquaintance with him. He was a widower with two sons aged fourteen and fifteen, but I'd been told that his health, of recent times, was poor. This was the reason he called on Gabriel Waller, a relative of his late wife, for assistance. It was a small farm, and I'd have thought two sturdy boys could probably manage the milking and the general day-to-day work around the place. However, they probably needed the occasional kick up the backside, or at any rate more vigorous oversight than Daniel, in his state of health, could give.

Having negotiated my way past a gaggle of unfriendly geese in his yard, I found Daniel at home alone, seated in his tidy but sparse kitchen. I could have guessed, without being told, that Daniel had no wife living. No bunches of herbs or bacon flitches hung from the beams, and what had once been an elegant China teapot had a broken and clumsily mended spout. He sat on an upright chair, his bandaged foot propped on another. 'Gout,' he said with a groan, 'and I never touch strong drink, so I hope that's not what tha's thinking!'

His lads, Timothy and Philip, he told me, had gone into Lancaster to the beast market. 'Not to buy, tha understands,' he said. 'Just to have a look, see. We lost one of our old milkers over the winter. Our Tim thinks we should get another, but I don't know.' He sighed deeply. 'If I were up to it, I'd go myself, but as tha can see, I'm in a poor way. Can't get my breath some days. I suffer something terrible with lumbago, tha knows? And now this gout is about killing me.'

Apart from his bandaged foot, he looked healthy enough. He had a decent amount of flesh on his bones, his eyes were clear, and his cheeks were ruddy. Indeed, when I had mentioned him to the Braithwaites or the Huttons, there had been some restraint in their replies. His poor health was alluded to, but without much concern, as though it was an unalterable fact of life, like the weather.

Lydia Hutton had pursed her lips a little, but all she said was, 'He doesn't make it to our First Day Meetings very often. One can worship alone at any time and in any place and find strength and guidance. However, it's so much better to come and sit *together* in God's Light and wait on the Lord.'

I had started out that day with some fellow feeling for another backslider in religion. However, once I'd sat through a half-hour's recital of his woes, all the while wanting simply to know how I could make contact with Gabriel Waller, I found my sympathy waning.

'Gabe?' He finally caught hold of the name. 'Oh, Gabe comes now and again to give my lads a hand. Not too often if I have any say in the matter. He eats us out of house and home. He lives down by Crook O' Lune. Why does tha want him? Has that bank slipped again?'

'No, it's holding well,' I assured him, 'but the wall just along from Lane End Farm is in a bad state of repair. I could use his expertise. Get it fixed while we have a few quiet weeks.'

'Aye, and with that withered hand o' thine...' He didn't finish the sentence, but he meant 'you're a cripple and good for nothing.' Rich, coming from the shirker I suspected *he* was! 'I daresay Gabe'd do it if tha paid him.'

I gulped a little, but of course it was reasonable. Gabriel Waller was not one of Sir John's tenants. His previous help must have been as a favour to Daniel. I would need to square the cost with

Sir John before I approached the man himself. I would write a note and give it to Lady Lavinia, whom I knew to be at Dalefoot just now. I had passed her parked carriage earlier in the day.

I took up my hat then, and thanked Daniel, intending to leave him to his woes, when he suddenly said, 'Should tha get some of them Frenchies to help fix yon wall? Happen they know nowt, but they'd be good enough to fetch and carry the stones for tha. Gabe said the Duke's men've been using 'em. Free and all! Gabe wasn't best pleased, but it seems they were just put to sorting and carrying stones. The Duke's agent still sent for him and paid him to do the laying.'

I was picturing the two ruffians with the gun, but then the conversation at Rush Ghyll came back to me. Young Wilf Hutton had thought French prisoners of war were being used on one of the great Bowland estates. I would mention this to Sir John. He was bound to welcome the possibility of free labour, and it would be better that he, rather than I, should approach the prison governor.

As I reached Dalefoot, James Carr was holding open the carriage door for Lady Lavinia. I broke into a jog trot, waving my hat aloft.

'If you please, my lady, may I write... a quick note to Sir John?' I panted. 'If you are not in too much of a hurry.'

James Carr raised his eyes to heaven. Lady Lavvy, however, was delighted to be 'at my service,' and ushered me indoors, where she pressed on me a pen and a sheet of her scented note paper. I think she sometimes forgot that she was the titled person, not I.

She then had to oversee what I wrote, fussing that she must hold the paper steady so that I didn't smudge it, 'with your poor arm,' as she put it, standing so close that I could feel her warm breath on my ear.

'Do you think Mr Higgins will allow Johnny some of these men?' she asked, reading over my shoulder. 'I'm sure it would be such a help to *you*. And I think the prisoners might like to be out in the fresh air, and not crowded together night and day in the castle's cells. Do you not agree? I've never been inside the castle, but they say it must be *very* damp.' She shuddered at the thought.

'Their help could be useful, Ma'am,' I said. 'These men are not criminals, but soldiers who happened to be fighting on the side of our enemies. There must be a corresponding number of British men languishing in French prisons. We would wish that *they* have access to fresh air and useful activity, would we not?'

'Yes, you must be right!' said Lady Lavinia Hathersage warmly, 'And we should treat these men well, in the hope that Napoleon will do the same for our poor fellows?'

'Exactly so,' I told her, moving towards the door. 'I won't hold you up any longer, Ma'am. I have the impression Carr wants to get you back to Lancaster without delay.'

'Does he?' she said, surprised, 'I suppose he thinks Johnny wants him for something this afternoon, although my husband said nothing to me. Or if he did, I've clean forgotten.'

Chapter Twenty-Four

Dorcas' Journal

1st Day, 2nd Week of 5th Month

A momentous day! Today, my sister Susannah married Nathaniel Braithwaite of Lane End Farm at our First Day Meeting. How lovely she looked in her gown of pale grey sateen silk, the bodice embroidered in matching silk thread. Her bonnet (with what some thought a shockingly high poke!) was covered in the fabric, and she had a long-fringed silk shawl around her shoulders which hung almost to her dainty feet in their fur-trimmed slippers. Nathaniel wore a coat and britches of brown superfine, white silk stockings, and a snowy-white stock. What a delightful picture they made as they spoke their vows.

'I, Nathaniel Braithwaite, do take thee, Susannah Hutton, to be my wife, promising through Divine assistance to be unto thee a loving and faithful husband as long as we both on earth shall live.'

And she answered, 'I, Susannah Hutton, do take thee Nathaniel Braithwaite to be my husband, promising through Divine assistance to be a loving and faithful wife as long as we both on earth shall live.'

And so they were married, and signed their names on the parchment on the table beside them, where later we would all sign our names as a token of our prayerful support for them throughout their married life and all their days to come.

Then came the ministry from those present. Anyone may speak in our Meetings, of course, but the Elders will always have plenty to say, and say it they did, one after another.

Papa and Rachel Stout spoke most movingly, I think, although I find it hard to recall exactly what they said. I had promised myself I would not cry. After all, I am not in the least jealous of Sukie's good fortune, and I wouldn't want anyone to suppose I am. Nat Braithwaite, no matter how rich he may grow with his silk manufacturing, would never do for me. Nonetheless, I felt my eyes begin to fill as they recited those beautiful, <u>beautiful</u> words. I blinked the moisture away, though when I saw tears running down Mama's cheeks, and quickly passed her my best handkerchief. She was sad to be losing Sukie, although she believes Nat will suit her well, but I think some of her tears were for George, our brother, who is still missing. Where <u>can</u> that silly boy be?

The Meeting House was as full as it could be. Every Quaker family for many miles around had made the journey. Braithwaites, Huttons, Kelsalls, Stouts, Tophams, Whalleys, Robinsons, and Satterthwaites, Fords and Lawsons, they were all there, a positive forest of bonnets and broad-brimmed hats. And dogs, amongst all the farmers, trying to squeeze under the benches so as not to have their tails and paws stepped on, should their master rise to speak. There were at least five farm collies, watching the proceedings with wary eyes.

In addition, I was astonished to see Hugh Armstrong, squeezed between Robert Topham and William Galbraith, and looking *most* uncomfortable. (We had trapped him into Silent

Worship again). I determined to speak to him, and assure him of his welcome, since he would not know many of these people.

Enough for now, I am too tired to write more tonight.

Chapter Twenty-Five

Hugh

Sunday, or 'First Day' as the Quakers insist on calling it, was fine and pleasant. No doubt, I thought sourly, Nathaniel had prayed on it and believed the Lord had provided this just for him and his bride. High clouds floated above the Trough. A cuckoo was calling in the woods, and the hay meadows smelt sweet in the warmth of the sun. It would be ready for the scythe very soon now.

I doubted my attendance at the wedding was a wise idea. I was in no position to take a wife, and in any case, had no beloved of my own in view. The occasion would only serve to remind me of this dismal fact.

I had mentioned, perhaps rashly, to Sir John and Lady Lavinia, that Nathaniel had invited me to his nuptials. Lady Lavvy was inclined to pout, offended that the two families had not thought to invite *her*, but Sir John said heartily that he was happy that I should go and represent them both.

'It's sure to be a long-winded affair,' he said. 'Those Quakers claim they meet in silence to hear God's guidance, but I doubt the Creator gets much of a word in. Some of those old fellows in their broad-brimmed hats can prose on for half an hour, if, as they say, 'the Lord moves them.' We must send a gift. Both families are good tenants, good farmers.

'Mind you, I doubt young Nathaniel is acting wisely, buying his way into that mill,' he went on. 'What can he know of silk manufacture? I, for one, will not be surprised if he suffers a mighty fall and has to crawl home to his father. Still, Susannah is a charming lass, pretty as a picture, and we must wish them both well, must we not, my love?'

'We'll send them a bundle of sheets,' said Lady Lavvy, brightening, 'the very best quality cotton percale, from our own mill in Preston,' she added. 'I should think they would be very pleased to have them.'

So, I went to the wedding and found the experience uncomfortable in every sense. I have to admit, Nathaniel, though a trifle pale after his illness, cut a fine, upstanding figure. The bride was lovely – how could she not be? However, I thought she looked a little anxious rather than radiant. Perhaps she was afraid of forgetting the words she had to recite, although she and Nathaniel remembered them perfectly.

It had been explained to me that Quaker couples married each other by this particular form of words; no one officiated, but everyone present was a witness to their spoken vows. An ink pot and parchment had been laid on the table in front of the couple. First, Susannah, and then Nathaniel signed their names.

My discomfort was caused not so much because Nathaniel had captured the loveliest lass in the dale, but because the room was packed. The narrow wooden benches were hard on one's posterior. I had the bony elbow of one old farmer pressed into my ribs on one side. The hat brim of another cut off my line of sight every time he bent forward in prayer, or simply to ease the pressure on his own hindquarters.

And lying across my feet was a dog. A collie who must have taken a swim in the Nether. Throughout the proceedings, his wet coat pressed against my stockings and the hem of my britches.

I suspected I would spend the rest of the day trailing this canine aroma wherever I went. He seemed a nice dog. From time to time, he raised his intelligent yellow eyes to meet mine and panted.

'What are we doing here, you and I?' he would have said, could he speak. 'Would we not both rather be out on the fellside with the sheep?' But we had no alternative but to sit this out.

An hour of extempore prayers from those gathered, and it was over. Two old fellows whom I took to be the Elders shook hands. People began to surge forward. I assumed this was just to congratulate the happy couple, but then I saw that the quill was being taken from the ink pot. The whole assembly – men, women, and children - were taking turns to inscribe their names on the parchment that the wedded pair had signed.

Not thinking this to be any business of ours, the dog and I remained seated.

After a while, I became aware of the rustle of skirts. A short figure appeared at my side and spoke.

'Hugh Armstrong?'

Dorcas Hutton, the sister of the bride. It took me a moment to recognise her, so neat, clean, and yes, elegant, did she look. She was dressed in a gown of fine-ribbed dark green fabric. Her Quaker bonnet was covered with the same stuff. Under this, she wore a cap edged with a narrow band of cream lace. These were hues I might have expected to see on an older matron rather than a young girl, but it struck me that she ought always to wear them. They suited her brown, gypsyish complexion. For some reason, I was reminded of larch trees.

'Miss D-dorcas? A d-delightful ceremony,' I stammered, 'I hope your s-sister and her husband will be very happy.'

'Oh, I feel sure they will,' she replied. 'Thee must come and wish them well, and sign thy name on their marriage certificate.'

I must have looked bewildered.

'It's our custom,' she said. 'Everyone present signs the marriage certificate, which is proof, should any be needed, that they are bound to one another, man and wife. Nat and Sukie will keep it as a memento of the occasion.'

'But I am not of your... persuasion.'

'Doesn't matter,' she assured me, gruffly. 'Thee is here, a witness to their vows. So come and sign thy name.'

I rose, carefully side-stepping the plumed tail of my canine friend, and began to follow Dorcas across the busy room. But, before we got anywhere near the certificate, an elderly lady in a dusty black bonnet seized Dorcas by the arm and began to gabble excitedly to her about how delightful this whole occasion was, and how pleased she was to see dearest Susannah wed. She led Dorcas aside, apparently to repeat what she had said over again. I was swept forward by the press of sturdy farmers and their plump wives, all making their way to the small table on which the certificate lay. It struck me as remarkable that no one upset the ink pot and spoiled the precious parchment. I finally added my own to the columns of names, many of which I recognised. The same ones were repeated again and again. Then I found myself swept out by the crush, into the sunny morning air.

There, I discovered, all were intending to make their way, either on foot or by pony trap, to Lane End Farm, where the wedding breakfast was to be held.

Perhaps Nathaniel had assumed I would attend the feast. Sir John had been eager for me to represent him at the wedding ceremony. But did he mean me to spend the rest of the day in his tenants' company, making polite conversation? I told myself I had things that needed my attention, but the truth was I would feel uncomfortable amongst these good people. I knew them only through my employment. And it was the Sabbath. Whatever these people chose to call it, it was *my* day of rest.

I could hear my grandmother's voice in my head. *Och, be honest wi yerself, Hugh! Ye're jealous o' yon laddie that's found his lassie. Ye dinae want tae see them sae happy taegether!*

I was on the point of making hasty farewells and bolting, but I hesitated just too long. Riding up the lane was Sir John Hathersage himself, a package tied behind him.

'All done, is it? They're wed?' he demanded as he saw me. 'Excellent! You can take this bundle from me.' He hitched it from behind his back and dropped it into my arms. 'Give it to the bride's mother or the groom's. Doesn't matter which. Our gift, my wife's and mine – the bedsheets you know – for the young couple. But that's not what I wanted to see you about, Armstrong.'

The wedding guests were fast disappearing around the bend in the lane. The wedding breakfast was being snatched away from me, whether I wanted it or not.

Sir John dismounted and led me aside so that we might speak in confidence. I would have liked to lay the bundle of sheeting down amongst the meadow flowers at the lane's edge, but we were also close to a number of fresh cowpats, so this seemed inadvisable. Instead, I stood as though cradling a large, swaddled baby in my arms, whilst the last of the farmers and their families streamed by.

'I've got 'em for you,' he said, and as I looked down at the bundle, 'No, no man, not the sheets, the *men* – a gang of prisoners to help you with the walling. I spoke with Governor Higgins, and he agreed most heartily. The place *is* very over-crowded, what with our own native miscreants, and a whole wing of the castle given over to debtors. I think the Governor fears a riot.

'The cells are overcrowded, he tells me, and the stink from the piss buckets is indescribable. There aren't very many French prisoners just now. Those that he has were bound for some new gaol in your homeland, but there's been a delay. No one's sure what is going on, now that old Boney is on his way to Elba.

'The men are discontented, of course, and those who have a few words of English are complaining about their conditions. The governor hopes sending them out into the countryside, and giving them something useful to do, will help to calm the situation. Meanwhile, some of the injured men can be set to cleaning the cells whilst they're gone. A dozen Frenchmen, you're to have! I *think* they're all French, but it doesn't matter, enemy prisoners anyway.' He paused for breath, while his horse snatched noisily at the wayside blooms.

'A couple of warders will bring them up on a cart first thing tomorrow to start the work. Can you get that fellow Gabriel Waller to come and to instruct them?'

I assured him that I would make every effort, mentally calculating whether it would be better to abstract one of Daniel Jackson's sons from the wedding feast, or saddle Polly and go to Crook O' Lune myself.

'Splendid!' said my employer, 'I shall ride up again in a day or two to see how things go. I feel I'll be doing my patriotic duty, relieving the people at the castle of these challenging prisoners.' He rubbed his nose thoughtfully and chuckled. 'Even the men our English regiments have been recruiting are a pretty variable lot, I daresay. Either side has to take what they can get, ha?'

'The Scottish regiments, too,' I said, thinking of my brothers.

Sir John Hathersage did not reply. Thoroughly satisfied with his morning's work, he remounted and rode away. I stood watching him for as long as it took the horse to carry him down the lane and out of my sight. As if I had a presentiment of what this commission would bring.

Chapter Twenty-Six

Hugh

Once Sir John had ridden off, I thought it would be rude to arrive at Lane End when the meal was already underway. Better that I should leave the parcel of sheets with a passing Quaker, and go in search of Gabriel Waller. He had told me he was 'inclined to Methodism.' I would probably find him singing his heart out with his dissenting congregation in Brookhouse or Caton. I would have to ask a villager which and catch him as he and his fellow worshippers disgorged from the service.

Besides, in the silence of the Quaker Meeting, something had surprised me. Into my head, two new lines for that verse of mine suddenly formed themselves. A gift from the Almighty? No, I assured myself, it was simply that, undistracted by everyday affairs, the mind may solve a problem, or in my case, produce lines that had hitherto escaped me.

They would only complete a single verse, but I was suddenly hopeful that it was a worthy start to something greater. I had originally written:

Evening draws on, as shadows cloak the fell,
O'er woods and dwellings sounds the evening bell,
And now within their stalls, all tired creatures
drink,
Into distant waters, the golden sun must sink.

Those last two lines were clumsy, both in meaning and rhyme, yet I had not found a way to improve them. Now I had:

In fields and stalls, all weary creatures rest,
Sinks now the golden sun in the waters of the West.

Rest and West. Much better rhymes than Drink and Sink. Was the whole verse better? Was I sure? Maybe that last line was a syllable too long. Perhaps further inspiration would improve it yet again. One verse alone can hardly be called a poem, but it was a better start than I had hitherto. I called in at my cottage and scribbled the lines down in a notebook before I forgot them.

'I hope,' I told Polly, as I saddled her and set off to find Gabriel Waller, 'that this does not mean I will find it necessary to attend the Quakers' Worship on a regular basis.'

On the road between Quernmore and Brookhouse, trotting gently through deserted lanes, between fragrant meadows, my pony and I were at peace with the world. A little wistful in my case now that the fair Susannah had wedded another, but not unhappy. A few lines had been bubbling in my brain for several days and now I had the poem.

Far from the haunts of man,
Beside a rushing stream,
A fair young maid was dwelling.
Her face was seldom seen,
Her eyes were blue as summer skies,
Her smiles would melt my heart.
But she is to another pledged,
And I must bear love's dart.
Now she is gone from this fair place.
I shall not see her more.
Another sees her lovely face,
And I, alone, endure.

Perhaps, critics might say, it was a little too similar to one by Mr William Wordsworth. I expect they would quibble also, remembering I said that all the Huttons had grey eyes. May I remind you that there is such a thing as poetic licence? I am inclined to dismiss this, reader, as mere carping on your part. *I* was rather pleased with it.

Polly and I ambled on. I, musing on my muse; she, snatching at occasional morsels from the hedgerow.

Suddenly, as we rounded a bend, there was a loud crack and a sharp stinging pain in my shoulder. My hat was blown from my head. Poor old Polly skittered in alarm. I slid sideways from the saddle and toppled ignominiously into the roadway.

Someone had actually shot me! As I scrambled to my feet, I felt blood dripping down my brow and under my coat and shirt. Ahead of me, armed with muskets, I could see a troop of men. My heart lurched in my chest, believing that these must be more escaped French prisoners.

But then I realised that they were nothing of the kind. There were half a dozen of them, dressed in heavy cloth jackets over collarless shirts, and wool britches tied at the knee with twine. Two wore a kind of cap, suggesting some sort of uniform, whilst the others were bareheaded. They were shod in the traditional footwear of Lancashire – heavy, iron-banded, wooden-soled clogs. Very effective, I thought bitterly, for kicking people if they ran short of shotgun pellets.

One of the others shouted 'Halt!' a command it seemed to the one who had fired on me, which, thank God, he did. Now the whole group assembled before me, barring the way.

'Who are you?' I gasped, 'Why are you shooting at me?'

''As Amos 'ere winged yer?' asked the fellow who had shouted. 'Sorry about that. 'E's over hasty, is Amos. Got no business afiring at yer before *I* gives the order.' He scowled at the shooter who was staring at me in open-mouthed idiocy. 'We're Officers from the prison,' he added, 'looking for escaped prisoners. Frenchies. They was being brought up from Preston this morning. Cart overturned on t' bend,' he nodded back over his shoulder, 'and they ran off. We're sent to get 'em back. But no sign of 'em hereabouts. Has tha seen any such?'

I had seen no one, and told him so, wiping blood from my brow. As I was still conscious, I assumed it had just been grazed by one of the pellets.

Polly, who had recovered from the shock more quickly than I had, was serenely pulling morsels of vegetation out of the hedge. 'A medal for you, Polly,' I thought, 'for gallantry. No, for *senselessness* under fire, which I suspect is the condition under which such are frequently won.'

I peeled off my coat and contorted myself so I could properly examine my shoulder. It didn't seem to occur to these louts to offer me assistance. The second musket ball was not, after all, lodged in it. Like the other, it had clipped me in its flight and passed on. Although it hurt abominably, it was a relief that this was my weak, left shoulder. Damage to the other would have rendered me helpless for weeks.

'Happen I've a kerchief I could let yer have. T' bind it?' The fellow who was evidently in charge of this band held out a grubby rag.

'Is the ball lodged like?'

'No, for which your colleague, Amos, may thank his Maker! I have my own kerchief,' I told him. 'But perhaps you could tie it for me?'

He stepped forward to perform an agonising procedure.

'That coat o' yours 'll need a few stitches to put it right,' he commented. 'You'll be making a report, like? To the Governor? About this 'ere incident?'

'Indeed, I will.'

He sighed. 'Aye, Ah supposed tha would. At least then mebbe I'll be spared lack-brains like Amos from now on. That can only be a benefit to the prison. We just can't get decent men. Any that's got any brains in their noddles get better money working at the mills. Or they've gone fer soldiers, or been pressed fer the navy.'

With a struggle, I pulled my coat around my shoulders, leaving my injured arm free. So, these were the gaolers, the turnkeys. They were a rough-looking lot! Seen close to, their skin and their clothing appeared ingrained with dirt. One had an empty eye socket. Another had a broken nose. These were the men put to guard the French soldiers captured by our army (or navy, as I gathered was often the case)? I thought of the Frenchman Dorcas Hutton had tried to question. Compared to these rogues, he had seemed halfway to a gentleman! If he and one of these men had stood before me and I had been asked to say which was the prisoner and which the gaoler, I would have placed the gaoler in the cell.

'How many prisoners are you missing?

This seemed to confuse them. I wondered if some of them could even count. 'Eleven' and 'a girt lot' were suggested. 'Girt' means a large object or number in these parts.

I told them I had ridden down from Netherdale and had met no one at all on the way.

'Where were yer goin' then? On the Sabbath an' all?' demanded their leader.

Although it was no affair of his and I disliked his manner of asking, I explained who I was, and that I was in search of a man named Gabriel Waller whom I had expected to find in Brookhouse or Crook O' Lune.

Heads were shaken. Gabriel's name meant nothing to them. They probably rarely strayed outside Lancaster. Tha'd best not go on,' their leader advised, 'seeing these Frenchies *must* be beyond here, since tha says tha hasn't seen them.'

He was probably right. My injuries were not serious, but even mounting Polly for the ride back to Netherdale would not be easy. I could not continue to search for Gabriel Waller today.

Chapter Twenty-Seven

Hugh

Polly ambled home, which was much her preferred style. She seemed to have dismissed the recent events from her equine mind. Meanwhile, I clung onto her back as best I could, my shoulder pain exacerbated by each jolt. Wherever these French prisoners had made their escape, it was not in the direction of Bowland. I thought it more likely that, catching sight of the seacoast, they would have run towards that. If so, they would most likely suffer a disappointment on discovering how far the tide retreats. And how long they would have to wait, exposed on the shore, for its return.

I had my own concerns. My head hurt, although not as much as my shoulder. I had been told to expect a band of men to start repairing the wall at Lane End tomorrow. Today I had achieved no Gabriel Waller, and had no clear plan.

Given today's events, would the prison Governor still be willing to send me a gang of Frenchmen? Was it not more likely that he would abandon the plan? With the return of those idiotic turnkeys, empty-handed, the idea of escape would spread throughout the prison. I imagined the Américain grinning in his cell at the news.

On reaching my cottage, I tumbled rather than dismounted from Polly's back.

'Sorry, old lady,' I told her. 'You served me well today, but I'm in no state to rub you down. All I can manage is to half fill your water bucket, toss you a bundle of hay, and one of last year's apples. Tomorrow, I hope to do better.'

Still out of doors, I managed to set the pump going and bathed my shoulder and scalp as well as I could.

Then I took to my bed, hoping that sleep, which 'knits up the ravelled sleeve of care', that 'balm of hurt minds', as Master Shakespeare says, might succeed in curing my hurts.

I assumed the discomfort of my wounds would keep me tossing and turning. But old W S was right as usual, and I woke at first light, feeling rested and, if not healed, at least ready to face what the day might bring.

It brought Gabriel Waller. I was gingerly stirring a pan of porridge, with my good but bruised arm, when there was a rap at the door.

''Ere, let me do that,' he said, when he saw what I was doing. 'What a crazy hullabaloo yer got yerself involved with yesterday.'

'How did you come to hear? I was looking for you, but never even got as far as Brookhouse.'

'Oh, 'tis all over the district,' he said airily. 'Word got around. Three o' them Frenchies were caught hiding in a barn. Them fools of prison guards! Fancy one of 'em firing off at yer. They should have guessed those men couldn't get far.'

He dumped the porridge into two bowls and set them on the table. Evidently, we were to eat breakfast together. Not an arrangement I had bargained for, but how could I refuse?

My bruises made me wince every time I lifted the spoon. Gabe watched me with apparent fascination.

'That arm's yer good 'un? Is the other paining yer much?'

I dismissed the question with a shrug and then wished I hadn't.

'How soon do you think these prisoners will arrive – if they come?' I asked. I had a horrid presentiment that if I didn't distract him, he might leap up and start spooning porridge into my mouth as though I were an infant.

He grunted, almost scraping the pattern off the bowl in his search for the last morsel. 'I reckon not before nine o' the clock. That's if the Governor fellow's arranged a cart for 'em. Still an' all, even if he sends 'em on the march, the days are longer now we're coming up to summertime. Happen if they don't get here 'til afternoon, we'd still get a lile bit o' work out of 'em.'

I was not at my best. I was paying toll for yesterday's alarms and my subsequent injuries. I ordered myself to rally. 'Whether they come today or not,' I said, pushing my bowl away, 'we had best go and look at the job and decide how to tackle it.' Gabriel eyed my dish for a moment, probably thinking he could scrape it cleaner, and said, 'Ah've already looked. On t' way up.'

He then proceeded to tell me how the prisoners should be employed – how they could sort and carry the existing stones – and how these should be placed close by, ready to be brought forward when required.

'Though 'tis not much used, we'd best not block the lane. Sam Braithwaite will more than likely tek it into his head to start moving his herd to new pasture if we do. I suppose there was high jollifications there at Lane End yesterday. For the wedding. High jollifications for *that* lot, any road. Did they sit the whole hour in their Meeting in silence?'

'The wedding wasn't entirely silent,' I told him. I might not be in sympathy with the Quaker way of worship, but I didn't intend to encourage Gabriel's disdain. 'The young couple stood to speak their vows, of course, and several of those present asked blessings on their future life together.'

'And the wedding breakfast?' he asked. 'They say Madam Hutton and Madam Braithwaite between them had baked for a girt number. People came from all over, even from as far as Slaidburn, as I heard. A good few will have stayed over.'

'That I can't tell you. I didn't stay to eat with the wedding party.'

I suppose it was natural for Gabe to be curious. After all, it must have been the biggest event in the neighbourhood for many a long day. But I sensed that he wanted me to join him in disparaging these people whose ways and beliefs he did not share.

'Sir John rode up immediately after the service with a gift for the couple, and the news that the prisoners were to come today. So, I set out to look for you.'

Gabriel chortled. "Bad luck then. You'll have missed a right good spread, and got yourself peppered with shot into the bargain.'

'Yes,' I sighed, 'and I'll not be a lot of use to you, building this wall, until my shoulder heals.'

I waited for him to say what he was no doubt thinking - that he didn't consider I would be of much use even uninjured. But he didn't.

We left Low Bield and walked to Lane End, arriving just in time to see a carriage and two men on horseback turn out into the lane from the farmyard.

'Not as many stopped over as I thought,' said Gabe. 'They'll be eating up the leftovers for many a day.' I wondered for a moment if he might turn in at the gate right then, and go into the farm kitchen and offer to help.

We made our way to the wall that needed rebuilding. On his way to my cottage that morning, Gabriel had pulled away some of the ivy and convolvulus that had pushed into the crevasses and dislodged the top stones. Now he attacked some of what remained, although I would have thought this was something the French prisoners could do.

'Might as well have it all down, from here... to hereabouts,' he said, gesturing a distance with spread arms. 'Get it right down to the ground and start again.'

I nodded. 'So, the first job for these prisoners is to take all the stones away, scrape them clean of moss, and put them in piles according to size. On the field side?'

We stood in contemplation for a space.

'Can tha speak this French talk?' Gabe asked eventually. 'Being an educated man?'

'Alas, no,' I replied. 'I never learned it. Perhaps I should go up to Rush Ghyll and borrow that book from Dorcas Hutton.'

'Can *she* talk it?' he asked, astonished. 'How'd the lass manage that?'

I had forgotten that Gabriel hadn't been present when we questioned the Américain.

'She doesn't exactly speak French, but she has a book,' I explained. 'A volume of useful phrases, things one might want to say to a French person. I doubt if many of them relate to wall building, but there might be a few words we can use. Lift, take, pass, large, small – words like that – only in French.'

Gabriel raised his eyebrows. 'That's goin' to be your job, then. For certain sure, I'm not up to any foreign talk. You'd best get up to Rush Ghyll and get the lass to lend you her book.'

The last thing I wanted was Gabriel Waller giving me orders. I certainly wasn't going to go running off up to Rush Ghyll at his behest. Yet I needed his expertise. So, for now, I pretended not to hear him. My pocket watch showed that it was less than eight o'clock. It seemed unlikely the prisoners would arrive for some time yet.

When it suited me, I *might* decide to go to Hutton Farm myself. Alternatively, I might find one of the younger Braithwaite lads and persuade him to go.

Another thought struck me. What with my mishap yesterday, I had forgotten to arrange for any provisions. As indeed I had on the day we shored up the riverbank, when Lydia Hutton had saved my credit.

'Do you suppose the prisoners will have brought their own rations? Sir John didn't mention anything about it. I should have asked him.'

Gabe grunted again. 'What do we care for that? If they've nothing and you ain't arranged any, they mun go without. There's water in t' beck.' Would *he* work all day on water alone? I doubted it.

I was determined to provide something for the men. Nathaniel's mother might be willing to give us something. I would have to pay her. I could hardly expect her to feed the men for free, but I had no means of contacting Sir John. Would his wife be coming up to Dalefoot again today? I glanced at my watch yet again. It was still early, but if I saw her carriage, I would go and ask her. Sir John might not approve the expenditure, but I was confident I could get around Lady Lavvy.

Chapter Twenty-Eight

Dorcas' Journal

1st Day, 2nd Week of 5th Month – evening of the wedding

It seems strange to sleep alone. I had thought, once Sukie was married, that Betsey would want to join me in the big double bed. She says that when winter comes again, she will come and snuggle in with me. Meanwhile, she says she prefers to stay in the truckle in the tiny room with the little bay window jutting out over the porch. People say some famous Quaker slept there once, years ago, when he came journeying in these parts, preaching to those who were open to convincement. Perhaps he left some of his words behind. Betsey has always had a ready tongue from babyhood and a way to get what she wants from people.

I quite like having the bed to myself. I can keep my candle burning on the night shelf while I write this journal – no need to hide away in the barn – but I must be careful not to let candle grease spot the sheets, or let Mama guess how long I sit up reading. (I have finished 'Pride and Prejudice', and thought it wonderous.) If she knew, Mama would read me a lecture about vain idleness and how I will spoil my eyesight.

I wonder how Susannah feels? How does it feel to be wed, sharing your bed with a man, and all that that entails? Sukie will know what to expect, of course. Mama has talked to us both about what it means to be a wife and how children are made. Growing up on a farm, we have seen how the animals mate. I should think Nathaniel will be quite considerate. I don't think he would treat her as roughly as the Braithwaites' old ram treats our young ewes.

I was meaning to write about the wedding breakfast and all the gifts and good wishes that were heaped on Sukie and Nat, but I can feel my own eyes closing and must leave that for another day.

Next day

The wedding breakfast went off delightfully too. Of course, Martha Braithwaite always provides a splendid repast whenever she has guests, but I was pleased to hear Mama's scones, patties, and fruit cake <u>much</u> praised by the assembled company. I'm sure she never expects compliments, but she truly deserved every word that was uttered. She has always taught us that everything we do is to serve our fellows in God's name.

I looked out for Hugh Armstrong, thinking I must try to make him feel at home amongst us, but he never came. Perhaps he did not realise the invitation was to the meal and not just the wedding ceremony. Perhaps he feared there would be another long period of silence before we ate. I will admit I was a trifle disappointed.

Well! To everyone's surprise, when the time came for Susannah and Nathaniel to set out on their wedding journey, we found that Nat (without telling a soul) had hired a smartly turned-out carriage and pair, and a man to drive them as far as Kendal for their first night's stay. When we heard it had arrived and was standing waiting, everyone rushed out to see them off. And then, almost before we could open our mouths to wish them well, they were gone. Nat had arranged for their luggage to be packed in advance. Mama must have helped him by packing Sukie's trousseau (all her pretty new underclothes).

I don't know how Mama and Papa felt, but this sudden departure quite distressed me. It seemed cruel somehow, giving us so little time to make our farewells and tell them how much we love them. Except, the truth is, I don't love Nat. I wouldn't dream of saying this aloud, but I can write the truth in this journal, can I not? I <u>don't</u> love him. I don't even like him very much. He is – dare I even write this? – so full of starch. No, that's not fair, he means so well, and I'm sure he loves Sukie – in his stuffy way. I hope he has not married her simply because she is the prettiest girl in Netherdale, will look so well on his arm, and behave so prettily to his guests and the men he hopes to do business with. Oh, it is very wicked of me to allow myself such thoughts.

I must go. I finished feeding the calf ages ago, and I promised Mama I would help her by churning some butter. After the wedding, we are quite out.

Chapter
Twenty-Nine

Hugh

The wagon carrying the prisoners drew up before the eighth hour was half gone. This was sooner than I had expected. And another surprise was in store for me. Amongst them were the two men who had held me up at gunpoint some weeks before. Their clothing was more disreputable than ever. At least they no longer had the gun.

'You two didn't get far!' I growled as they stood, dejected, at the end of the line whilst the warders counted them off. They acknowledged me with rueful grimaces.

The other prisoners seemed unwilling to even stand next to them. I wondered what they had done to earn this disdain until I remembered that they might well be Americans, French-speaking, but with accents unfamiliar to the rest. The others might well think they were spies, planted amongst them to report to the prison authorities.

Happily, for the success of today's enterprise, the two prison warders seemed brighter individuals than those from my previous day's misadventure. They commanded brisk control and perhaps even a measure of respect from their charges.

One of them, who told us his name was Jabez Hartley, had been a sailor and had plied the port of Calais before the war. He boasted that he had a few words of French, but he was unsure if all the men spoke it. 'This lot are off boats that've been captured by the navy. Off Ireland mainly,' he said, 'so they might be anything, speak any kind of gobbledygook.'

I called for attention and described the first task. The plan was to remove the stones from the section of wall to be rebuilt. The men would pass them from hand to hand to the back of the line. There, they would be divided into piles of large, medium, and small stones to be stacked in the nearby field until we needed them.

Jabez Hartley and his comrade soon had the men in a line, passing the stones from man to man. Then, he began to shout, 'Un, de, tra, catter!' and on, I think, to 'dicks' which must be ten. The men seemed mildly irritated. However, after much shrugging, they accepted it to keep the rhythm going as they passed the stones. The second warder made no stab at French but supervised the men at the back, who had the job of deciding whether a stone should be in the 'gross,' 'moyen,' or the 'petty' pile.

'This is gonna to tek a mighty long while!' grumbled Gabe, although they were doing just what he himself had suggested. 'O'course we'll have to sort 'em again for shape and quality once they're done.'

'*You* organise it then,' I snapped. '*I'll* go up to Rush Ghyll and borrow that phrase book. It was going to need more than French numbers to get the more complicated task of rebuilding done. Besides, standing around was uncomfortable. My back and arms were painfully stiff from yesterday's adventure. 'Once all the stones are in piles, you can get them scraping off the moss and cleaning them up. Between you and these warder fellows, you ought to be able to show them how.'

I slipped back to Low Bield and saddled Polly, congratulating myself that I had left Gabe with the most tedious part of the task. Let the annoying fellow do it his way.

Riding proved hardly more comfortable than standing, but I made it up to Rush Ghyll. This time I tethered Polly some distance from Lydia Hutton's flower border.

I found her alone, seated at the kitchen table, with a large basket of bread and other comestibles in front of her. I thought this busy, active woman looked, for once, a little sad, a little lost.

'Leftovers,' she told me, gesturing at the basket with a rueful smile. 'Might *thee* have a use for any of this?'

I'd completely forgotten not only to ask Martha Braithwaite if she could spare any leftovers but also to enquire if the warders had brought any food for the prisoners. I'd seen none being unloaded from the wagon. 'This must be the hand of Providence!' I said. 'As it so happens, I would be very grateful. I've been loaned a team of prisoners from Lancaster Gaol. They're rebuilding a wall for me down at Lane End. I believe they'd be happy to eat anything you can spare.

'This came from Lane End,' Lydia told me. 'I sent Betsey down earlier to ask Martha about some forks that have been mislaid. My lads will eat some of it, but we're in no need, and the bread and pastry will soon grow stale. If thy band of prisoners would like it, be pleased to take it.'

After a moment, she added, 'I don't suppose that's what thee came about, is it though?'

'No, I hoped I might borrow your daughter's French phrase book?' I said. 'Is she somewhere about, so I could ask her? I feel our wall building will go much better if we can communicate with the men. Even a few French phrases would be useful.'

Lydia Hutton held up her palms. 'I don't think Dorcas would have any objection, but it may take time to find her. She is inclined to disappear out into the fields, especially when she has things on her mind. Dorcas will miss Susannah sorely.'

She leaned back, gazing out of the window across the farmyard.

'It's a case of being in low spirits after the exhilaration of the wedding,' she said. 'Dorcas is feeling it. We all are. However, I know where she keeps the book, so perhaps...' She left the sentence unfinished.

'Will she be upset if I take it? Without asking?'

'If she wants it, she can easily walk down to Lane End and take it back from thee, can she not?'

'I'll only need it for a short while,' I assured her. 'I'll write down any words and phrases that may be useful and return it. As soon as this evening, if she wishes. Would that be satisfactory?'

Lydia rose from the table. 'It will be beside her bed, I think,' she said. 'Dorcas always has her nose in a book. Now that Susannah is married, she'll be reading through the night. She thinks I don't know, but I see all the candle ends.' She shook her head, smiling, and walked out of the room.

A few minutes later, she returned but without the book. 'Dorcas must have taken it out into the fields with her. I think she's been studying it quite frequently. She was so disappointed not to be able to provide any help for that American fellow at Dalefoot.'

What an extraordinary remark! 'But he attacked her father! Why did she want to help him?'

'Indeed, and my husband's head still aches, but there must have been a reason for his anger. Wilfred would have liked to know what it was.' She smiled at me. 'It is much easier to forgive someone who trespasses against one if one knows the reason. Often, it might help the sinner to understand where his anger came from. Does thee not think so?'

My immediate reaction was, 'No, I do not.' Although I had liked the man, I could not forget that, French or American, he was a supporter of the enemy who had killed one of my brothers and crippled the other.

I could understand that these sternly religious people might feel they ought to forgive someone who had sinned against them. Lydia could no doubt remind me of the chapter and verse where Jesus commands it. Knowing the reason for the attack might have helped Wilfred Hutton and his family to forgive, but they seemed to want to go further and *aid* the wretch!

I thanked Lydia for looking for the book and asked her to mention to Dorcas that I would like to borrow it. Then I thanked her once again for the basket of provisions and turned to leave. Lydia, however, called after me.

'I suppose... there is still no news of our son, George?'

I turned and shook my head. 'Nothing. I'm sorry, Ma'am.'

I rode down the track on Polly, the basket perched before me on the saddle, thinking about forgiveness. I had never forgiven my father for what he did to my mother and me. Even if I could bring myself to do that, *helping* him was a step further than I would ever be prepared to go.

'*No one*, not even these ridiculously devout folk, can expect that,' I muttered to myself. 'What he did to us was unforgivable. My mother died of a broken heart. All of us suffered abuse and ill-treatment. My brothers could not wait to join the army to get away from him. Now, one is dead, and the other lives in constant pain.'

My thoughts ran on. Young Dorcas shouldn't have been thinking of involving herself with that Américain. He had a violent temper. Her father could have been killed. That show of smiles – kissing her hand – he'd been trying to ingratiate himself with an innocent young woman. None of it was genuine. He was a rogue.

By the time I got back to Lane End, I'd worked myself up into quite a temper.

'What bit you?' demanded Gabriel Waller as soon as he saw my wrathful scowl. 'Would the lass not lend the book?'

'She wasn't there. It was a wasted journey,' I replied, dumping the basket of food on the ground and pulling the notebook I carried for poetic inspiration from my pocket. I tossed it on a portion of the wall that we were not planning to demolish. The prisoners, seated around on the lane's verges, scraping moss and lichen from some of the larger stones using smaller, sharper ones, watched our interaction with sullen interest.

'Miss Dorcas's mother didn't know where the book was?'

'When she sees her, she'll ask, so be quiet and let me make a note of the words we may need. This fellow, Jabez Hartley, probably knows some of them.' I found my pencil. 'Oh, and Mistress Hutton sent this. We'll ask the warders to share it out.'

I tried to think of suitable phrases we might need to have translated for us. This was no easy task. I fully understood how frustrated Dorcas must have felt, trying to interrogate the American seaman. That she had managed to find anything useful struck me as an accomplishment.

I recalled the kind of phrases that were usually to be found in the phrasebook a traveller to the continent would take with him. Phrases like 'Porter, kindly lift my portmanteau down from the carriage.' No use at all, complete. 'But if I said, "Please lift..." and pointed to a particular stone, that might help.' I wrote down other words and phrases as they occurred to me.

'Come off it!' grumbled Gabe, peering over my shoulder. 'Even if yer had the book, yer can't learn to speak foreign stuff in half an hour. From what you said, Miss Dorcas never got far with that seaman, and she'll have spent a lot more time conning that book than you're going ter have!'

'I'll do what I can with Hartley's help,' I snapped. 'Here,' I said, 'take this basket of provisions and get the guards to pass them out to the men.'

'Too soon,' he replied. 'They ain't done much yet. If yer let 'em eat now it'll waste time, and they'll want more come noon.'

Glancing at my pocket watch, I saw that it was still early. My excursion to Rush Ghyll had taken barely more than an hour. 'The guards can keep half back for noon.'

'They'll have a right hard job to do that!' said Gabe. 'From what I've heard, prison food's mostly cabbage water and stale crusts.' Yer could be starting a riot!'

He had a point. The men continued to scrape lichen from the stones, but since my return, I'd been aware of their eyes on me. Although Lydia Hutton had tied a cloth over the basket, they'd probably worked out what it contained. This did need careful handling.

I took a deep breath. 'Go and fetch one of the guards over here, I'll ask *him* what we should do.'

If I handled this in the wrong way, there could be fighting, even bloodshed.

Now I took the time to study them, they were a poor-looking lot. Many were painfully thin, their ribs showing where their uniform shirts were torn. The sores around some of their mouths spoke of undernourishment. I thought of the farm lads sent to repair the bank above the stream a month ago. Strong, healthy boys with good physiques and hearty appetites. These were the foot soldiers of Napoleon's army, who had probably joined through poverty and lack of work in their homeland. There must be many similar British prisoners in France, and in Spain and Portugal too. I hoped Boney fed his prisoners better than we did. These poor fellows hardly had the strength to hold the stones they were scraping.

I knew some French officers were allowed to live, after giving their 'parole', in small inland towns around England. Then, if luck (and money) ran their way, they would be exchanged for English officers held in France and Spain.

However, these poor specimens, mere foot soldiers, had little prospect of release. Lancaster was just a stopping point on the way to another prison in Scotland, far away from the continent.

When the younger guard came over at Gabe's summons, I asked him his name. 'Luke Johnson,' he replied. Asked about the prisoners, he confirmed what I'd thought, 'This lot should 'ave gone up to Scotland last week, but there's bin an 'old up. Dunno what, though I did hear,' he turned his head away and lowered his voice, 'people say they're talking in Paris. Talking *Peace*, that is, now Boney's sent to exile on that island, *Elbow* or some such name. Mebbe they'll all get sent home, and we can hope to get our own lads back. My brother's over there, somewhere, if he ain't bin killed.'

I said I hoped this too. When I mentioned the provisions, he shook his head. 'Leave it! Noonday's soon enough. They'll work all the harder and not be tempted to run off if they're waiting to get their fodder.'

'But did they eat anything before they set out this morning?

'The man looked mildly astonished at my question. 'Nay, Mister. The cookhouse ain't open afore seven, and they were riding on a wagon, not walking! Mind you, if it turns out warm by and by,' he added, 'we've a jug and a metal cup on the wagon. Could one of yer fetch water from t' beck? Give 'em a drink fr'm time to time? We don't want any fainters. Holds everyone else up if they pass out.'

This was something else I should have thought of. 'It's a fair step to the beck,' I told him, 'across that field. Is there a trusty amongst them we could send? One who could be relied on to take the jug and come back?' I wasn't about to run this errand myself. Gabe would certainly refuse, thinking it beneath an expert like himself. And I didn't want to risk losing control of the prisoners by sending one of the guards.

He jerked his head, deferring to his colleague, Jabez Hartley, who paused a moment in thought and then said, 'Yer could send one of the Yankees. *One* of them, mind you. *They'd* never run off, not the one without the other.'

Chapter Thirty

Dorcas' Journal

2nd Day, 2nd Week of 5th Month

Everything feels flat and dreary now that the wedding is past. Even though I had prepared for this feeling, it still rolled over me like the tide coming over the quick sands in Morecambe Bay. It dragged me down, no matter how I struggled against it.

Mama is much better than I am at pulling herself together and getting on with things. Busying herself, as she explains, so that she has no time to brood. This makes me feel worse because I can't seem to rise above it.

Later

This morning, once I had fed the calf, I forced myself to stay indoors to help Mama wash the last of the dishes, and polish the knives and forks we lent to Martha for the wedding breakfast. We have not got back everything we lent, and some of the returned forks are not ours. Ours are quite plain, whereas these have a tiny leaf engraved on the handle. Mama said, a little put out, that she was quite surprised that Martha did not check them over before she sent them. Now we shall have to return them and ask about our own, which Mama cherishes. They came from Aunt Hester and Uncle Josiah at Arkholme after they left us to dwell with Our Lord in Heaven.

Betsey, who was bored, immediately offered to catch the pony and ride down to Lane End, and rather to my surprise, Mama agreed.

'I have something to say to thee, Dorcas,' she murmured as she passed me a fresh polishing cloth. I must have looked alarmed because she chuckled, 'No, I'm not going to scold thee. I spoke briefly with Rachel Stout at the wedding, and she passed me this.' Mama took down a letter from the mantelpiece.

'Dorcas, Rachel says how pleased she and the other Elders were to see thy demeanour at the wedding.' Mama laughed. 'It is not like Rachel to praise *anyone* for their dress, *or* their smiles, but she says she was pleased to see thee looking so neat in thy new gown, smiling, and greeting everyone. She hopes this means thee is over thy disappointment about the school, and that thee has cast off melancholy. And that thee is ready to embrace whatever the Lord may require of thee. In a month or two, once the hay is in, she and Eliza would like thee to go and stay with them for a few weeks.'

Oh, how conflicted were my feelings! I must have shown something of this on my face because Mama then said, 'There will be no need for thee to go near the school, or meet with anyone there who might distress thee. Rachel and Eliza are busy with their charitable work, visiting the poor and sick in the town. Thee could help them, and perhaps by the summer's end, Rachel may hear of a family who requires a governess? Now that is something thee could do, Dorcas. Well, thee will see what she says in her letter.'

I took it aside to read it. Mama seemed not to mind that I wanted to peruse it privately.

It was quite short. I had little faith in Rachel's notion that some <u>good</u> family, by which she undoubtedly meant a Quaker Family, might wish to hire me as a governess. It was kindly meant, but I do <u>not</u> nurse any hopes in that direction. I have no skill in fine needlework, quilting, or patchwork, and I've been told that Italian is preferred to French. Besides, Quakers are always writing to one another. News of my departure from the Friends' School in Lancaster, and the reason for it, will already be known from Carlisle down to Manchester, and from Morecambe to Robin Hood's Bay.

Rachel suggested that I could help pack parcels of bread and basic foodstuffs, which we would then deliver to those in need. I know this to be good and necessary work in these hard times, but the prospect does not fill me with delight.

However, she then went on to say that she had called together a group of women Friends from Lancaster Meeting to discuss what they might be able to do for the prisoners at the castle. 'We have heard that conditions there are very harsh,' she wrote, 'especially for the Frenchmen and other foreigners caught up in the present wars. They have no relatives here who can bring them items such as soap, combs, and stockings. We have formed a small committee to try to alleviate their hardship. These men are not villains, but soldiers and seafarers far from their native lands.'

An image floated before my eyes of the Américain grinning, as he bent to kiss my hand.

'Perhaps... perhaps it would be right for me to go and help Rachel and Eliza,' I stammered. 'If thee can spare me, Mama?'

Mama smiled. 'Yes, Dorcas. In a few weeks. Thee would be doing God's work, and perhaps bringing some of those men to a measure of the Light.'

If she meant, as I suppose she did, that we would be showing the Frenchmen the way to true religious faith, as practised by

Quakers, I very much doubted it. I could in no way picture the Américain sitting in silence by the hour, 'waiting on the Lord.' But I admit it freely here, I am curious to see him again. Oh, Dorcas!

Rachel says I need not meet <u>that man</u>. But if I go to stay with them, they will expect me to accompany them to First Day Meeting, and <u>he</u> would certainly be there then, and so would those who did not believe me when I told them of his behaviour towards me.

Shall I go or not?

Later still

I would be glad to help them in their endeavours, especially if they are to collect things for the French prisoners. However, if I stay two weeks as Rachel suggests, there would be at least one First Day when I would be expected to attend Worship at Lancaster Meeting House. Could I invent something to prevent my going? A powerful headache or a stomach upset? It would be wrong of me, but I don't think I have the courage to go where <u>he</u> is sure to be. Where all those stern Quakers will be, who think me a wicked girl to suggest that this man behaved as I claimed? If they even admonished him, we have heard nothing of it. He is still there, teaching at the school.

I know, because I have heard Papa say so, that some in Lancaster Meeting are not so godly as they would have us think. They pretend that they detest slavery, as the Yearly Meeting of Friends has decreed we should, yet still receive remittances from plantations in the West Indies.

Mama saw the tear to my bodice and the pulled seam at my waist. Papa knows I wouldn't bear false witness, but I think even he thinks I made more of it than it warranted.

Rachel and Eliza Stout know that something happened to distress me, so that I left the school and insisted on returning to the farm. However, I never told them the whole story because I thought it would shock dear Eliza.

Mama says Rachel may know a little of it, as she is an Elder in the Lancaster Meeting. If I do go to visit them, I shall have to explain. It will take all my courage, and yet, why should I fear it? I know, and God in Heaven knows, the fault was <u>not</u> mine.

Chapter Thirty-One

Hugh

In my absence, the broken section of the wall had been dismantled. Preparations were in hand to build it up again, 'tying in' the new section to the remaining ends of the existing wall. This was where Gabriel Waller's skill was needed. If you are unfamiliar with drystone walls, no cement or binding is used. The stones are fitted together, two on one, and one on two, layered on top of one another. "Through stones" run across their width, tying them together. There should be only the slightest of gaps between each stone and the ones above, below, or beside it. To the uninitiated, it looks impossible. The individual stones are rough and irregular. Yet somehow, they must be slotted together so tightly that they withstand the harshest winters. Some, I'm told, have stood for centuries.

A waller needs an 'eye' to choose the shape and size of every stone, and I freely admit, this was where Gabe excelled. He knew, by look and feel, exactly where each stone could be deployed.

He seemed to glory in his expertise, and this the prisoners saw and appreciated. Perhaps they had once been craftsmen in trades of their own. Looking at their poorly healed wounds, their thin, skeletal forms, it was difficult to imagine what had prompted them to join Napoleon's army.

Was it the struggle to find work in their hometowns and villages? Or thoughts of glory, adventure, a patriotic love for La France? Whichever it was, I found I couldn't blame them. Many a Scot has joined the army of what had, not so long ago, been Scotland's greatest enemy. My brothers, one now dead, the other left with a crippled body and broken mind, had chosen this themselves. The alternative? To depart, as many had, across the ocean, leaving an impoverished Scotland for the unknown hazards of the West Indies and Canada.

I never had the option of a military career. And what could I, a cripple, have done in the colonies? I'd been grateful to obtain work as an under-factor on a modest estate in Fife until it was sold. The new owner had men of his own, and I was dismissed. Then, by a lucky chance, a friend of my late grandfather had recommended me to Sir John Hathersage.

I had always thought of my disablement as a bane, not a boon. Now I looked at these men in front of me and thought how easily their fate might have been mine.

They didn't lack intelligence, these Frenchmen. Just by watching Gabe, they understood what was needed. They placed themselves in ones and twos beside the differing piles of stones, ready to hand him whatever he called for or pointed to. Had I wasted my time going up to Rush Ghyll? Would we need the phrase book at all?

Gabe had somehow managed to 'grade' the stones, not only into large and small, but into piles of differing shapes: large, flattish ones to lie along the main body of the wall; long, narrow ones to run through it from side to side. He had acquired a bucket for the small "fillers" to dribble into any spaces to prevent the wet penetrating. On the top would be the tall upright "coping" stones.

Today, the work went surprisingly well. Men chose and proffered stones without being asked, sharing grins of satisfaction when Gabe accepted one.

He grunted. 'I'll mek decent wallers of 'em, even if they are dumb Frenchies!'

I hadn't dared hope that we could complete the work today. Now it looked as though we might – if the rain held off.

Then it happened. At one moment, all was a scene of industry; the next chaos, as two men jumped over the gap in the wall and ran as though a fiend of Hell was snapping at their heels.

'Hoy!' yelled Jabez Hartley, 'Come back, yer ruddy imbeciles!' But they were running faster than I would have thought such underfed creatures could. They disappeared around the bend in the lane. For a few seconds, Gabe, the warders, and I stood speechless.

Recovering first, Jabez Hartley asked me, 'Do yer want one of us to go after 'em? It's the Yankees. Why the devil would they take off like that?'

'The Américains? I thought you said they were trusties?'

'Thought they were, one at a time that is,' said Jabez. 'They stick together like fish glue. I doubt they'll get far.'

For a moment, I'd feared the others would down stones and follow, but all they did was shrug. (Frenchmen seem to have a particular and almost identical way of shrugging). Then they carried on proffering stones to Gabe.

I had to agree with Jabez. Those two probably wouldn't get far. They must have run almost straight into captivity on our previous encounter.

'You're sure this lot won't follow?' I asked.

'Doubt it.' He lowered his voice. 'It's all rumours you understand, but it could be that *these* fellows will be shipped home in a few weeks' time. *Rumours*, like I say, now we hear old Boney's done for. This 'ere Peace Treaty they're talking of *may* hold. That's what this lot are counting on. Free transport home.'

'They know that?'

Jabez shrugged. 'The talk is all round the castle. *I* don't know how they get to hear things. Letters come to one or two of 'em. From Paris maybe, seemingly harmless, but they could be in code – even a Frenchie newspaper gets to them now and then. This lot were being sent up to the Border. Then, orders. The transport was stopped. Word from London. Hang onto 'em in Lancaster. They *may* be going home.'

'So why would the Americans run off? Will they not be released too?'

Jabez shrugged again. He seemed to have caught it from the Frenchmen. 'No, not them. This Peace Treaty and the prisoner exchange, *if* it happens, don't affect them. They gotta stay. We ain't got a prisoner o' war exchange agreement with the Yankees like we have with the Frogs. They gotta stay until their government, or their families, pays to get 'em back. In the case of those two, I'd say that could be never.'

'But,' I began, but then thought better of speaking aloud. If, as I believed, the man in sea boots had been sent to rescue those two, he himself was now imprisoned. So, how did our two escapees imagine they could cross the wide Atlantic to Louisiana? They no longer had the gun. They were easily recognised in their prison garb. They almost certainly had no money.

'Will you be blamed for letting them escape?' I asked.

Another shrug. 'Can't be helped,' said Jabez Hartley. 'We lose a few regular. We lost some yesterday coming up from Preston. They glimpse a sight of the sea and think there'll be boats to take 'em off. When that lot saw what Morecambe Bay is like when the tide's out – a big puddle of mud – they came quietly.'

'Yes, I met up with some of the guards hunting for them yesterday. They managed to find them all?'

'Found them sitting on the shore, cursing their luck.' Jabez chuckled. 'When they were brought in and heard from the other prisoners that they might soon be returning home, they settled down, nice and peaceful. Those two will likely be caught again before they get far.'

The day had dawned fair, but heavy clouds had built over Clougha Pike. The wind was rising, blowing cold on our bare heads and necks. Spots of rain splattered dark splodges on the grey stones. The Frenchmen paused what they were doing and were now looking towards me.

'Is this going to come down heavily?' I asked Gabe.

'Very likely,' he grunted, examining the sky. He scanned the group in their torn and ragged tunics. 'They ain't dressed fer t' weather. Reckon we can go and stand in t' barn? While this passes over? Ah'd lay odds yer never thought t' ask Sam Braithwaite in case t' weather turned?'

I hadn't, of course.

It was no use standing on my dignity. I had better trudge up the track to Lane End Farm and do it now. However, before I could do so, the clouds above us burst asunder, and we were in the midst of a deluge. Nothing for it but to dive beneath the long bed of the prison wagon, signal to the prisoners that they might join us there, and wait for the sudden storm to pass.

Except that the men didn't seek shelter. Being the month of May, it wasn't particularly cold. They had been so long mewed up in dank airless cells that the freshness of the rain, the aroma of the damp grasses, and the honey scent of clover and meadowsweet was a novelty. Several of them tore off their shirts and threw them under the cart. Then they began to cavort beneath the rain, rubbing at their arms and torsos to wash themselves clean. One of the men produced a whistle, carved from what appeared to be a piece of bone, and piped up a tune.

And the prisoners danced!

Never in my life had I beheld such a thing. I shall never forget it. A bunch of half-starved semi-naked men in ragged yellow britches, barefoot, or in broken-down boots, dancing and whooping with laughter as the rain poured down. Great curtains of water now swept in across the fellside, flattening the bushes and the wild meadow grasses. Tree branches whipped back and forth in the sudden storm, and still those Frenchmen laughed and danced.

'They do this often, ye reckon?' Gabe enquired of the two warders.

Jabez shook his head in wonder. 'Never seen 'em do it before.'

The musician had started a new tune and piped it out merrily across the fields as the rain began to slacken. The dance went on.

'Where did they get that whistle from?'

Jabez's colleague, Luke Johnson, grunted. 'Beef bones. They fishes 'em out the stew. 'Wunnerful what they can mek outta bones and straw and a few bits o' wood, these Frenchies. Ain't supposed t' ave knives, but they gets hold of 'em somehow. Wunnerful things they meks. Lile models o' ships. Straw hats, if they can get enough straw. Lile boxes. I bought one fer my lass ter keep 'er bits o' finery in. Bits o' lace and that.'

'They're allowed to sell them?'

'Aye. Sundays, after Chapel. Folks come to see 'em, see fer themselves whether Frenchmen 'ave really got three heads or forked tails, and buy a few of what they call suveeneers.'

'Money?' I asked. 'They're allowed to keep it?'

The two warders shrugged. 'They can buy a few bits with it,' Jabez Hartley conceded, 'baked goods mostly. Pies. Stockings. Yer see, as well as the prisoners 'aving things to sell, some of the town's tradesmen set up stalls of a Sunday. It's quite the thing, the Sunday market. It's surprising what them that's in prison for debt can manage to lay out their blunt for. And the carriage folks that attend church at the Priory, *they* all like to come down after the service and view what's on offer.'

The rain was ceasing. The dance was winding down. A few men bent at the waist, breathless. The piper tootled on, seemingly for his own pleasure.

Then we saw someone approaching. A strange figure, I couldn't tell whether it was a man or woman. Its head and shoulders were wrapped in sacking, and it was hunched over as though to keep the rain off the treasure it clutched. I scrambled out from beneath the wagon and stepped forward. Then they pulled the sacking aside from their face. It was Dorcas Hutton.

'Mama said thee wanted to borrow my phrase book?' She stood blinking at me. raindrops dripping down her face from the edge of her sacking hood. 'I thought it might be urgent, so I brought it for thee.'

Chapter Thirty-Two

Dorcas' Journal

2nd Day, 2nd Week of 5th Month *continued*

I must have been leading the calf into the back meadow to join the herd when Hugh Armstrong came. I don't know why Mama didn't send him to look for me. She knew where I would most likely be. I think perhaps she wasn't inclined to help him. That isn't like Mama. However, I suspect she hoped that he might have news of our brother George and was disappointed when she learned that all he wanted was to borrow my book.

Susannah's wedding has left us all tired and a little out of temper. There is an empty place at the table, and in our hearts. I know this is foolishness: Nathaniel hasn't stolen her from us; they haven't set sail for Philadelphia, as Quakers of former times were wont to do. They will be with us again soon, and we shall hear about their journey in the Lake Country, and all that they saw and did there. Then, they will settle in their new home in Lancaster. Nathaniel will be going to the mill each day. Meanwhile, Sukie will be setting up her household and unwrapping all her wedding gifts. I cannot imagine her engaging a maidservant and a cook. How will she know how to choose? It would terrify me. Mama and Papa have rarely needed to employ more than the occasional hired hand at harvest time. When we were small, there were always relatives and neighbours to help whenever we were in need.

But Sukie is going to live a different kind of life. I am sure she will never grow too proud to acknowledge her childhood home or cease to love us, her family, but I wonder how often she will visit us, or we her? Nat has some plan to set her up with her own neat little carriage with a quiet mare to pull it, but will she risk driving up the rough track to the farm?

I'm trying, once more, to learn as much as I can of the French language. If I go to Rachel and Eliza, I hope to visit the French prisoners in the castle to see what can be done for them. So, I might need some phrases at my disposal. I must leave off writing now, Mama is calling me to help with the laundering of the tablecloths we lent for the wedding.

Later

Mama says Hugh Armstrong has a group of Frenchmen with him – more Frenchmen here in Netherdale! He and Gabriel Waller are teaching them how to lay a wall. I do not suppose the seaman is with them, or she would have warned me. What Mama called his familiar conduct towards me did <u>not</u> meet with her approval. I tried to tell her that it did not disturb me, unlike the behaviour of <u>that</u> man at the school. It is difficult to explain, even to satisfy my own notions, but the Frenchman seemed only to be trying to be gallant and show that he was grateful for my attempts to help. He was too exuberant for Mama's taste, but I felt perfectly comfortable. I'm sure he wished me no harm.

I will take the book to Hugh myself.

Chapter Thirty-Three

Hugh

Dorcas stood before me, proffering the book. 'I wrapped it as best I could, against the wet,' she said, but her eyes were on the prisoners. 'Why were those men dancing? In the rain? I could see them as I was walking down the fell. It looked so strange. Can thee not get them to do what thee wants? Is it... some kind of rebellion?

'No, not all,' I said, 'we're taking a break from our labours while the rain lasts. We British,' (I refused to say English), 'dived for shelter under the cart when the rain began, but it seems to delight these French fellows. I suppose it's a novelty. They've been locked in prison cells for a long time.'

I wondered how to tell her I didn't need the phrasebook – that we were getting on splendidly without it. I gestured to the partly completed wall. Beyond it, the prisoners were bending and stretching after their wild dance, some eyeing the newcomer with interest. 'As you see, we are managing better than I dared hope. Just by showing them what we want.'

Her face fell. 'So, thee doesn't need my book?'

'Oh, I'm sure there are words and phrases in there that might... that might hurry things along even faster,' I said hastily. 'If you can spare it for a little while, I could write down the words I think will be useful and return the book this evening.'

She nodded, but her mouth drooped in disappointment.

'Come and look at what we've done,' I offered. 'You probably know more about drystone walling than I do. In my previous work, in Scotland, most of the land was moorland or forested.'

I led her to the partially completed stretch. The prisoners were now all alert to this visitor. A female! Their eyes followed us, interested, speculative. Many, I realised, were still half naked. I felt a little uncomfortable on Dorcas's behalf, but she didn't appear to notice. Her head and shoulders were still partly concealed within her improvised cowl of sacking. She stood before the half-built wall, regarding it gravely.

'Will thee finish today?' No expressions of delight, no words of praise for our achievements.

'It depends on the weather,' I said. The rain had now lessened to a steady drizzle.

'Aye, if this lot stops, we will.' Gabe Waller jostled my elbow. '*I* can work in all weathers, as folks around here will tell tha, but if it chucks it down these fellows will start dropping stones on their feet. Heavy rain'll mak them slip out of their hands.'

'You could stop to eat.' She turned her grave eyes on each of us. 'Mama said she sent thee some of the leftovers from the wedding. Then maybe it will fair up afterwards?'

'It will be something of a crush, all of us beneath the wagon,' I said, but it was the sensible thing to do. The men, seeing me glance from the cart to the covered basket, rapidly divined my intention, and dived underneath, pulling on tunics, and those that had them, jackets.

'A good suggestion, we'll do that!' I said, smiling at Dorcas.

To my dismay, she took this as an invitation to join us and followed me, ducking under the cart tail, still clutching her French phrase book inside her sacking shawl.

Twelve rough prisoners, most of whom would not have been in company with a woman, possibly for years. In a confined space. Oh, Dorcas! How were we to deal with this?

The prisoners huddled together at one end of the big wagon, leaving what space they could for Dorcas, Gabe, and me at the other, while the two prison warders crouched behind the prison gang, trusting their greatcoats to give them protection from the driving rain.

'Bonjour, Messieurs,' Dorcas greeted the prisoners, and to my surprise, they made muttered replies, watching us, waiting to see what was going to happen.

Without consulting me, she took the basket, removed the cloth that covered it, and handed it to the nearest prisoner. 'Un!' she cautioned him, raising her finger, 'et merci de transmettre.'

Gabe at my elbow yelped in dismay, imagining, as indeed I did, that this was asking for a fight to break out, with the pastries scattered and trampled underfoot.

We were both wrong. The man took one and handed the basket to his neighbour. Each man took an item and passed it on. Soon, the huddle of prisoners had each taken a piece. Then the basket was returned to us, empty but for some broken crusts in the bottom.

'Oh, I'm so sorry,' said Dorcas, turning to Gabe and me. 'I thought there would be sufficient for everyone. But it worked, didn't it? As when Lord Jesus fed the five thousand? And I think they understood my French. A little. Enough anyway.'

'I'd forgotten you had experience as a schoolteacher, Miss Dorcas,' I said. 'Clearly you have a gift.'

She shook her head, blinking. Her fine eyes were troubled. 'No, no, I wasn't a success as a teacher. Perhaps I could have been if... if I had been able to continue.'

'Feeding the five thousand indeed!' grouched Gabe, 'Comparing tha self with Our Lord – that's blasphemy, young woman. And a pity tha didn't give us a chance at the victuals before this lot.' He scowled to himself, fishing every last scrap from the bottom of the basket and eating it.

'I wasn't comparing myself to Our Lord,' she retorted, 'merely following His example. I don't think that is blasphemy; does thee think so, Hugh Armstrong?'

'I'm afraid I'm no expert in religion, and this isn't the right time to have a deep discussion on such matters.' I sounded pompous, of course, even to my own ears, but neither said any more. I gave Dorcas a brief smile to show I wasn't angry. I didn't intend to be sidetracked by a squabble. This situation hummed with possible risk. If the prisoners saw us quarrelling, it might make it difficult to maintain discipline.

The men finished eating and then waited, cross-legged on the ground, to see what this strange young woman would do next.

Dorcas straightened her spine, opened her phrasebook, and addressed them, smiling.

'Bonjour, tout le monde,' she declaimed.

'Bonjour,' they muttered in response.

'Je m'appelle Dorcas. Et vous?' She pointed first at herself and then at a man in the front row.

Maybe it was luck, or maybe he was so surprised that he answered her automatically, 'Pierre.' These men had presumably answered many roll calls since they were captured and imprisoned.

'Bonjour, Pierre.' She smiled, and her finger moved to the next man, 'Et vous?'

'Henri.'

'Et vous?' The finger moved on.

'Michel.'

'Bernard.'

'André.'

'Philippe.'

'Whatever does she want all their names for?' Gabe muttered in my ear.

'I want to call them by their names,' she muttered back to him. 'They are men, human beings, not beasts of the field.' She recommenced flicking through the pages of the phrasebook. 'I want to ask them, what were, what *are*, their professions,'

'Vous etês un soldat?' she demanded of Pierre, prisoner number one.

He blinked, but then replied, 'Non, Mam'selle, je suis un marin.'

Dorcas flicked hastily through her book, which I now saw had a list of vocabulary at the back. 'Marin,' she murmured, 'Ah! A sailor! Bon, vous êtes un marin!'

Then she proceeded to question each one. She had memorised the names each had given, and questioned them in turn,

'Henri, vous et un soldat? Au un marin?'

Most replied that they were sailors, a few said 'soldier.' One, a big, raw-boned fellow, insisted that he was a 'cuisinier' and that this was 'sur un bateau'. While Dorcas skimmed through her phrase book to try to discover what this meant, he added, pointing to the empty food basket, 'trés bien!'

'He means 'e were a cook,' offered Jabez Hartley from the back of the group, 'I know that's so – there's a note of it on his record sheet. And he's saying 'e liked what tha mother sent. I'd guess you won't find that in tha book, lass.'

Dorcas, still searching, did not reply, but Gabe, who was growing more restless by the minute, said, 'She thinks she's running a Sunday school. She'll have us all praying and singing hymns next!'

'No, she won't,' I replied, 'because the rain has stopped. We need to get back to work.'

'Tha's right,' agreed Jabez. 'Come on, you lot! That's enough of the young lady's French lesson fer today. Happen she'll come another day if these fellas are to come agin? That's if yer 'ave more walls to mend?'

'Not here if we finish,' I replied, 'but at High Bield, a farm higher on the fell. A wall there collapsed under the weight of winter snow. I mean to ask the farmer if he would welcome help, supposing the Prison Governor will allow the men to come again.'

The two warders seemed hopeful. I supposed they liked the change in routine. Perhaps they embraced this chance to be outside the prison walls in the fresh air of the countryside as much as the prisoners did.

'Oh, Lord!' exclaimed Gabriel, 'not High Bield, not wi' Batty Trawden! 'Twas bad enough when we were mending yon bank above the beck. Wi' this lot, he'd likely start another war!'

'*If* we do go,' I said lightly, 'I'll get Matthew to lock him up.'

Dorcas overheard this. 'Matthew told my mother his brother does have to be restrained sometimes, for his own safety. They say the full moon affects him.'

The rain now stopped, she and I extracted ourselves from beneath the wagon. We walked side by side, back to the wall. Gabe was already signalling to the men to pass him more stones.

Dorcas sighed heavily. 'Some people can become very much afflicted in their minds. It is hard to understand the ways of God in such cases, does thee not think?'

I wholeheartedly agreed with her. 'I have a brother very much afflicted since he returned from the fighting on the Peninsula.'

'I am truly sorry to hear that,' she replied in her solemn way. 'It's a difficult matter, most especially for their families, who care

for them. My father says we must make safe havens for them –
not in prisons, not Bedlams, where all such people are thrown
together, the lost and fearful together with those who are
angry and violent. Papa has seen such sights as robbed him of
his sleep. Thy family are able to care for thy brother at home?'

'As best they can,' I said, ashamed to think that I had
rejoiced when offered work here and could leave my grandmother and her maidservant to manage Neil's rages. I had not
heard from Grandma lately. If matters had moved forward in
Dundee, surely, she would have let me know?

'Are you two set on spending the rest of t' day putting the
world to rights?' Gabriel Waller demanded.

'Oh, I must not hold you up.' Dorcas thrust the phrase
book into my arms. She stepped into the lane and headed up
the track to Rush Ghyll. She walked with grace, that Quaker
girl, the ends of her sacking shawl fluttering behind her in the
breeze like the wings of a meadow brown butterfly.

Some of the prisoners, seeing her go, uttered little cries of
pretended distress, and blew kisses after her before bursting
into laughter.

'Mais non!' the burly ship's cook admonished them, 'C'est
une gentille dame. Ne ridiculisez pas!'

'She's a solemn little piece, very *learned*,' said Gabe, 'but
mebbe *you* like that.'

'What I *would* like is to get this wall finished,' I replied,
determined not to suffer his insolence.

The clouds had rolled away inland over the Trough. Sunlight glinted on the windows of Lane End farmhouse and
illuminated great swathes of the fellside beyond. Do you see
that I was beginning to speak the local language without
thinking? The *fellside*, not the brae.

As it was May, the hours of daylight were lengthening. I now believed we could finish the wall today. I wanted to walk up to High Bield afterwards and ask Matthew Trawden if he would welcome a party of prisoners rebuilding his broken wall.

Chapter Thirty-Four

Dorcas' Journal

2nd Day, 2nd Week of 5th Month *continued*

Today, I conducted my first French lesson. The lesson was for me rather than for the Frenchmen. This is not the way lessons are usually carried out, with the teacher learning more than her pupils.

Hugh Armstrong seemed embarrassed that I had come, because it had turned out that he didn't need my book. Then he relented, and (I think) made me welcome. I don't have Sukie's winning manners around young men. I say too little, or too much and too strongly. I sense their discomfort and that they wish me away.

I wonder how she goes on? Is the married state all she hoped for? They are not to take a whole month on their honeymoon, of course. Just two weeks or perhaps a few days more if Nathaniel can be spared. He needs to be in attendance at the mill so that his partners see he is serious about the work.

I have never been to the Lake Country, although it is a little more than a day's journey north. I am told it is very beautiful. The hills there, which we can glimpse across Morecambe Bay on a fine, clear day, are much higher than our Pennine fells. Some of the stretches of lake water are said to be extensive. People compare it to Switzerland, but of course, I have never been there either, so I cannot tell if the comparison is just.

Travelling for pleasure, Mama and Papa consider an unnecessary vanity, unless for the purpose of bringing people to the Light, or attending to matters of Quaker business. The old Quakers of former times travelled a great deal 'in the ministry'. Some still do today, particularly when they need to bring injustices to our attention, such as slavery, conditions in the prisons, poverty, and, of course, the evils of warfare. I wish I had sufficient courage.

I hope Sukie is enjoying her wedding journey and that she will describe to me all the places she saw when she returns. However, I do not hold out great hopes. Sukie, when asked to describe somewhere she has been, is liable to reply only that it was 'most pleasant, you would have liked it, Dorcas.' Which is no help at all!

I must leave off. Something has happened; there are loud voices in the kitchen.

Chapter Thirty-Five

Hugh

I saw to the departure of the wagon with its load of prisoners. The drayhorses proved challenging to catch, having enjoyed their day of freedom grazing in the meadow. I inspected the finished work one last time and wrote out a note of hand for Gabe so that he could claim his fee.

So, it was later than I'd anticipated when I began the walk up the track to Rush Ghyll. I was determined to return Dorcas's book as I'd promised. However, by the time I reached High Bield, it would be dark. Perhaps it would be better to postpone my visit to the Trawdens. I rather imagined that the brothers retired to their sleeping quarters once darkness fell. Why would those two waste money on candles?

As I approached the Huttons' farmhouse, it was a surprise to hear, above a confused babble of sound, the raised voice of Matthew Trawden himself.

''E fell! T' hoss were spooked!' he was shouting. 'Our Batty never meant to, but 'e let off the gun sudden like, and the hoss were spooked and threw 'im. He fell agin the wall!'

Now what? Had Batty got hold of that gun again and killed someone?

I entered by the side door and followed the sound of raised voices to find a strange gathering in Lydia Hutton's kitchen. Laid upon a settle in the window embrasure was my employer, Sir John Hathersage. Lydia was engaged in bathing his brow. Young Wilf held a lantern aloft to aid her efforts. Sir John's eyes were closed, his cheeks ashen. He appeared lost to consciousness.

Standing around, adding anxious comments, were Wilfred Hutton, Jonathan and Betsey Hutton, Matthew Trawden, and Augustus Fenwick.

Dorcas alone had separated herself from this throng and stood at the kitchen table, engaged in trimming the wick of a second, larger lantern.

'John Hathersage has met with an accident,' she told me. 'It seems he rode up to High Bield with Augustus Fenwick, the detective, to see what more they might learn of that man found dead up there. This Augustus Fenwick is still convinced the man was a French spy. He believes the Trawdens must be involved in his spying, however much they deny it.' She shrugged, dismissing such a notion as absurd. As I had to agree, it was.

'It seems Bartholomew was out with a gun, hoping to get a rabbit. He was crouched on the ground behind a wall. John Hathersage and the detective rode up, just as he saw one and fired. The shot went nowhere near them, but the horses were startled. John Hathersage's reared, and he was thrown against the wall.' She finished trimming the wick, struck the tinder, and lit it.

'There. Now Mama will be able to see better.'

'How long has Sir John been unconscious?' I asked.

'I'm not sure. A while.' She passed her lantern to her brother, taking the smaller one from him. 'Since the middle of the afternoon, I think. Naturally, Batty would be no help in such circumstances, but he was persuaded to run and fetch his brother.'

Most farmers around here doctored their own animals and have an idea about human health. Matthew would have to, in particular, living in such a remote place.

'Matthew couldn't help?' I asked.

'So, they brought him here to Mama.'

'Your Mama?'

'With seven of us children, she has had enough experience. If your employer can be brought out of his swoon, Mama will do it.' Dorcas smiled.

'How did they manage to bring him down the fell?' I pictured Sir John thrust unceremoniously across his horse's back like a sack of barley. 'The Trawdens have no trap, I think. Being jolted down that track cannot have helped him.'

I was imagining Lady Lavinia's questions and struggling to frame answers. Where had *I* been when this happened? Why had she not been sent for immediately?

And – I fought to banish this last unworthy thought – if Sir John should die of his injuries, what then would become of me?

Somebody should be riding to fetch her now.

'The Trawdens have a hand cart, and they packed him about with some sacking they had. They did their best,' said Dorcas.

'He's breathing a little easier,' I could hear Lydia Hutton saying, 'and though conveying him here may have done no *further* harm, it would be best we put him to bed. A night's rest and quiet may help. Wilf and Jonathan, go and dismantle the frame bed and bring it down to the parlour. That will be better than carrying him upstairs. We must move him as little as we can.'

Little Betsey moved towards Dorcas and me and said, in what I suppose she thought was a whisper, 'I shall have to sleep with thee tonight, Dorcas.' For my benefit, she added, 'The frame bed is the one the old Quaker slept in, thee knows, Hugh Armstrong. He who travelled in the ministry one hundred years ago, and stayed here at Rush Ghyll. He was a good man, and so perhaps his bed will heal John Hathersage.'

I had grown used to plain speaking. I even found myself approving of it amongst the adults of this kindly and hardworking community. I accepted that they meant no disrespect by it, but bit back at my irritation that a child of Betsey's age should speak of my employer as though he were her social equal.

Dorcas shook her head at her little sister. 'Thee is too forward in thy speech, Betsey Hutton!' To me, she said, 'We do not ascribe healing properties to inanimate objects as I understand Catholics do. Is thy pony here? Will thee go tonight to let his wife know what has happened?'

'Polly is down at Low Bield.' I replied. 'I think I *must* go, but I don't know whether Lady Lavinia is at the Lancaster house or... no, she must be in Lancaster. I would have seen the carriage pass if she had come to Dalefoot today.'

'Thy poor pony is quite old to be ridden so far tonight,' said Dorcas in her frank way, 'also thee hast no gig to convey her if she wishes to come. Why not ask Papa if thee can borrow our horse and gig?'

Wilfred Hutton, applied to, immediately gave his permission. His own head was no longer bandaged. He seemed much his usual self, although gravely concerned for his landlord. 'This is a bad business,' he told me. 'No violence was intended, but a sad and testing thing to have happened. We must hold him in the Light and pray that no more such difficulties are visited upon our community.'

He, like me, must be wondering about the outcome when Sir John recovered. Or even worse if he didn't. Would Matthew and Bartholomew Trawden be turned out of High Bield? It wouldn't be easy to find new tenants for such a remote and unprofitable farm. But could Sir John excuse what had happened? I doubted it. Matthew, standing silently by, still wringing his hands in anguish, must be doubting it even more.

The bed was fetched and erected, and fresh lavender-scented linen found. Between them, Young Wilf and Jonathan gently lifted Sir John onto the mattress.

'I will take it upon myself to sit with him through the night,' said Augustus Fenwick, who up to that moment had said little. 'I feel a great responsibility. A very *great* responsibility. Of course, I could not have foreseen... but it was at my request that Sir John accompanied me to that farm. I thought it possible... but now I've seen your confounded brother.' He snarled at Matthew. 'He ought, in my opinion, to be put in an asylum. But never mind that. We are no further forward, and now this!'

Lydia Hutton thanked him gravely. This, I had discovered, was entirely typical of these Quaker families. If someone offered to do something they did not say, 'Are you sure? Are you quite certain? You must have had such a tiring day.' They assumed the person making the offer meant it to be accepted. 'Say what you mean, and mean what you say,' was how they saw it. I liked that. Much time is wasted in polite 'havering' as we say in Scotland. There was no havering in Netherdale.

Amid this busy activity, I'd failed to notice Dorcas slipping away. She returned, swinging a cloak around her shoulders and tying her bonnet strings.

'I have the horse harnessed and ready. I believe I should come with thee. Steadfast is a good creature, but driving down our track is not easy if thee has never done it. Also, if Lavinia Hathersage wishes to come, she would wish to have a woman with her for propriety, does thee not think?'

'But surely it is just as improper for *you*?' I stammered.

Lydia Hutton, her arms full of blankets, smiled wryly. 'My daughter does not regard that. She trusts thee, as indeed do I.'

We were almost out of the door when Matthew Trawden noticed that I was leaving and called after me. 'Mister Armstrong! I've got summat for tha.' He patted at the pockets of his frieze coat but then shook his head in annoyance. 'Ah must have left it on t' table.'

'Never mind!' I called back, not wanting to be delayed. Whatever it was could not be as urgent as bringing Lady Lavvy to the bedside of her sick husband.

'I shall come up to High Bield tomorrow,' I told him. 'You can give it to me then.'

Chapter Thirty-Six

Hugh

Dorcas was right. Guiding a strange horse and gig, with only one serviceable arm, down a steep track in the dark would have been an almost impossible task. And I needed the gig to bring Lady Lavinia back. James Carr could only get the carriage as far as Dalefoot. It would then have fallen to my lot to guide the lady up the fellside on foot.

I had difficulty just staying securely in my seat, but Steadfast was evidently as steady as his name and plodded on downwards whilst Dorcas gently applied the wheel brake. It did occur to me that perhaps either Young Wilf or Jonathan might have been spared to drive me, but she had seized the day before anyone had time to think.

'You drive well,' I said. We must find some unexceptional topics for the journey to justify her mother's faith in me, and this was the first that came to mind.

Dorcas chuckled. 'I believe I do,' she said, 'although my brothers pour scorn on my efforts. Everyone praises Susannah, because she looks so dainty sitting up in the driving seat with the reins in her hands, but she has always shied away from driving down this track, being afraid the horse may stumble, or the brake might fail.'

'But *you* place your faith in God so that such a thing will never happen to you?' I don't know why I said this. It was by no means an 'unexceptional topic'.

Dorcas said nothing. I sat in silence, ashamed of myself. My words had been rude and provocative. Hurtful. It wasn't her fault that she had been brought up in an atmosphere of piety and good works while I had suffered cruelty at the whim of a hypocrite.

'I'm sorry,' I finally said. 'I apologise. I'm afraid I have had bad experiences in childhood at the hands of a man who claimed to be a pious minister of religion, but who was nothing but a whited sepulchre!'

Dorcas remained silent. I assumed she was angry, offended. 'I'm sorry,' I repeated.

She turned so that her eyes met mine. This girl was no 'simpering miss'.

'I am sorry too,' she said. The starlight gleamed down on us, lighting her grave young face. 'I did not intend to imply that my courage comes from believing I have special protection from Our Lord. Nothing of the sort! I am fearful of many things, but driving down the fell doesn't happen to be one of them. Perhaps we Huttons do tend to speak as though we have God in our pockets.

'It must be very provoking for people like thee whose experiences have been very different. I fret about the restrictions in my life, about the boundaries that being a young woman from a Quaker family place upon me. But I know I am in many ways fortunate, truly.' She sighed. 'Did…did this man cause the injury to thy hand and arm?'

'My father? He did. Oh, not directly perhaps, although I did not escape the tawse entirely. No, he beat and abused my mother so badly that she had a difficult time giving birth to me – *that* was the cause.'

'And thee is angry because God did not punish him?'

'The laws of men finally caught up with him.' I said, grating out the words. 'When it was discovered that he had embezzled monies belonging to the kirk, he lost his living and was cast out of the community. So, I suppose one could say that God did punish him. If I found myself able to believe in God.'

'And that thee cannot do?'

I said nothing. Between us, we had stirred up a fierce storm of emotion. I was speechless with anger. Not with her, not even with my father anymore. He was serving out his doom. Perhaps it was my own weakness – the inner, craven terror of a helpless child – which I still carried within me.

'I apologise once again. I should not be inflicting my personal troubles on you, Dorcas. I was too emotional about what is past and gone.'

She did not reply, and I was grateful. We drove on in silence. Naturally, I thought, the girl can handle silence. In my head, I could hear Gabriel Waller's comment on this. 'Very unusual in a female.' I wondered if he had a wife. I had never asked him. Poor creature, if so.

After a while, Dorcas gathered the reins in her right hand and gestured to the heavens with the other. 'I, too, often doubt,' she said, 'but as my father says, *someone* or *something* made the stars.'

Now she'd drawn my attention to them, I saw that tonight the heavens were glorious – a thousand diamonds hanging above us, sending out shimmering flickers of light into the summer darkness.

'They say,' said Dorcas, 'that in the mill towns, thee can never see them clearly. Even on a cloudless night, the mills create a thin pall of smoke and dust that dims their brightness. Alas, Lancaster is like that now, with the new silk and flax mills springing up.'

'Such as the one your brother-in-law will be running,' I commented, 'hiding the stars.'

'Yes, I suppose so. But we cannot live on the beauty of the stars alone. Men and women must work to feed themselves, and the mills provide work.'

'For children, too, I hear. Will Nathaniel employ children?' I was still trying to provoke her. I cannot say why.

There was doubt and confusion in her voice. 'I heard him tell my father that youngsters can be very useful as runners – running up and down the spinning shed with the skeins to pull out the length of the silk thread – and of course, the boys are happy to be taking money home to their parents. Some are fatherless, he told Papa, and beg for the work, but I wish...'

'You will have to go and see for yourself,' I said.

'I will,' she replied. 'Nathaniel has invited us to see every inch of the mill as soon as he and Susannah are home and settled. Thee should come too. I'm sure the invitation could be extended to include thee. Nathaniel likes thee.'

'Does he?' I said, surprised. Apart from that one conversation on the fellside while I was assessing the broken stream bank, we had exchanged only a few words.

'He does,' she said gravely, but went on with a slight smile. 'I should not tell thee this – for we are warned against indulging in gossip and lightness of speech. He told Mama and Papa thee is a good man. *Sound*. He said John Hathersage chose well when he engaged thee, and that perhaps we might... No, I think Mama should not have repeated that to me!'

'Am I to understand that you do not care for your sister's husband?'

Dorcas turned her head away, but I saw that she was trying to suppress the urge to laugh. 'Nathaniel is a good man. He is *very* sound himself, very worthy, and he truly loves Sukie. I feel certain of that. I'm sure they will deal excellently together. I'm sure it is very wrong of me to find him dull.'

'You are all very worthy,' I said. 'All the families here in Netherdale.'

'And very dull?' she whipped back at me, smiling.

'No, I did not mean that. You are good people, good farmers, in harmony with nature, and all of you are content with your station in life. You care for one another, and there is laughter and good-natured teasing, and joyful occasions like your sister's wedding.'

I had not consciously thought this before, but it was true. They were good people, the farmers of Netherdale. There was no cruelty or back-biting amongst them, little prideful behaviour or striving to prove themselves better than anyone else. I had felt at home with them, that I could trust them, and should I ever need it, that I could call on them for help.

'Don't think too well of us,' said Dorcas gloomily, 'or thee will be disappointed. Quakers are not always as good as people think.'

We had reached the place where the track levelled off. I thought I might manage the gig from here and drew breath to say so, but Dorcas was looking straight ahead, eyes fixed on the horse's hindquarters. Once again, I worried that I had offended her. Perhaps with my words about her family and their neighbours. She drove on in silence. Lamplight flickered in the windows of Lane End farm, but Dalefoot lay in darkness.

'Should we call?' she asked.

'I was working on the wall here throughout today. If Lady Lavinia had come up to Dalefoot, I cannot believe her carriage could have passed by without me noticing.' Or, I thought, she have passed by without satisfying her curiosity to see the prisoners at work.

Dorcas and I seemed to have run out of ways to ruffle one another's feelings, so for the next few miles, we said nothing, and I fell to brooding on one of the first things Dorcas had mentioned. Nathaniel thought me a 'sound man,' a sentiment she had implied was shared by some (most?) of Sir John's tenants. *And perhaps we might— What* was the rest of that sentence? Did they hope to convert me to their faith? Were they hoping that I would take their side should any dispute arise with Sir John? I wasn't sure what to think.

The lights of Lancaster were now below us. Soon, we should have been bowling through the outskirts. Suddenly, however, the dark shapes of oncoming carts and covered wagons appeared, their side lanterns flickering dimly. Men pushing handbarrows with no lights at all blocked the road ahead. Dorcas slowed Steadfast to a halt, waiting while these vehicles swung across the roadway and turned in at a field gate. Were they setting up for a country fair or a market? There seemed to be too many for a gypsy encampment.

I broke our silence by saying so.

'Or it might be a travelling show with wild beasts,' said Dorcas, as the carts crossed our path. 'Oh, I hope they aren't exhibiting freaks. I think that's so cruel! Does thee not think so?'

'I don't know,' I replied, 'never having seen one. We have travelling shows in Scotland, but only in the vicinity of the larger towns. The showmen must be sure of a large audience to make the venture worthwhile.'

'Those poor people! They're slaves. Slaves to men who exhibit them like animals!'

'Indeed, along with two-headed calves and the like.'

Dorcas shuddered. 'I have heard they have growths on their faces and bodies, deformed legs, or have missing feet or hands. Or they have never grown in stature beyond the size of a three-year-old child. Yet people flock to see them and laugh and gawk at them. It is very wrong.'

'But,' I said, playing the devil's advocate, 'it may be the only way such people can earn money to support themselves. Rejected by their families, they have no other recourse but begging or the workhouse. The showmen at least feed and clothe them. I have heard some of them become famous and even wealthy.'

'Unlike the black slaves in the southern states of America and the West Indies, I suppose,' she agreed, 'but these people can no more escape from their "owners" than the slaves can.'

Short stakes were being hammered in the ground and flares set alight around the field where this travelling fair, or whatever it was, was being set up.

I could see that we were straying into deep waters. Dorcas was about to recount more of the opinions she had acquired from her father and his fellow Quaker Elders, but she was suddenly distracted. Catching sight of someone or something amongst the flare setters, she gasped aloud, thrust the reins at me, and leapt down from the gig.

Off she ran, into the dark 'show ground' and disappeared completely from my view.

Chapter Thirty-Seven

Hugh

Steadfast shuffled in his traces, stamped, and snorted softly. Possibly, he was as mystified as I was. Where had the wretched girl gone? Had she spied one of these human exhibits and dashed off to rescue them? Such faces as I had caught glimpses of by the light of the flares had not appeared in any way unusual to me. I was assailed by mild panic. I could not leave a valuable horse and gig to go after her. Judging by the eyes being cast in our direction, I suspected neither would be there on my return.

I felt conspicuous, so I climbed down from my perch and went to the horse's head.

'What do I do now?' I asked. Steadfast snorted. 'She does this often?' He blew gustily in my ear. 'Oh, nothing she does surprises you?' Steadfast shuffled his hooves, iron horseshoes clinking on the road surface. 'Or should I say nothing she does surprises *thee*?'

Steadfast didn't seem to have any answers, any more than Polly ever did.

Over the hedge, the wagons were being parked in a circle around a sizable sheet of canvas. As we had guessed, this was a travelling show. My crippled arm began to shake, as it does in distressing situations. Wretched girl! She could have no idea what danger she was putting herself into. These fairground workers were unlikely to deal 'politely' with a young woman straying into their midst.

A declaration on her part that she was there to rescue some mistreated animal or human freak would fall on extremely unreceptive ears. She would be lucky if she escaped with only insults and rough handling.

And what of Lady Lavvy, whom I had promised to take to the bedside of her sick husband? Dorcas had abandoned me. It would serve the stupid girl right if I put my employer's needs first and drove on, leaving her to her fate.

'We're going to have to go in there and try to find her,' I told Steadfast, 'even though we are likely to encounter people I fear may be more interested in stealing you than helping me.'

At this moment, however, a man on a stout pony with a young woman seated up behind him separated themselves from the last few oncoming wagons and rode towards us.

'Hey!' he demanded, 'what yer doing here? Running away to join the raree show, are yer?' His accent had slipped, but it was James Carr, Sir John's coachman.

'Waiting for Miss Dorcas Hutton,' I growled, 'who offered to drive me to your master's house. Sir John, I must tell you straight away, has met with a nasty accident, having been thrown from his horse. I need to inform Lady Lavinia and take her up to Rush Ghyll farm, where he is being cared for, but Dorcas...'

'Run out on yer? What yer do to her?'

I realised that Carr must have been drinking with the plump lassie who was clinging around his waist, and peeking flirtatiously at me over his shoulder.

'Ooh,' cried she, 'tha shouldn't ha' done that. 'Keep tha hands ter yerself!' That's what I says ter Jimmy here. Not that he pays me any mind!'

'Nothing like that!' I snapped. 'Miss Dorcas saw someone she recognised on this fairground they are setting up, and went rushing off, leaving me stranded.'

'What's this that's happened to his nibs then?' Carr demanded. He wasn't so flown with drink that he'd missed what I'd said. 'I seen he wasn't back when I set out to meet with Nancy here.'

'His mount shied and threw him against a wall whilst he was up at High Bield with Augustus Fenwick,' I told him. 'They brought him down to Rush Ghyll to seek Lydia Hutton's aid. I don't know how badly he's hurt. Dorcas offered to drive me into Lancaster so that we could bring Lady Lavinia back to be with him.'

'Tha needn't do that,' Carr shook his head. 'Waste o' tha time. Being as she ain't there. Gone to Preston to see what furniture she'll bring back from the house there, to put in the new place at Dalefoot.'

'Reet grand *she* is!' chimed in Nancy, clinging on to her swain, her chin resting on his shoulder, 'Got three 'ouses, she has. One 'ere in Lancaster, one in Preston, and this new 'un up in Netherdale. 'Ow's about that?'

Carr shook his head at her. 'Never mind that, Nance. I got ter get yer back 'ome, or yer dad 'll leather me.' To me, he said, 'Best wait for the lass to turn up. There's nay hurry since yer don't need to go to the Castle Hill house tonight. *I'll* tek t' carriage over to Preston first thing tomorrow and fetch 'er ladyship. Too late to go tonight.'

I reckoned up the distance, twenty miles and more. He was probably right. By the time I got to Preston with or without Dorcas – and I had no notion whereabouts the house was situated – it would be past midnight. A lengthy ride in an open gig in the early hours of the morning would not be pleasant for Lady

Lavvy. Much better to have Carr go for her with the carriage early tomorrow.

'I can rely on you absolutely to fetch her ladyship in the morning?' I asked.

'Believe me, I'll go.'

I sighed. 'So now I only have to wade into this fairground and find Dorcas, and we can return to Netherdale.'

'Ooh, can us come with yer?' asked Nancy. 'I never seen a travellin' show.'

'And you ain't goin' to see one now!' said her swain. 'I gotta get you 'ome or yer dad 'll kill me! It's a mite later than we said already.'

'Tell yer what,' he said to me, 'I'll tek Nance 'ome, and then I'll come back. 'Tis only a step,' he said, waving his hand towards a huddle of cottages set along a lane off to the other side of the road. 'If yer ain't found the Hutton lass by then, I'll come with yer and help yer look.'

This was a generous offer, but it still meant I would have to lead Steadfast and the gig onto the field, which I wasn't anxious to do. When I explained this, Carr nodded, saying after some thought, 'Swap over then. I'll tek Nance home in the gig,' and you ride this old slug onto the field to find the lass.'

I saw that this would have immediate advantages for both of us. Nancy, sulking because she couldn't come to the fair, perked up at the notion of being delivered to her dad in the Huttons' neat gig. Carr's slug, a shaggy, knock-kneed beast, at least as old as my Polly, would be less likely to excite acquisitive thoughts amongst the fairground workers.

So, the exchange was made. Bugle was not a beast designed or inclined for speed, but mounted on his back, I had the advantage of a commanding position to view the fairground.

I scanned the whole site without seeing anyone resembling Dorcas Hutton. Where on earth was she? I dreaded to think what might have happened to her.

The last of the carts and wagons must have arrived and were now neatly parked up in their appointed places on the field. Men were hauling up a billowing canvas tent with guy ropes, whilst others knocked stakes into the ground to hold it securely in place.

Bugle and I advanced. The men, sweating and straining to erect the tent, hardly glanced in our direction. Taking advantage of a young woman wasn't on their minds at the moment. I needed to seek out the animal tamers or – I shuddered at the thought – the guardians of the two-headed children. I set off towards some smaller tents and wheeled huts, such as gypsies and travellers call home, parked at the furthest edge of the field. There, I found a woman seated on a stool, peeling potatoes and dropping them into a bucket.

'Excuse me, Ma'am. Have you seen a young woman dressed in a russet cloak?' I realised as soon as I'd said it, it was too dark for anyone to be sure of the colour, despite the flares. This old dame squinted up at me with rheumy eyes. She might not be able to distinguish a cloak, let alone name it as russet.

'Youse a Scotchman.' She cackled, evidently pleased with her powers of aural deduction.

'Indeed, I am,' I agreed, restraining myself from correcting 'Scotch' with 'Scotsman,' as I hoped for co-operation. 'Have you seen a young woman? A stranger. Not someone who... travels with you people. She came running in here about half an hour ago, having perhaps seen someone she knew. Or something that alarmed her.'

The old woman shook her head. 'Ain't seen nobody that don't belong. Not yet. The whole town'll be coming once they find out we're 'ere.'

'I suppose so,' I agreed. 'What do you show? I mean, is it a fair? With stalls selling goods? Or performances with animals? Horse riding acts?'

'Bit o' this, bit o' that,' the auld 'un replied, cannily refusing to be specific. After all, I could be some local 'do-gooder' or official, here to discover reasons to move the fair on.

I smiled at her. 'I'll have to ask a few more people. I know she did come in here.'

I pressed my heels to Bugle's sides. As I departed, she called after me. 'Wouldn't give yer tuppence fer that old nag, Mister. *Our* 'osses is kept like kings!'

So, it was a horse show, she'd told me that much. Major Philip Astley had opened his so-called 'riding school' in London some forty years ago, where he and his wife had performed daring tricks on horseback. Their success had aroused many others to try to emulate them. Some had added balancing feats on a rope or a wire, or performing dogs taught clever tricks. Between the equestrian displays, there would be 'clowns' dressed in colourful motley, somersaulting to entertain the audience, playing the fool, pretending to be chased by a toothless bear. (It was always *said* to be toothless.) However, in recent years, as Dorcas had said, both children and adults, dwarves, outrageously fat people, and those with deformations, were increasingly 'shown'.

I rode a circuit of the field, glimpsing flickering lanterns in some of the wheeled huts, but apart from the old woman and the men erecting the main tent, no one else was out and about. There was the sound of horses stamping and shifting in a second marquee, but no sign of a young woman anywhere. Nor did I hear any cries of distress. Yet I knew Dorcas must be there. If she had passed out through the gate, I would have seen her. The field backed onto a dense wood surrounded by a high fence.

'No sign of 'er?' James Carr brought Steadfast and the gig to join me as I passed the entrance gate for a second time. This was fine, I reasoned now. With two of us here, I thought it unlikely that anyone would try to take it.

And I was beginning to feel that my assumptions about fairground folk might have been both hasty and unjust. These people were far too busy erecting their big show tent to concern themselves with interlopers. It was entirely possible that they were honest; they were certainly hardworking.

Their wives and mothers might at this moment be entertaining Dorcas to a polite dish of tea in one of the wagons. And telling her all about their enthralling lives as travelling folk. I supposed, sourly, that Dorcas might be enjoying herself – eagerly inquiring if any of them spoke French – without a thought for me.

We made another circuit of the field. The big tent was almost secure now. The last pegs were being driven into place, and the roustabouts were sending puzzled glances over their shoulders as we passed by yet again.

'She's got to be *somewhere* in here,' I said.

'I've heard tell that this lot has a performing bear. Perhaps it ate her?' Carr growled.

But before we could even contemplate the likelihood of this horrid fate, we heard loud voices arguing. Two people were coming towards us. The flares were dying, but I could see that one of them was Dorcas, quite unharmed and accompanied by a young man. He was rounder-faced than either of his brothers, but recognisably a Hutton.

'This is my brother George,' Dorcas exclaimed on seeing us. 'I've found him!'

George scowled. 'I don't want to be found. I like this life.'

'Oh, *do* tell him, Hugh Armstrong, how troubled poor Mama has been!'

'*Thee* can tell her I am well and doing as I wish,' her brother hissed in reply, '*You* can tell her, Dorcas! I've given up this theeing and thouing. It's... well, people don't do it anymore. Only old people in the countryside. It marks you for a dreary Quaker or a country bumpkin.'

'And you, George, don't want to be either of those!' I remarked, thinking I should help Dorcas out since she seemed to be on the verge of tears.

'I *don't* want to be stuck on a two-nag farm, miles from anywhere, at the constant beck and call of Papa and our Wilf, that's for certain. It came to me while I was trudging back and forth to Pontefract, taking our Isaac to school, that if I stayed in Netherdale on Papa's farm, I'd never have owt of my own worth more than a brass farthing. Jonathan can stick it if he likes. Isaac's set to be a scholar. Dorcas tells me Susannah's wed now, and Dorcas herself had a good place as a schoolteacher, but she threw it up for some daft reason.'

'It wasn't daft.' Dorcas was weeping now, tears coursing down her cheeks. 'Mama and Papa know the reason, and it's none of thy business!'

The recalcitrant George shrugged. 'If you won't tell anyone what it was, I'm bound to think that. Nor is it any business of *yours*, Mr Land Agent. Or *yours*, Jamie Carr.'

I gave him a brief bow of acknowledgement. 'Where did you meet up with the Fair people, George?' I asked.

'Just outside Leeds, and *that's* none o' your business either,' he snapped 'I'd set out early, fed up with those prosy old Quakers I'd been stuck with, 'walking in the Light', like they claim they do, and thinking themselves too godly to buy a second jug of ale. Their so-called 'simplicity' can look just plain mean. I met the fairground people on the road and got talking to them. I told them I was looking for work and was used to animals. They offered me a place, setting up the big tent, mucking out, grooming, and such like.'

'You'd say *that's* an easier life than on your father's farm?' Jamie Carr was incredulous.

'No, but they pay me,' George snapped, 'and when I'm not needed, I can do exactly as I like. Eat my food when I'm famished without having to pray over it. No sitting on a hard bench for an hour or more on First Day – *Sunday,* that is – while some pompous old Quaker tells us what the Lord wants, or what *he* believes the Lord should do about transgressors the likes of me!'

'So we should leave you here?' I asked.

'Exactly! Take my sister home,' he told me. 'Dorcas, tell Mama to stop fretting. I'm well and content. Doing what *I* want to do. Travelling up and down the land, seeing places I never knew of. Money in my pocket. Spending it on whatever I like.'

We stood in silence for a while. Dorcas wiped her eyes on her sleeve.

James jumped down from the gig. 'Seems like we aren't wanted here,' he said, handing me the reins. 'I'll go and fetch her Ladyship in the morning like I said, and bring her up to Rush Ghyll to see how things are.'

'Thank you,' I replied, sliding off Bugle and climbing into the gig. 'Come, Dorcas, let's go. Your parents will be wondering why we've been so long.'

Reluctantly, she scrambled up beside me, looking back at her brother, who watched us in mulish silence as we drove slowly out of the fairground. Then he turned back towards the big tent and his new life.

'I've failed Mama!' Dorcas sobbed. 'I was so excited when I saw him. I was sure I could persuade him to come home. If she'd been here, *she* would have persuaded him.'

'Possibly,' I agreed, 'but he seems to like his freedom, and perhaps it may do him good. You tried your best, Dorcas. Your parents will understand.'

'But surely the life he is leading is very wrong?'

I chose my words carefully. 'I would agree with you if he were living by dishonest dealing or amongst people who are cruel to their animals, but we don't know that they are. Do we?'

She was silent for a while and then asked, 'Does thee want me to drive?'

'Not at the moment. I can manage well enough one-handed on this straight stretch. You shall handle the reins when we reach a more difficult bit.'

Dorcas reached into her sleeve and at last found a handkerchief to wipe her eyes.

'At least you've found your brother,' I said. 'You can tell your mother where he is and that he seems well and happy.'

'I ought to have persuaded him to come home.'

We drove for a while in silence. Dorcas, exhausted by all that had happened, fell asleep, drooping sideways so that her head rested against my damaged arm and shoulder. This was acutely uncomfortable, but I didn't try to rouse her. Instead, I felt a small sensation of pride that I was able to manage Steadfast without her help. And I was even a little pleased to have a young woman lean on me. Not something that normally happens to a cripple.

I found I had some sympathy for George Hutton. He had convinced himself he was a general drudge about the farm, at everyone's beck and call, however kindly his family had actually treated him. It didn't surprise me that he'd yearned for freedom, money of his own, and a whole world out there to explore. At his age, I had longed for the same.

Chapter Thirty-Eight

Dorcas' Journal

5th Day, 3rd Week of 5th Month

Seeing me so weary and hardly able to string two sensible words together, Mama ordered me straight to bed. John Hathersage was no worse than when we left. If anything, she said, he was breathing more easily, and I was not to worry that we had not been able to bring his wife. Of course, I started to tell her about George, but she shushed me and sent me upstairs. She was glad, she said, that I had found him. The rest of the story could wait for the morning.

Squeezed in beside Betsey – I had forgotten how that child spreads herself across the bed, taking up more than her fair share – I lay awake for a time despite my tiredness, listening to the rise and fall of voices in the kitchen below.

By the time I rose the following morning, Mama knew everything about my discovery of George amongst the travelling fair people. I'd been sure she would be disappointed in my failure to persuade him to give up that foolish way of life, but she just shook her head and said she doubted anyone could have managed it.

'Your brother has always had an obstinate nature since he was a babe, and there is nothing to be done about it. We must pray that he will grow in wisdom and come to see the Light in God's good time. I was sorry to hear, Dorcas,' she went on, 'that thee worried Hugh Armstrong so, by thoughtlessly running off without a word. He told us he thought thee might have been eaten by a bear!'

'I believe they do have a bear, but George said he was old and nearly toothless. I didn't see him. They have horses, George says. Some of the men perform daring bareback acts or walk on the high wire. He said some of the young women perform too, in costumes sewn all over with sequins. George coloured up when he told me that, Mama. I think their costumes may be immodest.'

To my surprise, this made Mama laugh. 'George is seeing something very different from the life he has been used to,' she said, 'but I believe God's hand is over him, and he will come to no harm.'

I should have been happy that she seemed so unconcerned. Of course, the Prodigal Son stayed away from his family, wasting his inheritance, but was welcomed by his father with open arms. The story is meant to show us that, however far we fall from grace, we can still be forgiven, but George is *so* annoying! On the other hand, I suspect the Prodigal Son was annoying, too. The Bible doesn't mention any sisters, only that his older brother disapproved of his father forgiving him so easily. Well, I am an older sister who wishes the fairground people might let loose that bear, and that the bear would chase George, and if not eat him, at least give him a big fright.

Later

George is right, of course, that it's considered old-fashioned nowadays to use thee and thou when speaking to people. 'Thou' is awkward. The old Quakers would have said, 'What <u>canst</u> thou do?' We shorten it to 'what can *thee* do?'

Although he has never said so, I think Hugh Armstrong might agree with George. I'm not sure what I think. Maybe we <u>are</u> old-fashioned, and the need for it isn't what it once was. Everyone else says 'you' and 'yours', to all but God, no matter what their station in life. I've noticed that even Nathaniel says 'you' on occasion now that he engages in the world of business. Perhaps I will grow used to it.

I'm truly sorry I worried Hugh Armstrong. When I see him next, I will make my apologies. I am self-conscious in his company and do not show myself in my best light.

Mama is very busy, of course, caring for John Hathersage and making food for everyone else, including Augustus Fenwick. She murmured to me that Augustus has the appetite of a carthorse. She said she was glad to have me at home to help her, and that made *me* glad, although I know I am not such a help as Susannah would be if she were here.

I asked if we had heard anything from Nat and Sukie, but Mama shook her head. I hope we will hear soon. I miss Sukie so much, especially now that I am sharing a bed with Betsey. I never knew a child of nine could snore as she does.

Chapter Thirty-Nine

Hugh

It had been a relief to hear that Sir John was no worse when I returned from my fruitless attempt to find his wife. Lydia Hutton seemed confident that he would soon regain consciousness, and, with luck, this morning, James Carr was already on his way to fetch Lady Lavinia. There was nothing more I could do.

I was just about to leave the Huttons when Lydia reminded me that Matthew Trawden had said he had something for me – something Bartholomew had found. 'He seemed very anxious that thee should have it,' she said. 'I know those brothers are a strange pair, but I also know them to be honest.'

I couldn't imagine what Batty Trawden could have found that was mine. I had lost nothing, not so much as a handkerchief, but the only way to find out would be to talk to Matthew. If we were to go ahead with rebuilding the wall, I needed to speak to him anyway, and at least I hoped to be able to give the brothers reassuring news of their landlord. Nevertheless, my mind kept returning to what this item might be that belonged to me.

I missed no sleep over it, but the next morning set out early, first for Rush Ghyll and then for High Bield. My pony turned an uncooperative rump on me as soon as I entered her stable, 'Polly,' I said, 'now that I have made the acquaintance of Steadfast, the Huttons' most excellent and *worthy* beast, I shall require better behaviour from you.' As I fully expected, she was unimpressed, but I saddled her up and set out.

As I rode, I glanced down the dale to see Sam Braithwaite, two of his sons, and a couple of their cousins out studying the hay in the bottom meadow. With the wedding over, the natural rhythm of the year was urging them on. This year's weather had so far remained promising for a good crop, rain showers giving way to hours of breezy sunlight. In a few weeks, Wilfred Hutton and his family would be ready to start on their own fields.

If the Trawdens had land down to hay, I'd never seen it, but they must have some source of fodder for their beasts. Perhaps they traded with their neighbours in exchange for eggs or fleeces.

Lydia Hutton was standing at her kitchen door watching as Dorcas and Betsey spread fresh washing on the bushes.

On this occasion, it seemed to consist of linen sheets or possibly tablecloths, nothing to embarrass any of us, so I rode up to speak to her.

'How is the patient?'

'He passed a reasonably comfortable night, she replied, 'and seems to know where he is and that he is being cared for. He hasn't spoken yet, but I believe he understands what we say to him. We have told him that thee is to arrange to bring his wife to him today. He has no fever, which is a good sign.'

Mischievous Betsey grinned and said, 'That friend of his, Augustus Fenwick, was snoring in the chair by the bed when Mama and I went just now to see how they went on.'

Dorcas shook her head. 'Betsey, thee must not say such things. It is not respectful, and if we are to speak of snoring, *thee* should have nothing to say since thee snores like a sailor who has taken too much ale.'

'Daughters! Daughters!' But I could see that their mother was trying not to laugh. 'Thee need not worry, Hugh Armstrong.

John Hathersage is doing as well as can be expected after such a nasty accident.'

'That relieves me greatly,' I said, 'and I thank you once again for your care.' To another person, I might have said I thanked her "from the bottom of my heart," or some such fulsome phrase, but I knew it wasn't necessary. Lydia Hutton smiled and nodded.

'I am on my way to see Matthew,' I said. 'I cannot imagine what he's found of mine is anything of value, but I do need to arrange for another band of prisoners to come and rebuild one of their walls. I expect Lady Lavinia will soon be here,' I added. 'James Carr promised to go and fetch her from Preston this morning. I hope he does not have too much difficulty with the carriage.'

I wondered, as I left them, whether I should have asked to see Sir John myself. He might be offended that I had not done so. I could hear my grandmother's voice in my head. *Allus worriting, wee Hughie!*

As the track turned from stones to grass, I pondered. How was my grandmother? What was happening in Fife? I'd not had a letter for several weeks now, but letters from Scotland could be delayed for any number of reasons. There might even be some languishing at one of the coaching inns in Lancaster, which no one had thought to collect and bring up to Netherdale. This was partly my own fault. Nathaniel Braithwaite had asked me if there was anything he could do for me when he went down to Lancaster, and I, feeling irritated for some reason, had told him no.

I found Matthew Trawden feeding his poultry, his dogs waiting patiently at the gate to the hen run. I assured him at once that Sir John was on the mend, but he seemed more anxious to excuse his present occupation.

'This is Batty's work,' he said, 'but he's taken a sulk on him, and t' fowls were squawking for their mash.'

'He's not here then?'

'He's legged it, run away over the fell in one of his moods,' said Matthew. 'Which he does whenever I finds him out in wrongdoing. Same as he did when our father was alive, fearing a thrashing. *I* don't beat the fool, being as he *is* a fool and beatings never changed owt, but I've kept his rations short.'

'Because of shooting at the rabbit and causing Sir John's fall?'

'Nay, nay! About them coins o' thine! I tried to tell tha last night.'

Now I was utterly at sea. Batty had found some coins, but why did he think them to be any concern of mine?

'In a lile leather bag,' said Matthew. 'Gold, mark tha! Money fascinates that fool brother o' mine. It ain't no use to him. What can he do with it, situated as we are up here on the heights? I asked him what did he want 'em for, but he just looked at me stupid. Like he does.'

'A bag of gold coins?' I said. 'Where?'

'On t' corpse, like. In the pocket of the fellow's coat. After Batty showed that dead 'un to thee that time. Before Hathersage sent those Lancaster fellers to fetch him away. Ah reckon they'd have searched his pockets while they'd the chance, but they'd have found nowt. Batty had been there afore 'em.'

'Ah, I see. Your brother found some money in the pocket of the dead man and kept it without telling you. And now you, being an honest man, want me to take it to Sir John, or Fenwick, the detective.'

'No, no!' replied Matthew, shaking his head in exasperation at my idiocy. 'Nowt to do with either o' them. I reckon 'tis *thine*.'

I stared at him, more bewildered than ever. '*Mine?*'

'The letter's addressed to thee,' he said, as though this should have been obvious. 'Ah figured out it's got tha name on it – Hugh Armstrong.'

'A letter?'

'Ah, 'tis in the kitchen, on the shelf behind the flour crock. That's where I found it when I came to fill the crock. Batty must have tossed it there, thinking Ah wouldn't find it. Letters mean nowt to Batty, and I'd not noticed it before. He can't read.'

He led me into the farmhouse kitchen, the dogs following rather closer than I would have preferred. It was a bleak place, dark, dusty, and bare, although I do not say that it was especially dirty. There was little sign, other than an upturned frying pan on a wooden drying rack, that anyone carried out any household tasks here. How did the Trawden brothers feed themselves?

Matthew seemed to read my mind. 'Ah makes bread in the bread oven and fries it up with bacon. Porridge oats fer breakfast, fried bread, and bacon at five o' the clock. Our own pig,' he gestured to a fitch hanging in a dark corner of the room. 'It keeps us well enough,' he added.

The flour crock stood on a shelf in another gloomy corner of the kitchen. Matthew produced a folded sheet of paper from behind it. Having first peered closely to see if the inscription was still on the outer fold, he handed it to me.

The paper had a crumpled appearance as though from damp. It had once been sealed with a blob of sealing wax, which was now broken.

I carried it to the dusty window, opened it, and squinted at what was written. All at once, a strange, cold feeling crept up my spine. I recognised this scrawl, the wobbly remains of an educated hand destroyed by drink and ill-living. Only too well.

Hugh Armstrong Esquire, High Bield, Netherdale, via Lancaster, Lancashire, England. The address had originally said 'Low', but that had been scratched out and 'High' substituted. Slowly, I unfolded the sheet and read.

To my son, Hugh,

I shall trouble you no more, since I fear I shall die, either of the poor diet in this place, or gaol fever. The magistrates at my trial spoke of hanging or transportation, but I think, while I still have money, the Governor, crafty fellow, will keep me here.

You seemed to me to be a weakling, the runt of the litter, and I doubted you would ever amount to anything. But I have to acknowledge that at least you have found employment and are making shift to feed and clothe yourself, and have not stayed around to gloat over my downfall as your grandmother and your brother have done. If you choose to take my advice, you will not marry. Women and children are a burden, and from my experience, you will be better off without them.

The house will go to Neil, with your grandmother installed there to keep house for him, since he was wounded in the Peninsula, and she says he can do nothing, his wits being astray. There is little enough left, but perhaps your grandmother is right that something is due to my younger surviving son. Therefore, I am sending the sum of thirty guineas enclosed with this letter, which I am entrusting to Ranald Duff. A drunkard, but one of the few men I can trust.

I can do no more, and I fear this may be the last you will ever hear from me.

Your unfortunate Father,
Walter Armstrong.

Postscript: I trust you will take note that you are in receipt of 30 pieces of gold rather than 30 pieces of silver.

Eventually, I spoke aloud. 'It seems the corpse's name was Ranald Duff.'

'Who, the dead 'un?' Matthew proffered up the stained leather bag.

The contents of the stained leather bag chinked against one another as I took it. I felt a strong urge to laugh (but also to weep). My grandmother had seen Father after all. She'd probably told him the correct address, but he had misremembered it. He would always prefer things to be 'high' rather than 'low' – that was his nature. Grandma had mentioned in one of her letters his intention to send me a legacy, but neither she nor I had believed he would actually do so.

'Yes. The dead man. He was bringing this money to me, a gift from my father, but he had the wrong address, High Bield instead of Low.'

Chapter Forty

Dorcas' Journal

6th day, 3rd week, 5th Month

If this journal recorded real spiritual progress, I know I should be humbly asking for God's guidance instead of shedding tears of vexation. I ought to bow my head and accept martyrdom if that is to be my portion, but I find I am so angry I cannot. That George should shame our family by running off to join a travelling show, and then to have Mama and Papa shrug their shoulders when I told them! And Mama even laughed! The story is sure to get about. We shall be fortunate if we do not receive a deputation from the Elders of Lancaster Monthly Meeting, demanding that we fetch him away from such corrupting and un-Godly influences.

Later

Mama called me to help wring out the washing. I told her how upset I feel, and she shook her head and said I was overtired and overwrought. That may be so. I do not sleep well sharing a bed with Betsey – she sprawls about so. Yesterday, I was not very civil with Hugh Armstrong, and then I dozed on the drive home, so he had to take the reins despite his crippled arm and hand. And in my sleep, I accidentally leaned on his shoulder. Perhaps I am not as ashamed of that as I should be. When I woke and realised, I found I rather liked the sensation of resting against him as we jogged along. Can this mean I am 'forward' as *that man* accused me of being? Is that why I enjoy saying uncivil things to Hugh?

Later again

Mama does not believe that anyone will think badly of our family because George has joined a travelling show. I thought Rachel Stout would be much grieved and might withdraw the invitation for me to stay with her and Eliza. (Although Eliza might be secretly amused, and want me to tell her about the bear!) I also wonder if their brother and his wife will be less inclined to let our Wilf court their daughter. Mama says this is nonsense.

We Huttons have always lived orderly lives and walked in the Light (so far as we were able), and now we are to be humbled before everyone. There are those, I fear, who will gain some satisfaction from a member of our family falling from Grace. Martha Braithwaite, for one, as Mama will come to realise. Mama says I am dramatising and not to be so silly. How it will affect Nathanial and Susannah, I cannot think.

I do not believe Hugh Armstrong is the kind who delights in spreading gossip, but if someone asked him what happened, I suppose he would tell them. As for James Carr and his sweet-heart, it would not surprise me if they tattled the tale all over Lancaster.

Chapter Forty-One

Hugh

I stood, weighing the bag of coins in my hand, a hundred disjointed thoughts running through my brain. Meanwhile, Matthew Trawden stood patiently at my side, awaiting my next word or move.

'I must tell Sir John and Augustus Fenwick who the dead man was,' I said, shoving the bag into my satchel. 'Then they will trouble you no more, Matthew. This Ranald Duff was a Scotsman of my father's acquaintance.'

'He weren't a French spy?' said Matthew. 'Batty and me never set eyes on him. Not alive, we never. Tha'll tell 'em that?'

Absently, I promised I would.

Now, I must somehow find a way to tell my employer and Fenwick that their French spy was no such thing. *But how?* Without revealing the truth? My father's letter, I was determined never to show to anyone.

I roused myself from my state of stupefaction to hear my own voice quite calmly saying, 'Let us go and look at your broken wall, Matthew. In a day or two, if the weather holds, I can bring some of those prisoners of war to repair it. They did a good job at Sam Braithwaite's place.'

'Aye, I heard that, and fer free,' admitted Matthew. 'Although I don't know as I wants any Frenchmen here. I don't hold with Frenchmen, be they spies or no.'

We trudged across his land, through a flock of incurious sheep, to the wall, under which Ranald Duff had lain buried in the snow for months. Surely only a hopeless drunkard would have struggled up here in a snowstorm. Now, at least, I thought, we can inform the Authorities and give the fellow a proper burial.

The wall was damaged in several places. Having agreed with Matthew that a day's work by a team of men could put it right, I reclaimed Polly, mounted, and set her plodding downhill, my mind awhirl with conflicting thoughts. I had no clear idea where I wanted to go, so she had to find her own way. Naturally enough, she made towards home.

Father's letter was in my breast pocket. I had always known how little he thought of me. But to see myself described as 'the runt of the litter' pierced my heart like the stab of a Highlander's dirk.

There was no one to whom I could ever tell my story. Sir John Hathersage had given me employment on the recommendation of a man who had stood as my friend. He, good fellow, must never have mentioned my father's misdeeds, and news of them had never yet reached Lancashire. I had hoped, prayed even, that they never would.

I doubted Sir John would have taken me on if he had known that my father was a thief. That he had persuaded trusting members of his congregation to invest in fraudulent schemes, and embezzled every penny. A man who had many times physically attacked his own family whilst under the influence of drink. That his cruel treatment had undoubtedly hastened my mother's death.

My father's evil reputation had hung over me all my life. I'd always dreaded that it might follow me here to Lancashire.

The golden guineas chinked against one another in my satchel. If I burned the letter and hid the money, perhaps no one needed to know about it. I doubted if either of the Trawdens could read more than the inscription.

However, even if Matthew and his crazy brother never said a word to anyone, how could I keep the coins a secret? I couldn't carry the money around with me like this.

Yet, I had never locked up my cottage. If I now did so, wouldn't folk wonder why?

Wild ideas flitted through my head. Could I bury the bag of coins in my strip of neglected garden? Under the straw in Polly's stable? Could I *spend* thirty guineas, and thus rid myself of them? Some new shirts and under drawers I could certainly do with, but they could be purchased for a couple of guineas at most.

If I suddenly appeared in a new suit of clothes and new boots, people would notice and ask me about my sudden good fortune.

I laughed aloud, startling Polly, who snorted her disapproval. Who would have thought that the sudden possession of a large sum of money would present a problem? What, I wondered, *did* Judas do with those thirty pieces of silver?

I was quite unaware of where we were going, so that when Polly drew to an abrupt stop, I nearly slid over her head. I righted myself to see Wilfred Hutton in front of me. I dismounted, embarrassed.

'My apologies,' I gasped, 'I wasn't paying attention. My pony realised she couldn't carry me down so steep an incline, and refused to try.'

Polly and Wilfred bore remarkably similar expressions of be-musement. They seemed to both be pondering what ailed this poor fool. Yet I sensed that neither wished me ill.

Wilfred Hutton was the one man in this district whom I instinctively trusted. I might not share his religious convictions, and he might deplore my lack of them, but here was a good man and a wise one. One day, when I had taken time to reflect, I might share my present problems with him.

However, this was not the moment. Tactfully, he changed the subject. 'I've been looking over the crop,' he said, indicating the meadow with a sweep of his arm. 'Young Wilf thinks another two weeks before we mow. But I say let's go to it next week while the weather seems likely to stand our friend.'

'I agree,' I said, glad to be speaking of the ordinary, sane, everyday things of Netherdale. 'I saw Sam Braithwaite earlier. He's already made a start. Will you have enough hands for the work?'

'That we will,' he replied. 'Young Wilf and Jonathan, and two sons of my wife's cousins at Caton are to come over. And Sam will lend his lads, if need be, although they'll likely be tossing and stooking their own crop still. I could have done with George,' he shook his head, smiling, 'but seemingly he's found a home amongst acrobats and fancy equestrian acts.' He laughed. 'A foolish life to my mind, but his sister says he's set on it.'

'It does seem strange,' I said. 'It seemed to me that it would be a much harder life than he had on your farm.'

'And just as many people giving him orders, by what Dorcas told us. But my wife and I know he's safe and well, and we give thanks to God for that.'

We stood awhile in silence, until we became aware of movement on the track above us. A carriage, drawn by two bays, was struggling up the steep incline.

'This must be Sir John's wife,' I said, 'come to take him home. I'd better go. Lady Lavinia will expect me to help if he's well enough to be moved.'

Unless the carriage was better sprung than I suspected, it wouldn't be a comfortable journey home for the poor man.

I rode across the meadow to Rush Ghyll, arriving just as the heavy vehicle made an awkward turn into the farm yard. James Carr raised his eyes to heaven when he saw me.

'She would do it,' he hissed as he climbed down from the box. 'Ain't done the hosses nor the landeau any good, but she would do it!'

The door opened, and Carr helped Lady Lavvy alight, this time without any disastrous consequences for her modesty.

The noise of the carriage's arrival had alerted Lydia Hutton and her daughters, who stood waiting to greet their visitor.

Seeing them together with Sir John's wife, I could hardly contain a smile. Lady Lavinia was dressed in purple silk, the hem adorned with row upon row of frills above her white kid boots. Her huge straw bonnet concealed not only her head but her shoulders, as though she were hiding inside an overturned bucket, its downturned rim adorned with feathers.

In contrast, Lydia, Dorcas, and young Betsey wore workaday round gowns in plain dull colours and white aprons. Lydia wore a plain linen cap, and the two girls went bareheaded, their dark hair glossy in the spring sunlight.

The Hutton women greeted her ladyship with polite smiles and tiny inclinations of their heads. No curtseys. No words of welcome or flattering greetings. Instead, they waited for her to speak first.

Lady Lavvy did not seem to know what to do. The farmyard on that sunny day was dry, tidy, and beset by neither cow pats nor farm implements, but it was uneven. She looked around for James Carr. Having helped her to alight, however, he was fully occupied in calming the horses, which were still blowing, quivering, and tossing their heads from the effort of bringing the carriage up the rough track. So, I slid down from Polly's back and stepped forward.

'We have good news for thee,' Lydia now greeted her. 'Thy husband is much improved. Be pleased to come this way and see for thyself.'

Lady Lavvy clung to my arm, determined that I should accompany her into the farmhouse. Why, I could not tell. Did she imagine that the Huttons lived in squalor or kept savage beasts indoors? Was it that inside her enormous hat, she could not see where she was going?

Or was she afraid to see her husband's injuries?

Lydia led the way into the parlour. On the truckle bed, propped up with cushions, we found Sir John. His head was swathed in bandages, the side of his face black with bruising, but when he saw his wife, his face lit up.

'Johnny! Oh, Johnny!' Lady Lavvy cried, dropping my arm and rushing to his side. Lydia Hutton and I glanced at one another. Without a word, we turned and withdrew.

Chapter Forty-Two

Hugh

I had assumed Lady Lavvy would take Sir John only as far as the new house at Dalefoot, an uncomfortable journey in itself. However, she insisted on taking him to Lancaster. He must see his doctor straightaway, she said. She wouldn't hear of waiting while Carr fetched him from town. Doctor Whalley, she told us, had gone to the prison to attend to one of the Frenchmen who was said to be dying. He could not be found and brought away.

'So unkind of him,' she said, tearfully, 'when they say this prisoner is at death's door from consumption. There is nothing the doctor can do for him, while my poor Johnny needs him to make him well again. Anyway, he cannot rest at Dalefoot, because the beds have not yet arrived.'

The Hutton lads helped to carry Sir John out to the carriage and propped him up in a corner seat against the squabs. Then the womenfolk tucked blankets and quilts around him. I had to hide a smile, because he looked exactly like a giant baby, cocooned inside all his wrappings!

I feared that Lady Lavvy might demand that I accompany them on their journey, and was relieved when we waved them off. James Carr's face and shoulders were taut with the strain of guiding the horses down that steep, uneven track. Despite their careful efforts, it cannot have been comfortable for the poor man.

I continued to watch the coach's slow descent, fearing that the brake might slip or the carriage overbalance, but all went well, and soon they reached the foot of the track and disappeared over the Nether Beck bridge.

When I turned to comment on this, I found I was alone. The entire Hutton family, having done what they could for the Hathersages, had disappeared to continue with tasks about the farm. So, I collected Polly and let her choose her own way home. It was too late to do anything myself, even if I were clear in my mind about what that should be. Naturally enough, my thoughts travelled back to earlier that day. The coins in my satchel still clinked faintly as I rode.

Ranald Duff – it was now May, and the man may have died perhaps as long ago as December. In an apparent effort to reach me, he had died of the bitter cold. Or perhaps as a result of that great wound on his brow – a stone flung at a stranger's head, much as the sea captain, or whatever he was, had flung the doorstop at Wilfred Hutton. I could imagine Batty doing such a thing.

Fenwick had thought nothing of it, 'an old injury,' he had said dismissively, 'long healed,' and there had been no sign that it had broken open and bled. But after such a long time, could anyone be sure? Were the Trawdens innocent? Had I been right to give Matthew that reassurance?

My father had given Duff the wrong address, but even if it had been the right one, why had he pressed on in a raging snowstorm? I wondered what hold my father had over him.

Some clue to all this might lie with my grandmother. However, I had heard nothing further from her.

'Polly,' I said to my ambling pony, 'Tomorrow we must go to Lancaster and make enquiries at the tavern where the post is held.'

Polly's ears twitched, and she made a small snort. Perhaps she understood from the tone of my voice that I was planning an excursion.

Whilst in Lancaster, I could also go to the castle and arrange for a band of prisoners to come and repair High Bield's wall. The very wall under which Ranald Duff's corpse had lain.

And enquire too, at Castle Hill, after Sir John's health once he was home.

Into my mind crept the disloyal thought that now I had sufficient money to purchase that young horse of Nathaniel Braithwaite's. This I did not say aloud, but perhaps Polly sensed it because she snorted.

The next morning, I saddled up. Only to see ahead of us, as we left Low Bield, a lost-looking youth with a bag slung across his body.

The post had come to Netherdale!

I slid down from Polly's back.

'Yer know any o' these, Mister?' He pulled a sheaf of letters out of the bag and shoved them into my hands.

This lad was not an official post-boy, such as one sees waiting for the mail coach to arrive at the coaching inn, or walking about the streets of towns and cities delivering the mail. For a start, he had no scarlet jacket. He looked no more than fourteen, and his feet were encased in battered clogs that looked too large for him. They must be raising blisters on his heels. Someone must have paid him to tramp up here, not wishing to journey the seven miles themselves. Having got here, though, he was now quite lost.

'Fella told me he'd give me a lift,' he explained. 'He were comin' up here with a message, but he dint want to come all the way. He'd picked up all the Netherdale post from the King's Arms, but then these two Quaker ladies – he rolled his eyes – stopped him just as he was leaving the inn yard, and gave him some money to bring two more. Right strict they were, especially the one! Said it was urgent, wouldn't tek no for an answer! But this fella, Jim, he said his name is, wanted to tek his lass to the fair. So, he gave me a bob and dropped me off at the ground. This place is a might further on than he said.'

I scrutinised the directions on the letters, while he jingled a few coins at the bottom of his bag in a manner that suggested hope that I would add to them. The lad would certainly want to be paid again once he found the recipients. *If*, left to himself, he ever did. The sparsely populated dale was as strange to him as the back streets of Jericho. He knew none of the inhabitants or the whereabouts of their houses and farms.

'*You* knows any o' em?' he repeated.

'Fortunately for you, laddie, I do. *These* four are for me.' I held them up. 'There is my name – see? – Hugh Armstrong Esquire.' (In my grandmother's hand, and correctly inscribed, 'Low Bield.' Thank goodness! Perhaps all would now be explained. 'And this one too.' (It had about it the air of a lawyer's epistle, from Edinburgh). '*This* one (the direction was printed in a shaky hand) is a note from my employer in Lancaster.'

'Yeah,' said the boy, unimpressed, 'and that means you owe me four shillin' an' fourpunce.'

My heart had long formed the habit of sinking into my boots when faced with sudden demands, and it duly did so now. Just as suddenly, up it rose again. I was now a man of means! I could pass over four shillings and fourpence without a qualm.

'Four shillin' an' fourpunce,' repeated the post-boy, a lad whose mind clearly ploughed a straight furrow. 'And what about these others?'

I dearly wished to open my own letters straightaway and devour the contents, but I laid them on a gatepost and leafed through the others. The first was what looked like a dunning letter for Daniel Jackson at Quernstones. Then two in the same rather wobbly copperplate, one for Sam and Martha, and another for the family at Rush Ghyll.

'Them old Quaker ladies sent those,' said the post-boy, watching my reaction. 'Come right in to the yard at the King's Arms, they did, amongst all the dirt. And all o' them rough fellas drinking, an' smoking, an' talking in right coarse language. Paid no heed to the cat calls. Mortal anxious they were that Jim should bring those letters. Thanked God out loud, they did, that they'd met up with him. Reckon someone's bin taken sick.'

'Something like that,' I agreed, unwilling to gossip. 'I'll tell you what, laddie, suppose I first pay you for my own letters?' I took the four shillings and fourpence from the purse in my pocket, and laid the coins out along the top of the gate so that he could count them. 'Then I'll show you how to get to Lane End Farm with their letter. They'll tell you how to go on across the fields to Quernstones. Meanwhile, to save you a stiff climb, I'll lay out the money for this letter for the Huttons at Rush Ghyll, and take it myself.'

'I ain't supposed to do that – give over letters to any folk but the Ouseholder. You ain't Wil-fred and Lyd-ya Hutton,' he spelt out. 'You ain't, cos you said your name was Arm-strong.'

'I am a close friend of the family,' I said, 'I'll deliver this without fail, and save you a good deal of time and effort.'

He didn't want to let me have the letter, but I laid out a further shilling along the top bar of the gate, and, when he still hesitated, another one after that.

'This is obviously pressing,' I said. 'The Huttons need to have it at once.'

At this, he succumbed and handed it over.

Since there was an almost identical letter for the Braithwaites, I concluded that it concerned Susannah and Nathaniel. Had there been an accident?

'I'll go up there straight away.'

'Right you are,' said the post-boy. 'I'm suited. I'd like to get back, mebbe look in at the fairground. That fella, Jim, said they got a dancin' bear, and I ain't never seen one.'

Chapter Forty-Three

Dorcas' Journal

Tuesday May 24th

Papa has always said we Quakers don't use the names the world uses for days, weeks, and months – because they date from pagan times and are the names of false gods. Numbering is accurate and honest, as we must always strive to be. However, like using thee and thou, I find it doesn't answer well outside our own circle. So, I'm trying a new way.

But this is not what I should be writing about. Hugh Armstrong came up to the farm this morning with a letter from Susannah. We immediately feared an accident amongst the mountains, but it was no such thing. They have returned early to Lancaster because Nat had word that there had been a fire at the silk mill. He dashed off to see the damage as soon as he had deposited Sukie and the luggage at their new house, leaving her in a great state of anxiety, not knowing what to do. She had never even seen the house before. There is very little furniture other than two chairs and a bed. All the rest were to be delivered on the day of their intended return.

It appeared that Nathaniel had found the fire largely put out, but some of the beams still smouldered. These he had, so a messenger said, attempted to cut away. Alas, the ladder had slipped, and he had suffered a painful injury to his shoulder. Susannah, unable to go to him, had been convinced he would be brought home on a trestle to die.

Poor Sukie, how upset she must have been, her honeymoon coming to such an abrupt end. Her letter was splotched with tears, and her handwriting, which she usually counts as one of her accomplishments, was blotted in her haste.

Fortunately, Nat has hired a house in the street below the castle where Rachel and Eliza Stout live. They had seen Nat's flight from their window, but at that time, hadn't liked to interfere. But when they saw the mill hand arrive and Sukie's distress at his message, they called round immediately to see if they could help.

Rachel Stout, ever practical in a crisis, had waylaid the man. Assured the doctor had been summoned, she urged Sukie to write to us. Then she and Eliza braved the King's Arms to find someone to bring her note up to Netherdale.

That is, it was brave of Eliza. I do not believe Rachel is afraid of anyone. There is a story we are told of previous times when a Quaker woman, Mary Fisher, without even another Friend to support her, went to Constantinople to visit the Sultan of the Ottomans and tell him about her faith. How she dared to, I do not know. He might have had her executed, or even thrown her into his harem. However, I imagine he probably didn't understand a word she said, but politely dismissed her with a pair of silken slippers to take home. I can imagine Rachel doing just that, and when she came back, she would have given the slippers to some poor person (who would be very puzzled about what to do with them).

Naturally, Susannah had written to Nathaniel's parents as well, so there ensued a tussle over which mother should rush to her aid. In the end, both of them went, with Sam Braithwaite driving their new dog cart, which is roomier and more comfortable than ours. Hugh Armstrong went with them, seated on the tailboard. He said he needed to speak to his employer. So, there wasn't room for me, although I would have liked to go and comfort Sukie. Because we are so very different, people forget that we are twins.

Chapter Forty-Four

Hugh

Those letters from Scotland were burning holes in my pocket as we jogged down to Lancaster. All three appeared lengthy, and reading them would have to wait until we stopped moving. Meanwhile, I distracted myself by observing the mild rivalry between the Braithwaite and Hutton households. Anxious as they must have been about their son, both Sam and Martha were very eager to tell Lydia about the dogcart's finer points. It has metal-rimmed wheels, although Sam said he'd read that it might soon be possible to have the rims covered with rubber, as wagon makers are experimenting with this substance. He thought he might have the alteration made, if and when such a thing became available.

'It would be worth the expense,' said Martha smugly, 'to give our friends a really comfortable ride, instead of this bump, bump, bumping over the stones.'

Then, recalling the errand they were on, she said, 'What a pity we cannot obtain them at present, when we may have to bring dear Nathaniel home. Susannah is *such* a new bride. She must hardly know what to do for his comfort!'

Lydia gave a slight smile, lifted her chin, but made no comment. Lydia Hutton, I could confidently predict, would consider boastfulness about one's possessions unseemly – especially when it was their son, not her daughter, who had met with a mishap of his own making. (Although, I thought, she will never blame Nathaniel for his foolishness, not aloud.)

'Thee has news of John Hathersage?' she asked me.

'I think he is progressing. I have a note from Lady Lavinia,' I told her. 'She is passing on a message from the prison Governor, Mr Higgins, which she would hardly do if she were worrying about Sir John. Higgins plans to send a party of prisoners up to High Bield two days hence. This was what I was going to Lancaster to arrange. I will call on Sir John, but perhaps I can offer some assistance to Nathaniel and Susannah?'

'Perhaps thee may,' said Martha brightly. 'I was just thinking that to transfer him up into the cart may be quite difficult. He must be in great pain. We should have brought Joseph and Henry, Sam. Why didn't we?'

'Because then we could not have brought Lydia,' he replied, 'let alone Hathersage's man.' Sam turned and lowered an eyelid for me to see. A solid fellow and an upstanding member of the Netherdale Quaker Meeting did not wink, but he wanted me to know that here we were dealing with the vagaries of women.

'It may be that Hugh and I will need to walk back,' Lydia smiled at me. I thought it was the first time she had called me Hugh, and not Hugh Armstrong. Perhaps I was becoming 'a close friend of the family' as I had suggested to the post-boy. 'Although I *hope*, she emphasised, 'that we may find Nathaniel not so bad as we fear, and can lend him assistance where he is, and not subject him to an uncomfortable ride.'

Not the most tactful comment, Lydia, when your neighbours have been making so much of the superior qualities of their new equipage! Even a Quaker lady, I was discovering, can sometimes let her exasperation show.

I grinned at her. 'I'll walk if anyone has to,' I promised, 'and I'd think there'll be room for Nathaniel to rest on a bed of blankets, if some can be found.' Lydia gave me a tiny smile and a nod. 'With God's Grace,' she murmured.

Privately, I was wondering if I might borrow James Carr's pony, Bugle. I didn't think he'd have taken the old nag to the fair. Surely, he couldn't have ridden out with Nancy and the post boy all three atop such a venerable beast.

We were approaching the field where the fair had been set up. I sensed Lydia tensing, perhaps hoping to catch a glimpse of George, her wandering boy. Martha turned and stared at her, expecting some reaction, but she said nothing.

Bunches of townspeople were wandering about the fairground. Some were trying to peer under the flaps of canvas into the big tent. We heard snatches of music drifting out, perhaps a band warming up before a performance.

Lydia gave only the tiniest of sighs as Sam drove on.

We traversed the streets of Lancaster. Sam drove us straight to Nathaniel and Susannah's house in the shadow of the castle, only to find that far from Nathaniel being 'brought home on a trestle', as Sukie had predicted, he had not been brought home at all. The little house beneath the shadowy walls of the great medieval castle lay deserted.

'Oh,' cried Martha, 'he must be in such pain that they could not move him!'

'I pray it may not be worse than that,' said her husband. Just then, however, a door across the street opened, and a little lady in a grey bonnet and shawl came bustling out. I recognised her from Susannah and Nathaniel's wedding – the one who monopolised Dorcas and talked and talked.

'Oh, my dears! Oh, my dears!' cried she. 'But you must not fear anything *terrible*. The poor boy's shoulder is quite dislocated, and he was in such agony that they decided they could not move him. They sent for Dr Whalley, because you know, they say he is quite the best doctor in the town, and he came as soon as he could, and pushed the joint back where it should be. Poor Nathaniel. The man who came to tell us said he fainted clean away with the pain of it. They'd sent for Susannah, but she was in such a state, the poor dear girl, that my sister called on Thomas Parkinson to drive them, and went with Sukie to keep her spirits up. So that is where you will find them, out at the mill.'

Sam Braithwaite thanked her and turned the dog cart. 'Oh, do hurry!' cried his wife. 'Does thee know how far it is?'

'Nigh on three miles,' replied her spouse, 'but we do not need to gallop to the rescue, wife, since it appears the doctor has done all that was necessary.'

I knew the mill was in a settlement just south of the town, and I wondered if I should ask Sam to set me down. It seemed hardly necessary for me to make one of the party. However, Lydia and I exchanged glances, and I gained the impression that she would be pleased if I stayed with her.

'I apologise that I insisted on coming,' I said quietly. 'It would have been more useful for you to have Dorcas with you.'

'However, I am happy to have thee, Hugh,' she replied.

I was curious, having never had an opportunity to see a silk mill before. I had heard that some enterprising people in Scotland had taken to spinning and weaving silk in Renfrew, a town close to Glasgow, where there was a market for silk garments amongst the wealthy merchants' wives. But in Fife, jute was king.

This mill was smaller than I expected, a square building with a high roof and a tall chimney at one end. It was close to the banks of a stream, and the space around it was filled with a number of sheds. These, I assumed, were for storing the bales of unprocessed silk, or perhaps the finished product, awaiting despatch to the buyers. I had no time for more than fleeting impressions, as I followed my companions as they hurried inside the building.

Here, in a high room, propped against the end of one of the looms, lay Nathaniel. It now became clear why the lad had not been taken home. Firstly, the doctor expected to be paid for his ministrations – Nat had rushed to the mill without a penny in his pockets. Secondly, he had hired a horse to make the journey, for which he had not yet paid either, and which, as a result of the doctor's ministrations, was in no state to ride home.

Sam Braithwaite pulled a purse from his coat and took the doctor aside to begin negotiations.

Susannah, who had been crouched beside her husband, holding his undamaged hand, now threw herself, weeping, into Lydia's arms. Martha took Susannah's place and began exclaiming over her stricken son. The woman whom I now knew to be Rachel Stout, rather stern sister of the little lady who had told us where to come, now intervened. She pulled Martha to her feet and led her some distance off, explaining what the doctor had done and that the injury – an arm wrenched from his socket – though painful, would heal in time.

I stood looking down on Nat.

'My own fault, entirely,' he said through gritted teeth. 'I thought I could shave those smouldering bits off the beam, and so I did. It would have cost a great deal to have men come back to finish the job, which they ought to have done in the first place. Unfortunately, to reach the last section was a longer stretch than I realised. I jumped free when my ladder slipped, but my shoulder— Poor Sukie, what a shock for my poor girl!'

'Yes,' I remarked, 'not the best start to married life.' I found myself thinking that if such a thing happened to me, I would much prefer the practical Dorcas to rush to my side, and felt guilty again that I had selfishly denied her the chance to come. 'But now people are here to take you home. You rode out here?'

'Yes,' he said, wincing. 'I persuaded the fellow at the livery stable to let me take him without payment, promising faithfully that I would do so on my return. He took me on trust because of my Quaker hat. I had visions of the whole mill burning to the ground, thee understands. The new Jacquard looms are here, ready to be installed, already paid for. What a disaster that would have been.'

'I'm glad to see it is not so bad,' I said, glancing around at the weaving frames with the pattern cards laid on the weave so that the weavers could continue the work once their stricken employer was no longer in the way. At other looms, further off, men continued to pass the shuttles rhythmically across the frames. Work could not be entirely abandoned because one of the 'masters' had pulled his shoulder out of joint.

'We weave mainly in self-colour, simple patterns which repeat, and add interest to the fabric,' Nathaniel explained from his lowly position. He managed a small, rueful grin. 'My partners aren't too happy with Quaker plainness. They want to sell more widely, certainly not only to Quakers, so I've agreed to compromise. The Jacquard system will greatly increase our range.'

'I liked the corded effect you produced,' I said, trying to sound knowledgeable. 'The dark green cloth Dorcas and Betsey wore for the wedding.'

'Not mine.' He shifted slightly, squeezing his eyes against the pain from his shoulder. 'One of my partners produced that. Part of the length was spoiled – there was some trouble. The men grew angry, thinking these new looms, which don't require so many hands, would put them out of work. However, we managed to cut away sufficient of the spoiled cloth to make gowns for my sisters-in-law. I still have a huge amount to learn. I won't have endeared myself to my associates by having this daft accident.'

'But you were able to prevent a further fire.'

'That at least. It was fortunate I was not too far off. Both my partners are in London, showing samples of our goods to potential buyers. They'll only hear what happened on their return.'

His father had concluded his business with the doctor. Some of the mill hands gathered round to help Nathaniel out to the dog cart. I wouldn't be needed for this after all. It was time to make myself scarce.

'Shall I return your mount to the livery stable?' I suggested. 'There won't be room for me in your father's vehicle.'

I was half tempted to ride the animal up to Netherdale. It was growing late, and there was little I could do here today. But Nathaniel might be accused of horse theft, and he had troubles enough without that.

In the end, I rode alongside a smart trap containing Rachel Stout and Lydia. This was driven by a man called Thomas Parkinson, who had apparently been waiting, unacknowledged, to do Miss Rachel's bidding. I was surprised to discover that he was no hired man, but a very well-dressed fellow in correct Quaker costume. He seemed anxious to please the lady, although she acknowledged him with the merest of polite nods.

Chapter Forty-Five

Hugh

I returned the horse and paid Nathaniel's shot, explaining what had happened.

'I knew I could trust 'im,' said the stableman. 'They're a strange lot, them Quakers, but they've done a lot for the town, helping to bring in prosperity.'

At the mill, plans had been agreed. Lydia would spend the night with the Stout sisters. Sam and Martha Braithwaite were to take the young couple to their new home and help put Nathaniel to bed. The doctor would call tomorrow to see how he fared. Thomas Parkinson had offered to send round extra furnishing and bedding from his own home. The Braithwaites accepted, I thought, rather grudgingly. I wondered what he had done to offend.

As it was growing late, I took myself to the King's Arms and bespoke a bed for myself – a cheap garret under the roof.

There, I lay awake listening to the tumultuous snores of the man next door.

This caused me to reflect that now I had money, I was finding myself strangely unwilling to part with it. Thirty guineas were more than half my year's salary, but they wouldn't last me a lifetime. I ought to invest, and thereby obtain interest. A good plan, but in what? I should choose something worthy if I wished to maintain good relations with the Quakers of Netherdale. And I found I did so wish.

On the other hand, I could now afford to look for other employment and free myself from the moods of Sir John Hathersage. I could even return to Scotland, although folk there might still shun me because of my father. And it no longer felt like home. Had Netherdale become that?

By the light of a faltering candle, grudgingly supplied by the landlord, I read first the lawyer's missive, then the two from my grandmother, long delayed.

The lawyer told of my father's attempts to prevent his sentence of deportation, which had, ultimately, proved futile. There was a receipted bill enclosed for the legal fees. It was noted, with a suggestion of censure, that my grandmother had paid. If Neil had refused to pay, I couldn't blame him. He, too, had suffered at the tawse end as a boy.

One of the letters from Grandma was from months before, wondering how I was. Was my new position still suiting me? Was everything in England as 'dear tae buy' as she had been told? If so, she apologised that she couldn't send me money.

> *Your father is demanding that I pay his lawyer. He supposes, the blackmailing rogue, that I will, 'to save our family's name.' Although what name do we have left to save? But for your sake and Neil's, I'll do it. Neil's money gaes to the drink, but it keeps him quiet. It was a black day when I agreed to Effie marrying Walter Armstrong. Your mother thought, poor fool, it would be a fine thing to be the Minister's lady. Aye, well. She made her bed, and there she had to lie, poor lass!*

This letter concluded:

> *I've not heard from you lately, Hughie.*
> *I'm hoping you are well and satisfied with your*
> *employment. Perhaps ye'll take a fancy tae marry*
> *with one o' these Quaker lassies ye mentioned. They*
> *say they're a warm people, the Quakers. And they*
> *have no ministers to rob ye of your money or your*
> *soul!*

My grandfather had sold jute. He hadn't been a rich man, but he had been 'comfortable'. No doubt, Walter Armstrong had married my mother to get his hands on her inheritance. He'd quickly drunk through that. Grandma had rescued my mother, my brothers, and me many times from penury. If anyone deserved money from him, it was her. So, why had the thirty guineas been entrusted to me? Perhaps the second letter would give the answer.

Could I bear to read it and find out? I read it. And I found out.

I won't lay every word before you, but the last sheet started thus:

> *Ye'll perhaps remember Ranald Duff. We*
> *used to call him your father's slave. Walter told me*
> *once, when he'd drink taken, that he'd saved the*
> *man's life when he was accused of murder. That*
> *was why the craven fellow did whatever he asked,*
> *no, ordered him to do. If your father owed money*
> *for his gambling at cards, he would send Ranald to*
> *give the man he owed a thrashing, and no more was*
> *said of the debt. As for the husband of any wife, or*

279

father of any lass that your father dishonoured, he would get the same to keep his mouth shut. Not to mention those folk whose black secrets Walter had learned, and who were paying him to keep quiet. Folks were mortally afraid to cross him lest he send Ranald Duff round.

So, this was the source of my legacy: blackmail and threats. We have an expression in Scotland, 'I wa' gae dumbfungled.' It means that one is rendered too shocked, too tired, and too low-spirited to do anything about a situation.

With my neighbour snoring next door, and with the contents of Grandma's letters on my mind, I lost all hope of repose. But sometimes 'dumbfunglement' is a blessing; a man's brain absorbs the information but declines to deal with it. I was granted deep sleep bordering on unconsciousness.

I woke as the summer light penetrated the blinds that served the upper windows of the inn. I pushed back the ragged fabric. The sun had risen over the Pennine hills to the East and glinted on the yellow sands of Morecambe Bay to the West.

I washed my face, pulled on my britches, and descended to the inn's coffee room. I would re-read Grandma's letter after I reviewed my plans for the day – the plans of a man with a modest fortune in his pocket. Best not think too hard about its source. I'd go to the tailors and order two shirts. I'd bargain for a new pair of britches, lined with a well-padded seat, which would make riding more comfortable. As it would sitting through another Quaker Meeting, should I ever have reason to do so.

Then I intended to visit Sir John to confirm the plan for the next phase of wall building at High Bield. After this, I'd hire a ride back to Netherdale to prepare for the prisoners' arrival.

I'd been looking forward to this meeting with Sir John, and, having received my inheritance, appearing a more confident fellow, less craven. A man who intends to give good service, but is not afraid of dismissal. Now, however, I knew the source of my gold, I no longer felt so haughty.

The coffee room at the inn was empty but for one man, who was seated in the window, consuming a plate of ham and eggs.

'Good morning to thee,' said Thomas Parkinson. 'Not yet returned to Netherdale? Very wise of thee. Start fresh upon a journey, that's what I say – not that anyone listens to me. I'll ring for the manservant. The ham is on the fatty side, but the eggs are fresh.'

He reached for the handbell.

'I did not catch thy name?' he asked once the servant had taken my order. I told him.

'I am surprised to see you here,' I said, 'because I understood you lived in town.'

He chewed mournfully. 'I do, but having no wife or family, I dislike eating alone. My house is close by, so I choose to break my fast here.'

'I see. Tell me,' I said. 'I understood from things that were mentioned yesterday that you no longer follow the Quaker's religion. Yet you maintain their way of dress and speech.'

'Wrong,' he said with a sigh. 'Quite wrong, young fellow. I follow Quaker precepts assiduously. I worship faithfully amongst them every First Day. They cannot forbid me that, for Quaker Worship is open to all. I adhere to their strictness in matters of dress. I give to every needy cause, but because of my late father's business dealings, I am *disowned.*'

'Your parent did things of which other Quakers disapproved?' I was interested to discover someone besides myself who had an unsatisfactory father.

'Indeed, and it seems I can never live them down.'

'He owned slaves?'

'He owned *shares* in a plantation. It was well run. The slaves were well-treated, I assure thee. I travelled there, though I suffered mightily from seasickness on the journey, to see for myself. It would have been foolish to have treated them badly. Half-starved men cannot work efficiently, and having already been brought there from Africa by others, it was not in our power to release them. Where could they go? How could they earn enough to feed and clothe themselves?' His face grew flushed, indignant that other people had failed to understand.

'And believe me, young fellow, factories are springing up in this very town where the conditions are far worse than on a well-run sugar plantation. In a healthful climate! The one thee was shown yesterday may look good, I grant, and I'm sure young Braithwaite means well, but now I hear his partners have bought these Jacquard looms. Once the weavers have learned to use them, they'll find they need only half as many men. And thee will see men and young lads turned off who can ill afford to lose their employment.' He emitted a gusty sigh.

'The Quakers still shun you?'

'Yes. Our family's money is, they say, contaminated. Besides, the ownership of the plantation was not the main cause of our being denied Membership. Papa also had shares in a ship. A ship that brought cotton, sugar, and molasses here, which everyone in this town, Quakers included, was glad to have. But, because it was in danger of being beset by pirates, the ship's captain arranged to fit it with cannons. They were never fired, but were there as a warning to those rogues. When *this* was discovered, Papa and I were called before the Elders, and disowned.'

'So,' I said slowly, 'the Quakers considered the ownership of cannons, weapons of war, a more serious thing than owning slaves?'

'It would seem so.' He shook his head as though the whole thing was incomprehensible.

I looked at Thomas's natty dove-grey coat, his starched stock, his well-polished boots, his black felt, wide-brimmed hat. 'I understood from Wilfred Hutton that *benefitting* from goods produced by slaves, even though none are owned directly, is unacceptable?'

'Oh, very likely *he* would say so,' he said. 'They're good people up there in Netherdale. I don't deny it. They live simply and honestly, but they're too apt to preach on things about which they know little.'

'You no longer trade with the Indies yourself?'

'*I* have invested in shares in a bank, young man,' he snapped. 'All perfectly sound and above board. My partners and I never lend to unsatisfactory or unsavoury businesses. No one ever suggested any dishonesty in our dealings. Indeed, if you ever have money to invest, I strongly recommend our company.'

'I'll remember,' I said. He had at least checked to see that the slaves were well-treated. My fortune, such as it was, had been amassed by the wicked schemes of one man (my father) and brought to me by his evil accomplice. A man who was acknowledged to be a murderer.

Chapter Forty-Six

Hugh

It was still early when I parted from Thomas Parkinson – too soon to call on Sir John. The tailor would hardly welcome me at such an hour, either. I walked up Castle Hill and stood awhile under the stone arch that held the castle's great, forbidding entrance doors and looked down on the city. To the East, the Pennine hills were emerging from the mist. Below me, men, women, and children were making their way through the streets to their work.

A prosperous city, as Thomas had told me. These mill hands looked reasonably fed. Most of their children were shod, if only in well-worn clogs. The mills here were sited away from the town centre, where the shopkeepers would be opening up for the new day's trade, laying out enticing goods for sale – bread, fruits, and cones of sugar wrapped in blue paper.

The river Lune slid softly through the town, silvered in the morning light, on its way to the sea. Mill chimneys thrust out smoke, creating a light haze which partly obscured the sun. However, compared to Dundee and Paisley, this still looked a clean and healthful place.

I thought of Mr Wordsworth's poem on beholding London in the beauty of early morning, and wondered if he would have written something similar of Lancaster.

I tried, standing before the castle gates, to create a few lines in imitation:

Hath on this morning, bright and fair,
On earth, a place more sweet, more rare?
Than this city which doth wear,
Like a garment, the silver shawl of Lune.

But there I was stumped. Mr Wordsworth was much better than I at this stuff. But he was unencumbered by an exacting employer, eccentric farmers, and a horde of French prisoners, and had more time to practise his art.

And yet, was Lancaster as fair as it appeared? If Thomas Parkinson was right, mill owners, greedy for profit, were investing in new inventions, new machinery, which would throw many folk out of work, bringing about great poverty.

A sudden cough roused me from these reflections.

'Yer want ter get in?' I turned to see Jabez Hartley, prison guard, at my elbow.

'I'd like a word with Mr Higgins, or if not him, then the head warder,' I said. 'I want to check the arrangements. Some of the Frenchmen are supposed to come up to Netherdale tomorrow. It's a different farm we'll be working on.'

'C'mon then, I'll tek tha round to the side postern,' he said. 'I don't know about tomorrow. They say the Frenchies are being shipped home.'

I had never been in any place where prisoners were held. The first thing that struck me was the smell of unwashed bodies, human waste, and unattended sores. As we passed the small windows in the cell doors, I caught glimpses of men, dead-eyed, peering out hopelessly to see who passed by. I pushed aside the thought that my father spent his days thus.

To my surprise, Jabez ushered me straight to the presence of the Governor. Mr John Higgins was a stolid fellow who looked as though he would be just as much at home growing turnips or running a pig farm.

'You're the agent with walls to repair?' he asked me. 'A good plan, I liked it from the first. Useful employment. Fresh air and exercise. Just the thing for 'em. However, I can only let you have a rag-bag collection of men tomorrow. The lading bills have come through. There's a ship waiting on the dock below us as we speak. We've instructions to send most of 'em back to France. War's over! Boney's exiled! Big celebrations are planned, or so I'm told. I myself have doubts. Elba don't sound far enough off to me! Of course, they're not all going, only the men who can prove they're French *and* served in Bonaparte's army. Half of 'em are ship's cooks or the like.'

'There are still a number of men remaining?'

'Enough for your purposes. A couple of Dutch. Some Belgians. You can have those French-speaking fellows who reckon they're Americans.'

I let out a mild guffaw at this. 'Those two ran off last time.'

'Did they? Oh well, we must have caught 'em again. Would you object?'

I shrugged. 'If you send them, I can use them, but I make no promise to prevent them from escaping. I believe,' I added, 'that they were hoping to meet up with a fellow American – a seaman, who was here to take them off on his vessel. Perhaps you still have him? It was suspected that he was a spy.'

'Him! Good heavens! We can't get a word out of him, English or French, but Sir John Hathersage – he's your employer, is he not? – assured me he was one.'

'So he thought.'

'You have reason to doubt it? We were going to send him down to Dartmoor to see what they could get out of him.'

'I may be wrong,' I said carefully, although more boldly than I might have done a week ago (money, even tainted money, I found, gave a man confidence), but I believe him to be a privateer. I think he's been trying to find those two idiots and take them aboard his sloop. Someone in Louisiana must have paid him good money to find them and take them back.'

'Ah,' exclaimed Mr Higgins, as though a great light had dawned. 'I think you could be right, young man. I've been enquiring where those two rascals came from. The only men matching their descriptions seem to have escaped from Norman Cross in Huntingdonshire several weeks ago. How they ended up here, I cannot imagine.'

'The camp at Norman Cross is close to the Great North Road, I believe?'

'It is. So they escaped with instructions to travel north. Goodness knows how these scoundrels get word. Any letters are supposed to be censored. Then they discovered they needed to be on the West Coast, not the East.'

'And after reaching Yorkshire, somehow made their way through the Trough of Bowland,' I finished for him, 'where I encountered them, on foot. They expected to find their deliverer's ship anchored in the bay.'

'His name isn't John Paul Jones, is it? No, that was years back. The fellow tried to burn down Whitehaven. I've relatives there who haven't forgotten.'

I grinned at this. That was over thirty years ago. In Scotland. Jones was attempting to kidnap the Earl of Selkirk.

'I imagine this man is another of his stamp,' I said. 'A man of charm, but daring and ruthless when deprived of his goal.'

Higgins grimaced. 'We should have found this out for our-selves, but this is a busy prison. The prisoners of war are the smallest proportion of our inmates. Would you believe we some-times have as many as three hundred debtors incarcerated here? And a frightful nuisance they are. They whine day and night be-cause their friends will not stand bail. I'll order the two Louisiana rogues put in the same cell with this seaman, if that's what he is, and see if they show that they know one another.'

Before I left him, he confirmed that prisoners would be sent to High Bield on the morrow. Then, to my surprise, he handed me a purse with instructions to purchase rations for them.

I walked back through the prison, wishing I could close my nostrils to the smell. And my ears to the cries of anger and dis-tress. This, my father must have endured. Might still be enduring. I found I could summon pity, though not forgiveness. However, for the first time, I wondered if I would, one day.

The house Sir John had rented was some way down Castle Hill, a tall and narrow terraced building in the modern style. As I approached, the front door opened, and Augustus Fenwick emerged. He didn't look happy.

I hailed him. 'Sir John is recovering, I hope?'

'That wife of his won't let me see him,' he snarled. 'Says he needs complete rest and quiet. I could hear him calling out when the bedroom door was opened. Didn't sound too weak to me. *Lady Lavinia* says he's decided those Trawden brothers knew nothing about the spy.' He stared at me, challenging me to dis-agree.

'They're a simple-minded pair, those two,' I said. 'I'm certain no spy would trust them with any great matter.'

'Because they're soft in the head, you mean? Mind you aren't deceived. That corpse was on their land. Must be a reason he ended up there.'

There was something in his tone that worried me. Spy or actual detective, he would have already made enquiries about me – the land agent, a fresh arrival in the district, with no kith or kin nearby. Lady Lavinia had just sent him packing, but he might still find out more and make the connection with my family.

I made a quick decision. It would look less suspicious if Sir John heard about Ranald Duff from me.

'Actually, I was hoping to see Sir John. I've discovered the dead man was looking for me. Wrong address – High Bield when he should have been seeking Low Bield.'

'And you didn't recognise him when you viewed the corpse? Didn't wonder why he never found you?'

'I had no idea who he was, or that he was coming. Letters from Scotland never reached me. He was bringing a message about a family matter. Very unfortunate that the poor fellow was caught in the snow.'

'Ah, yes, letters from Scotland,' Augustus Fenwick gave me a look that said he knew something about the communications I might or might not have received from Scotland. Had an account of my father's crimes been reported in the newspapers? Had he even wondered about blackmailing me? However, when he saw that I didn't intend to elaborate, he seemed to come to a decision. Evidently, I was not worth the trouble. He turned on his heel and walked away.

As he left, the side door of Sir John's house opened, and James Carr looked out.

'Has 'e gone? Mister Spy Catcher Fenwick?' He grinned and wrinkled his nose.

'Yes. Not best pleased, I gather.'

'Her ladyship don't care for 'im. Reckons he gets the master all wound-up about spies when there ain't no spies. She's handed him his hat this time, and no mistake!'

Well done, Lady Lavvy, I thought. 'Why are you answering the door, James? Do they not have a butler?'

'Still at the Preston 'ouse.'

I imagined the Hathersages might have some difficulty in persuading their servants to leave the urban delights of Preston for a remote manor house in Bowland.

I considered leaving a note, but dismissed the idea. Sir John should have his rest. I might enquire at the printer's about having a card made for future use. I could hear my grandmother's voice in my head, *Grand ideas that money's gae ye!*

'I won't trouble Sir John now,' I said. 'Let him know I called, please, and that I'm off back to Netherdale.'

'Watch where you go through the town, then. I hear the fairground folk have brought that bear to dance in the market square.'

'Did you see him yesterday? The postboy told me that you went to see the show.'

'Mangy ol' creature he looked to me,' he replied, 'but them horse acts were good, when the men stood up on their backs. And the clowns. Nancy nearly bust her stays, hooting at those!'

I laughed and went on my way. An appearance by the bear in the marketplace seemed an ingenious advertising ploy on the part of the fairground people. Not something that would interfere with my plans. I set out for the tailor's shop and the wholesale grocer's to arrange for victuals to be sent up to High Bield for tomorrow's work gang. Then home to Netherdale. However, as Auld Rab told us, 'The best laid plans o' mice and men gang oft astray.'

Chapter Forty-Seven

Hugh

The tailor seemed puzzled by my order for padded britches. 'With the weather warming and summer coming on?' he asked.

Then, in Church Street, outside the grocer's shop, I found Lydia Hutton, examining sacks of cornmeal. She looked troubled. I asked if Nathaniel had a bad night.

'Not at all. He will soon be on his feet again. I need not stay. Martha is to remain and support Susannah for a few days.' She pulled a wry face, 'I must school myself not to be an interfering mother. My daughter is perfectly capable, and after all, Nathaniel is Martha's son. We were all overcome yesterday, thinking the poor boy was at death's door. There was no need for me to be here. I must learn to walk more humbly.'

Then she said, 'Sam Braithwaite is returning to Netherdale. He has offered to drive me back later, after he has attended the men's Morning Meeting.' Noting my bafflement, she explained, 'The men Friends are meeting to consider repairs to the building in Meeting House Lane. They offer prayer, and then consider where the money can be found. If it is God's will, it will be located somewhere.' She chuckled. 'They know full well where money will be found. In Ephraim Bleasdale's pocket! He is a warm man, as we say in these parts. He has lately abandoned all connections with the West Indian trade and is anxious to be seen to walk straightly in the Lord's way. However, my time can be usefully spent buying foodstuffs to take home. Having the use of Sam's trap will be a blessing.'

'I'm on a similar errand,' I told her. 'I have a group of prisoners coming up to the dale tomorrow and instructions to buy supplies for them.'

The glorious scent of fresh ground coffee wafted from the shop's doorway. We both stood transfixed.

Lydia sighed. 'Oh, that smell, so enticing. I can never buy it, as Wilfred thinks it an unnecessary luxury. And, of course, we refrain from buying any goods from the West Indian Isles, because they are sure to have been produced by slaves.' She paused, firming her lips against temptation. 'But do not let me stop thee buying whatever thee needs. Then surely thee could travel back with Sam and me? If thee buys flour, I'd be happy to raise some bread overnight. Those poor soldiers. So far from their homes and loved ones! Although Rachel Stout tells me they have agreed in Paris that the war is now at an end. The Lord be praised indeed, if that is so. Those imprisoned here will soon be going home.'

'So the Governor has assured me,' I replied, 'although there is to be a delay for some while their nationality is confirmed. A party will still come wall-building tomorrow.'

We entered the shop, and each approached one of the aproned assistants to purchase the foodstuffs we required. Lydia's offer to make fresh bread was a boon, and the opportunity to travel, with all my purchases in Sam Braithwaites' cart, very welcome. I was grateful, having thought I would need to hire a carrier to take my goods up to Netherdale.

Almost, I felt myself a carefree and happy man. Until I came to pay for my purchases. Passing over the coins from Governor Higgins, I remembered the other money in my pocket. My grandma's words came back to me: *He got it by blackmail, and by sending Ranald Duff tae beat the monies out of them.* Last night, I had felt a wild urge to open the window and hurl it down on the heads of the passers-by. But I still had it.

Lydia and I met again in the doorway, burdened with packages. It seemed neither of us had needed to bargain with the shopkeeper as I usually did.

'Is thee ready?' Lydia asked. 'Sam said I should meet him in the marketplace. Or perhaps lower down the street if the market is too crowded. He may be there now, waiting.'

Side by side, our arms full of packages, we strolled to the meeting place, I thinking how different Lydia Hutton was from my own mother who would surely have forgone the best coffee beans the merchants of Cupar and Dundee could provide, for Lydia's peace of mind.

May sunshine warmed our backs. Market Street was busy with commerce, and people haggled with the shopkeepers. Other scents drifted from doorways – fresh-baked bread, the tang of new cheeses, and sweet pastries.

Sam's cart was not visible along this section of the street, so we turned into the town square.

At first glance, the place looked deserted. Laden stalls had been abandoned in haste, leaving the goods in disarray. The traders and their customers had fled to the far side of the square, where they stood bunched together in alarm. The cause of their dismay was in the cleared space in front of the town hall.

The bear!

He was more than six feet tall on his hind legs. Swaying from side to side, he roared. He was not entirely toothless. And by no means clawless. He wasn't dancing. He was raging – raging as perhaps all wild things do against captivity, and the cruelty of humankind – against kicks, pokes, blows, and the torments we force them to endure.

'Oh, poor creature!' Lydia's normally soft voice sounded loud in the sudden quiet of the square. 'What have they been doing to him to make him so angry?'

It was obvious how he had got loose. The rope around his head, threaded through a hole drilled in his snout, had frayed and broken. It now lay useless on the ground, together with the whistle required to accompany the dance.

Holding a long cane, the lad who had brought him from the fairground now made sporadic sallies to keep the animal away from the throng without going close enough himself to risk those claws. There seemed little chance of his persuading – or goading – the animal into the wicker cage on the hand-cart that stood waiting.

The bear dropped onto his forepaws and swivelled towards us. His eyes, deep in his fur, were reddish, small, and malevolent.

'Don't move!' the lad with the stick yelled. 'Fer Gawd's sake, don't move!'

Lydia's packages slipped to the ground. As the bear growled, mine followed suit. He lumbered forward a few paces and then sat up on his rump, perhaps considering how he might best kill us.

The crowd shifted and murmured amongst themselves. Suddenly, a ragged urchin, with no understanding of danger, crawled from between the legs of adults. He darted across the paving stones, seized the whistle, and blew a few discordant notes. With a snarl, the bear loped towards him. The child scuttled in our direction and hurled himself into Lydia's outstretched arms. Deftly, she passed him behind her body so that he was hidden by her skirts.

We were face-to-face and dangerously close to an infuriated bear.

Neither of us dared make the slightest twitch of limb. Standing as still as rocks was our only chance. The bear sat back on his haunches again. Even if I were a whole man with two strong arms and a weapon to aid me, I could see no way out of this situation. I prayed inwardly that the boy would stay still and out of sight.

The lad with the cane called and whistled. The bear ignored him.

Now, however, there were exclamations and movement on the other side of the square. A horse and cart was trying to push through the crowd, with voices around berating them. I hoped against hope that it was Sam Braithwaite coming to our rescue. But when the vehicle finally forced a way through, I recognised not Sam's Zebedee, but Rush Ghyll's Steadfast.

And atop the cart were two figures we both knew. Dorcas Hutton held the reins. Beside her was her brother. George jumped down and rushed at the lad with the cane. 'Gibbie, you fool!' he hissed. 'Why'd thee bring him on tha own? Thee knew Mopso was laid up sick. Gimme that cane. I've got honey cakes. Here, give it to me!'

The bear rose up, ready to attack these new foes.

Beside me, I heard George's mother gasp. Lunatics was my thought. They will both be killed.

George wrestled the stick from the lad. He took something brown and sticky from a bag lying in the bed of the Rush Ghyll cart and rammed it onto the end. Advancing, he held it out to the bear.

Another silence had fallen amongst the spectators. The bear, now facing away from us, sat back on his haunches. Lydia, the urchin, and I should have turned and fled. Instead, we stayed, spellbound.

George took a step closer to the bear. 'Here Arktos, good fellow. Here's a bun for you. My sister made 'em, and she ain't such a good cook as my mother. But I think tha'll like it.'

The bear still had his back to us, but I thought he was considering the offer. Dorcas, still seated on the cart, turned huge, anxious eyes in our direction. Steadfast shifted his hooves as though he thought it was time to move on.

Up rose the bear, jaws agape, but just as he was about to seize the bun, George flicked it into the air. Arktos caught it and gulped it down. The crowd, thinking the entertainment had resumed, clapped and cheered.

George repeated this, and again Arktos caught the bun and swallowed it. With the bear distracted, he sidled closer to the hand cart and flicked the next one into it. Arktos paused, head on one side, looking puzzled. Then he lumbered over to the cart. He clambered aboard, scooped up the bun, and settled down, suddenly content. George and the other lad then walked in a business-like fashion over to the cart and fastened up the tailboard. They didn't attempt to pull the hood-like wicker cage over the bear. 'No.' I thought. 'He'll realise he's trapped and scramble out.'

However, Arktos seemed to feel the show was over and continued to enjoy the rest of the buns George had thrown into the cart.

The two lads began to wheel the cart away. The crowd pressed back against the shop fronts, letting them through. Then George turned to flick a hand of farewell towards his mother and sister, and was gone.

Down from the cart leapt Dorcas. She ran across to her mother and flung her arms around her. 'Mama! Mama! I was so afraid the bear would kill thee!'

'No, dearest,' said Lydia, laughing. 'Today my life was not required of me, but why did thee come, and why has thee been cooking sugar buns?'

'It is such a tale!' Dorcas turned to me. 'I started out to see whether I would meet one or both of you on the way – and then I met with George, who was hurrying into town because the boy, Gibbie, had stolen off with the bear,' she said breathlessly. 'Oh, so much has happened! Hugh, your grandmother has come. She is here, at Rush Ghyll, but not well – the journey was too much for her, and she begged me to find you!'

Chapter Forty-Eight

Hugh

Grandma was here in Netherdale! The events of the morning, startling as they had seemed at the time, immediately faded from my mind.

'When did she come? Where did you leave her? I must hire a mount at once and hurry to her.' Words tumbled from my mouth as I tried to make sense of this development.

'No need for that, surely?' said Lydia Hutton. 'Sam Braithwaite promised to drive me home with my packages. His horse will be fresh, having rested overnight, and he can take me and thee back to the farm as quickly as may be. Dorcas can follow after. Having driven Steadfast so fast, as I'm sure thee did, my dear,' she told her daughter, 'it will be better if thee returns more slowly.'

I could see that Dorcas was disappointed, but she accepted her mother's ruling. 'We dashed past Sam on the corner of Penny Street,' she said. 'George was in such a panic about the bear, thinking it might have savaged half the population of the town. I expect Sam is still waiting there, wondering what we were about.'

'Yes,' said her mother, thoughtfully, 'and I want an opportunity to talk with Sam. Rachel Stout had much of interest to impart from her correspondence with Friends in other parts of the country. Oh!' she exclaimed suddenly, remembering the reason she was here in the first place. 'Dorcas, thee must have no further worry about Nathaniel. His shoulder was pulled out of joint, and they had some difficulty moving him, but once the doctor had pushed it back into place, he was much improved. He should be well again in no time. There was no need for me to have come at all. It was unfortunate that they were newly returned, earlier than they intended. Even their furniture hadn't arrived, and poor Sukie didn't know what to do.'

Since riding back with Sam and Lydia would be quicker than going to the livery stables, I agreed to go with them. We walked together down the street, Dorcas leading Steadfast and describing Grandmother's dramatic arrival as we went.

We found Sam Braithwaite where Dorcas had said. Lydia and I stowed our purchases and climbed aboard, Lydia beside Sam and me on the back seat. Everyone had accepted immediately that Lydia would be the one to go to my grandmother's aid.

'We must hurry,' Lydia told Sam. 'Hugh's grandmother has come down from Scotland, and has had a slight attack to her heart.' She smiled at me. 'It is no wonder such a journey has fatigued her. Sam's Zebedee will get us there more speedily than Steadfast.'

Then she turned to Sam Braithwaite. 'As it happens, I want to talk with thee as we go, about starting some schooling for youths in the village. Perhaps an adult class,' she said, as he took up the reins. 'Rachel has been corresponding with Friends in Nottingham and Birmingham, and I believe it is something *we* should do.'

'Mama!' said Dorcas, clearly exasperated with this irrelevance, when an old woman lay sick at Rush Ghyll.

I felt a bit sorry for Dorcas as we bowled away. She had rushed to fetch me, and now she was left to follow on as best she might. Steadfast was indeed a steady animal, but he had already covered seven miles today, and no doubt, George, in his anxiety about Arktos, had insisted on pushing him to the limit.

I returned to fretting about my grandmother. I knew she had some weakness of the heart.

Lydia Hutton spoke over her shoulder. 'I'm sure we'll find it is just the strain and fatigue of travelling. From what Dorcas told me, she tried to find thee at Low Bield. Did thee know she was coming?'

'Letters seem to have gone astray,' I began, but as the houses of the town fell away, Zebedee further quickened his pace, and my voice was carried off by the wind. We passed the travelling fair. I saw no sign of George and the bear. Nothing was said.

Sam and Lydia's voices blew back to me, somewhat disjointedly, on the breeze.

She was enlarging, enthusiastically, about a school for the youth of the neighbourhood, her friend Rachel Stout's idea. Sam merely grunted from time to time.

We passed through an avenue of trees, which lessened the noise of the wind.

'Who would be the instructor?' I heard him say. 'We'd have to pay out a tidy sum to get someone to come up the dale to take these classes.'

This seemed to quell Lydia. 'Perhaps,' she began, but we were back in the open, and the wind took her voice away.

'Thy lass, Dorcas?'

'I don't know,' Lydia replied. 'If I could persuade her...'

'Martha's always thought she made too much of that trouble at the school,' said Sam. 'She must have given him some encouragement. Innocent like, I'm sure.'

The wind was rushing into my ears, drowning out most of what they said, but what I did catch distracted me from thoughts of Grandmother.

Lydia was sighing. 'An inexperienced girl, asking for his help with managing the children. He is older, a married man... They chose to believe his denials.'

'They felt they couldn't dismiss him,' said Sam. 'He's said to be good at his work and has a wife and young children to support.'

'He should not have behaved so!' snapped Lydia, her voice rising. 'Why would Dorcas invent such a story? It was his word against hers. It broke my poor girl's heart and destroyed her courage.'

Lydia glanced back over her shoulder. I pretended to be absorbed in my thoughts, watching the passing scene as though the burgeoning hedgerows, heavy now with dogrose and climbing vetch, had all my attention. I sensed this was not to be discussed further in my hearing.

I had somehow assumed that Dorcas had been dismissed from her post because she had no aptitude for it and could not control a class of lively children. What she had said suggested that she believed this herself.

Yet of late, it had puzzled me. From what I had seen, first with the seaman and then with the prisoners of war, she seemed to have a natural aptitude for teaching. Now it appeared that some man had made improper advances to the poor girl, and it was she, and not he, who had been forced to give up her employment in the school. No wonder she had appeared so angry and lost during our early encounters.

I was truly sorry for her. I looked back the way we had come to see her slowly driving Steadfast home through the verdant lanes. Poor lassie. I, too, had had unfortunate things in my life to overcome. However, I had been lucky to find work far away from people who knew about them. It must be doubly hard to be part of a small circle of people who knew only part of the story and judged you for it. Yet, she continued to hold her head high.

Surely there must be some second chance for her. I vowed to ask her to come and meet with the prisoners on the morrow and practice her French again.

I had come to expect people, particularly young women, to recoil from the sight of my withered hand. Although Dorcas had sometimes given the impression that she disliked me, it was not because I was a cripple. Lately, especially since our night-time expedition and the discovery of her missing brother, I believed we had found a way of dealing with one another, even a measure of friendship – friendly combat, perhaps – *Quakerly* combat. I smiled at my own feeble witticism.

Lydia broke my reverie. 'Does thy grandmother suffer often with her health?' she called back to me. 'Is she under a doctor's care?'

I roused myself. 'Not if she can help it! She thinks the man a quack, just out to make money from folks' ailments. Although being over sixty years of age and having had a hard life, and, as you say, having undertaken a long and perhaps unwise journey...'

'I'm sure we will find she had good reason,' Lydia said.

We fell silent as Zebedee, sensing that we were approaching the mouth of Netherdale, quickened his pace, only to come to a determined halt at the gate to Lane End Farm.

Then ensued a gentle argument between Lydia and Sam about whether we two would walk the rest of the way up to Rush Ghyll. Lydia, in her firm but gentle way, insisted on walking.

'I knew when I married Wilfred that I would always have this climb before me,' she told Sam, 'and I am not yet so old that I cannot undertake it.'

Sam, smiling, raised his hands in submission, and off we set. An intriguing thought. Had Lydia once chosen Wilfred Hutton

over Sam Braithwaite? But no time for idle speculation, we must
hurry to Grandma.

Chapter Forty-Nine

Dorcas' Journal

Wednesday, May 25th, otherwise 6th Day, late evening in my bedchamber

(Betsey is asleep. I hope she will not wake.)

It was so strange to wake this morning and find no Mama in the kitchen setting breakfast for Papa, Wilf, Jonathan, Betsey, and me. She had hurried off to Lancaster to see what had happened to Nathaniel and to help and support Susannah.

I spent the rest of the day in worry, and I must confess, resentment, because I had not been allowed to go and be with my sister.

However, it was up to me to take Mama's place and attend to the needs of the rest of our family. So, I rose early and set out a breakfast of hot milk, bread, butter, cheese, and Mama's blackberry preserve. When they came in from milking, my brothers asked where the porridge was. I had to admit that I had forgotten to set the oats to soak overnight. I fear I shall never make a true housewife.

When Wilf and Jonathan grumbled, Papa said, 'Leave your sister be. The two of you will not starve for want of a bowl of porridge. Think instead of the poor who live in the alleys of the big cities, yes, even in the back streets of Lancaster. Some of those youngsters have already risen and found not even a crust to fill their bellies. Even now, the poor creatures are making their way to the mills, where they will slave all day to earn one slice of stale bread.'

This is what we call Papa's 'testifying voice'. My brothers know it is best to stay quiet and not argue.

He called for a period of silent waiting on the Lord. This lasted for quite ten minutes before we were allowed to eat. I gave my brothers a look that said, 'If there <u>had</u> been porridge, it would now be cold.'

Papa told us he was going to the Fourth Day morning Meeting in the village. Then he and one of the other Elders had been appointed to go to speak with Daniel Jackson at Quernstones. We knew this was because his sons are thought to be behaving in a wild and unruly fashion. They have been seen spending time at an ale house. Papa's absence meant that Wilf and Jonathan would be doing all the work of the farm. Meanwhile, Betsey and I were to take Mama's place indoors.

During our time of prayer, I had determined to do better and pay proper attention to the tasks of the day, even bake a batch of sugar buns to make up for my failure to prepare the oats. Wilf and Jonathan both have a sweet tooth.

So, once the lads had gone to their work, I built up the fire beneath the brick oven, took down the flour crock and the sugar loaf, and sent Betsey out to fetch eggs. She jiggled them in her apron, but I didn't chide her as only two were cracked.

Susannah is usually the one to make sugar buns. Mama considers them too much of an indulgence to bake herself, but I knew the recipe, so I set to.

The first batch turned out very well. I sprinkled a little extra sugar on the tops while they were hot so that it half-melted into the crust. A real treat for my brothers, I thought. And when I emptied those from the pannikins to cool, I had enough for a second batch while the oven was hot.

But 'pride goeth before a fall', as is truly said. Although it was hardly my fault that there was a commotion outside just when I should have been removing this second baking. Betsey (who had been scraping the bowl and licking the spoon) and I went running out to see what had happened.

A dilapidated cart had driven into our yard. The rough track up to the farm had jolted it so much that a wheel had now come off, nearly depositing two old ladies onto the ground.

The older lady scrambled out without help, although her maid (as it turned out she was) sat in the collapsed cart, whimpering about a knock to her knee. An elderly nag was struggling in the broken traces.

'Ma'am, what happened?' I cried, although it was perfectly obvious.

'Ach, the wheel's come off. That disna surprise me,' the old lady said, shaking out her dusty skirts. ''Tis a wonder it brought us thus far. That man was a skellum that hired it to me. There was nought else to be had. Katie! Whisht! Ye're no dead!'

Wilf and Jonathan had gone over the fields to see to a gap in a hedge where they thought the cows might push through. Papa had put on his broad-brimmed hat and walked down to the Meeting House to meet with those who attended the Men's Morning Meeting. There was no one but Betsey and me to pick our visitors up and dust them off.

The old lady looked us up and down, and said, 'Ye'd be daughters o' the Hutton family? Aye, Ah've heard o' ye, frae Hugh. Whisht, Katie! Ye're all right. Naething's broken, auld lass. I daresay these lassies will give ye a cup o' tea and a dab o' the witch hazel. I'm Elspeth Muir, seeking my grandson, Hugh

Armstrong. Would ye know where he's likely tae be? We found the place where he bides, Low Bield, but he's no there.'

She had such a strange way of speaking, more Scottish than Hugh.

I told her he was in Lancaster. 'He will probably be back today. He went to see his employer, and also—'

But Katie was moaning about her hurts, and the old woman shushed me.

'Tell me in a wee while, lassie. My ears are good, but I cannae listen tae two of ye at once. Will ye see to the poor beast?' For a moment, I thought she was talking about Katie, but of course, she meant the pony.

And that's how the second batch of sugar buns came to be a little burnt.

It is late, and Betsey is stirring. So much has happened, I must leave this account for now.

Later still

I find myself still wakeful and thinking of all that has passed, although the tall clock in the passageway has chimed two. The whole household is asleep, so I have relit my candle and will explain how it fell out that I went to fetch Hugh and Mama home.

To cut my long tale short, I released the pony into the meadow. Hugh's grandmother said, 'He'll no bolt, he has nae the energy,' and we took our visitors indoors. Betsey declared she would boil water to make tea, which she was able to do, the kettle being already on the hob. I made a pad of arnica, as I had seen Mama do, for Katie's swollen knee. Having made the sugar buns, I thought it right to offer them to our visitors.

'Hmm, no bad, no bad at all,' declared Elspeth Muir when she tasted hers, and she looked me up and down in a very 'meaning way' which puzzled me. Does she think we Quakers are so strict and severe that such treats are forbidden? Or maybe she caught the whiff of burning from the second batch and was surprised that these were not scorched.

Feeling ashamed of the burnt ones, I hid them away in an old flour bag and opened the kitchen window to let out the smell.

I was feeling happy and even proud of myself, playing the hostess. I should have realised. Elspeth Muir is an old lady, and the shock of the cart's collapse had affected her more than she or any of us had realised. She began to suffer pains in her chest.

'Och, it'll be the indigestion,' she said, but I saw her breath was coming short. Katie looked worried. This was serious. What were we to do?

'Mebbe you'll gae and search for my grandson?' said Elspeth. 'Katie'll get my heart medicine frae the baggage? I'll bide awhile and rest.'

What to do? I supposed Hugh might be on his way back from Lancaster, but I had no idea how close he was. My father was away across the dale. Jonathan returned, panting. Some of the cows had indeed strayed into the wheat. He and Wilf needed to drive them out again. He wanted Betsey and me to go and help, but I told him no. We had a sick woman on our hands.

We persuaded Elspeth Muir to lie down. Katie found the heart medicine. She and Betsey soothed her brow and gave her drinks of water, but still she fretted for her grandson.

'Did that divil o' a man bring him the watch or no?' she muttered. 'If I knew that, I could rest easy.'

It was up to me to find Hugh. Ashamed of the scorched buns, I took them with me. I suppose I had some notion that I might give them to tramping men along the way, but the Lord's hand must have been over me, for they proved very useful.

Chapter Fifty

Hugh

'Ah, Hughie, the Lord be praised!' my grandmother greeted me. 'I'm aw reet. There was no need for the lassie, Dorcas, tae go fer ye. I'm sorry I sent her pelting off. T'was only the heartburn. Katie found my medicine, and it had me right in a trice.'

She was half lying, half seated, propped about with pillows, on the settle in the Huttons' parlour, a room I guessed they rarely used except when they had visitors. The truckle bed where Sir John had lain was still here, stripped of its sheets. Lydia, calling Grandma Elspeth, as though they had known each other for years, insisted she should lie down and try to sleep.

'Ach no,' Grandma insisted, 'there's a good bed in Hughie's wee hoose, and if the sheets are no sae clean, they'll do. Katie and I will bide there. The good Lord knows we've slept in worse along the way.'

Grandma had already taken advantage of my unlocked house and inspected it from top to bottom.

'An' if ye'd be kind enough tae lend that bed over yonder,' she added, meaning the truckle. 'Hughie can sleep on that.'

Wilfred Hutton ordered his sons to dismantle the bed and carry it down to Low Bield. 'While you two do that, I'll start on the milking,' he said, 'and Betsey, thee is old enough to see to Steadfast.

313

'I hope all of you will stay to eat something. A bowl of broth at least.' said Lydia. She smiled at me, 'For I don't suppose thee had planned to cook for three?'

She served up bread and broth, and after we had eaten, we set out for my cottage. Grandma insisted she was well enough to walk, but she leaned heavily on my arm.

'Ah, Hughie,' she sighed as we progressed slowly down the rough track, Katie burdened with their baggage. 'I've terrible things tae tell ye. Terrible things! I couldna speak o' them in front of those good people.'

'Wait until we're there,' I said. 'Then you can sit quiet and tell me.'

'That's what they do, isn't it?' she asked, glancing back towards Rush Ghyll, 'sit quiet and tell it tae God, and He taks away their troubles? Ah, I wish it were so.'

Home to Low Bield. I lit a wax candle in Grandma's honour, and settled her in my favourite chair with a cushion behind her. I had but two chairs in the house. Katie refused to take the other and seated herself on the floor. With her back against the wall, she promptly fell asleep.

'Dinna mind her,' said Grandma, 'She can sleep anywhere if she's a mind to.'

'Then, tell me,' I said. 'Tell me what brought you on this crazy journey, and then you can both rest in bed.'

'First things first,' said she. 'You've no been answering my letters.'

'I hadn't received any for months until two days ago.'

'So did that skellum Ranald Duff come tae ye, nye on the New Year, or did he not?'

'I believe he did, but I never saw him.'

'Did ye get whatever it was your father sent?'

'I did. I have it here.' I patted the pocket of my coat.

'There's a miracle! Your father was wild when the man niver came back, and him due to go to Australia, not knowing if the rogue had kept his word.'

'I believe he intended to,' I said. 'Nobody here remembers speaking to him. He must have come in January or February and was lost in a snowstorm. When they found him, he'd perished. Father had given him the wrong address, High Bield instead of Low Bield. High Bield is a farm much higher up the fell – the brae.'

Grandma mumbled her mouth awhile as she digested this. 'Years back, Ranald Duff murdered his wife and bairns, cut their poor throats. But Walter told the police he had been with him at the time, receiving religious instruction. Religious instruction! Ranald Duff? He knew if Walter told the truth, he would hang. Walter held that over him for years, making the man carry out any wicked acts he wanted done – the beatings he gave to folks to whom your father owed money! I think he even thought of taking Duff with him to Australia if the ship's crew could be bribed. When he didn't come back, and Walter was due to sail, Walter thought himself betrayed. He thought Ranald had stolen the package and maybe taken ship to America instead.'

'No, Ranald Duff was dead. I saw his body after they dug it out from under the snow, but I didn't know who he was.'

'Aye, you wouldn't,' said Grandma grimly, 'I niver let that dirty skellum near you or your brothers.' When she said this, I recalled dim memories of a man coming to the house at night, after dark, and my father talking to him at the door, never bringing him inside.

We were interrupted by a loud snore from Katie.

'Poor lassie,' I said. 'Should we not let her go to bed?'

'Ach, no. She'll no wake,' my grandmother continued unconcerned, 'I've no told you yet what befell your father and your brother. *Then* she and I can take our rest.'

'My father and Neil?' I asked. 'Has something happened to both of them? I thought you'd come to tell me Father had been deported at last?'

'So he would have been. But then, when we heard the ship was riding at anchor in the Tay, and the convicts were to be taken aboard once the tide was right, Neil took it into his head to go to Dundee and see him go aboard with his own eyes. You know how it was with your poor brother? He came back from Spain with part of his foot blown off, and most times out of his proper wits. And the rest of the time completely out of them wi' the drink.'

I nodded. My brother and I had had little love for one another when we were younger, but I understood his injuries and the terrible sights he must have witnessed in Spain.

'Neil determined to see your father aboard. "And shout a curse after him," was what he said. I tried to dissuade him, but no, he would go. And go he did.' My grandmother closed her eyes and for a moment seemed unable to continue.

'What happened, Grandma?'

'The convict ship had come close into the harbour,' she continued, her eyes still closed as though to shut out forever what she had witnessed. 'They had the prisoners already lined up on the quay, to be taken out to it in small boats. The men were in prison clothing, almost in rags, with their hands and ankles shackled so they couldna run off. I didna pick your father out at first, but Neil's eyes, being younger, spotted him.

'And would ye believe, Hughie, there was a *Minister* there, in his white bands, giving those men a blessing. *That* was more than Neil could bear.

'Of course, Neil couldna walk wi' out a crutch, but off he set, hurpling along the pier. I called after him, but he took no notice, set on giving Walter his curse.' She stopped and sighed again.

'And did he?'

'Oh, he surely did. At any rate, he went towards Walter and began shouting. Walter tried to back away from him, but Neil grabbed his arm. Maybe the crutch caught in the ankle shackle – if Neil hit him, I didn't see. There were too many folk, besides the prisoners, around. When I got through, nobody could say what happened exactly. They were gone.'

'And? I asked, already guessing the answer, but needing to hear it.

'Both were dead when they fished them out of the harbour. Walter was weighted down with his shackles. They said Neil must have hit his head on the pilings below the pier, or maybe on rocks beneath the water.' She sighed. 'What could it matter? I told the prison people to bury Walter in the prison cemetery where he richly deserved to be, but I took Neil home and laid him to rest in the kirkyard beside your mother.'

We sat a while, wordless, because there was nothing to say. Perhaps, in time, I would feel sorrow, but now all I felt, and yes, I am ashamed to acknowledge it, was relief that Walter's deeds would trouble me no more. The only sounds in the room were Katie's snores. Her head had fallen to one side, and her mouth hung open.

'Ach, poor lass!' said Grandma at last. 'I told her I didna need her wi' me, but she would come. She thought that once I crossed the border into England, she might niver set eyes on me again. We left her sister Jinny tae mind the hoose.'

'Is there need for you to give up the house? You've enough money to live on. It wasn't his watch. Father sent me thirty guineas. I could spare some of that if you need it.'

I was a little worried, I confess, that Grandma had come to take up permanent residence with me.

'No need.' She waved this away. 'I niver let Walter know the whereabouts of *all* that your grandfather left. I'll miss Neil's army pension, but now he's gone and not spending most of it on the whisky anyway. We'll get by, Katie and me.'

She yawned hugely, then grinned, revealing many missing teeth.

'Ah'll be snoring along o' Katie soon. Well, away tae that bed o' yours.'

Chapter Fifty-One

Hugh

I didn't find much repose on the Hutton's truckle bed. Horrid dreams haunted me. Several times, I saw Father falling from the pier, tumbling, and turning in the air. Except that it wasn't with Neil but myself – falling, dropping, into a sea that churned angrily below. Yet each time, before the waters engulfed me, I woke, drenched in sweat. In another dream after this, I stood on a deserted headland while a huge bear lurched towards me, fangs bared, claws outstretched.

I woke properly to the sound of raised voices in Low Bield's kitchen.

Of course – Grandma was here! She'd be wanting her porridge, but I could hear a man's voice as well. Then I remembered Gabriel Waller. Today, the prisoners were coming to High Bield. I had forgotten all about them.

When I stumbled into the kitchen, it was to find them arguing. It seemed they disagreed on a number of points with regard to how porridge should be made, in what direction it ought to be stirred, and whether it should be served with salt or sugar and milk.

'There you are at last,' said Grandma, slapping a ladle full into a bowl and pushing it in my direction. 'I hear you're to go wall building today, or so this mannie here tells me.'

'There are men coming from the prison,' I began.

'Has tha remembered ter get victuals fer 'em?' interrupted Gabe.

'I have,' I replied, then recalled that all my supplies were still up at Rush Ghyll. 'Lydia Hutton promised me she would make bread for us. We'll collect them on the way.'

'And since when was it the business o' an agent tae build walls?' demanded Grandma. 'I thought 'twas an occupation ter mak ye a gentleman.' She slapped down bowls of porridge in front of Katie and Gabe. Gabe gave me a look, but he settled to eat it without sugar as he had on the previous occasion. Katie added a liberal sprinkling of salt.

'I don't have to build the wall myself, Grandma.' I explained about the French prisoners. 'Gabriel, here is the expert. My job is to supervise the work.'

'And arrange victuals. He forgot last time,' Gabe added gloomily, 'but there'd been a wedding, so we got the leftovers. Don't let that Hutton lass give it all out today. All I got were 'broken meats', as it says in the Good Book, Matthew 15, verse 37.' The rascal must have looked it up.

'Gabe is inclined to Methodism,' I told my grandmother.

Grandma raised her eyes to Heaven. She had suffered enough Bible-quoting from my father. 'Katie and I will bide here, and turn this place out,' she announced. 'That man, Sir Whosit, that pays yer wages, should gae ye enough to employ a scrubbing woman.'

I had known Grandma would be unimpressed by my house-keeping. 'It's hard to find anyone in this lonely place,' I said. 'I'm lucky that a woman from the village takes my washing.' I scraped my bowl clean like a good child and stood up. 'Come on, Gabe, or the prisoners will be there before we are.'

'Is the Hutton lass coming wi' her French book?'

'If she wishes,' I said, but amongst yesterday's excitements, I hadn't asked her.

'That's young Dorcas?' asked Grandma. 'She knows French? Then you'd best take her along. She's a good wee lassie that one. Mind those Frenchmen dinna carry her off!'

Gabe and I reached the place on High Bield's land where the wall had collapsed just before the prisoners. From that windy height, we could see a line of them trudging uphill. Evidently, the warders had decided not to bring the wagon the full distance up the steep and uneven fellside. I waved my hat to indicate where we were waiting for them.

'What'll we do if it pelts it down like last time?' asked Gabe, ever the pessimist.

'Find what shelter we can. The prisoners didn't mind the rain before. Dancing about half naked like they were in Bedlam!'

'Nae rain today, Ah reckon,' said a voice from behind. As we turned, Matthew Trawden gestured to the clouds above us, racing southeast towards Preston. 'Too high for it today.'

Gabe continued to mutter doubts. There was no sign of Batty. I hoped Matthew had locked him in the house.

The prisoners, struggling up the slope into view, were just such a motley crew as before. Some, like the two Américains, I knew already. I wondered if they would run off, but why come so far if that was their intention? Some I did not recognise at all. There was no sign of the fellow I thought of as the sea captain.

'Mostly Belgians and Dutch, these are,' panted Jabez Hartley, recovering from the climb. He and Luke Johnson were escorting them again. 'Try English on 'em, try French. Some of 'em that came before'll know what tha wants. Some won't.'

'Gabe is here to show them,' I said. As I had told my grandmother, I was here only to supervise. I wondered how she was getting on with 'supervising' my house in her turn. I also wondered how long she intended to stay. Rather guiltily, because Grandma had been my sure and certain champion in childhood against my father's ill-treatment and my brothers' bullying.

We soon had the men lined up and passing the stones to one another.

'Is the young lady coming today?' Luke Johnson asked.

One or two of the men looked round at this. Their English was improving, and Dorcas had made an impression.

'I think she may,' I told him. 'Her mother has undertaken to bring us food at midday, and perhaps she'll come then.'

We'd been greeted by the smell of baking bread when we called at Rush Ghyll. Yesterday's several shocks and alarms did not appear to have troubled Lydia Hutton at all. Dorcas was not visible, and with Gabe glowering over my shoulder, I hadn't felt I could ask about her plans. I didn't relish giving him the chance for waggish remarks.

And so, the work of rebuilding a long section of wall at High Bield began. We had all learned from the previous occasion. Gabe was more patient, more willing to demonstrate what was wanted. Those men who had come before eagerly shared their skill with the others, and even seemed to recognise some of the terms for the stones, footers, long stones, tie, and top stones, fillers, and so forth. The warders trusted the new men to learn from watching Gabe and their comrades, rather than barking out orders in their own limited French. I suppose, too, I was less fearful that the whole exercise would be a disaster.

However, it caused me some surprise and discomfiture to see Sir John and his lady approach on horseback. Sir John's head was still bandaged, his face still pale. Lady Lavvy wore a ruby velvet riding habit, no doubt the height of fashion, but quite unsuitable for an excursion over the moors on a warm spring day.

'Johnny would come,' she told me as they dismounted. 'And I came with the old fool in case he takes another tumble, although I hate to be up on a hoss.' Her eyes eagerly scanned the prisoners.

Frowning, Sir John looked around for the Trawden brothers, I suppose afraid they might be firing at rabbits again. However, Matthew had wandered away to see to his fowl and left us to it. No explanation of Batty's whereabouts had been offered. He could still be 'legging it' over the fells in one of his moods.

'All going well here?' Sir John asked. 'You'll finish today?'

I said I thought we would.

'You know, I had quite decided to give Trawden, and his idiot brother notice to quit,' he said, 'but m'wife won't hear of it.' He gazed around at the bleak spread of moorland. 'She doubts I could get a decent tenant for this place, the land being very inferior at this height.'

'That's right,' said Lady Lavinia, 'Those brothers can surely scrape only the barest of livings. I was a farmer's daughter. I know starvation land when I see it.'

I hastened to assure Sir John that if they remained, henceforth I intended to keep a closer eye on them. 'Matthew isn't a bad sort of fellow,' I said, 'and provided he keeps that gun locked away, there should be no more trouble with Bartholomew. He is simple-minded, it's true, but not, I believe, intentionally murderous.' I forbore to mention that on my very first encounter with them, Batty had just shot his brother.

The Hathersages seemed satisfied with what they had seen and made to remount and leave, but just then, we saw people approaching from the direction of Rush Ghyll. Coming up the final slope and out onto the moor were Lydia, Dorcas, and Betsey Hutton, with baskets of food. With them was Grandma, hobbling on a stick, and her faithful Katie, carrying a stool. So much for setting my house to rights. Curiosity had triumphed.

'What a good idea,' said Lady Lavinia, eyeing the stool, 'but I don't recognise this person.'

'My grandmother,' I told her, sketching a bow, 'here on a visit.' I wasn't about to mention the deaths of my father and brother, but Grandma immediately piped up, 'Yes, wi' sad tidings – his father's gone at last!'

'Oh!' exclaimed Lady Lavvy, 'how sad, Hugh. Had your father suffered long?'

I shook my head and sighed, thus avoiding an answer to this. I attempted to quell Grandma with a frown, although I'm certain she muttered, ʼTwas *we* suffered long!'

The prisoners dropped their stones where they were, eager for their share of food.

The scent from the baskets also seemed to decide the Hathersages to stay. Lady Lavinia perched on a protruding 'step' in the still-standing section of the wall. Sir John leaned against it. Grandma planted her stool and spread her skirts. The rest of us sat on the ground, prisoners and warders, the Rush Ghyll womenfolk, Grandma's maid, a waller, and the wall builders' supervisor, all of us ready to share this outdoor feast.

'Is it loaves and fishes, then?' demanded Gabe, but even he was grinning as the tasty treats were brought forth and passed around.

'Have I agreed to pay for this?' Sir John seemed puzzled rather than angry.

I assured him he had not, that Mr Higgins had done so.

Keen to prevent Lydia Hutton from refusing it, I had placed the money down firmly on her kitchen table and indicated that we would not discuss the matter.

'Before we eat, we must give thanks unto God,' she now began in her gentle voice.

'Indeed, we must,' said Grandma, and proceeded to astonish everyone by seizing the initiative and reciting,

> *O thou who kindly dost provide,*
> *For every creature's want!*
> *We bless Thee, God of Nature wide,*
> *For all Thy goodness lent,*
> *And if it please Thee, Heavenly Guide,*
> *May never worse be sent,*
> *But whether granted or denied,*
> *Lord, bless us with content. Amen!*

'Amen!' we all responded, even the prisoners, who could not have understood much of her Scottish brogue.

'That was lovely!' exclaimed Dorcas. 'I've never heard it before.'

'Ach, t'was our Rabbie himself that penned it – Robert Burns, our national bard,' said Grandma. 'My Grandson,' she went on, between mouthfuls of bread and cheese, 'aspires tae be a poet, but he'll no match our Rabbie.'

Oh, Grandmothers! How apt they are to embarrass us before everyone. No one else knew how to respond. I pretended to be profoundly interested in what I was eating.

Lady Lavvy then asked Grandma what part of Scotland she came from. Was it very wild?

Grandma replied that Fife was 'as douce as ye could wish, but,' she added darkly, 'she couldna say the same of the folk.'

The last thing I wanted her to discover was that she was seated not many yards from where Ranald Duff's body had lain, buried in the snow. I imagined her enumerating his iniquities and inadvertently mentioning my father's role.

Dorcas was on her feet, passing amongst the men, handing out food, and greeting the ones she recognised with 'Bonjour, Henri! Bonjour, Pierre! Bonjour, Bernard! Comment allez-vous aujourd'hui?'

When she's happy, as she is today, trying out her French and getting responses to her greetings, I found myself thinking, *she is a very handsome girl.*

Chapter Fifty-Two

Dorcas' Journal

Thursday, 26th May, evening, the barn

There is just enough light in here to write my journal now that the days and nights are drawing close to midsummer. I thought I wanted to cry where no one could see me, but no tears have come. It has been a beautiful day, such a happy pique-nique (if that is the correct word). The prisoners were, I believe, pleased to see me. But the warders told me that the governor has had word from London that all of them are to be sent home, or as far as Brussels, from where I suppose they must make their own way. I shan't see them again.

Of course, I must be happy that the war is over, but now Rachel Stout's plan for us to visit the prisoners will come to nothing.

So far, it seems nothing further has come of the suggestion that I might go as a governess to a Quaker family. I feel my life is a wasteland, unprofitable. Mama keeps insisting that the Lord will show me a way, but none has opened. Haytiming will soon be here. I will do my part, but with nothing to look forward to but a genteel visit to Rachel and Eliza in a few weeks' time.

Dorcas, thee must <u>not</u> give way to self-pity. One amusing thing did happen today. Hugh Armstrong's Grandmother (who now seems quite well) demanded of Mama whether she might attend our Meeting on First Day. Mama, of course, said yes. Elspeth Muir said she had never attended one. How long would it last? Could she bring her maid? She did not have any grey clothing, would that matter? Mama tried to reassure her on all these points. What made me nearly laugh out loud were the expressions of horror on the faces of Hugh and the maid, Katie. Meeting will be <u>interesting</u> if she comes. I hope it will not be entirely silent. Papa hears Daniel Jackson's sons think they may leave the Quakers for the Methodists because <u>they</u> are not so solemn and boring, and at least sing rousing choruses. However, Papa doesn't believe they will, as the Methodists are dead set against ale houses.

Chapter Fifty-Three

The wall at High Bield was repaired, and the prisoners had gone. It seemed they were to be shipped out within days. I was strangely moved, seeing the last of them, knowing they were bound for their homelands, and we would never see them again. It would have been useful to have borrowed some of them to help with the hay. I knew Wilfred Hutton would have been glad to have extra men. Sam Braithwaite would lend his younger sons, and the womenfolk would help. Haytiming could be amongst the hardest few weeks of the farming year. Yet winter without it would be a disaster for the Netherdale farms.

'You could hire a few Irishmen was Sir John's response. 'I understand they come over in droves at this time of year, hoping to find work. They're all rogues of course, but I rely on you to choose the best.

When I suggested this to Wilfred Hutton, he shook his head.

'I doubt they'd come up to Netherdale,' he said, 'We're too far from taverns. We'll manage, with my wife, Dorcas, and young Betsey lending a hand. Some of Lydia's cousins will come once they've carried their own crop. They farm in the Lune valley, and their hay is ready before ours. We all help one another.'

Meanwhile, Grandma seemed to be settling in for a long stay at Low Bield, still full of disparaging remarks about my housekeeping. Her maid drooped in her wake, homesick for Scotland.

'At least she hasn't dragged you to the Quakers' Meeting yet,' I teased.

'She's no forgotten,' Katie grumbled. 'She only gave up the notion last week because all that stravaiging up the brae tae see the Frenchmen tired her oot.'

'If she wants to go, I'll take her,' I said, hoping, of course, that she'd forget.

I don't know whether Katie mentioned my offer to Grandma or not, but when the next Sunday came around, she appeared in her best black gown, draped in shawls, with Bible in hand, ready to go to Meeting.

'It's a long walk,' I said, 'shall I put the old side saddle on Polly?'

If I'd thought this would discourage her, I was wrong. The side saddle had been here in Low Bield's makeshift stable since before my time. The leather girth was stiff with disuse, and the wooden foot platform riddled with worm. I also feared serious rebellion from Polly, but to my surprise, she seemed to have taken a liking to Grandma and made no fuss.

'Why do you want to go?' I asked, as we set out, Grandma aboard Polly, I on foot.

'To see what it's like,' she replied. 'If you're to stay here, you canna remain a heathen all your life.'

'What! You think I should become a Quaker?'

She was silent for a few minutes as we ambled through lanes fragrant with honeysuckle, dogrose, and wild broom.

'Your father gave ye a strong abhorrence o' religion,' she said, 'and no wonder. But in country places, where ye'll likely always be working, it will count against ye if ye dinna go to church at all.

'Tis expected, or folk will shun ye. The folk who matter, like that Sir John and his lady wife.'

'They've never mentioned it. Never asked if I'm a churchgoer. I don't even know if they go to church themselves.'

'Maybe not when they're living in the town, with churches all around. Who is to miss them at this one or that? But now they're moving into this wee manor house at the foot of the glen, ye'll find they gae to yon village kirk every Sabbath day. 'Tis expected of anyone who likes to think they're part of local society. And soon they'll be asking why ye dinna go too?'

'I'll say I'm a Methodist,' I said, laughing, 'and it's too far to walk to Brookhouse on a Sunday. It's Polly's day of rest, too.'

Grandma dismissed this with a snort to match one of Polly's.

'By what I hear, Methody is all enthusiasm, hymn singing, Bible reading, and long sermons telling folk what wicked sinners they are, bound for Hell. Your father did a might o' that, whited sepulchre that he was. Ye wouldn't want to have all that again, surely?'

'No, I would not!' I had no intention of joining Gabriel Waller and his fellow worshippers. Nor did what I had seen of Parson Chorley from the Anglicans appeal to me. 'But I am not about to become a Quaker.'

'They seem good people, and they dinna allow anyone tae wear the white bands and stand in a pulpit, and think himself holier than they are,' she said.

As we entered the village, we found ourselves following two children on a skinny donkey, a little girl in front, with her younger brother clinging on behind. The little girl turned huge, anxious eyes on us as we drew level. '

'Are you coming to the Quakers' Meeting, Sir?' she asked.

'We are,' I said.

'That's good,' the child replied, 'because it means we're not late. Mama is too sick to come, and we haven't any food in the house. We aren't *really* Quakers, but there is a lady there called Mary Grundy, and she was kind when Mama was sick before, and Mama said she is sure to ask how Mama is, and perhaps she may give us something to eat, or some money to buy bread.'

'Dearie me,' said Grandma, 'that's a hard tale. We're new in this place. What is your name, lassie?'

'I'm Minnie, and my brother is Edgar.'

Grandma glanced at me, eyebrows raised.

'If this Mary Grundy is there, I suppose she will know their circumstances,' was all I could say.

Many people had already gathered outside the little stone-built Meeting House. A tall Quaker whose back looked familiar was dismounting from his horse by way of a mounting block. Others were lining up dogcarts, tethering their horses against the side of the building. I saw Sam Braithwaite's shiny new vehicle amongst them. The Hutton family had chosen to walk and were already entering the building without seeing us. They were dressed in the same clothes they had worn for the wedding.

'We should tether Tinker,' said little Minnie, anxiously, 'or he'll wander. Would you do it for me, please, Sir?'

'You're coming into the service?' I asked the child. 'You don't see the lady you were looking for? Will it not be too long a time for you and your brother to sit still?'

I looked at Grandma, but she was fully engaged in getting down from Polly's back. I had coins in my pocket. Should I give one to this waif, and save her having to sit an hour or more? Minnie, however, seemed determined, and taking her brother's hand, walked on in through the doorway, her little head held high as though she was going to her martyrdom, certain of salvation.

'Where should we sit?' hissed Grandma.

'Anywhere at the back,' I murmured.

Most of the Quakers were now seating themselves in family groups, with Mama at one end of a bench, the youngest children nearest to her, and Papa with the older ones at the other. Those without children sat separately, men with men, and women with women, although three men and one woman sat on a slightly raised platform at the front. I presumed these were the elders

The benches at the back of the room were left free for villagers who had come along out of curiosity, like us. Little Minnie patted the seat beside her, solemnly urging us to join her.

Silence fell. Grandma closed her eyes. It was warm in this plain, whitewashed room, with only a tiny breeze through the open window. I hoped she wouldn't fall asleep and topple over. I hoped I wouldn't either. Little Edgar's legs swung to and fro beside me.

After some minutes, I realised with surprise that Susannah and Nathaniel were here, visiting with his family. He looked pale and strained, as though his shoulder still pained him. Martha Braithwaite glanced at him anxiously.

After about a quarter of an hour, one of the elders rose to his feet and read an unfamiliar section (to me) from the Book of Timothy, about 'not muzzling thine ox when he treads the grain, because the labourer is worthy of his hire.' Grandma scrabbled through her own Bible to find the verses. He proceeded to tell us what he believed the passage contained for us, in which explanation he rather lost me, except that we should respect 'those who serve us, and those who seek to encourage our feet on the path of righteousness.'

Grandma was frowning. Placing one's personal interpretation on Holy Scripture was a foreign notion for her. I could imagine a fine argument arising. I just hoped she would conduct it with me, after this, and not attack this worthy man.

He sat down, and the silence continued. A bee blundered in through the window and buzzed lazily against the glass, unable to find its way out. One of the farm dogs yawned at his master's feet. Little Edgar had fallen fast asleep, his sister's arm around him.

I'd wondered if perhaps poetic inspiration would be granted to me a second time, but this seemed unlikely with Grandma fidgeting at my elbow. I prepared to sit the hour out, wishing for those new padded britches, still at the tailor's shop. The insect seemed to buzz louder.

There was a sudden stirring. A young woman was on her feet. I saw to my astonishment that it was Dorcas Hutton.

'The passage our Friend has shared with us has raised questions in my mind.' Her voice wavered a little. 'Young though I am, I believed I was worthy of my hire at the school in Lancaster. I understood that although I was a beginner and had much to learn, with God's blessing, I could give good service. Yet when I sought guidance from one more experienced than myself, I was treated disrespectfully. When I protested, my word was discredited, and I was shunned. Did I misunderstand God's Word for me, the leadings I felt in my heart?'

Backs grew taut, and hasty glances were exchanged. The woman elder leaned forward in her seat, as though ready to rise and command Dorcas to be quiet.

But Dorcas sat down again. Still, the air hummed with disquiet. This was not the kind of message the worshippers had wanted to hear.

Then, to my horror, Grandma rose to her feet, Bible raised aloft.

'I am a stranger in your midst,' she declared. 'I dinna ken what happened to this puir lassie, or why it was that not one o' ye took her part. Although I might guess. However, I have seen enough o' her tae ken she's a guid wee lass, truly a labourer worthy of her hire. When I needed help, she gave it, although she'd never seen me before in her life. Did not Our Lord tell us,' she shook her Bible at them, 'that we should nae pass by on the other side?'

Oh, Grandmother! I thought. If you truly wished me to join the Quakers, you have just destroyed any chance of my doing so! Should I rise and lead her out? A few heads turned and stared at us for a brief moment, but no one signalled that we should go. The man who had expounded on the Book of Timothy sat still as stone, expressionless, only blinking his eyes from time to time. The silence deepened, the room grew still, as though some Presence did indeed enfold us and command us.

Then two of the elders shook hands, and the Meeting seemed to be over.

Chapter Fifty-Four

Hugh

However, as in any church, there were notices to be given out. Friends were asked to support those who were sick in prayer. Mary Grundy was named. It seemed Minnie's friend was not here to help her. A women's Meeting would be held there on Fourth Day to consider assistance to the poor and sick of the district. This received some murmurings. 'Surely we should postpone now we're haytiming,' said somebody behind me.

Then we were dismissed, out into the morning sunshine. After her embarrassing intervention, I had hoped to hurry Grandma away. However, she would have none of it. I think she intended to tackle Lydia Hutton, but the woman Elder had trapped Lydia and her husband at the door.

The younger Quakers, including Susannah and Nathaniel, were massed together amongst the plain tombstones. I wondered if this was always the case after the period of worship. Or if Dorcas's words had subdued them as well as their parents. I couldn't see Dorcas to begin with and assumed she'd already left, embarrassed by her temerity, and fled for Rush Ghyll.

But then I saw her, standing with Susannah's arm protectively around her shoulders, her face pale but defiant.

I began to move towards them, but my grandmother swooped in.

'Whatever he did, lassie, you hold your head high!' she declared, loud enough for everyone present to hear her.

It was sweet Susannah who replied.

'It was not what he did, though that was very bad, it was that the governors of the school did not believe my sister!' I would not have supposed her capable of such vehemence.

'Thee should have given a great scream, Dorcas,' said Nathaniel. 'Then he would not have tried it. The governors felt sorry for him,' he explained to my grandmother. 'He has a sickly wife and young children. If they dismissed him, his family would be destitute. We are counselled against seeking retribution, but...'

'He told a lie,' said Dorcas. 'He said it was I who had made advances to him.'

Grandma nodded. 'Such men will always contrive to blame the woman. My own Effie's husband was just such a one.'

To my great relief, the tall man in the broad beaver approached the group. Seeing him from the front, I realised it was Thomas Parkinson.

He nodded to me and held out a hand to Dorcas. Rather doubtfully, she took it. 'I thank thee for thy ministry,' he said, squeezing hers so vigorously that she winced. 'I have felt anger that I was blamed for sins committed by my father, but I see now what I should have done. I should have started a school in Barbados. I could have done so, even after we sold our shares in the plantation. But it seemed difficult at such a distance, and I gave up the idea. However, this morning during the worship, I felt a call to make some kind of recompense. I believe thee might be able to help me.'

Dorcas looked bewildered. Was he about to suggest sending her to Barbados? The older members of the Meeting came closer now, wondering what on earth was happening.

However, it seemed Thomas had Netherdale rather than the West Indies in mind. 'I sensed the Lord's presence today, and felt called to do something, here in the dale, for the children and youth. Such schemes require time, money, and commitment. And teachers with knowledge and patience. So, I would like to try a small experiment. If I can hire a suitable room for a school and pay thee a small salary, Dorcas, would thee be willing to be the first teacher?'

For a moment, we were all struck dumb. Minnie, who had wriggled through the surrounding crowd, spoke first. 'Our Mammie's sick,' she stated, 'and we think my Papa is lost in the war, so us couldn't afford for me and Edgar to go to school.' Her tone seemed to say that to even suggest such a thing was ridiculous.

I felt Grandma's eyes on me. *Father's golden guineas.* It would mean sacrificing the idea of purchasing the new young horse, even the coat and neck cloths I'd hoped to buy. But like Thomas Parkinson, we, *I*, needed to right old wrongs – become the opposite of what my father had been – do some good in this world for children like Minnie and Edgar. And, of course, for Dorcas. With that, into my mind shot a further thought, so startling that I was afraid to examine it further.

'I'm sure, if Dorcas is willing,' I found myself saying, 'and a suitable schoolroom can be found, it ought to be possible to set up a fund to help children whose parents cannot afford their lessons.'

But before I could even unscramble my thoughts, the Elder who had started all this with his choice of scripture, spoke up.

'I thank Thomas Parkinson for his generous suggestion,' he said gravely, 'but if this is to be an undertaking with the approval and support of this Meeting, it must surely be discussed at our next monthly Meeting for business.'

'And before that, at our women's Meeting on Fourth Day,' said Lydia Hutton. 'I am sure my daughter would be interested in assisting in setting up such a school, but it must be done with proper consideration.'

'In right ordering, prayerfully, and under God's guidance, added her husband. Had Thomas offended the gathering by raising matters in the wrong way? Or could the son really never be forgiven for the sins of his father?

I asked Nathaniel about this as we proceeded up the dale with the younger members of Braithwaite and the Hutton families. Grandma was on horseback, the rest of us on foot. 'It's not that,' he replied. 'My father-in-law may see him as too full of enthusiasm, too hasty to do good without first thinking it over. We call it discernment. Every detail of any plan must be carefully considered several times over. Is it truly the Lord's will? Are we fully clear? Who will commit time and money to such a scheme? I accept it is right to do so, but it can be mightily frustrating,' he told me with a sigh.

'That's right, said Young Wilf. 'Papa and the other elders will say, "Is it in right ordering?" when everyone can see 'tis the answer. Drives thee mad it does, at times.'

'There is no problem, surely, about there being a commitment of time and money for a school?' I asked. 'This Thomas Parkinson seems prosperous, and eager to pay for it.'

'Aye, and to get back into the Lancaster elders' good books,' said Nathaniel.

'And perhaps he'll get to marry Rachel Stout at last,' Susannah giggled.

'But he seems a good man, surely they'll accept him?' Grandma demanded, from her seat atop Polly. 'Is it not possible to cleanse bad money by doing some good?' I prayed that she would refrain from saying more.

'What do you feel about this?' I asked Dorcas, trudging beside me, silent until now.

'There is much to consider,' she said gravely. 'I'm in sympathy with the idea of holding classes for the children and young people of Netherdale, or even any adults who've never had a chance of schooling. However, I was not a success with the younger children, as I told thee. They would much rather have been playing with their hoops and spinning tops than learning the alphabet and chalking their slates. That was why I asked – for help and advice, and he – that man – chose to misunderstand me.'

It was fortunate that she walked on the side of my crippled arm because I felt an urge to give her a comforting squeeze.

We walked on in silence until we reached the turning for Low Bield. Home. I expected that we would part here, allowing Grandma and me to discover what Katie had cooked for lunch. Meanwhile, the Braithwaites would turn aside towards their farm, and the Huttons would carry on up the fellside to Rush Ghyll.

But up ahead stood three figures, obviously waiting to speak to us. Two were skinny fellows dressed in a multifarious collection of clothing. One was a much larger man in a greatcoat and seaboots. He held the reins of a pony trap in one hand and patted the pocket of his coat with the other. The pocket bulged as though it contained something hard and bulky.

The Américains!

'Bonjour mes amis,' boomed the Sea Captain, for it was undoubtedly he. He swept off his hat in an extravagant bow. 'Nous sommes libres! Now free! Prison n'est plus! Take ship back to America. Louisiana.'

So, someone had decided to let these fellows go free.

The rascally Captain had, I suppose, every right to be pleased with himself. He'd reclaimed his two missing men. His ship presumably still waited in the bay. He had endured imprisonment and given away nothing to the enemy. And now he had come to say goodbye. Or had he? His eyes, agleam with mischief, sought out one person. Dorcas Hutton. With his free hand, he indicated the cart.

Instinctively, Dorcas stepped forward. 'Bonjour, Monsieur,' she said, 'Vous sont partir?'

He nodded, smiling, all the while gesturing to the pony cart, signalling that she might, if she wished, step aboard.

I think Dorcas understood more quickly than the rest of us, and for a second or two, she even considered his offer, but then she shook her head, laughing. 'Mais non, je vous remercie! Bon voyage.'

Then the three men leapt aboard the cart, and the Captain shook the reins. Off they went, bowling down the lane, past Dalefoot, past Lane End farm, towards Morecambe Bay and the sea. Bound for Louisiana. As they rounded a bend and disappeared from view, Dorcas's Sea Captain dragged a pistol from his pocket and fired a shot in the air, sending the rooks in the tree tops shrieking in alarm.

'Sensible of ye, to turn him down,' said Grandma. 'Likely he has a wife and six or seven bairns at home.'

Chapter Fifty-Five

Dorcas' Journal

Sunday, 12th June

I did not intend to speak in Meeting, but I suddenly found myself on my feet, compelled. It was Abraham Wilson's ministry that brought it all into my heart, the Bible passage from the letters of Timothy. I had sought to be worthy of my hire, but was prevented. As Susannah rightly said, my story should at least have been heard, but the governors and the elders brushed it aside.

Well, my speaking caused a storm. Hugh Armstrong's grandmother, Elspeth Muir, who doesn't quite understand our ways, ministered in my support. She has been very kind to me. And then, afterwards, Thomas Parkinson, a banker in Lancaster, whom I hardly know, proposed starting a school here in the dale, and asked would I care to become the teacher.

Mama and Papa say this needs careful consideration. We must not be swept away by notions which have not been properly tested. We do not even know whether the people of the village and surrounding farms feel the need for such a thing. While it might be welcomed for the young children, the young adults might find studying difficult after a long day's work in the fields.

Papa says there could even be ill feeling. It seems Theophilus Chorley (I believe that's his name), urged by his parishioners, already has plans for a day school where the families would pay a small fee. He would be very offended if we started a rival, free one. In his eyes, it would be taking the children away from his 'true church'.

Certainly, nothing can happen, not even serious discussions, before the wheat is harvested.

Later

I don't know what to write, or even what to think about the Captain. For a moment, I thought he meant his offer to take me to America, and wondered if I should climb up into his cart and go – leaving all these considerations about my life and what I am called by God to do behind. However, it must have been a jest. I never even learned his name. Also, I'm sure Elspeth Muir is right, and he very likely has a wife and children in Louisiana. As he drove away, he fired a pistol in the air, scaring everybody and sending up all the birds for miles around.

It was a surprise to see Hugh and his grandmother at Meeting. Hugh came to Sukie's wedding, of course. However, I suspect that although he likes our family, even, I believe, quite likes me, and does not despise our strange ways, he still finds silent Worship uncomfortable. I will never forget his first meal at the farm, when we gave him the wobbly chair.

Chapter Fifty-Six

Hugh

September

The year had moved on. Two more months, I thought, and I will have been a whole year in Netherdale.

Yesterday, I had found Lydia Hutton in her kitchen, surrounded by preserving jars.

'Ah, there thee is Hugh.' She hardly paused to look up, almost as though I was one of her children. 'Thy grandmother got off safely?'

'Yes, I put them on the stage at the King's Arms. Katie was the picture of misery, of course.'

At this, she looked up properly and laughed. 'Elspeth gave up the idea of going on to London then?'

'Greatly to Katie's relief. Grandma had some idea of seeing the sights, but now and then her heart reminds her that she isn't a young woman anymore.'

'Will she come back again?'

'I don't know. As we know, her heart is not strong. And Katie is most unhappy travelling. The motion of the coach makes her sick.'

'Poor creature! Elspeth told me she rescued her from an evil situation.'

'She did, and makes a slave of the lass, but I doubt Katie will ever leave her. For all she complains, she knows she'll always have a roof over her head and food on her plate with Grandma.'

'Ah, yes. It's more than so many poor creatures can hope for in this world. Thee delivered those things I sent to Rachel and Eliza Stout?'

'I did. And those for your daughter Susannah, and I managed to bring the horse and cart back safely. I handed Steadfast over to Young Wilf just now. I hear your husband is going with Jonathan to take Isaac back to school.' I'd noticed that we were not mentioning Dorcas, who I had left with the Stout sisters along with two baskets of apples, a smaller one of hazel nuts, and a round of cheese.

Lydia smiled. 'Not because we fear Jonathan would be tempted to run off with the travelling fair! He would happily have gone on his own. However, Wilfred plans to meet with the superintendent at the school to discuss Isaac's progress and ask his advice about Betsey, who's eager to go, but still very young to leave home. I want her to wait, but Wilfred thinks perhaps she should go next year. She could have some time at the Friends' School in Lancaster, but...' She twisted her mouth. 'We are counselled against bearing grudges. However, matters there were not dealt with as they should have been. Of course, we suggested her sister could teach Betsey, but Betsey scorns that idea.'

'I don't think I would have responded well if one of my brothers had tried to teach me,' I said, laughing.

'Thy brothers are both dead?'

'Yes,' I replied, 'one on a Spanish battlefield and the other as the result of an accident. Together with my father.'

I suspected Grandma might have told Lydia Hutton something of our family's troubles. I didn't want to dwell on them myself.

'Your husband is out somewhere about the farm?'

'He's watching Jonathan rebuilding part of the wall in the upper meadow.' She smiled again. 'Jonathan learned a lot from Gabriel Waller that time when they reinforced the bank up on the fell road. And also, from watching those Frenchmen at work. He's eager to do some walling himself.'

'Good. Gabe had better watch out,' I said. 'It sounds as though he has a rival!'

Inspecting walls was something I must do. The 'back end,' as the farmers here call this time of year, was almost upon us. Once the harvest was in from the fields, and the stores replenished, all outstanding structural work, walls, gates, dykes and draining ditches must be made good. Already, old men were shaking their heads, predicting another harsh winter.

Soon, I thought, Sir John Hathersage would be demanding reports from me – although, since his accident, he was a quieter man, somehow less sure of himself. Nowadays, it was often Lady Hathersage who gave the orders. Which, as I was a firm favourite with the lady, made my life easier, most of the time. She was still inclined to trap me in her drawing room at Dalefoot and stand too close while she gave me instructions.

Sir John had recently bought another farm, near a place called Claughton. I hadn't yet ridden up to see it, but I must attend to that too.

Today, I found Wilfred Hutton standing in the meadow watching Jonathan at work. Beside him stood a younger boy, his daughter Betsey, and, cropping at his feet, a large Swaledale ram.

'Good day to thee!' said the farmer. 'Thee has met my son Isaac, home from school?'

I nodded to the boy, 'I saw you at Meeting last week, did I not?' Grandma had insisted on a final visit, 'to wish those good people farewell.'

'*This* is the one,' whispered Betsey to her brother behind my back, 'that they hoped might marry Dorcas.'

'Betsey! What have I said to thee about holding thy tongue?' her father snapped. 'Hugh, what does thee think of this fellow?'

'The ram?' I asked in confusion. 'A handsome beast. You've purchased him?'

'Borrowed only,' said the farmer, 'from my wife's people. Last year, we lost quite a few lambs. The bitter weather was largely to blame, but Sam Braithwaite's ram is getting on in years. It's good to bring new blood, a new strain, into the flock.'

'Yes,' I mumbled, feeling the heat rising around my collar. Was he saying he hoped I would bring new blood into a human flock, his family? Probably, I thought, he means nothing by it. Even if he did, he could not know that my grandmother's parting words had been to counsel me to 'marry that lass'.

'Why not?' said she, when I demurred. 'She's a good wee lassie, not so pretty as that sister of hers, but well enough. She's no insipid miss without a thought in her head. *And* she's been brought up to 'live simply' as these Quaker folk say. She's even set to earn her own living as an instructress with this new school they're talking of.'

'Not possible,' I had replied. 'I don't share the Quakers' beliefs. Even if her family were to give their blessing, she wouldn't be allowed to marry a heathen like me.'

'Ach, nonsense!' Grandma had said. 'Ye're nae a heathen, and would it hurt ye to sit on a hard bench for an hour once a week? Especially now ye've those new britches.'

We'd had this argument many times, Grandma and I, about my failure to attend a house of God, of any persuasion. She knew, none better, how my father had stifled any infant faith of mine, but always her argument was, 'How will it look, laddie? What'll the carriage folk hereabouts think o' ye, if ye dinna go tae church at all?'

We could name a Duke, and even a Royal landowner over towards Clitheroe. However, apart from my employer and his wife, there were few people hereabouts I would class as 'carriage folk'. Just farmers, and one or two families who thought of themselves as genteel.

Indeed, Lady Lavvy had already complained to me that the district was woefully thin of 'company'. She had seen 'nothing but dowdies' in the pews at the village church. As Grandma had predicted, she and Sir John had begun to drive there every Sunday. However, now that the excitement of furnishing Dalefoot had receded, I thought they would retreat to their townhouse in Preston once winter closed in on the dale. The one in Lancaster had been given up. (To my advantage, I may say. Lady Lavvy had given me carpets and several items of furniture, including a fine new bed.)

'Made thyself reet comfortable here, I see,' commented James Carr, who had been charged with delivering them. 'Buying that young horse from Nat Braithwaite, they say! Tha'll be getting wed next.'

'I'm in no hurry,' I said, through gritted teeth.

'Nor me.' He laughed as he drove away.

Dorcas had driven us down to Lancaster and delivered Grandma and Katie to the coach at the King's Arms before I'd dropped her off. Both of us received a parting hug from Grandma and a wan smile apiece from Katie. Perhaps it was just relief on the maid's part that they were bound for Fife at last.

I missed my grandmother, but part of me was thankful to have my home back; to please myself, to enjoy my solitary existence at Low Bield again. Perhaps I would at last draft another poem. Composition had been impossible with Grandma ever present.

As we crossed the town to our next destination, the home of the Stout sisters, I found myself saying as much to Dorcas.

'I should like to read one of your poems,' she said, gravely. 'I had no idea thee wrote them until Elspeth Muir mentioned it.' Then, seeing that I was loath to discuss it further, she said, 'We Quakers are not encouraged to read fiction or poetry, but I... I have a liking for stories.' She indicated a bundle at her feet. 'I'm returning a book dear Eliza Stout lent me. *Pride and Prejudice, by a Lady.* Has thee heard of it?'

'A novel? Isn't that forbidden?'

'Not forbidden exactly, but discouraged.' She chuckled. 'I'm afraid it's my secret sin. I love novels too much to give them up. I've never had sight of much poetry, but I believe I would like it. That prayer Elspeth Muir recited up at High Bield – when we were all there with the Frenchmen – by the Scottish bard, Robert Burns? It had nothing exalted about it, nothing 'poetic'. It was very humble and sincere. I plan to seek out a book of his poems while I'm staying with Rachel and Eliza.'

'I could lend you one,' I said, and was rewarded with a smile.

We arrived at the house of the Stout sisters and found Susannah there too, waiting to greet us. There, I left the womenfolk disputing in which of their houses they should drink tea. I declined for myself, saying I must take Steadfast and the cart away.

I may have imagined it, but I thought the women exchanged disappointed glances. But balancing a tea cup, whilst parrying intimate questions about one's future intentions, is a situation a man, especially a man with a crippled arm, will, if he is wise, avoid.

Chapter Fifty-Seven

Dorcas' Journal

Thursday, 8th September, Lancaster

It has been good to spend two weeks with dear Eliza Stout, and especially to have Susannah so close. However, she is still worried about Nathaniel. It seems he has a persistent cough and a fluctuating mild fever, which he cannot throw off. Several people have told her it may be that the atmosphere in the mill doesn't suit him. I must agree that when Sukie and I drove out to see it, I found the workrooms uncomfortably damp and, strangely, at the same time, dusty. It seems that in the weaving process, the threads rub against one another, creating constant dust. This is barely visible to the eye but is easily inhaled. Most of the workers seem untroubled by it, insisting that silk is easier to work with than cotton, but it may be that Nat is more susceptible. To comfort her, I reminded Sukie that he had never before lived in the town, amongst the dirt from coal fires and manufactory, as well as constant dust at the mill. I do pray it may not prove to be the start of something more serious, because it would break my sister's heart to lose him.

My own future has taken a strange turn. Since Elspeth Muir spoke up for me at that memorable First Day Meeting, all our friends and acquaintances have sought to find a way forward for me. I believe the Lord has indeed had a hand in it.

It happened that, very soon after Abraham Wilson spoke on that passage from Timothy, he and his wife were suddenly asked to take in their three grandchildren. Their mama is sick, and their governess has given notice. Her husband is taking her to Harrogate for the cure. So, I am to teach Tobias, and Sarah, twins of eleven, and Amelia, who is nine. The women's Fourth Day morning Meeting has suggested that I might include Minnie Ryeland, and Betsey too, if she would like it. Betsey is torn. She has always resisted my efforts to instruct her, but she dislikes thinking she is missing anything. Our classes are to be held, for the time being, every weekday morning in the Wilsons' parlour in the village, and the Wilsons are to pay me a small salary.

As yet, there is no news of when we may start our experiment with the Adult School. Friends are still 'discerning the way forward', just as we all feared. However, this coming winter, I am determined to try it in a small way. Papa has offered to help me. I do think he would have been an excellent teacher if he had not been a farmer.

The last days of my stay in Lancaster have been a whirl of acquiring copy books, pens, pencils, a globe, and other supplies, such as a French dictionary, for my little school.

Tomorrow, I have heard that someone is coming to drive me and my packages home. Mama's note did not say who this might be. Eliza, hearing this, gave me very meaningful glances. She has taken a great fancy to Hugh Armstrong, and keeps hinting that perhaps he and I might...? Susannah has also dropped hints, but I pretend to be deaf. I do not think what they hope will ever happen.

Thursday, 20th October.

I have not had time of late to write my journal. Every evening, I prepare lessons for the following day, and have little time to record my thoughts and feelings. I think my little school is progressing satisfactorily. The Wilsons' grandchildren are well-behaved and easy to manage, though not clever. Betsey could easily outsmart them, but her pride is held in check by Minnie Ryeland. At nine years old, she is the sharpest of them all. When I reported this, the women's Fourth Day Meeting decided to recommend that Monthly Meeting pay for her to go to Ackworth with Betsey next year. Her mother continues very sick and melancholic, and we do not see her, although Minnie always comes and brings her little brother on First Day.

When Elspeth Muir went home, she left behind the old pony and the broken cart she had hired to bring her up the dale. The pony, having spent the summer eating its head off in our meadow, is much improved in health and now quite lively. Wilf and Jonathan mended the cart. Papa decreed that we ought to return the pony and cart to their owner, but Elspeth Muir said she didn't know the man's name. 'And why should ye?' she said. 'That skellum likely stole it in the first place!' Her view of honest dealing did not quite align with Papa's.

However, despite making enquiries at the beast market and roundabout, no one could find the owner. So, the pony, whom we called 'Elspeth's mare' and, once she left, just Elspeth, is loaned to me. She carries me and my basket of school books to and from the village each day. It is pleasant to have my own means of transport.

Chapter Fifty-Eight

Hugh

November

The day was dry, but cold and windy. Winter would soon be upon us. I tramped, heavy-hearted, across the dale from Quernstones farm, where I had been impressing on Daniel Jackson the need to clear a drainage ditch on his land.

'With the next heavy rainfall, it will back up and flood the garden at Dalefoot – and displease Lady Lavinia.'

'I'm not feeling too well,' he croaked. 'My old trouble, the quinsy. I don't know if my lads could do it – if tha was to supervise them. Or I could send fer Gabriel. Only he's allus on at Tim and Phil to join his chapel.'

We both grimaced.

'Didn't I hear tha's joined our lot?' he enquired. I declined to satisfy his curiosity. 'Ah heard tha's been at Meeting a few First Days? I reckon the Huttons will be disappointed if tha doesn't wed that lass of theirs.'

I dragged him back to the subject of the collapsed drainage ditch. 'Have Timothy and Philip come and find me tomorrow. *Fourth* day, if you will, bringing trenching spades if you have them – if not, I'll borrow some from Sam Braithwaite – and I'll see if we can clear it.'

'Tha'll see if *they* can clear it,' he replied, looking at my useless arm in a meaningful fashion.

Holding on to my hat (the wind was blustery) and my temper, I left him.

My pocket contained a letter. In a barely legible hand, Jinny, Katie's sister, had written to inform me that my grandmother had suffered a heart attack and was very sick. Grandma's triumphant return to Scotland must have been too much for her. Jinny urged me to make haste back to Fife. Poor Katie had scrawled her name at the bottom.

Setting out immediately was impossible. First, I must get permission from Sir John and Lady Lavvy. They were in Preston – as I'd predicted, now that colder weather had arrived, country living had lost its appeal. And even if I left today, I might be too late.

Pale beams of sunlight broke through the clouds, pointing to the place I was making for. It was a small enclosure, an unproductive corner of Daniel's land, walled and gated, the entrance guarded by a single Scots pine. Little grew here except coarse grass and stunted saplings. Yet it had an atmosphere of warmth and peace. I leant on the narrow gate, waiting for the calm I always found here to wash over me. Whenever I came to this place, I felt it possible that I might recapture that faith I had lost in infancy – the faith my grandmother still had, despite everything.

Dorcas had told me that this was where the first Quakers in Netherdale were buried. 'When George Fox and his followers first came to Netherdale,' she said, 'many were convinced by his teachings, but when they died, the priests would not accept them in the churchyard. So, an ancestor of Daniel's gave them this plot.'

'There are no headstones. Did they not believe in the Second Coming?'

'They didn't think them necessary,' she replied. 'God would know where to find them.'

'Quakers no longer believe in the Second Coming?'

She had frowned. 'I cannot think it is *imminent*, because there are still so many wrongs to be righted.'

'And you, Dorcas Hutton, intend to right them.' I said in a mischievous tone.

'We must each do what we can,' she'd replied, looking hurt.

That was one of our many misunderstandings.

Today, I became aware of the sound of hooves. A cart stopped in the lane below. Someone got down, and the pony moved off. Betsey Hutton sat triumphant in the driving seat. She waved as Dorcas came walking up the slope.

'Your last lesson with the Wilson grandchildren?' I asked when she joined me at the gate.

'Yes. Their mother is well again. They go home next week.'

'So, your little school is at an end?'

'No, the Wilsons say I may go on using their parlour for Minnie, Betsey, and Minnie's little brother, on two mornings each week. And I am planning for the new school, now that Thomas Parkinson has purchased the land, as he promised.'

We stood in silence for some minutes, gazing over the little graveyard.

'Hugh, I have thought about what thee asked me...' she began.

'There is no hurry for your answer,' I interrupted. I took the letter from my pocket and gave it to her. She read it in silence.

'I'm so sorry,' she said. 'We all liked your grandmother so much. She is a good woman, a fine person. Thee is going to her?'

'I must. Even if I'm too late, there will be much to do. The house must be sold. I think Jinny will give Katie a home if I settle some money on her.'

'And will thee come back to Netherdale?'

'I will. And perhaps... perhaps I will apply to join the Quaker Meeting, if they will accept a Doubting Thomas?'

'Oh, that would be–' The wind rose, snatching her words.

'You'll miss me? And think about me. Think about *us*?' I was almost shouting now, the wind was so loud.

'I do think about thee, Hugh. All the time,' she replied. 'While thee is away, I will have the chance to practice the skills a good wife should have. Thee deserves a *good* wife, Hugh.'

'Those things don't matter.'

Above our heads, the old pine was now swaying dangerously. With a loud crack, a branch broke off and began to drop. I snatched her arm to pull her away, and we both tumbled over a tussock of grass, where we lay, breathless and laughing.

The broken branch had lodged across the wall. A few top stones had been pushed aside but could be quickly put right. No need to send for Gabriel Waller.

As soon as we had our breath back and had risen to our feet, I said, 'Dorcas, I *know* you will always be busy in the schoolroom, or running off to rescue unfortunates. I know my supper will sometimes be no more than bread and cheese. I want you for my wife. I want you just as you are.'

'Thee believes we can find a way to live in love and harmony?'

'Yes, I believe, together we can.'

She laid her head on my good shoulder and took my hand. 'Yes, dear Hugh. Go safely to Scotland and return. We will find a way.'

Author's Notes

This story is set in the Forest of Bowland, a geographical district set between Lancashire and Yorkshire, running through the Pennine fells, connecting Lancashire and Yorkshire. Netherdale, supposedly a side valley, is purely fictitious. The farming families in the story are also figments of my imagination and bear no relation to the present-day inhabitants of Bowland.

Prisoners of the Napoleonic Wars (1803 – 1815):

This was the first war in history in which soldiers (and sailors) captured by either side in a conflict were held prisoner rather than executed. Captured Frenchmen of the 'officer-class' were allowed to live in designated small towns up and down the UK until they could be 'exchanged' for British officers held in France or Spain. Ordinary soldiers, seamen, and people of various nationalities caught up in the conflict were imprisoned, often in dire conditions. Men from the newly formed United States of America sometimes became involved in the war on either the French or the British side, and it is known that Americans imprisoned on Dartmoor were employed to build the prison, which still stands today. I have no actual evidence that French speakers from Louisiana took part in the war on either side, but why not? Just about everyone else did.

The staff of Lancaster Castle confirmed that French Prisoners of war were incarcerated there, but there are no records available. The castle was actually used as a prison until 2011. Conditions there would have been grim, and the overcrowding in the early 1800s would have been further exacerbated by the great number of English debtors held there.

Walls:

As a child I was told that the drystone walls that snake their way over the fells throughout the North of England were built by French prisoners of war. Modern experts dismiss this as 'folk myth', although the myth also exists in North Wales and other parts of the North of England. It is unlikely that such men built complete walls (many walls have been shown to date to medieval times), but I believe it is possible that 'work gangs' of prisoners were taken out onto the fells to make repairs to existing walls. Excursions into the countryside must have seemed preferable to being stuck in stinking, overcrowded cells. Interestingly, nowadays, UNHCR runs a 'wall building programme' for Refugees and Asylum Seekers in Yorkshire.

Quakers:

The *Religious Society of Friends*, or *Friends of the Truth*. Their founder, George Fox, made many converts in North Lancashire and Westmorland in the C17th. The nickname 'Quaker' is now used more frequently than the original name. It may have arisen when George Fox urged his hearers to 'quake before the Lord.' Alternatively, his followers were seen to tremble when rising to speak during Worship (as they were encouraged to do if they felt 'the power of the Lord'). By the 1800s, what had been a radical religious group had become more staid. Great attention was paid to 'simplicity of living', particularly in dress, where dark plain colours were encouraged. Failing to 'walk orderly,' for example, by spending too much time in alehouses, gambling, or indulging in frivolous pursuits such as novel reading, and benefitting financially from the proceeds of slavery, could lead to expulsion. Marrying a non-Quaker meant having one's membership terminated too.

Plain speech:

Quakers originally used the singular form, 'thee and thou' rather than 'you' as a sign of their equality with everyone. 'You' indicated that someone was your social superior. However, by the C19th, this distinction was disappearing in general society. Quakers retained elements of plain speech, but used 'thee' more frequently than others. For instance, 'Does thee need my help?' rather than the old grammatical formation 'Needest thou my help?'

For Book Groups

Characters

1. Hugh arrives hoping for order and respectability. In what ways is he seeking stability – and in what ways is he avoiding his past?

2. How does Dorcas challenge Hugh's assumptions about authority, Religion, and himself?

3. The Quaker community values peace, integrity, and plain dealing. How do these principles influence the characters' decisions? Where do they create tension?

4. Love in the novel develops gently rather than dramatically. How does this slow unfolding shape your experience of the story?

Setting

1. *Clouds Over Bowland* is set in 1814, towards the end of the Napoleonic Wars. How does that wider conflict shape life in the valley, even though the setting feels remote and self-contained?

2. Suspicion spreads easily in small communities. How does fear – of outsiders, of war, of scandal – affect relationships in the valley?

3. Landscape plays a strong role in the book. How does the valley itself reflect the emotional lives of the characters?

Themes

1. The presence of French prisoners unsettles the community. What does the novel suggest about seeing an 'enemy' as human?

2. How does the novel portray the tension between personal conviction and communal expectation?

3. If the story were set today, which conflicts would feel different – and which would remain the same?

About the author

Rosemary Sturge is a British historical novelist with a keen interest in people as well as the past. After working for many years in nursery, further-education and youth-club settings, she returned to writing and has since produced fiction set in a range of periods, from 18th-century Venice to medieval England.

Her research for *Clouds Over Bowland* led her deep into the world of 1814 Lancashire, its rural communities, local Quaker meetings, and the little-known history of French prisoners of war held in the region. While Rosemary has been a Quaker from childhood, her husband's family have practised Quakerism since the 17th century.

www.historical-novels.co.uk

Thank you for reading.
If you enjoyed this novel, please consider leaving a review on
Goodreads or a sales platform like Amazon.

SOLD

by Sue Barrow

a thriller suitable for adults and teens

15-year-old Roza thinks she's leaving Albania for better things in the UK. As she arrives, she realises her father has sold her to get out of debt.

Adelina and Jozif Braka now consider Roza their property. They work her hard, beat and starve her, and refuse to let her go out. But she must tell people they are her parents. She runs to the police, but the Brakas produce a forged birth certificate. She is dismissed as attention-seeking and returned to them for punishment.

She doesn't think life can get much worse. However, when she tries to escape, she's sent to a holding house full of other enslaved girls.

2024 Read For Empathy collection

'Compulsively readable, harrowing yet hopeful... shines a fierce light into the shadows of child trafficking.'
THE GUARDIAN

Rosemary's self-published books

Northampton 1290

A tale of history, mystery, and a little bit of romance, in the England of King Edward I.

Give Me Again All That Was There

The story of Flora Macdonald as seen through the eyes of her maidservant Betty.

Black Nazareth

A mystery set in the 19th century in Schiedam, Holland, the capital of the gin trade.

A Storm in Summer

A mystery set on the edge of the Yorkshire Dales in the final months of the English Civil War.

Death of a Daughter of Venice

Set in the Pieta Orphanage at the time when Vivaldi was writing music for them.

www.cadencepublishing.com/rosemary-sturge

Careful!

Richard Madelin

PUBLISHING

Brooklyn, New York

Careful!

Printed in Canada

Published in the United States of America
by
Ig Publishing
www.igpub.com

ISBN 0-9703125-6-3

10 9 8 7 6 5 4 3 2 1

Madelin, Richard.
Careful! / by Richard Madelin.
p. cm.
ISBN 0-9703125-6-3 (pbk. : alk. paper)

1. People with mental disabilities—Fiction. 2. Parent and adult child—
Fiction. 3. Police—England—Fiction. 4. Mothers and sons—Fiction.
5. Accident victim—Fiction. 6. Torture victims—Fiction. 7. Kidnapping—
Fiction. 8. Brothers—Fiction. 9. England—Fiction. I. Title.

PR6113.A33C37 2004
823'.982—dc22

Cover and interior design by
Joseph Tullman

For Tom and Kate

1.

Careful! This car goes as smooth as hell. Fucking good car. Yes it is. If Jimmy could see him now, the tips of his fingers on the wheel, just like Jimmy. Give it the gun. Mum never tells him how to drive. No one can tell him what to do in this car, nobody can. Well, Jimmy sometimes. That's all right because Jimmy's his mate. They're best mates. Jimmy says so. It's true. But Mum never tells him. Never.

He touches the burn on the back of his hand. It hurts. It hurts like hell. He likes to touch it because then it isn't a cigarette burn, it's only a pain that hurts. He can do it with one hand on the wheel, touch it. That's how good a driver he is. Bleedin' good. Careful!

This car changed his life, that's what Mum says. This car changed your life, Lenny. Changed it forever and ever. A BMW, a B reg, bought at Arnie's. Big Arnie who knows a good car when he sees one, all right. Jimmy went with him so it was OK. And Jimmy knows Big Arnie. Jimmy knows what's what. Mum wouldn't want Jimmy to go with him but Mr. Wyatt said go, damn you, go and get rid of that thing, I don't want to see it again, go, go, go. And so he went. Jimmy drove with him in the

Metro, down to Big Arnie's, to see what they had.

He chose the BMW. It was the only one there. Big Arnie had only the one, the one. It was lucky. He chose it. Nobody else. He's not stupid. He's not dumb. He isn't. The color, bright red, as red as you can get. It's a good color. Like a dog's dick, Jimmy says.

He's had it for a month now. He is so cool, so cool, when he drives it. He has new boots as well. Mum bought him new boots to go with the car. He's really cool. He can drive the car everywhere. For a month he's been to places he's never been before. Mum says this car has changed his life. That's so cool. Jimmy says it's cool as well. Jimmy drives the car sometimes. He doesn't tell Mum.

Mum says now there's one thing, one thing, I want you to do, my son, now you've got the car. It's all worked out just fine. Coming together nicely. All right, all right, Mum. It's today, Lenny, she says. Today. Careful! Today he's a good boy. He's not an idiot. He passed his driving test, he did. He could do the reading, all the letters and the numbers. He could. He could. Mum went with him. She smiled at the man. Today he goes only where Mum tells him to go. All right, Mum. Careful! There's one thing, one thing, I want you to do, my son. I'm a good boy, Mummy. You're a good boy, my son. One thing, and one thing only.

2.

Alice watches, holding her breath, waiting for sunlight to shine through the trees, waiting for a shaft of light that will tell her that she does the right thing, that will tell her something, bloody anything. She won't see it. She knows full well she won't see it. She watches because she has to. God forgive her for what she is about to do. Or has already done. Lenny, my son, she thinks.

She waits, afraid to breathe, because even her breath, like butterfly wings, can change what is about to happen, can change the world. She sees Lenny turn the wheel, move out to overtake. She sees the car jerk, a spasm, twisted metal, oil on the road. She puts this aside. There is no danger. Not if you can believe it.

She closes her eyes and thinks that this is what it has to be because there is no other way. She thinks of Lenny's body settled into the seat of the car, the splay of his thighs, the weight of him. She takes in a breath that is for her own good and for his good, as it always has been. It will be all right in the end.

Think about anything. Think about the bloody weather. No sun today. No light. Rain squalling in. October is the worst and with the sun the best month.

She runs hot water into the bowl, squirts in washing-up liquid, watches the green squiggle disperse. She dips in the cloth, closes her eyes, and rubs at the stainless steel draining board, rubs as hard and as brisk as she can.

God forgive her she is not a religious woman. At fifty she feels she is too young to be intimidated into belief, but she knows that every act should be bathed in a special light to show that it is something that is lived rather than not lived. Where does the light come from? She can't answer this. She is scared, haunted by a conviction that people reach the ends of their lives and never see the light.

She opens her eyes and scrubs along the edge of the draining board, scrubs down to the edge of the sink and around the taps. These smooth lines, these worked surfaces, they upset her now where once they were comforting in themselves, in what they were, in what they told her of the world. Now she thinks how can things be so fixed, so determined, so damn sure of themselves?

She moves her fingers within the dishcloth, feels its texture, feels the hard edge of the metal, looking for reassurance. She picks up the washing-up bowl, empties it, turns on the cold tap, runs it hard, to hear the splatter in the sink, the rumble of metal.

The car is running smoothly out on the ring road. She knows this as much as she knows that by turning the tap the water will stop. She stiffens her fingers, holds them in front of her. If she could hold them still enough, poised in the air, it would be all right. It would all be all right and it would be done.

She runs the dishcloth along the edge of the table. She runs along it again. She is worried that she has missed something in the cleaning. You never can be too sure. She continues around the table. Does the same thing again. It would be a wonderful thing, to know where to draw the line. To know when a thing was finished. For good and all.

She looks through the window. The cat is darting from one place to another, picking up its paws in the sodden grass, making a run for home. She thinks it is one of those days. She goes to the cupboard and takes out a bottle. She pours a small measure into a glass, stops, but pours in more until the liquid tips the brim, a meniscus bulge that brings deep pleasure. She touches the surface with the tip of her tongue because it is good to wait. She thinks about the tongue of God. She wants to be licked by the tongue of God, which is a fearful thing. God give her strength. That is what her mother used to say. But she does not know who God is. Perhaps He is the pain in her chest as she reaches for the glass, something so close that it is a part of her. Perhaps He is the tremble in her fingers. Perhaps He is so close He will never go away. She drinks the contents of the glass, knocks it back in one, and there is a roaring in her throat and in her stomach. She pours another measure, up to the brim. Just one more, just another, because today is what it is.

3.

Before this car he had a beat-up crap Metro that was shit. That's what Jimmy said. Everybody knows about Metros. He drove Mum round in that crap car, wherever she wanted to go. It was her car, really. Sometimes Mum drove herself. Now this car is his. Even Mum says so, and it's up to him. He goes where he wants to go. This car has power, it's got guts, it motors. Except today. He's a good boy. I'm a good boy, Mummy. If you're good, nothing horrible happens. Careful!

He stops in a lay-by. A tractor and trailer in a field, a dog that barks. Seagulls. The taste in his mouth. He's still got the taste in his mouth. Mum says that's silly, it's too long ago now. He gets the can of baked beans and the tin opener off the back seat. He loves beans. He loves, loves beans. More than anything. He doesn't like chips. He's not going back to town. Never.

Open the can quick. Don't spill the juice. Keep it off the seat. It's his car and it's up to him to keep it clean. That's what Mum says. Shovel up the beans with his fingers, tip the can back and drink the juice, the few beans left, there's always some, lick his fingers. He likes licking his fingers. It's like licking the car. He doesn't do that. He could if he wanted. If he really wanted to. He might. But he isn't an idiot. It's his car. It is. Yes it is. The juice is on his jeans. Jimmy says no bird likes a dirty car.

Jimmy gets birds. He'll get birds soon. After he's fucked Maudie. Maudie's old. It doesn't matter. A bird's a bird. You've got to start somewhere, my son. That's what Jimmy says. Maudie said come down here when Susan, her daughter, is away. Maudie says people don't understand. Squeeze the empty can of beans, squeeze it up tight, put it on the floor behind the seat, next to the Belter. Touch the Belter. He's killed so many rabbits with the Belter. They get trapped in the net. He gets rabbits with Mr. Wyatt and Jimmy, and Pat, Mr. Wyatt's dog. Pat the dog. Get it? Pat the dog, pat the dog. It's not cruel, killing rabbits. They don't feel it, not one bit. So that's all right, then.

Touching the Belter makes him want to drive fast. Take the Belter, son, Mum said. Mr. Wyatt said get rid of the Metro. He shouted at him, and Pat the dog barked. Mr. Wyatt said he was going to buy him a new car. Get rid of the Metro, bloody get rid of it, you stupid sod, get rid of it as fast as you can. Mr. Wyatt told him he was a bloody fool to use his car to carry all that stuff up to the top field. Didn't he know there was a tractor and trailer for the sacks of fertilizers? But he was in a hurry, a great big hurry. Taking his car meant he could drive straight back to see Maudie. She said he could fuck her. Maudie's old, but it's all right. White stuff seeped out of slits in the sacks. The slits shouldn't have been there. White dust coated the windows so that he polished a hole to look through, like he was using his initiative, like Mum said, like Mr. Wyatt said, use your initiative, to see where he was going. His eyes stung and his throat was sore and it wouldn't go away. So he didn't go to Maudie's. Maudie didn't mind. She says he's a good boy. Maudie doesn't hurt him. She teaches him to draw.

He was pleased the next day because he stacked the sacks in the field, all neat, like Mr. Wyatt liked. But he couldn't clean the inside of the car. He couldn't get the white off the seats and out of all the cracks. It stayed and there was nothing he could do. That was when Mr. Wyatt got mad, the next day. Get that bloody car out of my sight, Mr. Wyatt said when he saw it. But it wasn't his fault. It wasn't.

When Mr. Wyatt speaks his teeth click. It's funny, but Lenny doesn't laugh. Mum said not to. Mr. Wyatt said take the Metro up to Big Arnie's yard smartish. Big Arnie breaks cars, piles of them, smashes them up because they're crap. But sometimes he sells them. Mr. Wyatt told him to choose a car, any car that Big Arnie said was all right, with the price, the money from Mr. Wyatt, which he said over the phone, the money, he did. Just get rid of the Metro.

He could have cleaned it and it would have been all right. But Mr. Wyatt said no. Pat barked and jumped up at him. Pat wanted to play but Mr. Wyatt wouldn't let him. Mr. Wyatt asked what he was doing still hanging about. He drove up to Big Arnie's. Didn't stop on the way, not to look at the chicks in the box in the yard by the house, not to drive the wrong way in the lay-by where the bus stops, not to look in the stream where Jimmy says the big fish live although he's never seen them, never. Jimmy tells lies sometimes. He doesn't mind. Lying's cool.

The taste in his mouth, on his tongue, at the back of his throat. Like some sweets are, only more. It hurts. It's sharp like an apple but he's never tasted an apple so sharp. The can of beans makes no difference. It doesn't take the taste away like he wants it to. There's a pain in his guts. There's a pain, Mum. Oh, shut up, Lenny. I've got more to think about than you. Today's the day. That's what Mum says. He's a good boy. This is a good motor. Careful!

The empty can, pick it up. He promised Mum he'd keep this car clean. No sacks, no fertilizers. Nothing else too. But there's nothing wrong with being hungry, and there's the taste in his mouth. He has to eat, must eat to keep up his strength. There's nothing wrong, Mum.

The engine purring. Throw the can away and keep the car clean. He'll do it. It's a good car. He could lick it all over. The windows, the doors, the bonnet, the boot, the tires, the seats. He likes licking. But he isn't an idiot. Pick up the can, reach for it, hold the wheel. Wait until there's a gap in the traffic and open the window and throw the can out. Good boy. Careful!

He knows where he has to go. He went there with Mum. She wouldn't stroke his arm on the way. She shouted at him to remember. Don't shout, Mum. She told him what to look for when he turned off. Where to turn down the lane. Where the gate was. Where the space on the grass was, to park the car. Stroke my arm, Mum. Not unless you listen. Listen to me, Lenny.

He feels the pain in his guts to go with the taste in mouth. Sometimes he wants to drive away, like Jimmy's going to do, one day. He could if he wanted. Mum says he could never drive to get away, not that far, not far enough, not while she's alive. Mum isn't going to die. It's a trick.

He knows he could drive far away. He's a good driver. But Mum won't die. The pain in his guts is worse, worse than the taste. Sometimes Mum says she'll send him back into town to live. She did that once. But he won't go again.

He's never had a car like this before. He's seen a new dent at the back. Jimmy didn't do it, not when he drove it to town from the farm. Jimmy says things like that happen. But he knows what he has to do to fix it. Jimmy said he'd help. You use filler.

Sometimes Jimmy says this car's not up to much but he's only joking. It's a trick. Lenny likes tricks, they're good. Sometimes he doesn't like them. It depends. You can have things like that, both at the same time. And anyway, you can't really see it much, the dent. He won't touch it. But he knows it's there, like it's in his head. Things are always there and not there. Like it's a trick.

4.

Alice cleans as she waits. Something for her hands to do. She is a sum of too many parts, divided, incomplete. Harold kissed her for the first few years, but those years didn't count. His stubbled chin on her cheek, his grizzled moods. After Lenny was born, he wouldn't touch her. But you'd expect that, wouldn't you?

She cleans the kitchen because everything eventually has to fall into place. She moves the pepper pot and the saltcellar, each a fraction of an inch. She moves a small plastic ornament that has played no part in her life. Fills the plastic red bowl again with hot water to the brim. Squeezes in washing-up liquid. Finds a sponge under the sink, balls it up into the palm of her hand and plunges it into the water. She shouts, waiting for the pain to hit her. She releases the sponge and it uncurls, reverts to the shape it has.

She stands on a chair and pushes the sponge along the wall above the curtain rail where cobwebs collect. Black cobwebs are a sign, they've always been a sign. Too many signs, not enough meaning. She scrubs but the blackened spiders' legs are laminated onto the wall. She lives in a world where things do not always follow one another in the way that they should. That world was abandoned in the park when Lenny was on the swings.

She pauses halfway along the rail, the sponge leaking hot water. She thinks back to the swings but she pushes the sponge past the moment, pushes it hard, against the wall, against dead spiders' legs. She gets off the chair and squeezes the sponge into the bucket, scoops it briefly into the water to replenish it. She picks off dead spiders' legs as water drips onto the chair. The hardest thing is to know where to draw the line.

You can rearrange the world if you have a mind to, but the world has a way of rearranging it back. She called her first son Jack, after Jack Kerouac and *On the Road*. She liked to think she was a freewheeler. It was a time she wouldn't forget. She called her second son Lenny after Lenny Bruce, the comedian. She loved Lenny Bruce because he wouldn't give up, however hopeless it was. After the swings, after the accident, it became Lenny in *Of Mice and Men*. That's irony for you. That's sarcasm. That's wit. She didn't know then that the world's not easily rearranged.

Today, it's up to her Lenny. She can't be a part of this. She doesn't have the capacity to do such a thing. But she tries to not think of it as a failing in herself. A wise person knows her strengths and weaknesses. She sighs. Sometimes a sigh will take you from one moment to another. It will keep you going.

Harold's weight pushes down hard onto her as he

gets up from the bed. She turns away from him, does not want to see. She used to forgive him before the boys came along, because then there was a sense of give and take, something between them that could get better or worse. But afterward neither of them had anything to trade. Harold stood cupping his cock and balls and she saw menace but she knows now that menace was the last thing on his mind. Harold was helpless. That was why he cupped his cock and his balls. He didn't know what else to do.

She scrubs the faded wood at the side of the window. The sponge slides easily but she's not fooled. She knows that anything that is easily done is stored up for trouble later. She hopes Lenny remembers the turning. She's told him enough times. She thinks of his pudgy face, sweat shining as he tries to remember, as he searches for the right place. The white of the scar at the side of his forehead shining through as a reminder. Everything he does, he does with her consent. But there is nothing wrong with that. She makes it happen. Without her, he is nothing.

Sometimes when Lenny is in the bathroom she goes in and holds him and pushes her face, her nose, her chin, against his face as hard as she can until it hurts. She wants to be with him so that he knows it's all right. She wants to smell him, the worst of him, so that he knows that there's nothing he can do that will stop her from loving him. She wants to hurt him to let him know that nothing will come between them. She wants to hurt him sometimes so much that she grits her teeth and thinks of nasty things. She pinches him, a layer of his fat between her forefinger and thumb, and she will not let go. This is how much I love you, son, she says. He whimpers. He doesn't understand. Pain is part of love. The mutt, the fool. Don't you fucking see? she says. Don't you see? Well do you? Speak to me, my stupid son.

She pushes the sponge along the windowsill. She looks outside. Rain hits the flagstones in the yard. Water streams from a split in the downpipe on the barn wall and hammers against the water butt. She stops with the sponge raised, dripping. She thinks perhaps it is a good thing that it rains. It fills up the spaces, helps you forget.

Her hands feel cold and unattached. She knows that when everything is all right they will belong to her. Sometimes you have to do something to lay claim to your body. Sometimes she washes herself all over in scalding water. Sometimes she does this several times a day. Sometimes it hurts so much that she has to smear cream between her legs, onto her thighs, sitting at the kitchen table, the light weak from the bulb high up above her, and not speak to Lenny as he asks his dumb questions. Her stupid son. She does not want to attach blame. She does not want to blame Lenny. It's too easy to do that. Lenny is not stupid. It's just that the sense is trapped in his body and won't come out.

Above all else, she likes the idea of revelation. The

idea that a moment can be divorced from the one that precedes it, and the one that comes after it, and exists with a life of its own, and nothing is then ever the same again. She believes that Lenny seeks some sort of release, as he drives, as he bends down to pick up a sack, as he wipes away sweat, as he touches his scar. She believes that it will come. She believes that somehow, in his own way, he knows this. It is his part of the bargain between them. The light will shine on Lenny. She has waited for the last twelve years.

5.

Today is different. He drives in the rain. He likes his hands on the wheel. They feel good. He looks in the mirror and sees the line of stickers in the back window. He likes colors, greens and reds and blues. He likes Big Arnie, who sells cars, although it isn't allowed. Sometimes he drives to the yard and talks to him. He didn't see Arnie smash up the Metro. Mr. Wyatt told Big Arnie to do it that day. He didn't see it. He went back to work. Big Arnie is his friend now. Hello, Lenny, he says. You need friends in this world. Jimmy is his friend. Pat the dog is his friend.

He's got the day off. He asked Mr. Wyatt. He didn't ask Jimmy. He didn't have to do that. Mum said today is special. But not to say. He didn't tell, not even Jimmy. He's a good boy. Mum said today was different. It is different. Careful!

He looks for a big sign that tells him where to turn, a big sign on a corner that Mum showed him, where a horse puts its head over a gate, by a shed, a bathtub, a wooden fence. The horse drinks from the tub, he knows it because he saw him. He wants to see him drink today. It's a friendly horse, but it's sad. You can tell.

He drives along the straight road, past a hedge, and he strokes the dashboard. It feels good. He looks in the mirror. He presses his foot down but there's no sign.

He stops in a lay-by and starts to cry. A white space fills the car. It won't go away, ever. He puts his hands on his face and looks at the floor of the car through his fingers. The white is sticking to his face. Go away, go away. He cries and he hits the dashboard. He does it again. Careful! He thinks he'll go back now to look for where he missed where he was going.

He turns the car around in the road. He loves it when the car turns, how it sounds. He doesn't mind the creak he hears as he turns the steering wheel. He doesn't mind the noise of a wheel. This is a good car, Jimmy says so. It's red.

Maybe he won't see the turning. His nose starts to run. But he'll see the horse. He likes the horse. He'll see it drinking. He looks in the mirror, clicks the signal and passes a lorry. He's good at overtaking. He likes to talk to Mum when he drives, even when she's not there. He's a good driver, she says, even though she's not there in the car.

He's crying again. He missed the turning. He missed the horse. Mum said he'd like the horse. He wants to stop and stroke it. Mum said not today. But she's not here. He can do it if he wants to. He can. The horse will like him.

He speeds up. Careful!, Mum says, even though

she isn't there. He sees a herd of cows and looks to see if there's a horse in them, hiding. They have their heads down to the grass. He could be friends with them. He could pat them. But they don't know about the horse. He cries harder now, because he knows about the seconds, minutes, and the hours, the things that roll in his head.

He has to do this. Mum said so. Seconds, minutes, hours. The white space. There's a clock in the car but he won't look. It's got hands. He doesn't like hands, the big one and the little one. Why doesn't this car have a clock with numbers that will tell him what to do? Seconds, minutes. He feels the burn on the back of his hand. It doesn't hurt. It doesn't. Not anymore. Careful!

He sees a horse at a corner, a gate, a horse. It isn't the one. He sees the shed and the bath. It is the one. He signals. You have to do that. He waits for traffic and turns, both hands on the wheel. He hears the car moaning. It's all right. It's a good car. Jimmy says so. Big Arnie says so.

He slows at the corner to see the horse but he knows he can't do that now. There's only one turning, she said. You can't miss it. Why isn't she with him? There could be another turning, one that's there to trick him. There could be turnings both sides. There could be another horse, back the other way. Which way does he go then? What if the horse isn't there when he comes back? Will it be the wrong turning?

He stops with the wheels on the verge. It is the

lane. He switches off the engine and squeezes the steering wheel so that it hurts. The burn on his hand doesn't hurt. Not really. The one on his face was worse, when she did it there. He made her really mad. I'm sorry, Mum. Darling, she said. That's his head against her arm then, the smell of her so that he can't move. Don't let me go, Mum. Her fingers on his arm, the first two fingers on his wrist. Don't move, Lenny. I won't move, Mum. The pain is what joins things together, son, nothing else. It's good then. I love you, my son. I love you, Mum. Careful!

He starts the car and moves it forward ever so slow. He turns to see the horse. He drives along the road but things fill up his head so he can't see it. He keeps going. Mum told him to. I love you, Mum. Careful!

6.

The swing goes back and it comes forward and it goes back and it comes forward again. It stops, suspended, the chains shivering, and there's nothing that can be done. Alice sees wet flagstones outside, water glistening on the grass under the trees, rain hitting hard against the window. The car is moving on the ring road, then off the ring road, down through the lane, and the swing is moving, Lenny's hands on the chains, his fingers, squeezing. Catch hold, my son. She is looking through a hedge, dreaming, paralyzed by the weak light of the sun. Turn around. Look, for God's sake, look now. This is when you have to look.

Lenny's hands are on the wheel, she knows it, and he will do this thing now. He will do it and that will be an end to it. But of course it will not be an end. It will be a beginning. She is not sure if she likes beginnings.

She stands on the chair and feels more detached than at any other time in her life. More than the years with Harold. More than the time on her own with Lenny, when it was all she could do to stay here with him, with the smell of him, his big body, his hot cheek pressed against her arm. He went back to nappies for a time.

Thank God he soon got over that. It wasn't the smell. She could love him even for that. It was just the having to do it.

She feels detached, floating, between the commissioning of the act and the act itself. The cat is crying at the door but she will not get down. She has to feel this now. Getting down does not come into it. She thinks of the cat's spiked, sodden fur, the lifting of its paw, its insistent cry. She will not get down. She is stuck where she is.

She listens. Listening is something in itself, true to itself. She listens to the cat and something beyond it and below it, deeper. She listens for spiders, a movement of the curtains, a creak of water in the pipes, the creak of the chair, wind in the chimney. She listens for Maude Edgecombe who visits her when she least expects it. Maude Edgecombe, who thinks of her as a friend because they share secrets. Maude does not know that she prepares these secrets, that they are something she trades in order to keep who she is intact. Alice tells her of a woman in another village who is pregnant and gives birth and does not know she is pregnant until her water breaks. Maude wants to know the woman's name. That is the point of a story like this. But she will not tell her. There is no woman. There is no name. There is no point. Maude does not see things like that.

Standing on the chair she thinks that perhaps, in her turn, Maude makes allowances for her. Thinks of her as a close friend and thus forgives her. This tilts her world and she is in danger of falling. The window lurches and the cat's cry changes to a scream. The swing moves forward and it goes back and there is nothing she can do.

She steadies herself and listens but there is no Maude. She listens and wonders how many other allowances have been made for her in her life. By Harold, and by Jack, and by Lenny, perhaps. Even by Lenny. By her parents, her grandparents, her friends. She knows she is trapped, everyone is, but it is knowing what to do with it that counts.

She stands on the chair and listens, trapped by the weather, the time of day, wind that whips through the branches of the trees, Lenny in the car. She wants to get down but still there are things to do. The secret, she knows, is where to draw the line. That is what she has to find out, what she has to know. How to act, when to act, when to bide her time.

7.

He slows down in the lane, goes past a car on the verge. A woman stands in the rain pointing into the field, her arm held up in the air. What is the woman pointing at? Why is she doing that? A girl stands by the woman. The girl doesn't mind the rain. He can tell. Why are they there? It's always like this, the things that people know, the things he doesn't.

He drives on. Careful! He brakes on the hill. He wants to go faster but he's not allowed. Not today, my lad. He opens the glove compartment but there's no can of beans, no packet of pork scratchings, no pork pie. He licks his fingers instead. It isn't as good.

He drives until the road curves, past the stream and the pond and the white ducks. Mum told him not to stop at the ducks today. He wants to stop and see them swim and waddle when they walk, wag their tails. But he's a good boy. Careful!

He likes the note of the engine. Jimmy says it purrs. He likes the way the windshield wipers go, slapping, slap, slapping. He likes the feel of the passenger seat under his hand. He likes the speed of the car with his foot on the pedal. He doesn't care about the rumble in the wheel. It's nothing. He wishes that Mr. Wyatt could see him now. Mr. Wyatt and Pat the dog. And Jimmy. Jimmy says the car's all right, that it purrs. Nothing to worry about. It's good to have friends.

He touches the burn on the back of his hand. It hurts. It won't go away. Don't touch it, Mum said. But he can touch it if he wants. Mum put a plaster on it. He took it off. It didn't hurt. He's a big boy. The pain on his leg, the burn, it doesn't hurt.

How will he know the right place? Places are all different but all the same too. How will he know the right car? So many cars. He knows lots. He knows it's a police car. He wishes it wasn't. He doesn't like police cars but he does as well. Perhaps Mum got it wrong. She said police-men know what he thinks, every little thing, no matter how tiny, those nasty little things, like if it was him who farted. That's what Mum said. Mum knows what he thinks and says policemen know what he thinks as well.

Mum told him what to do and he will do it but he doesn't want to see the white car with the badge on the door, not the man sitting in the seat without his helmet. If he were a policeman he would never take his helmet off. He doesn't want to see the man reading the newspa-per, eating his sandwiches. Does he know what he thinks? He wants to turn around and go and talk to the ducks and the horse at the corner.

Make sure it's him, Mum said. But how does he know? How does he know? Careful! How do you know policemen? Policemen don't have faces like people. They're policemen. Mum smiled and stroked his arm and said that he'd know. How does he know?

Last month she drove him to work at the farm each day and drove off. She did it every day, all the days. He knows the days, each day, Monday, then Tuesday, then Wednesday, all the rest, but she didn't say where she was going. She wouldn't talk to him for days. She stayed up in her bedroom. She was crying. He could tell. He knocked on the door but she told him to go away. He took the cat up to her, he held it so it couldn't get away. She wouldn't open the door. He stood outside the door and sang to her, her favorite song, about the good ship sailing, but she didn't open the door. The cat ran away. Open the door, Mum.

He heard her moving in the night when he couldn't sleep. She wouldn't talk to him and he was scared. He was scared because he was filled by the white spaces. Mr. Wyatt came in the morning because he hadn't gone to the farm. Mr. Wyatt shouted up the stairs to Mum but she wouldn't come down.

One night Mum sat at the kitchen table, her knee touching his, her hand on his hand, and she talked to him. She drank her whisky but wouldn't give him any. She doesn't let him drink beer and things like that. She asked him if he remembered somebody else in the house. He said there was nobody else. Don't be silly, Mum. He didn't say Maudie because she only comes sometimes.

Careful!

There is a thing, something, but he doesn't know what it is. Like when he was bending in the big field picking up spuds and the ground rose up at the end. Something. Picking up a spud but it wasn't a spud. It was a stone, a big heavy stone, heavy in his hand, mud on his boots, the sky loud, a bird screaming, going up, and there was something but it went away. It was nothing. The stone in his hand. Don't get lathered up, she says. Horses get lathered up, he says. Mr. Wyatt told him. But she doesn't want to know. It makes her angry. Listen, she says. Shall I sing, Mum?

A brother, she said. He knows people with brothers. Brothers play with you. No one has played with him at home. Except Mum. A brother, she said. Her knee touched his knee.

She told him what to do, held his hand tight, held her glass tight, pressed it hard down onto the table with her other hand, and she was shaking, her knee against his, telling him what to do. He's a good boy. But it's all right because he knows it's a trick. You don't hit policemen. Careful!

8.

Harold's hands are pinning her down. He thinks she likes this. Shadows on the walls, a gap in the curtains, his hand moving from her arm to her breasts and she coughs, loses her breath, tells him that this is not right. He takes a nipple between his forefinger and thumb and squeezes gently, showing as best he can all his love for her. But it's not what she wants. How does she tell him that she wants something that is not him? That the sad, little creature that lives inside him will never win her over?

She pushes him off, gets up from the bed and goes and sits at the dressing table. She releases her hair, lets it fall onto her shoulders. She doesn't like to do this when he is there. It's too intimate. He stands behind her and strokes the length of it, presses his hands to her cheeks, her forehead, as if he can redeem himself and tell her who he really is. But he doesn't know a thing about her. She looks in the mirror into the darkened room and sees a thin strip of light under the door. You left the landing light on, she says.

The first child is always the closest, he says later. At this time of night there is nothing between them that matters at all but she has learned how to avoid hurting him. Children are sent to judge us, he says, as if that might endear him to her. Perhaps a second one has to be treated differently. She thinks that he looks for some way to get closer to her, but she knows that he does not have the guile to do this and she hates him all the more. Children are nothing of the sort, she says. They do what they do because there is nothing else for them to do. They can't judge us. They don't have the means to do so. Children are just bloody kids, she says.

9.

When he wouldn't stop laughing she shouted at him and lit a cigarette and twisted it in the ashtray so the ash sharpened to a point. You weren't listening, Lenny. No, don't do that, Mummy. Make sure it is him, she said. But he doesn't know. He wants to cry because she thinks he knows him. He's a policeman, she said. He's a policeman in a car.

He switches off the wipers to see if he can see without them but the rain makes it look funny and he doesn't like it because this car is supposed to be good. He turns the wipers back on and they work and the rain goes. Rain, rain, go away.

Make sure it is him, Lenny, she says. She grins but it's not a grin. It's something else. Please, Mum, he says. Careful! she says. But he doesn't want to play that. Not now, Mum. Oh, yes, Lenny, she says. You have to listen to me. She catches hold of his hand and she asks him what will he do down the lane? He says he doesn't know but he does, really. It was a trick. She slaps his hand. Careful! she says.

One, Lenny, she says. No, I didn't mean it, he says. It's not fair. Start again. Where will you turn off the ring road, Lenny? Tell me. Where will you turn off the bloody road? He can't think because she's so angry. Where? he says. Careful! Lenny, she says. That's two. No, no, no, Mum, he says. It isn't two. Two, Lenny, she says. Careful! Where will the police car be, Lenny? He can't think because it's two and he has only one left. Where will the police car be? Tell me! He remembers the horse and the ducks and the lane and the first turning left, this is his left hand, and the tub where the horse drinks but he can't say it because there's too much to think. Tell me, Lenny, she says. The words fill his mouth and he wants to spit them out but he can't. Careful! Lenny, she says, and she holds his hand down hard on the table. No, Mum, he says. Yes, son, you have to listen to me. That's three.

She takes her cigarette, sucks on it, sharpens the tip of the ash again, pushes it hard into the top of his hand. No, Mum, no, he shouts. But she holds it there. Careful! Lenny, she says. You have to learn. You have to know what's good for you. Careful!

Sometimes he goes down to see Maudie Edgecombe. Mum says it's not Maudie, it's Maude, that he mustn't call her that. But Maudie doesn't mind. She likes it. She smiles at him. She says that he can call her whatever he likes. He doesn't tell that to Mum. He likes calling her Maudie because it's like then they're friends, which they are too. Maudie says he can ask her anything. He asked her about the sacks in the car, dust all over the place, and he wants to cry because he doesn't know what to do in the car and he is trapped, but she doesn't mind. Maudie has an arm that doesn't work, that she holds in front of her. He asked her if he could touch it and she pulled up her sleeve and let him. It was funny. It was the same except he knew he could pinch her and she wouldn't feel it. He didn't do this because Mum wouldn't like it but Maudie would laugh. If he pinched Mum's arm she'd feel it. She'd tell him. People can do that. They can feel.

Sometimes when things are bad he goes down to Maudie's. He sits at the table and talks. Maudie likes that. She says he's a good boy. He is a good boy. He does what he's told. Careful!

He sees the police car in the place by the gate where Mum said it would be. The policeman is eating his sandwiches like Mum said. He doesn't wear a helmet. If Lenny were a policeman he'd wear his helmet all the time. He would even wear it in the lav and in bed. In the lav. That'd be a laugh. He wonders if policemen are allowed to wear helmets in bed. He'd wear his and they'd never find out. It would be a trick. Unless someone told. Careful!

He drives past the police car and stops down the lane in another patch. He puts on the handbrake, gets out and shuts the door. But he doesn't lock it. Mum told him to leave the key in the ignition, that's what it's called. He knows he shouldn't do that but he'll do it now because he's a good boy. Careful! He asked Maudie about leaving the key in and she asked why. He didn't tell her. He didn't say that sometimes you have to. He's a good boy. He does what he's told. Careful!

He gets out and walks back along the lane and it's stopped raining. He likes it, the time after rain, the smell. He knows it'll start again any time now. He likes the smell of Pat the dog when it's rained.

He stands by the side of the car. Don't say anything to him. That's what Mum said. The policeman takes the top slice of bread off his sandwich. Lenny sees it's corned beef and tomato. He likes corned beef, he hates tomatoes. The policeman puts the piece of bread back and bites into it. A line of spit joins the policeman's sandwich to his lip.

"Yeah?" the policeman says. The spit's gone but a piece of tomato sticks to his teeth.

"Where's your helmet?" Lenny says. "Why aren't you wearing your helmet?" The policeman points to the backseat.

"It's there," he says. "Why do you want to know?" The policeman knows he wants to wear it. He didn't tell him, but the policeman knows. Careful!

"Want to try it on?"

"I can't wear it," Lenny says. "I'm not a policeman. It's not allowed."

"It's all right," the policeman says. "Go on, have a go. I can let you."

Lenny steps back from the car.

"I can't," he says. "I'm not allowed. I'm not

allowed to talk."

He knows something is wrong, something is missing. It's the Belter. He should have the Belter. He should be hiding it in his hand behind his back. Sometimes there's nothing and there should be something. Like when he feels a space under his feet and he's falling. Like when he was in the field with the potatoes. He hates falling because everything turns and he can't see what it is. It goes and comes back and goes. That's what happens with the white space.

He walks away from the car.

"It's all right," the policeman says. "It doesn't matter."

Lenny goes back to his car. The policeman gets out. He isn't supposed to do that. Mum said. Lenny knows what to do. He shouldn't have talked to the policeman. That's what started all this.

"It's all right," the policeman shouts down the road. "Look, here's my helmet. I'll put it on." The policeman puts his helmet on, cups the strap under his chin. Lenny opens the back door of his car. He's looking for the Belter. The policeman walks toward him. He isn't supposed to do that. All this trouble and now he wants to pee.

"It's all right," the policeman says. "You don't have to worry." He's coming nearer. He won't wear the helmet. He can't find the Belter. He knows it's there. Mum put it there. She knew where it was.

Careful!

"What are you doing? Are you all right?" the policeman says. "Can I help you?"

He's holding the Belter now. Good. He kills rabbits. He's good at killing rabbits. That's all right. He's holding it tight. Mum held it with him. Tighter, she said, her fingers on his. It felt funny to have her fingers on it. Mum, he said, don't be silly. Tighter, she said. On the back of the neck. Don't hit him anywhere else, and you must only do it once. Like killing a rabbit, she says, only you don't kill him. Do you hear me? she said. He won't have his helmet on, she said. Hit him, she said. Just enough to get his hands tied and into the back of your car. Hit him.

They practiced tying. They had a rope that he had to tie around her wrists. Tighter, she said. You have to do it tighter. He mustn't get away. But he didn't want to hurt her. Bloody tighter, bloody tight, son, she said, swearing with her cigarette in her mouth, the ash dropping. Then she spit the tip of the cigarette out. Pick it up, Lenny, she said, put it in the ashtray. We keep doing this until you get it right, until you can do it properly and do it good and quick.

He wouldn't do it to her. He saw red marks on her skin. Lenny, she said, this doesn't hurt me at all. Don't worry, son. Do it for me. I won't do it any more, he said. Do it, she said. He cried. And he did it to her, tied the rope tight around her wrists. He tied the knot again and again but he couldn't do it the way she wanted. Lenny, she said, we have to get this right. He cried. She wouldn't stop. We do this until you get it right. Do it again, she said. Left over right and right over left. But he forgot left and right. He knew them really. In the car, she said, you'll know it in the car. You turn left and right. Then he did it like she wanted.

But after, when he untied her, he didn't want to touch the rope. No, I don't like it. Pick it up, she said. I don't like it. Pick it up and put it on the floor of the car with the Belter. That's where you'll put him. You're a good boy, Lenny, she said. And don't tell Maude Edgecombe.

The policeman is bending down, his helmet on his head, looking into the BMW. Lenny has the Belter in his hand. He's holding it tight, just like she said.

It's all right, though. He knows. Because it's a trick to play on the policeman. He likes tricks. Mum likes tricks too. Everybody likes tricks.

10.

Susan Edgecombe runs with a weighted pack on her back. She pounds the roads and lanes and footpaths in pink stretch lycra running shorts and green and white bulbous trainers. She stands out in the lanes. Alice asks Maude about this but Maude won't comment because that would be to commit herself to her daughter in a way Alice knows that she hates. Alice persists just to see the woman's discomfort.

Alice knows that Susan Edgecombe is a politico of the old sort. She would have demanded to fight in the Spanish Civil War, for the comrades, and for the good of women everywhere. She is no revisionist. She runs each day that she is home, in the mornings and the afternoons, runs to keep fit, in order to be in trim for the fight, for the revolution. She moves from one political action to another and is a serious young woman. There is a desperation about her, her hands holding the straps of the backpack, her eyes locked forward. She would be a good model for a Russian poster, looking out and up. All shoulders to the wheel. But Alice thinks that her outfit is the outfit of a desperate woman. How much better if she had kitted herself out in khaki shorts, a khaki shirt, big boots and thick socks. That would show real political commitment and courage. Alice thinks that Susan does not want to know where she is when she runs.

Alice stands by the big front window and watches Susan as she goes by. She wants no one to call today, and thankfully Susan is the last person who would do such a thing. She has her own agenda. Alice hates that word. *Agenda.* Maude uses it and she guesses that she must have learned it from Susan. But it's plural, Maude, she wants to say. It means more than one thing. But she doesn't because it is comforting to have that knowledge to spare. Maude talks about the agenda as she sits at the table and taps her cigarette on the side of the ashtray. What fucking agenda, Maude? Alice has an agenda but she will discuss it with no one. It has to be that way.

She looks at the old, plastic, battery-operated clock above the fireplace, its marks for numbers, its sweeping second hand. She wonders how far the clock is from Greenwich Mean Time. But it doesn't bloody matter. You have to draw the line. She thinks about Susan's jogging in the lanes. There's no possibility that Susan could run as far as the place where Lenny is. No one could run that far in the time given. Not out of the village to the main road and down to the ring road and then some more. But it might be done. And anybody could go down that lane. But they won't. That's why the spot is so good, why it was so good to find him there. Nobody goes down there.

Careful!

She's put Maude Edgecombe off for today. Told her that she'll be out. But she wouldn't put it past Maude to come around. Alice stands to one side of the window, her shoulder against the wall. She presses her forehead to the plaster just for the feel of it, cold plaster against her skin.

She was coming out of Boots in town when she saw him. Just another policeman and she thought nothing of it. But she looked again. Too much water under the bridge for such a thing to happen, and besides a policeman. She took hold of Lenny's hand. She walked back. Lenny pulled away. Let me hold you, she said. Stop playing around. Stop it, Lenny.

She knew. It didn't matter about the uniform, or the ten years that had passed. She could forgive him that. She looked for him on other days. She dropped Lenny off at work and drove into town. She knew the spots, the vantage points, the hidden corners, the doorways to stand in. She kept out of sight. She just wanted to see him. To know it was her son.

She stands now with her head pressed to the plaster, feeling the cold, and looks out the window for Susan. The girl is long gone. Alice knows that one form of intensity can easily replace another. She could run around the lanes, she could pound the roads, as urgently as Susan does. It would not take a lot. After all, they are together in the sisterhood that does not know where to draw the line.

11.

The policeman stands beside him. Mum didn't say anything about this. He wants to talk to him, so they can be friends. Tell him about the car, the BMW. People don't talk to him. They pretend, he knows. Mum listens but sometimes she doesn't because she has other things on her mind. Sometimes he sits at the table and watches the big, red hand of the clock go around. He hates it because it makes him itch. But sometimes he has to do it because the clock won't go away. The red hand is there. Mum slaps his wrist when he scratches. He likes it. Sometimes they laugh and then he scratches again to make her laugh some more. But then she stops. She won't laugh any more. Don't scratch, Lenny. For God's sake. It gets on my nerves. Then he licks his fingers.

The policeman is talking to him but he can't listen because there's something in his head. Why isn't Mum here? Why can he smell the car? Why is his head like that, why is the door of the car on its side? The policeman puts his hand on his shoulder.

"It's all right," he says. "Don't get worried." Lenny holds the Belter as hard as he can. The policeman's hand is on his shoulder. They could be friends. But the white

Careful!

shapes are there. They won't go away.

When they play Careful! sometimes Lenny talks and Mum listens. Sometimes it's the other way around. Most times Mum wants him to tell her what he's done in the day and what he's going to do the next day. She listens. Sometimes she laughs and it makes a tickle in his belly. He likes it, but not when she gets angry. Then she does it nasty with the cigarette. She doesn't want to. He makes her do it. He will be the death of her. But she's not going to die. She isn't.

Sometimes Mum won't play Careful! Even if she hurts him he likes it really. Sometimes she doesn't know that. When she burns him she cries. He asked her to stop crying but she said it was part of the game. Don't cry, Mum. It doesn't hurt. I'm a brave boy.

Rain splashes on the windshield. The policeman doesn't mind the rain. Lenny grips the Belter as hard as he can because that's what Mum said. Don't cry, Mum. The policeman is smiling even though it's raining. He has white teeth and a bit of tomato. The rain makes dark marks on his shirt. He shouldn't get wet. But he can't tell him when he has the Belter in his hand. It's not allowed. You can't talk to him. You can't tell him you've got it. Don't talk to him, Lenny. Just do it.

Lenny's leg feels wet. He knows it's not the rain. Careful! If Mum were here she'd slap his wrist. The policeman isn't smiling now. He's seen something. He can't hit him on the back of the neck like Mum said because he's got his helmet on. He shouldn't have it on. It's his fault. The only place he can hit him is in the face. You wouldn't do it to a rabbit.

He hits him. Careful!

He hits him hard. Careful!

He sees blood coming from the policeman's lips, his teeth, his nose. It's red. Careful! The policeman shouts, screams, and puts his hand up to his face. Lenny wants to cry. He didn't want to do it. He didn't mean it. The policeman's kneeling now. Lenny stands in front of him and pulls at the helmet. It won't come off. He pulls harder and the policeman puts his hands up to it. Lenny sees blood on the policeman's fingers. It's red. Careful!

He hits the policeman in the face again. The policeman shouts and lets go of the helmet, puts his hands on his face. They're bloody. The strap of the helmet goes under the policeman's chin. He pulls it and the helmet tips forward. It's easy to take off. Easy peasy. The policeman doesn't try to stop him now. He holds the policeman's shoulder. His shirt is wet. He puts his hand on the back of his head and pushes down so that the policeman's neck is where he can see it.

"It's all right," he says. Once he saw Mr. Wyatt kill a deer. He shot it but he only hit it in the leg. Mr. Wyatt knelt on the deer and pulled back on its neck and snapped it. Afterward the deer was dead. When the deer was dead it didn't breathe, anywhere in its body. Its leg kicked but it wasn't a real kick. Mr. Wyatt said that was a bit of life left in him. Sometimes rabbits have bits of life left in them. Lenny holds them up until it's all drained out, the life draining from their legs, their bodies, down through their heads, out through the tips of their ears.

With the helmet off Lenny sees the policeman's neck. It's white. Mr. Wyatt had that once where his neck was white. Mr. Wyatt has lots of little holes in his neck.

Lenny raises the Belter and hits down hard on the policeman's neck. He hits down hard again because he's not sure. You do it with rabbits. Yes, you do.

Careful!

The policeman falls forward onto the ground. Lenny sees rain shining on the policeman's hair. He sees it on a small patch of white at the back of the policeman's head where he has no hair. If he'd kept his helmet on he would have kept his hair dry. Lenny touches his own hair. It's wet. He doesn't mind. He lets it get wet when it rains. He tells Mum, he tells Mr. Wyatt, he's not scared of a bit of rain, not one bit. Rain doesn't hurt.

Lenny puts the Belter on the floor of the car. The policeman's shirt is wet all over and it has changed color. He puts his hands under the policeman's arms and lifts him. He's not heavy, not really heavy, not what they call heavy on the farm. Not as heavy as fertilizer sacks. He opens the back door and tries to push the policeman in but he won't go.

"Come on, help me." The policeman does nothing. He can't make him put his arms and legs where he wants them to be. He gets into the car, one foot on the seat, the other on the floor, and pulls him onto the backseat. That does it. Mum said to put him on the floor of the car but he won't go. Lenny stands beside the back door. Closes it. He's a good boy.

On the floor of the car. On the floor of the car, for goodness sake, son. Don't you know anything? Can't you do anything? You'll be the death of me. She won't die. He can kill rabbits. He can break up crates and burn them. He's good at doing it. Mr. Wyatt says he is. He's got new boots. He can drive the car. He's good at that. They said he couldn't do it but he did. He can read. Mum taught him, and Maudie. Mum doesn't know. They said he couldn't take the test but Mum made them let him. She taught him. She smiled at the man in the car. He smiled at her. They said he wouldn't be allowed but Mum made them. She shouted. She did.

Lenny stands by the back door and looks in. He hears a car. He opens the back door and pulls the police-man by his shoulders. His body is wedged against the seat and won't go down. He pulls him and turns his shoulders so that the body slips down. The arms stick up. He pushes at them and still they stick up. He hears a car. It's not a car. It's a tractor in a field. A Massey. Anybody knows that. He's a good boy. He knows he's a good boy.

He closes the door, gets in and starts the engine. It's a good trick. He likes tricks.

12.

Lenny and Lenny.

Irony is the discrepancy, the difference, between the way things are and the way they're supposed to be. Before the day it happened she thought that life was a slow process. Before, she would walk in the fields in the rain with the kids, holding Lenny as close to her as she could. Before it she would be surprised by a glimpse of the church tower through the trees. Before it she bought a cheap camera and took pictures of the church from all angles, some near, some so far that the church tower was a tiny thing in the corner of the viewfinder.

Before the day it happened she dressed the kids, listened to Lenny gurgle, watched Jack strut from one end of the room to the other. Before it she tasted everything as pungent as you like. Before it life was as slow as she wanted it to be. Life with the kids accumulated, one thing on top of another, one good thing and then another.

There is a moment and after it a stillness that leaves her empty. Emptiness is blue. With white clouds. But it's not a blue you would bet on.

Afterward life developed at its own pace. She saw it as a series of contractions, as if she were about to give birth. It took hold of her and let her go, played with her, and there was nothing she could do.

Lenny and Lenny. Irony of ironies.

Before the kids she liked the idea of comedy so much. She liked a burst of laughter, a howl. But it was with Lenny Bruce that she saw what comedy could be. It was more than laughter. He was the one who knew what mattered most. He was the one who could see it the way it was. Dear old Lenny Bruce, trying so hard.

Harold didn't see it about Lenny Bruce at all. Harold said the man was a fool. She told Harold that if he could understand something of what Lenny Bruce was saying, just one tiny bit of it, it would make him a different man. But Harold didn't want to be a different man. Harold wanted to suffer as he was, thank you very much indeed. Lenny Bruce suffered because he wanted to know who was doing it to him and who was doing it to everybody else. Lenny Bruce wasn't in it for the laughs. Lenny Bruce was in it for the defining moment, the flash that would show why things were like they were, explain it. Lenny Bruce was the person who said it isn't happening like you think it is. She knew that. Lenny Bruce said it's worse and this is how bad it is and this is how it's going to be and she could take it because she could laugh about the cosmic stupidity of it all.

But after it, and there's irony for you, she really knew what Lenny Bruce meant. Lenny Bruce would have seen the arc of the swing, the rough concrete, the shake of the chains, he would have to see the face of the kid, and he wouldn't have looked away. He'd have got down on his knees to take a closer look. He'd have looked into his eyes, at the blood on his lips. He wouldn't have talked about Life, Life with a capital L. He would have talked about the swings and the chains and the concrete. He'd have talked about the color of the grass, the color of blood on the concrete, say did you notice the shade of the red, you don't get red like that very often, it's a moment, it's curious, what about your grief, he would fix it in time, pin it, because he knew about the moment, he knew about pain. He would have said look at it. This is it. He would have said did you think about it before it happened? Did you ever think it might happen? What if it did? What might it mean? And she would say she never gave it a thought because she was in a state of grace that could not be altered. He would have said now you take it further to where it goes. She never did that. But come on, come on, damn it, there is nothing she doesn't know about the moment. Isn't that enough? Lenny would say you're running away. She would say don't tell me that. I've lived with it for years. Lenny would say is that so? Is that really fucking so?

She doesn't play her Lenny Bruce records anymore.

Life isn't poetic. Life is contractions forever and ever. Waiting and hoping and not getting there. Isn't that the irony? Lenny Bruce knew it and she knows it now. It's

Harold on the bed wanting to talk to her and her hand on his arm and Harold not knowing what to say and the kid is in the hospital and all she wants is for him to be with her, but Harold's on the bed, his arms all over her but he's not feeling her, the poor sod. All she wants to know is that they can help each other so that they can get on with it. Jack is asleep in his room, knocked out with sleeping draught, the poor kid, and Harold's arms wave around the room. All she wants is to know that they can work at it, that no matter how bad it is they can be together, they can be in it together. But Harold might as well stand on the bed and yell into her face, because that's all there is in the man.

This is it, this is the moment, the moment that wraps up all those years, and all she can do is scream. In the middle of the night. Scream and scream.

She sits at the table and waits and thinks about Lenny. She has been with him every day through the years. Except for the time when they took him to town. She wonders why Jack came back to the area. Perhaps he thought that she would never see him. She never goes to town. But she did go to town and she did see him. Which goes to show. Perhaps he came back because he wanted to come back. Perhaps he came back because he wanted to put it right. Perhaps he came back because he didn't give a damn. She knows that one moment doesn't follow another, that one thing is not linked to another. It expands and it contracts. It's a lurch and the sky is mottled with clouds, the grass is green, and the chains of the swings are rattling.

She opens the cupboard in the dresser. Puts in her head and sniffs. Smells keep their attachments. They never let go, not for as long as you can smell them. She takes out cups and saucers, crockery, dishes, a box with envelopes in it. She puts them onto the table. She runs hot water and squirts in washing-up liquid. Lenny could be back at any moment but she knows about moments and she has to do something. She has to stroke surfaces, wash and rinse, scour and clean.

She went with Lenny once to see Robert De Niro in a film. De Niro played an armed robber. He told a woman that he never gets into a relationship that he isn't prepared to drop, to walk away from, in thirty seconds. Lenny liked the film because he loved the gunfire, the noise, the business of the guns. He wanted Mr. Wyatt to get a machine gun. Think, Mr. Wyatt, of killing rabbits. Lenny made a guttural noise that started in his stomach and came up to his throat and rattled through his teeth.

In the cinema toward the end of the film Lenny wanted to go to the toilet. He insisted that she go with him. She stood outside waiting for him. While she waited she thought about dropping everything and leaving. When they got back to their seats, De Niro was walking into a trap in a hotel. There were policemen everywhere. He couldn't get away. He was trapped. Because of a woman. Lenny Bruce would have laughed.

She washes cups and saucers, dishes, washes something from them. It's not dust, it's not grime. She washes them too often for that. What is it? It's something hidden that might make a difference. She does this with everything, all of her life. She has to make sure.

As she washes she waits for the noise of the car. She throws a cup away, a white, fine porcelain cup with yellow piping, drops it into the bin, not because it is cracked but because she has never liked the sodding thing and besides it looks dirty. It does not smash. She takes it out and drops it again. Still it doesn't smash. She takes it out and drops it onto the floor. This time it smashes. She likes the sound it makes. She brushes up the pieces with a dustpan and brush. It is like she is brushing up the sound.

At first the doctors said there was nothing wrong with him. She knew they were wrong. She talked to a surgeon. He sat behind a desk, placed one hand on top of the other, a mole on his left cheekbone, skin peeling on his scalp, a striped shirt with a spot of blood on the collar. Yes they did have the results, the X-rays, the other tests. Such cases were difficult, extraordinarily difficult, to diagnose. It wasn't a matter of all of one thing or all of another. It was a case of compromise and hope. It took time. Things developed. She looked at the blank hospital wall behind him, a file on the desk. His words drifted past her. The surgeon separated his hands and stroked the top of his desk with the tips of his fingers. She could have stroked his hands, she thought, and then none of this would have happened. There is always hope, he said. He has a long way to go but perhaps he has the will to do it. I need to know, she said. I need you to tell me. I need to know if he will ever be all right.

The surgeon tapped his desk. Look, he said, why don't I give you something that will help you? You need it. We all need a little help at times like this. Then he lifted a finger to his mouth to bite a nail. Such nice nails. He would go outside, get in his car, and drive home. You have to hope, he said.

She should have gone in the car with Lenny. She knows she should have gone with him. She has asked too much. She has gone too far. But she has a great deal of faith in her son. He has the will and the doggedness. He will kill a rabbit in a field and think nothing of it. But he has never hit a man.

13.

He stops the car and turns off the engine. The policeman's helmet is in the road. He gets out. The police car door is open. If Mr. Wyatt were here, Mr. Wyatt and Pat, and Jimmy, they'd tell him what to do. Get on with it, kid. Don't dawdle. The hedges in this lane are too high. They should cut the hedges because then he could see. But if they did he might get a puncture. The splinters get in the road. There's no one here to help him. No one comes here. Grass grows in the middle of the road, it comes out of the tarmac.

He stands and listens. The radio in the police car makes a noise. He hears a woman's voice coming out of it. It's not his fault. Mum said drive away, don't hang about. But what about the helmet? What about the door? And what would it be like if Mr. Wyatt were his dad? His dad would tell him what to do.

He stands in the road and moves his toes in his boots. The boots squeak. He bought them with Mum when they went to town. Yellow laces. He wanted to get them and she said they would but she didn't care when they got to the precinct. Not after they'd crossed the road and walked past the burger bar. Not after they'd gone past the sweety shop. She'd changed her mind. Come on, Mum, he said. He pulled her but she wouldn't. Mum, I want them. You said so. Mr. Wyatt said I need new ones. It's true.

He pulled her to the shop. He knew the right shop because Jimmy told him, down the road from the burger bar, crap burgers, and he was going to get boots just like Jimmy's with yellow laces. Mum said so. But she stopped at the door. You said, Mum. She was looking down the road, past the shops. Mum, listen, you stupid bitch. Don't call me that, don't you dare call me that. Call you what? It's here, Mum. This is the shop. Jimmy said it was. Bugger Jimmy, Mum said. I want them, Mum. You said I could have them. Shut up, she said. Shut up, shut bloody up, you fool. You don't want me to have them, he said. This is where Jimmy got his boots. I want the boots. You said I could. Shut up, she said.

It was all right then because she held his hand and smiled and they went into the shop. He got it right first time because he knew his size. He told the girl, size ten. The ones like Jimmy. Jimmy bought his here. With yellow laces. She got them. He tried them on. It was right first time. Then Mum asked him for the money. I haven't got it, Mum. Where is it? she said. I lost it, he said. He started to cry. But she was joking because she laughed and gave him the money. It was a trick. But she didn't smile. Sometimes he doesn't like tricks.

He hears his shoes squeaking. Jimmy's don't

squeak. His shoes may be wrong. You can get them wrong. He kneels to test them out, presses at them with his thumb. You press them there, where Jimmy presses his. They look the same as Jimmy's. Perhaps Mum put the laces in wrong. But they look right. He looks up and down the lane. He doesn't like it. The hedges are too high.

He picks up the helmet. It's empty. He puts his hand into it. Nothing happens. He carries it over to his car and puts it on the front passenger seat. The radio in the police car squawks like a bird. He wants to stop it, like you'd stop a bird. Like if Mr. Wyatt said it was getting on his nerves. Like lots of things get on Mr. Wyatt's nerves. Mrs. Wyatt's canary got on Mr. Wyatt's nerves. It said things.

The policeman's arms are sticking up in the back. They aren't supposed to. They're supposed to be on the floor behind the seats. He opens the back door and holds the policeman's arm. He's never touched a policeman before. It feels the same. His arm is warm. The policeman has rolled his shirtsleeves up. He likes that. He doesn't roll his sleeves up because in summer he wears short-sleeved shirts. They're best for him, Mum says. And in winter he wears long-sleeved shirts under his pullover. He'd like to roll his sleeves up. He wants to wear long sleeves in the summer and roll them up like Jimmy and put his cigarettes in the rolled-up sleeve. Except he doesn't smoke. But he could if he wanted. It's like his belt. He can wear a belt now. He doesn't have to wear braces. Jimmy wears his sleeves rolled up but he won't tell Mum.

He catches hold of the policeman's arm and pulls. It's hard to move him. It's like he doesn't want to move. Come on, he says, be a good chap. Don't mess me around, you naughty boy. He puts his foot onto the seat and heaves. The policeman's arms fold onto his chest. Good chap, he says. Well done.

Lenny closes the door and gets in, starts the engine. It's a good car. Listen to the engine. It'll do a ton easy enough. Jimmy and him are going to the motorway one day after work. He'll drive, not Jimmy anymore. Not in the new car.

They're good boots. But he doesn't want them to squeak. Jimmy's don't. Jimmy will tell him what to do. He drives down the lane away from the police car. Straight home now. Good boy.

Careful!

He knows he should have done something. He hears a noise in the engine. He hears a rumble, rumbling in the wheels. A white space in his head rattles.

14.

Two fifteen. He should be back by now. She ought to have gone with him. But it was right in the thinking, in the bloody moment. Like there's always a right thing in the moment if you know what it is. Like fuck off Harold, or like sticking her face as close to Lenny as she can, her cheek pushed against his skin so she can't breathe. Not like standing in the park and listening to the faraway creak of the swings, creak, not like standing on the chair in the kitchen and looking through the window.

Two seventeen. Anything could have happened. She can't get away from it, in washing the woodwork, in looking through the window. None of these is a moment. They're one thing joined to another, joined so that every-thing is stuck and can't be itself. Hell, she didn't go because she thought he would recognize her. But she hadn't thought this when she'd driven the car around the town all those times, when she had followed him, when she had parked and walked or when she had driven out into the country and down to the lane, thank God in the old Metro not that bright red thing he has now, hadn't worried when she had gone past him three times, three separate days, turned at the end because it goes nowhere and driven back past him, in between the high hedges, her head lowered so that she would not be seen. She hadn't thought it then.

She didn't go because Lenny would do it without fussing if she weren't there. Like the rabbits. He'd get on with it. Lenny doesn't have her scruples. He has his own, but they're different. Sometimes it's a blessing.

To be honest, it's better this way. There's a feel to it. She likes the idea of the two sons together. Neither of them has the key. She's the one who has that. It's up to her. Lenny doesn't know, and Jack, who has the capacity to know, won't recognize his brother after all this time, she thinks, but she's not sure. She likes to think, in one way, he will recognize him, that blood binds them. But she knows that that would be disaster too.

Two twenty-two. His room is ready. Not his bedroom. That would be a mistake. Not the single bed and the cartoon curtains, the cricket bat, the radio with the aerial that sticks up askew from the back, the poster of the floating astronaut with the reflection in his visor, the reflection that says it's all right as long as you can see that. No, Lenny will take him to the room at the top of the house where there is a window that looks out over the road, a bare wooden floor. That's the room. She wants it there because it's part of the house but not a part of their lives. No-man's-land. Harold never went into that room. He stayed in the rooms he knew and liked. The kids played in the attic. They had the space there.

Two twenty-four and still no noise in the drive. She can hear cars turn the corner at the top of the village. She listens to them come down the road, listens to the swish of the tires and the roar of the engines. She thinks she will know the sound of Lenny's new car, its engine as it turns into the drive.

She didn't want the house. It was too big. She preferred the two up, two down terraced house they had in town. She was happy there. And it was just the right size, even when the kids came along. It had a number, forty-three. She liked that. Having a number was part of who you were. More than a name. A name means nothing if you had nothing to do with the choosing of it. And worse if you did. You always see nameplates, varnished slices of pine, the Raydors, the Shanors, the Shirbens.

Harold was sniffy from the start in number forty-three. He said he wasn't, but he wouldn't speak to the neighbors. That was all right, he wasn't the social sort. But he wouldn't go in the garden, the small handkerchief they had at the back. When they moved in, married six months, the first time inside the door when it was theirs, only renting though, he screwed her up against the wall in the hallway, as hard as he could. But it wasn't like Harold. He wasn't the spontaneous type. He was telling her something.

He thought he was too good for the house. His parents put that into his mind and they didn't have a penny to scratch their asses. Small rooms, the hallway,

Careful!

the bathroom at the back of the kitchen. Number forty-three.

Two twenty-nine. She can hear nothing. Back in number forty-three she was part of the road, knew the neighbors and everyone else. Could name them from one end of the road to the other. But that was what it was like then.

And then out of the blue Harold got a legacy from a relative, someone he never knew. He didn't tell her. The first thing he must have done after he put the money into the bank was to go around the estate agents. She can see him doing it, his chest puffed out, the stuck-up little bastard. Licking his lips and putting on that voice to the woman behind the counter. He didn't ask her, didn't even tell her. He bought the house. Shetland House, the house that stands by itself with no neighbors. An eighteenth-century, three-story desirable residence with four bedrooms, in its own grounds with barns and two acres of land. She had never lived in a place so big. She had been brought up in a terraced house in another part of the same town. That was why she liked forty-three so much.

He didn't tell her, didn't show her the estate agent's description, didn't show her a picture of the house, didn't show her an advert in the paper. He didn't tell her he was thinking of it, didn't whisper it at night in bed. Nothing.

Two thirty-three. She remembers when he finally

told her, his face as he told it to her sitting at the table in the evening, sweat on his nose, his teeth showing. She saw a hole in his jacket. She didn't tell him. Let that hole stay there, let it be. He didn't buy new clothes with the legacy. He was too mean. He didn't offer to buy her new clothes or toys for the boys. The new house was enough. Take it or leave it.

Two thirty-five. Where the hell is he? Where the hell are they, more to the point?

15.

Driving the car up the lane. The horse will be at the corner. He can stop and look at it. He can stroke it. Mum would let him. He's a good boy. Careful!

He wants to talk to the policeman. Do policemen likes horses? Some policemen like horses because they ride them. Police horses don't care about fireworks. He likes fireworks when they go bang, like a gun, like it hits you right in the guts. Mr. Wyatt won't have fireworks. No fireworks, he says. That's because of the animals. That's right.

He speeds up over the hill because he knows that he's going to stop at the end of the lane and get out and go to the gate. He feels a space in his belly. He's forgotten something. He is a very naughty boy. There's the white stuff. Careful!

He stops the car at the gate. He sees the horse. It shakes its head and laughs. Perhaps if he gets out and goes over to the gate it will come to him. He opens the door. Rain hits his leg. His leg is wet but not from the rain. Naughty boy. I told you and told you, Lenny. He hears something and he turns around. The policeman moves his head. He's a naughty boy. He feels the pain in his belly. You have to watch it. He puts his leg back in the car. He won't go to the horse even if it wants him to because he has something very important to do. He wishes the white shapes weren't there. He doesn't like white shapes. That's when his mother shouts Careful!

He looks both ways at the big road. He has to do that. He sees a line of cars and lorries and they all have their wipers going. He moves his fingers to the switch but his wipers are already slapping the screen. He's a good boy. Careful! He sees a space. He drives quickly out and joins the end of a line of cars. He keeps his distance. Not too near, not too near. He knows. Jimmy doesn't care about things like that. He wishes he were Jimmy so that he didn't care. He could do what he wanted. Anything. Who gives a shit? Not me, Jimmy. I don't give a shit.

He hears a noise in the car. He puts his foot down but that brings him too close to the car in front. A Fiat Uno. Crap car. He wants to overtake. Crap car, mate, he and Jimmy would shout now. Crap car, mate. Jimmy would stomp his feet.

White space. White space.

He hears the noise again. He'll have to stop but he's not supposed to do that. It's not allowed. He wants to pee again. He wants to pee so much. Naughty boy. He turns and sees the white rope on the floor. It's coiled up flat like a snake. He doesn't like snakes. His mother coiled it after she showed him what to do. He likes the coils in the rope. He doesn't like snakes. No, he doesn't.

Careful!

It's big.

He had to tie the policeman's wrists. He knows he has to stop. Tying the policeman's wrists is a piece of piss. That's what he told Mum. Left over right and right over left except he can't remember. Sorry, Mum. He wants to pee so bad. Left over right and right over left. He won't overtake. It's not allowed. He'll drive into a lay-by. He knows there's a lay-by up ahead by the big sign that says things. Come straight home. Straight home. Once he didn't pee for days.

He remembers things. The white shapes make him remember. Things that happened but he won't say because Mum gets mad. She says he's making it up. He wants to tell someone. He tried to tell Jimmy but Jimmy laughed at him. He tells Maudie now. Mum asks him if he has secrets and he says no, but he does. It's a trick. Maudie is going to let him fuck her. She says he needs to know. Jimmy has secrets because sometimes he taps the side of his nose. Mr. Wyatt does it. Mum doesn't do it. Sometimes he taps his nose for Maudie. She laughs. She taps the side of her nose, but only for him. They do it together. Careful!

He pulls into the lay-by and switches off the engine. The Fiat goes on. So what? He could have overtaken that crap if he wanted to. A piece of piss. He didn't want to. This car'll do a ton, easy. A ton ten, a ton twenty, a ton thirty. What comes after a ton thirty? He turns around. The policeman has his hand on the back seat. He shouldn't do that. It's not right. Lenny gets out. Bloody rain, but it's good for the crops. He opens the back door, the inside one, the one by the hedge, and he picks up the cord. Don't do that. DON'T DO THAT.

It's all right, policeman. He sees a red mark on the back of his neck. He hit him good. He isn't a rabbit. He puts the cord on the seat and takes hold of the policeman's hand, then the other one, but they won't come together. He has to get them together to tie them behind his back. He kneels on the policeman and pulls. This gets his wrists together and the policeman groans. He mustn't do that. He mustn't make a sound. Don't make a move, my boy. He picks up the cord and wraps it around the policeman's wrists. Round and round but he has to stop this, he has to tie it. Left over right and right over left. Which is left, which is left and which is right?

A car turns into the lay-by and parks farther up. A red car but not one like his. A Ford, an Escort. Maybe an XR3. Jimmy would know. It's raining hard and he can't see the car through the windshield because he's stopped his engine and the wipers stop when you do that. He can't see through the raindrops. Why do the wipers stop? Because the electric is stopped. Electric is different from water and petrol. People don't have electric. It kills them through the holes.

Left, but which is left? Which is right? He wants to piss. Once he didn't do it. He pulls hard on the cord. The policeman groans. He's not supposed to do that. He sees

Careful!

the car through the raindrops on the glass. It's an XR3. He hears the swish and the roar of the cars and the lorries on the road. He didn't stop for the horse. Left is the side of the car on the inside of the road, but he is looking the wrong way, it's not that side. He doesn't want to tie a granny knot. A granny knot is wrong. Careful! He's a good boy. He twists the cord around itself but that doesn't make a knot, does it? No, it doesn't. The policeman groans again. He's a good boy. Mummy, he's a good boy. Jimmy, a ton thirty. What comes after that?

Left over right and left over right. He twists the ends of the cord, one over the other, one over the first one, and he tucks one inside. There is no left and no right. They're both left and right now. He pulls at the cord around the wrist. It's tight. He's a good boy. He is.

He shuts the back door. He's hungry. He could eat a horse. But not the horse at the corner. Not the nice one. Another horse. Start the engine, look both ways. Look up and down the road. There's a space coming. Wait. Careful! And . . . go. Not far now. Keep the speed down, keep it steady. Hands at the top of the wheel. Jimmy laughs when he does that, hands at the top of the wheel, like a ponce, he says. But you can drive like that if you want to. He moves his hands to the bottom of the wheel, his fingertips on it, just so, just right. That's how Jimmy does it. They're mates.

Not far to go. He's done what Mum wanted. He's a good boy, for sure. Careful! His hand hurts. Once she burnt him on the bum. Made him take his trousers down. Naughty boy. You nasty thing. You evil bastard. He's not a bastard. He's a good boy. He thinks he'll cry. He wants a pee. He thinks he will cry. He can if he wants. He wants a pee.

16.

Two thirty-seven. She isn't sure, what with the clock being like it is. She should have got rid of the clock years ago. It was one of the first things she bought after Harold died. She had to buy something. Where the hell are they?

She has set the table for tea. Only two places, as she usually does. Two plates. The pure white ones with the yellow and gold edging. No significance in this. Knives and forks and glasses. A bottle of lemonade for Lenny. Wine for her. No chance of Jack joining them, even if that were the plan, which it isn't, even if he wanted to, which he won't. It would be good to celebrate, though. So much to celebrate.

Jack began to eat alone after Lenny was born. He ate in the back room with the high window, next to the old larder. He sat at a small green beige-topped card table, under the window. His feet hardly touched the floor. He sat holding his knife and fork, staring at the food. She didn't press him to join them. She let him get on with it.

Jack likes to eat alone still. She knew it when she saw him down the lane in the car. His head tucked over his lap, a sandwich at his mouth, just the way he was doing it. Looking around to see who was there, like he was still a kid. He'd never let her stand over him. He always waited for her to leave the room. That's if he ate at all. Does he have a wife now? Has she changed him? Doesn't something happen to you as you grow older? Surely he has kids? Is she a grandmother? Has this wife rubbed off his hard edges? Someone has to.

Two thirty-eight. You set a table because it adds to the shape of your life, that extra little bit. It matters. She picks up the tea towel and polishes the plates then the glasses, then the knives and the forks. She moves the plates. Gets them just so, just right. It matters.

They should be here by now.

She struggles for breath. A pain in the ribs, a constriction at her throat. It's sent to show her. She knows. She should let sleeping dogs lie.

Two forty. They should be here by now, for sure. She shouldn't have let Lenny go on his own. But she wanted to do something to show that she knew her son, that it was what she wanted it to be. If you want something enough you will get it. Lenny, my son, come to me and I will kiss you and make it better. I will make you whole. I can do this, I know I can, if I want it enough. I can change my life so that yours is changed along with it.

Years ago she walked around the house in her nightdress on the coldest of cold nights because it was what she wanted to do. She could do what she had to do because it was what she wanted, it was one and the same thing. Funny really, because when you are in the moment you don't will it. You are there and that's it. She had looked in on the two kids, checked the small, blue flame in the paraffin heater, no real heat, but she was trying. She walked along the landing and down the stairs, through the kitchen into the hallway and out the front door. She went out onto the road, into the cold rain, her nightdress cold and wet, tight against her skin. Down the village and into the high-banked, hedged lane that twisted on itself. Through the hedge she could see the line of orange lights on the hill. She walked and walked. Her mind was the shiver of the orange lights, the coldness that kept them so bright, the rain that washed them, the darkness that suspended them, looping up the hill.

She walked and walked. Then there were lights behind her on the road, in the rain, and the rattle of an engine. She walked on down the narrow lane and the car followed her, its engine burbling, its wipers clacking. She walked and walked and there was no way the car could pass. She didn't care. She was looking for the moment, in it and of it, through pain and cold and wet, because only then can there be change.

She came to the end of the lane, past the house where the dog always barks, past the stream, through the puddles, and up to the intersection. She walked around the corner and the car drew beside her and stopped. A window slid open and she saw a face. A man was shouting. She couldn't hear him. She didn't want to hear him.

She walked past. The man shouted. She knew he was angry but she didn't know why. She had to carry on. She did this, and had to do it, and could he not bloody see that she had to do it? The man opened and slammed shut the door and the engine roared through a busted exhaust pipe, gurgled and rattled, and then was gone.

She wanted to be the rain and the cold and the stinging on her arms and legs, the nightdress against her skin, her bare feet, a stubbed toe, the dark, the high hedges and the light on a telephone pole, the light in the upstairs window of a house, a high brick wall. Those things were joined in some way and she wanted to be joined, to be of them.

She saw the taillights of the car as it turned the corner at the top. She watched the headlights wash the hedges up the high hill. She closed her eyes and clenched her teeth, shivered. It is, after all, only where you draw the line.

After the accident she had to put the world to rights. If only Jack would eat with her, if only he would talk to her, then perhaps it might be different. If only she could place the cups and saucers in a different way. If only the washing-up water were hotter. But there was always something that was not in place, that was not quite right. Waiting for the light to shine. The light that shineth in the darkness. Two forty-three, or is it two forty-four? Who gives a shit?

She came back to the house and slept in the wet

nightdress, pushing her palms hard against her body. Shivering in bed she attached blame to everything and everybody. She blamed poor, dead Harold. She blamed the house. She blamed her mother who had moved from the town to the seaside far away in another country. She could always shout at her mother but she was paddling in a warm sea, up to her knees and not bothering to listen, a hot, thick towel waiting on the sand, a flask with a cold drink, ice that chinked. She blamed Thatcher most of all. Lenny was one of Thatcher's children, a casualty of what it takes. She blamed Thatcher because Thatcher was filled with herself and that did not allow her to know. She blamed Thatcher because of her teeth, that mean beak of a nose, that airy wave. She blamed Thatcher for Lenny and as she shivered she thought, yes, she was right. If she tried hard enough everything would be all right. It was the hardness of her hands against her body, pressing, pressing, her teeth chattering, her wet hair, her hand cold between her legs. It was the pain. Everything could be all right. But that was Thatcher for you. Thatcher in her bed, her teeth clenched. Thatcher, the smell of Thatcher. The light that shineth in the darkness.

Two forty-five. Let him do it. Please let him do it. He can do it if you let him have his head. She laughs at that. She does it like this because she is afraid. Let the light shine in the darkness.

She wants no one to call. Let no one come. She does not want to see Maude Edgecombe today. But how does she keep the woman away? She can forgive Susan. However wrong-headed she might be, she does at least try. Maude allows things to happen. How can she do that?

It's the same in Martin's bookshop where Alice sometimes works. How can Martin allow it to get the way it is? She's told him a thousand times that classification is the key, not only to the bookshop, Martin, but to life. Everybody knows that. You have to draw a line. That's what classification is. You make a decision, it's here rather than there, that's all. It's only a fucking decision, Martin. It's only one fucking way.

But, oh no, Martin knows better. He does it by feel. And you can't find any damn thing. She does her best to rearrange the books but it's a thankless task. Martin says that life's like that. She says only if you let it get like that. He laughs. How can he laugh? A book can be in science fiction or it can be in fiction or it can even be in travel. How can you work with a system like that? He says you can't pin life down. You shouldn't try. It's like a butterfly. You destroy its beauty if you catch it and pin it down. He says it's a phenomenon, which means it's something that happens, not a thing. It terrifies her. Life has to be pinned down or where would we be? Where would you draw the line?

Two forty-seven. How she hates the creaking movement of the clock. A digital would be so much bet-ter. No two ways about the time then. It either is or it

isn't. Come on, kid. Get back here. I need you back here.
I can't go on like this.

17.

He's a good boy. He knows where he is. Drive through the village. The policeman moans. Mum will sort him out if he doesn't stop it. Watch it, young man. Don't stop. Don't talk to anybody. Not Mr. Wyatt. Not Jimmy. Not Maude. What is wrong with talking to them? They're his friends. Maudie's his friend. But it's a secret. He could stop and talk to her and it'd be all right. Maudie lives in the house he's passing. She will touch him on the shoulder with her good hand and say hello, sailor. He's not a sailor. She knows. It's a trick. He tells her and tells her but she always calls him that. I'm not a sailor, Maudie. I don't have a uniform. I don't go on a ship. She laughs. You're my sailor, Lenny, she says.

He can stop and talk to anybody. He likes to do that. But he won't stop today. He'll go the long way round, like Mum said. Not through the middle of the village past the shop where Mum works. They sell books. He likes books. Mum says so. Not past the farm where he works. Not past the house by the yard where Mr. and Mrs. Wyatt live. Not past Pat the dog. He'll go the long way round.

He wants a dog. A big dog that will do what he

says. Down, boy, down. Good boy. Lay down. Come here. Heel. But Mum won't let him. He says he can look after him but she says he forgets and she doesn't want an animal around the house. Ha, caught you, Mum, he says. Caught you there. The cat's an animal. We've got a cat. The cat is here. They call him cat, which isn't a name, but it is as well. She doesn't answer sometimes because she forgets. She's old. But she won't die.

Up the hill, round the corner. Mum's waiting. What does she want him to do this for? Naughty boy. Shut up and do what you're told. You try my patience sometimes. Maudie says that Mum's a saint. What are saints, Maudie? Maudie says saints are people who don't care what other people think, no matter what. Maudie holds his hand. She sits him in the big chair or on the sofa and she holds his hand and talks. Sometimes she asks him questions. Oh, Maudie, you are a caution. What do you know? Tell me a story. He told her about the vids. About the way the women did things. He said Jimmy would find a woman for him. She said no. He could do it to her. She said he could fuck her. She did. It's true. It is.

The policeman groans. He shouldn't do that. They're nearly home now. He must keep quiet. He won't stop, he won't stop. He'll keep going. He's a good boy. He needs a pee. Down around the corner and he's almost there. Careful! A big cat sits in the road. He brakes. It runs across the road and jumps up into the hedge. Good cat. There's a hole in the hedge where the fox jumps through. Look out, cat. The fox will get you. It isn't their cat.

Maudie says there's nothing to be afraid of, not in this world, not in this life. What world? he says. What life? He does this because she laughs. It's his trick. She says there's only one world, one life. What world, he says. That's enough, Lenny, she says. Enough is enough. She strokes him on the back of the hand, touches him with the tips of the fingers of her good hand like it's a feather and it feels like she's touching him and not doing it. She doesn't look at him when she does it. Because it's something else no one knows about. Your time will come, she says.

Mum doesn't like Maudie. She doesn't say it but he knows. He knows it because his body hurts when Mum is with Maudie.

He won't tell Mum. Why should he tell her that? What for? He changes down. Too fast. The car shudders. Today it doesn't do what he wants it to do. Stupid car. He changes back up but the car won't have this and he changes down again.

Nearly there. He'll be glad to be home all right. He's a good boy. Careful! Sometimes Mum hits him when he's done nothing at all. He hates that. You try me, she says. You really try me. He scratches his arms. I'm a good boy, he says. You try me, she says.

18.

Two fifty. She changes the plates. The same plates with the same pattern but sometimes she thinks she is not sure which one is which. Sometimes she avoids thinking about it, but sometimes it's just the tip of a thought that makes her do it.

Two fifty-one. It was worse with the kids. Especially Jack, when she first had him. His head peeping from the bedclothes and she felt something was wrong. She had to move everything. Wake him and the kid was squalling and she had to change the bedclothes, change his nappy, wash her hands, wash the sink, change the soap, wipe the tip of his head just in case there could be something there, and then, just because she had done that, she had to wipe the rest of him and then wash him, and then she was putting him into his small bath at three in the morning, it was so dark outside, and he was still crying and she was squeezing the sponge, trickling warm water over his head and down his back, splashing his toes to make it all right, but after this there were always gaps that needed filling. And she filled them.

Two fifty-two and she hears them.

She looks through the window, waiting to see the

car, to make sure. Come on, son, nudge it a bit farther forward, get it out of sight. It is you, isn't it? You're a good boy. She looks at herself in the small, mottled mirror over the sink. She pushes her hair from her eyes. Would it be better cut really short? Would that make her more herself, who she really is? But hair is just one thing.

Two fifty-three. The car's parked across the yard. She can see Lenny at the wheel. She puts her hand to her collar, holds it tight. She looks for Jack. He'll be in the back if Lenny has done it right. She waits for him to walk across, comes to the door, opens it for him.

"Well?" she says. "Was it all right?"

"Careful!" Lenny says, his finger to his lips.

"What's wrong?" she says.

"I'm a good boy, Mum," Lenny says. "My car can do a ton. Jimmy said that too. But I didn't. I did what you said. It could do more if I wanted it to. I didn't stop to stroke the horse."

She runs out and opens the back door of the car. She sees him on the floor between the seats, his wrists bound by the white cord. Lenny walks over.

"Is he all right?" she says.

"I'm a good boy. I am a good boy, Mum." She strokes Lenny's cheek, puts her hand onto his shoulder, hugs him.

"You're my good, good boy," she says.

"Mum," he says. "I want a doggy. Jimmy says I could have a dog. It would be good fun, wouldn't it? It would be mine, wouldn't it? It wouldn't be anybody else's. Nobody else's at all. It could come in the car."

"Let's get him inside," she says.

"I want a pee, Mum," he says.

"Not now, Lenny," she says.

"I'm a good boy, Mum," Lenny says. "I'm a good boy, aren't I?"

"You get hold of his shoulders, Lenny, I'll take his feet. Be careful."

"Careful!" he says.

"It's not a game, son."

"Careful!" he says.

"I said it wasn't a bloody game."

They lift him out of the car, but she can't hold him. His feet slip from her hands.

"Take care," she says.

"Careful!" Lenny says. He stands with his hands under Jack's shoulders. Does he have an inkling? She takes hold of Jack's ankles again. She lifts and they carry him into the hallway. He groans.

"You didn't hit him too hard, Lenny?" she says.

"I'm a good boy, Mum."

"You're a very good boy. Now, come on. Let's get him upstairs. I don't want anybody seeing this. You're not to say anything about this to anyone. You hear me, Lenny?" He nods.

"Did you hear me?" she says.

"Careful!" Lenny says.

They carry him past the hall stand and the chest of drawers. She drops his feet when they get to the stairs.

"There has to be another way to do this," she says. "Lenny, could you carry him over your shoulder?"

Lenny lowers Jack's head and shoulders to the floor. She won't look at Jack's face. She's seen blood on his mouth and on his nose. She wants to touch him, to make up for it, to make good. No one, no one, can touch him like she can.

"Turn him over," she says. "He has to be the other way to carry him on your shoulder." Lenny pushes him over and pulls him up onto his shoulder. He stops halfway up the stairs but not for long. She knows she invests him with strength to make up for his weaknesses when, in fact, he's probably no stronger than anyone else of his build. And he has a tendency to run to fat. Sometimes she tries to look after what he eats but he puts away a lot at work.

She follows on the stairs. She can see the back of Jack's head. Blood on Lenny's shirt.

"It's all right," she says on the landing. "Stop for a rest."

"I'm a good boy," Lenny says.

"You're a very good boy," she says. "Stop on this landing before you go to the next. We'll have a rest."

Jack groans.

"You didn't hit him too hard?" she says.

"I'm a good boy," Lenny says.

Careful!

"Lenny," she says. "Don't keep saying that. You're a very good boy. How many times did you hit him?" Lenny whimpers.

"We can carry on now," she says. "Up to the next landing."

"I don't like it up here," Lenny says.

"Of course you do. Don't be silly. Now let's get him up to the attic."

"Hello, hello?" A voice calls from the foot of the stairs.

"Keep going," she says. "I'll be back. Don't come down. Did you hear what I said? Don't come down." She runs down the stairs.

"The door was open," Maude Edgecombe says. "And the door of the car. I wondered if you were all right."

"It's OK," Alice says. "Just doing a bit of rearranging. Nothing to worry about."

"Is Lenny not at work? I see his car here."

"He's had a day off. He's staying home with me."

"I expect he likes that," Maude Edgecombe says. "Shall I shut the car door?"

"I'll do it," Alice says.

Will the news be out? Is there anything on the radio? Surely too early for that? She goes out to the car. Wind throws the rain at her. She slams the door and runs back inside. Where is Maude Edgecombe now? She runs to the stairs. "Maude," she shouts. "Don't go upstairs.

Lenny's up there. He needs to be alone." But Maude is not upstairs. She is standing out in the passageway by the cupboard door, looking at the rain as it splashes from the gutter onto the paving stones.

"He's not quite himself," she says. Maude touches her forearm.

"Don't worry," she says. "I won't bother you. You get on with what you have to do."

She waits for Maude to leave. Watches her walk along the drive through the rain, watches her pick her way daintily through the puddles, damn the woman. Under the trees, under the splattering rain, out onto the road.

She runs up the stairs. Lenny stands with Jack over his shoulder outside the attic door.

"Go in, damn you," she shouts. "What are you waiting for?"

"I'm a good boy," he says.

"Yes, of course," she says, "of course you are, Lenny."

The smell of the room as she goes in. Smell is always the thing that gets her most. Something about the smell of a room that is never used. The day before she was up here and had unfolded the camp bed, put a blanket on it, a sheet over that, another blanket and a pillow. But she didn't make it up, didn't want it to seem too permanent, that she was taking it for granted, that it could go only one way. No, not that. There has to be some leeway. After all, he has a mind of his own. She will take it as slowly as it needs to be taken.

She brought up a plastic bucket. She brought up a chair. She brought up a thin silk scarf. She sat on the bed and cried. She went downstairs and put on an old rain-coat. She came back up to the room, sat on the bed, pulled up the collar, did up the belt, pushed her hands down into the pockets. She waited, alone, uselessly, but of course nothing happened. Sometimes she does things like this.

Lenny settles Jack belly-down on the chair. Jack's head lolls, his feet touching the floor.

"Not like that," she says. "Sit him up properly." Jack is groaning. Lenny sits him in the chair.

"Out of the way," she says. She has to do it now. She picks up the silk scarf. Sees blood around his mouth. A broken tooth. A bruise under his eye.

She pushes her fingers into Jack's mouth, works the scarf between his teeth, like a bit for a horse, ties it at the back of his head. It's too intimate, too intrusive, at this stage, to have to put her fingers into his mouth.

"I'm sorry," she whispers. She wipes her fingers on her sleeves. She can see the bruise on his neck now.

"Right," she says to Lenny. "You can go."

"I'm going to Maudie's," he says.

"You're not," she says. "I want you to stay in the house for a bit. It's very important, son."

"Very important," he says. "I'm a good boy, Mum."

"Come here," she says. She catches hold of his wrist.

"What did I say to you?"

"I'm a good boy," he says.

"No, no, the other bit."

"Not go to Maudie's."

"And the other thing?"

"Stay in the house. I'm a good boy."

"That's right. You're a good boy." She touches the back of his hand.

"That hurts," he says. "But I can go to work tomorrow. Yes?"

"No, I don't think so, darling. We'll let that go for a bit. Go on downstairs now."

"But I have to stomp the crates. I have to burn them."

He stands with his hands at his sides.

"Don't dribble," she says. "Go on down." He stands with his fingers on his lips. "What is it? What do you want?" He looks at her. "What is it? What the bloody hell is it?" she says.

"The policeman," he says.

"Yes, he's a policeman. But don't tell anybody about him. Do you hear me? What is it, Lenny?"

"He said I could wear his helmet."

"I don't expect so. You imagined that, darling. You can't wear his helmet. Where is it?" Lenny fingers his scar, the white ridge of flesh.

Careful!

"I said where is it, darling? His helmet? You brought it with you, didn't you?" He shuffles his feet. Jack groans.

"What is it?" she says.

"He said I could wear it. He said, he did."

"Where is it, darling? It's in your car, isn't it? Tell me it is." He shrugs. "Tell me, darling." Nothing worse than a policeman's helmet lolling in the road.

She runs down the stairs, through the kitchen, and out into the rain. Finds it on the front seat. Anybody could have seen it there. She smells it, puts her hand into it, takes it inside. She opens the door of the cupboard under the stairs, puts it on the floor at the back of it, buries it under boxes, old forgotten things, anything she can find.

The phone rings just as she closes the cupboard door. She waits by it, trying not to pick it up. She puts her hand on it counting the rings. It might be something. She has to do it. Otherwise it's something left undone.

"Hello Alice," Martin says. "I have to go out. I wondered if you could look after the shop for a couple of hours before closing."

"I'm sorry, Martin. Not today. I can't today. Any other day would be fine."

"Are you sure? I really do have to get out."

"Not today, Martin. Something's come up."

"Are you all right? Is there anything I can do?"

"It's all right. Ask me another day."

"Are you absolutely sure that I can't press you on

this one? Just this once? Honestly, just this once."

"I can't. I really can't. If I could I would, so don't ask me about it again."

"It's this house I've seen. I told you I was looking, didn't I? I have to see it soon. It's a snip and someone is sure to snap it up."

"No, Martin. I can't do it. Not today. I can't today."

"Pretty please?"

"For God's sake, didn't you hear me? I fucking said no." She slams the phone down and runs back upstairs. Lenny is standing where she left him.

"He said I could wear it," he says.

"Forget about it now," she says. "We'll talk about it later. You go downstairs and wait. I'll make a cup of tea. We'll have a cup of tea together. That'll be nice, won't it?" He stands with his fingers in his mouth.

"Don't do that," she says. "What is it?"

He points at Jack.

"Will you make a cup of tea for him?" he says.

"Not now," she says. "Perhaps tomorrow, but he doesn't want one now. Go downstairs. Don't come back up. I'll come down. Wait for me in the kitchen."

"Shall I switch the kettle on?"

"Yes, darling. And listen. You don't come up here again without me. Do you understand that?" He nods his head, his fingers in his mouth.

"Go on down, then," she says.

"I want to pee," he says.

19.

He won't, not if he doesn't want to. He doesn't have to, the white stuff that spurts out the end. Mum doesn't know because he doesn't tell her. Mum, I can't, not like Jimmy does. It's a trick. It is. Tell him, Mum. Sometimes he can, he can, he nearly can. It's there, it's what Jimmy says.

Sometimes he strokes the vids, licks them to taste what's inside. They don't taste. He doesn't tell Jimmy. Jimmy lends him the vids. Not to your mother, you stupid fucker. Stupid, stupid fucker. Naughty boy. Not to her, oh no. It's a trick. It is.

20.

She hears the phone, a faint ringing at the bottom of the house. Don't answer it, Lenny. Don't answer it, son.

Dust in the air. A cobweb in a corner. Twisted beams across the ceiling. A small, blue glass jar on the windowsill. A rusted can on the floor in a corner.

He sits with his head on his chest, his hands tied behind his back. She sees a ring on his left hand, a scuffed shoe, blood on his collar. Dried blood on his face, dark, scabbed into a shape that will tell her something if she has the wit to understand. A bruise on his cheek by his nose, under his eyes, a cut on his lip.

She steps forward. He moves his head. She puts her hand under his chin, lifts it, and she hits him as hard as she can on his cheek. She does it again. Her hand on his cheek, the impact, the touch, her skin on his. It's all his fault. He made her do it, and he should know that.

"You know what that's for," she says. "Who the hell do you think you are?"

She hits him again.

"No more," she says. "Not now. I've done it. You sit there and think about it, about what you've done."

She goes to the window. She touches the grime on

the glass and thinks she should have cleaned the room, made a job of it. Rain streaks the glass, batters the trees. It would be easy to let go, but this is about not letting go. Not about that at all.

"I could have just not bothered," she says. "It takes a lot to bother. It takes a bloody lot to care. But what do you know about that?" He stands up, unsteady on his feet, but he does not open his eyes.

"No," she says. "Stay there, where I've got you." She goes to the bed, reaches under it and pulls out the rest of the white cord. Pushes him back into the chair, easy to do it with him like he is. Wraps the cord around his body and around the back of the chair. She can hear his breathing. Close to him she wants to say something intimate but the knot has to be tied tight enough not to worry. She tests the tension of the cord. It's tight enough to show that she means what she says.

She goes back to the window. Rain softens everything but nothing stops her worrying. She wants to say that all those things, all those past things, they're all gone. But with her fingers on the glass she knows she can't let go. It will take more than this. She draws her finger down the pane. She can feel the coldness of the outside air on the glass. She sees the cat in the road. She sees it stop, stare at something, lash its tail and move on.

She never saw him eat after he had moved to the other room. He never talked about it. It was a part of him that he kept to himself. A young boy, doing that. Just think of it. He wanted to sit with a knife and fork in his hands, the plate in front of him and chew and swallow in his own way. It wasn't the eating. She knew that. It was the start of who he was. How often do people see something that changes their lives in an instant, just a moment, and it's done? He did.

She rubs the window with the palm of her hand, wipes it as clean as she can. Nothing is ever as fixed as you want it to be. Nothing keeps on and on, not in the way you think that it's going to, but sometimes it does.

It wasn't that he wanted more to eat. It wasn't that he was hungry. It was nothing like that. She imagines herself standing over him as he eats. She tries to convince herself that she did this. Makes herself believe she did. That she watched him as he quietly took his time, as he gently prodded the food on his plate, as he chewed it. But of course she did nothing of the sort. He wouldn't let her. It wasn't the eating at all, really. It was something else.

He pushed his hair out of his eyes as he sat at the table. It started with that. No, it started before that. It started with small things and she had neither the wit nor the wisdom to notice that she was adding one thing to another, joining them for him. It started with Jack in her lap, the sudden snatching of his hand to her breast, a movement that hurt. No intent to hurt but she stored it away to add to the next thing.

She draws the tip of her finger around the windowpane and then places her hand on her breast. She cries because light through the window on the boards on a cold day is a beautiful thing. Because the air in the attic is sharp and she feels it on her skin. Because light through the trees makes patterns. Because her other son is a galumphing fool whom she loves. Because she wants him to be someone he is not. She cries because she remembers Jack's face looking up at her before he could walk. Because she worries to think of how many things like this there can be. She cries because if she can find the end of the thread that is tangled through all of these things, she can pull it and everything will be sorted. But she is afraid that she will not try hard enough to find it, now she has come this far.

She goes to the bed and rearranges the blanket. She goes to the corner of the room and tries to brush the cobweb from the ceiling but she is too short to reach it. Now it is in her mind and like all cobwebs it will stay and grow.

She walks down to the next landing, takes a chair from the bedroom and carries it upstairs. She stands on it in the corner and knocks the cobweb away. It is nothing in her hand, blackened threads sticking to her skin. She carries the chair around the room combing the corners for cobwebs. And then she stands holding the chair in front of him. She could hit him with it. It would be a thing to do. This might be the time, the opening, her chance. She will see the end of the thread and pull at it and at that moment it will happen. What if she misses her chance? She puts the chair down and walks a step toward him. Then she turns, picks up the chair and carries it out of the room.

21.

He stands in the kitchen pulling the curtain. It's untidy. Outside rain hits the top of the car and the stones in the yard. At work he'd be in the barn. Mr. Wyatt would find them something to do. He says there's always something to do on a farm. He likes it in the barn. They talk. Jimmy tells him things, about the girls, the women, the bitches, who go to his house. Jimmy tells him about pubs, films he's seen, movies, cars he's had, real, good motors, places he's been abroad, in France. Jimmy went to France once on a boat and there were hundreds of cars on the boat. Tell me, Jimmy, but Jimmy talks about his bitches.

Sometimes when they're splitting crates Jimmy tells him about the night before. He likes it, but sometimes he doesn't like it because it gives him a hard-on and it's not right, not there in the barn. He has to hide it. Sometimes he doesn't like what Jimmy says. When Jimmy starts to talk he doesn't know what he will say. Jimmy's not very big. He has short hair, an earring, and new boots he didn't tell him about. Jimmy says that you can tell a man from his boots. Mr. Wyatt says you can tell a cowboy from his boots. That's silly, Mr. Wyatt. You don't have cowboys in England. They live in America.

Don't you know that, silly?

Jimmy stomps on the crates in his boots. Take care with your boots, Jimmy, but he doesn't mind. Mr. Wyatt says that cowboys are like that. They get splinters in their hands if they don't wear gloves. He has gloves. Jimmy never wears gloves. Mr. Wyatt tells him to wear gloves and he does until Mr. Wyatt goes away. Then he takes them off. Lenny takes off his gloves like Jimmy. He likes stomping on the crates in the big barn where the sparrows fly in and sit on the rafters, chirp and rattle and skitter about.

Sometimes Jimmy cocks his leg and farts, a great, big raspberry that shakes his trousers. Beat that, he says. Lenny tries but it doesn't work like Jimmy's does, it doesn't beat it. It's a trick. Teach me the trick, Jimmy. Jimmy says you know why women can't fart like men? They never stop talking long enough to build up the pressure. What pressure, Jimmy? Jimmy stomps the crates. He says he'll teach him farting like that one day.

His new boots aren't like cowboy boots. They aren't like Jimmy's new boots. Jimmy should have told him he was changing. But Jimmy says that Lenny's boots are great. Sometimes Jimmy wears his old boots and he likes that because that means they have the same. Him and Jimmy together. Look, Jimmy, he says. Look at me stomping. These boots are great. They're great, aren't they, Jimmy? Aren't they? Aren't they?

Listen to me, Jimmy says. I fucked this woman

last night. I screwed her to the floor. Mr. Wyatt wants this done by dinnertime, Jimmy. Oh, slow down, Jimmy says. What's the rush? This woman, see, this bitch, and he knows what Jimmy's going to tell him. The bitch will take off her clothes and ask Jimmy to do things to her, naked, with nothing on, she's panting for it, really panting, and she's naked with nothing on, and she doesn't mind, and Jimmy will say not yet, and he doesn't want to know because it hurts him in his belly, because of the waiting. That's what gets women, big boy, Jimmy says. They love the tension, that's what gets them every time. Like in the vids, Jimmy. Yeah, that's it, kid, Jimmy says.

He stomps on the crates, as hard as he can, and throws them in the fire. Listen, big boy. It's human. Everybody wants it. You included. There's nothing you can do about it. You're the same as all the rest. And he is, he's the same as the rest, there's nothing he can do and there's nothing they can do, whatever they say they can. It's true. He's the same.

Jimmy taught him how to wank properly. He wasn't doing it right before. You've got to hold it this way. Jimmy said everybody does it. There's an art to everything, big boy. Jimmy gave him magazines and said he had to practice, that he had to learn. Jimmy said not in the barn, you stupid sod, not when the boss is around, not when Mrs. Wyatt gets out here. For fuck's sake. Put it away.

Jimmy calls it his mighty sword. Is this my mighty

sword, Jimmy? Put it away, for fuck's sake, you moron. I'm not a moron, am I Jimmy? I'm not. Put it away. Is this a big one, Jimmy? Put it away. For fuck's sake. But everybody does it, including him.

He's stomping on the crates and Jimmy is telling him about the bitch with black hair and all he sees is the bitch's body doing things and Jimmy is giving it to her, giving it to her good. Stop it, Jimmy, stop it, that's what the bitch says, it's too much. And he wants to say stop it, Jimmy, but he won't say it because Jimmy is his friend, and Jimmy wants to do it, and Jimmy tells him things he tells nobody else. And Mum says he needs friends. She's not sure about Jimmy. Giving it to her good between the legs, this tart. Stop it Jimmy, please.

Jimmy told him he'd give him videos. You've got a video player? In your own room, kid? Mum, I want a video in my room. What for, darling? I want to see videos. Well, you can see them down here. I want to see them up there. I want to see them in my room. What videos, Lenny? Where will you get them, love? You get them in the video shop in the village. I don't want you watching them. Well, everybody else does. Everybody? Who's everybody? Everybody, Mum. I have to think about this, she says. You try me, you really do.

Jimmy's giving it to her good, right between the legs, and then he takes it out, you take it out and you tease them big boy, they say they don't like it, but they do. Jimmy is a red-hot lover, he's taking it out and putting it in and giving it to her good. Jimmy says he gives her one for him. For me Jimmy? Thank you very much. Jimmy's his friend.

He's stomping hard on the crates, stomping them to fill his head. Hold up, big boy, says Jimmy, he doesn't pay you to work like a nigger. Hold up. Jimmy tells him that he gives it to her up the ass. Up the ass, Jimmy? He's stomping as hard as he can, he doesn't want to stop the stomping. Stomping hard. Give it a rest, kid. He's stomping. He likes his boots. They're good boots. They're good boots for doing this. She wanted it like that, I'm telling you, she was screaming for it. He's stomping the crates.

Mum let him buy his video. It's my money. I want one, Mum. I'm not sure about this, Lenny. Everybody has one. Don't lick your fingers. I want one in my room. Then take this one up. I want my own. You stupid boy. No, you're not a stupid boy. I'm sorry. I'm sorry, Lenny. I'm not sure about this. He bought one in town. Mum went with him. He bought it with his money, his own money. It's his video.

Jimmy lends him the vids. He doesn't like to look at them but he has to because of what he can see. He does like to look but he doesn't. He likes the bitches. Maudie says they're not bitches. But she hasn't seen the vids so how can she tell? They look nice. They could ride in his car. He wouldn't tell Mum. He covers his eyes just to see and not see what's there. He wants to look at the women and the men but he doesn't know what to do when they're doing it. He doesn't like the men. They scare him. He rubs and rubs and thinks about his new car or Susan or the girl who serves in the post office or his new boots. He thinks things he could say. There's too much to see. It won't stop. He wants to ask. But he won't.

Once in a vid there was a girl who looked like Susan. He took his fingers from his eyes and he paused it and watched it flicker. It could be Susan. Her face is like that. It could be. Look at my tits, big boy. No, I don't want to, Susan. Look at them, look at my tits. Aren't they nice? Don't you want to stroke them? Don't you want to do things to me? Don't you want to do something between my legs? Where's your mighty sword, big boy? No, no, no, no, no. He didn't watch the rest of it. It wasn't Susan. It wasn't. Who can he ask? Don't say those things.

He looks through the window and watches the rain. He has a vid to watch but not now. He goes out to the car. He opens the door and gets in. It's nice in the car, out of the rain. He listens to the rain hitting the roof. Spots of rain. Lots of spots. He looks at the cat sitting in the barn. Nice cat. He wants to drive away. He could go to France on a boat with Jimmy. They take cars, hundreds of them, more than you think. He would go with him if he asked. They would go everywhere in his car.

Now a white space in his head. He turns as fast as he can to lose it but it follows him. He shakes his head and hits it with his fist but it stays. He thinks there's something he should do. Mum, I'm a good boy. He turns the key but he doesn't start the car. It's the wrong time to start it. The red light and the orange light come on. Don't do that. Just don't do it.

Maybe tomorrow he'll stomp crates. His boots are great. They're not cowboy boots but they're good for stomping crates. Jimmy told him. Jimmy doesn't like stomping on crates in his new boots. He doesn't say, but Lenny knows. Jimmy likes driving the tractor best. Sometimes Mr. Wyatt won't let him. Jimmy swears at Mr. Wyatt when he's gone. He doesn't care, not one bit. Sometimes Lenny tries to swear when Mr. Wyatt has gone but he can't do it like Jimmy. Jimmy rolls a cigarette and lights it and swears between his teeth, and it's like the swear words are smoke in his mouth. Swear for me, Jimmy. I like it. Fuck off, kid.

22.

She stands outside the door and listens for his breathing. She wants to hear him breathe, she wants to hear who he is, who he really is, after all this time. She puts her ear close to the door but she can hear nothing. She has to open the door, just to see what she's done. He hasn't moved. He can't. Funny how she has imagined him big in his life, filling out who he is, strong in everything he does. Now here he is trussed up, stuck in this room.

She hears something, a knock perhaps? Is it Maude Edgecombe? Alice suspects that Maude knows what's going on when in fact she really doesn't know a damn thing. Maude hints that she has powers. Maude thinks nothing in the world is extraordinary. For Alice too much is extraordinary. Bloody Maude and her arm across her chest, her silences, her grace, damn it, her poise. Funny in a woman who gossips so much. Perhaps this is what her arm is for. It's an antenna, listening to what's happening, gleaning extraordinary things. Alice's world is full of sensation, but nothing stands still, remains for long enough for her to make sense of it. That's why she cleans and tidies like she does.

She hears the slam of a door. Only Lenny, the poor

boy. He did it, didn't he? He did what she wanted. It's time for the news. She has to watch to see what they say. First she has to go in to see Jack. She wants to hear him breathe. She wants to hear his breath in the room, see it in the cold air, because his breath is her breath. Nothing else matters. That will help to put it right.

She opens the door wider. He is seated on the chair, his hands tied behind his back. His head droops on his chest, his eyes are closed. She tiptoes toward him, lifts her hand to touch his arm. He moves his head. She steps back. She can't touch him in the way she wants to, not now, not yet. The bruise on his face, the side of his nose, underneath his eye, a mottled red turning to purple, the cut on his lip an ugly swollen line. She wants to hit him again, hard, because so much has happened.

She balls her hand into a fist but then it goes. She wants to stroke his cheek. He lifts his head, opens his eyes, and makes a noise through the scarf. She can do anything she wants to him in this room.

She tiptoes in near, puts her head as close as she can to his without touching. But Harold intervenes. He always does. Bloody Harold, keep out of this. Nothing to do with you. Harold's hands on her knees, his arms rigid, Harold taut as taut can be, his wired body. Harold tied to the world, pushing down on her because he wants to get past this moment to a place where things are better than they are, where he does not hate her or the kids or himself, where it's as right as right can be. Please stop

Harold, we can do whatever you want, it's only the two of us together. Harold, do what you have to do. Harold crops up at these moments. It's nothing to do with her.

She lifts a finger to Jack's cheek, holds it as close as she can. She wants to stroke him so that he will know who she is again. She puts her face close to his, to feel his closeness. It's something animals do, isn't it? Deeper than thought. So much gets in the way. Animals don't have that. Harold, not now, you poor sod.

She has to watch the news, she has to leave him here, but she wants to talk, to go beyond what they used to be to what they are now. Before she goes she will say something that will matter. But what is there to say, after all this time? *I wanted to make it right. That's why you're here. You can't understand why I've done this. Your brother needs healing. My life needs healing. You can't stay apart. Why did you do it? I could see this coming, I've seen it for ten years. There was no getting away from it. I am so sorry it happened like it did. But there was no other way. I know what you are going to say. I could have talked to you. But that's not true. You stopped talking to me when you were eight. You wouldn't talk. I could have gone up to you in the precinct in town and put my arms around you. But we aren't like that, are we? Why did you come back to this area? You must have wanted to see us, whatever you say. You know it's true.*

She knows she cannot start like that. She has to

start somewhere else. "Open your eyes," she says. "You have to open them sometime. If you open your eyes, I'll take the scarf out of your mouth." He keeps his eyes closed. One of his eyelids flickers and she takes this as a sign. She likes signs.

"Right," she says. "I have to go if you won't cooperate." She turns but she goes back and kisses him lightly on the cheek. Then she hits him as hard as she can, a ringing blow.

"I had to do that," she says. "You know why, don't you, son?"

23.

It's his bedroom and he can do what he likes. He doesn't want to watch the vid, not now. He has the white space, inside his head and outside, sticking to his face. It won't go away. He's a good boy. Careful! Sometimes he doesn't turn off the tape. But only sometimes. He steals things in the shop but only because he forgets to pay. He let the chickens out but only because he didn't shut the door. He dribbles but that's because it happens. He pees on the floor, not in the toilet. That's only because he forgets. It's easy to forget.

He sits down and takes out his pecker. That's what Jimmy calls it. He calls it his mighty sword as well. He calls it two things. Jimmy says he has two peckers, one for peeing and one for shagging. That's not true. It's a trick. He rubs his pecker but nothing happens. It should but it doesn't. Jimmy says that's always the fault of the bitch. Some women step out of line. He rubs and rubs. It feels sore now. There's a red patch. The bitch. Jimmy says women tease. What's tease, Jimmy? It's sore. The white space howls. Go away!

He's hungry. He goes downstairs, past the window on the side of the stairs. He hates the window. He hates the plant on the sill, the dark green leaves. Careful!

He hurries down the stairs into the kitchen. Nothing on the stove, nothing in the oven. He won't touch the stove. He won't touch the oven. He can cook. Mum taught him a long time ago. She said there was nothing he couldn't do. She said he was her son. He is her son. She taught him everything. She didn't touch anything. She said he had to do that or it wouldn't work.

She left him to look after himself. She said he was grown up now. That was when the policeman came. After the firemen. He liked the firemen. They put out the fire. A good job Maudie came when he was cooking. She phoned 999. He knows the number. 999. It's the same number you dial again. It's made that way. It's easy. He can cook.

The policeman wouldn't let him live in the house by himself. Mum said he could. The policeman said he was a good boy but he couldn't stay there by himself. Where's your Mum? She's gone away for a few days. I get on her nerves. She'll soon be back. It's all right. Maudie said he could stay with her but the policeman sent a woman.

The woman talked to him. She took him to an office with bright lights, a plant by a window that was all right, a calendar with a funny man, and the woman talked to him in another room without anybody else. She gave him a cup of tea. She said he could have as many cups of tea as he liked. He was hungry. He liked the woman. She gave him some chewing gum. He's not allowed chewing gum. Jimmy chews it and gives him a piece. You can't swallow it, it hurts you if you do. He didn't tell the woman he wasn't allowed. He tricked her.

The woman took him to a house in the town where a man and a woman lived. He didn't like them. He had to sleep in their house even after Mum came back. They wouldn't let him home. They didn't talk to him. Mum cried when he came back. Don't cry, Mum.

The trouble was the smoke in the kitchen. It went everywhere and he couldn't stop it. He tried and he tried ever so hard. It went on the ceiling and the walls and the doors and the windows and the plates and cups, everywhere it wanted to. He couldn't see anything. It was so big. It was on the windows and he couldn't see out. He wanted to make chips like Mum did. Chips in the chip pan. That was when the policeman came. The policeman said he was lucky.

Mum comes in. She's crying. Hug, Mum. Hug.

"Don't cry, Mum. I'm a good boy. I can cook, can't I?"

"Lenny, I'm sorry. I've made nothing for tea. I set the table. Look, it's all set, but I didn't do anything. What shall we have? Chips and beans?"

"Not chips," he says. "Not chips. Mashed potatoes."

"Sorry, Lenny," she says. "I forgot." He doesn't eat chips, not anymore. He doesn't like them. "Mashed potatoes and beans, then? Good boy."

"I'll do it, Mum. I'll do it good."

"You sit down and wait. We have to watch the telly. Watch telly, Lenny."

He switches on the old set on the sideboard. It's useless. It's crap. Who wants to watch a thing like that?

"Oh fuck, that's crap," he says.

"What did you say, Lenny? Did you swear?"

"It's crap."

"Don't say that, Lenny. That's swearing. Don't swear."

"It's not, Mum. Jimmy says it."

"I want a word with that young man."

He watches the telly. It's boring. But then it's like something he's seen before. He sees the place. He knows the place. The car. He sees the car. The door's open. It wasn't him.

"I closed the door. Mum, I closed the door. Look, it's the place." Mum comes over from the stove. She looks at the telly.

"I did, Mum. I did."

"Quiet, Lenny, I want to hear this. Let Mum hear."

"It's the place, Mum. I'm a good boy." He sees lots of policemen. He hears the voice of a man. A man is talking to another man. Farther on down the road are the ducks. He hopes they show the ducks.

"Will they show the ducks, Mum? I want them to show the ducks."

"Quiet, Lenny. I want to hear this."

"It's the car, Mum. I closed the door. They opened it. Not me. They opened it. It wasn't me. It wasn't me."

"For fuck's sake, give it a rest, Lenny. I want to hear what they say."

"You swore."

"Fucking shut up." He wants to pee.

"I want to pee, Mum."

"Well, go and do it. You're big enough now."

"I am, aren't I? Tell me if they show the ducks."

He takes down his trousers and sits on the seat. He is a good boy. He didn't pee when they took him to the woman and the man. He couldn't. He stayed in the room and sat on the bed. If he closed his eyes hard enough he'd be home but he wasn't. The woman with the plant sat on the bed and talked to him but he didn't listen. She put her hand on his shoulder. He cried, he didn't listen. He's a good boy. When the woman went away in her car the woman in the house said he'd been a naughty boy, a very naughty boy indeed. The man said he was a naughty boy too.

But he's a good boy. He can cook. Mum won't let him anymore. The woman with the plant came and took him to the office. She didn't give him gum. Then she took him home. The woman made Mum sign a form. That meant she could look after him but not let him cook. And she couldn't go away. Not ever. And not die. But he can cook if he wants to. No one can stop him.

Careful!

When it ends he leaves the seat down. He doesn't put it up. Jimmy leaves it up in the lav at work. Sometimes he leaves it up too. Jimmy says he doesn't fucking care. He didn't pee when he was at the woman and man's house. He didn't tell them. It was a trick. But it hurt.

"Mum," he says when he gets back to the kitchen.

"Shut up," she says. But she's not doing anything. Why does she say that? She's switched off the telly and she's sitting down.

"Mum," he says.

"Not now," she says. She's thinking. He knows. She looks at her hands. But perhaps she isn't thinking at all. You never know. You never, ever know.

"Mum," he says. "I want to see the ducks. Can I see the ducks?" He remembers the horse standing in the field in the rain. It will still be there, in the rain, shaking its head. "And I didn't see the horse. I want to see the horse. Can I see the horse?"

"Lenny," she says. "Come and sit at the table. I want to talk to you."

"Can we have the mashed potatoes and beans now?"

He sits beside her. He sees the plates and knives and forks on the table. He likes the yellow edge on the plates. It's an outline. Maudie taught him that word. Sometimes she gives him paper and he draws. He's good at outlines. He's good at outlines of trees and cars. Soon he will be good at filling them in. Maudie says she's going to buy him some paints.

Sometimes when he's in the fields he looks up and sees an outline. A tree or a hedge. He likes it because he sees it then, not like other times when he doesn't see it. Tree. Hedge. Car. Police car. Next time he'll draw a police car. He'll draw it with the door closed. He's going to fuck Maudie. He is. She said so.

"Lenny," Mum says. "Listen to me. You aren't listening to me."

"I am. I'm a good boy, Mum."

"Listen to me. You know about the policeman?"

"I didn't wear the helmet."

"No, you did what you were told. You were a good boy. But you know he's upstairs?"

"We carried him upstairs. I carried him, up to the room."

She strokes the back of his hand. He likes it when she does that.

"You don't know who he is, do you, Lenny?" Lenny smiles.

"He's a policeman. I didn't hurt him."

"Besides that. You don't know him?" Lenny smiles.

"He's a policeman. He's a policeman. I didn't wear his helmet. He said I could."

"Good boy. Listen to me."

"Can I have mashed potatoes and beans now?"

Careful!

"You can have them when we've finished." She moves her fingers from his hand to touch a plate. He does the same. He likes it. It's a game.

"Stop it," she says. She moves her hand back to his, covers his hands with hers.

"Listen, Lenny," she says. "You have to listen to this. Really listen. You mustn't say anything about this to anybody. Do you understand me? Do you know what I am saying?" He nods. He's a good boy.

"If Maude asks you, or Susan or Jimmy or Mr. Wyatt or Mrs. Wyatt, if they ask you anything, you know nothing. You've seen nothing and you've heard nothing. If anyone says anything about a missing policeman, you know nothing. You didn't go there today. You stayed home with me."

"Mum," he says. "That hurts. You're hurting me. Don't do that. Let me go. Your nails are sharp. Please."

"Careful!" she says.

"I'm a good boy," he says.

"You're a bloody bad boy if you say anything about this. If you say anything then you'll be sent back to the woman in town."

"It was a man as well. I want to pee," he says.

"You've only just been."

"I want to go again."

"Lenny, stop your crying. There's no need to cry. I mean what I say."

"I want to pee. I want to pee."

He sits in the lav and he wants to pee but he can't do it. He tries because he's a good boy. The lav is tall and thin. The ceiling is a long, long way away. In the corners are funny things he can't see but he knows they're there so he closes his eyes. Sometimes they're going to come down. That's why he does number twos, Jimmy says crap, number twos, upstairs in the bathroom. It takes longer. He can't pee. He goes back to the kitchen. Mum's cooking.

"I can cook, Mum," he says.

"Lenny," she says. "Look at me, son. You'll never cook again in this house. Do you understand me?" She holds his shoulders so it hurts. She shouldn't do that.

"Do you understand me?" she says. "Do you know what I mean?"

"I'm a good boy, Mum."

"You remember that. You don't want to go to that house in town again, do you?" He puts his arms around her, hugs her.

"Hug. I love you, Mummy."

"Never again, do you hear me, son?" He nods his head.

"Say it," she says. He shakes his head.

"No," he says.

"Say it, Lenny."

"That was a trick, Mum. I was going to say it."

"Say it, son."

"What? Say what?"

Careful!

"Say, you know. Say you will never cook again in this kitchen."

"I'm a good boy."

"Say it, son. Say it or you won't get your meal."

"I'm hungry."

"Say it."

"I won't cook again because I don't want to go to the nasty man and the nasty lady's house."

"Good boy. Now I'll do the meal."

"I'm hungry, Mum."

"Lenny, listen to me. You don't say anything about what you did today. You hear me? Not to Maude, not to Jimmy, not to Mr. Wyatt. Not a word. If you do then you'll have to go back to the house in town."

"I'm a good boy, Mum. Careful!"

24.

Lenny shovels in his mashed potatoes and beans. He's as hungry as a horse. Jack must be hungry as well. She wants to do a plate for him, take it up, the plate hot in her hand, the beans steaming. Here you are, son. But maybe he's not hungry. It was a shock after all.

Lenny picks up his remaining beans with his fingers.

"Don't do that, son. Use the fork."

The news was just what she thought it would be. Some local, overstated guff about a missing policeman, the police are doing all they can, most unusual, appeal for information, etc. They want to play it both ways. The man could just be missing, having decided to take off. On the other hand it could be a serious crime. They don't know what to do. The police are so thick. Except for Jack, of course.

"Mum, why can't I eat the beans with my fingers?"

"Because you can't. Shut up. Don't keep on. Oh hell, just do what you want to do. I don't care."

"That's swearing. Hell is swearing. Can I have some more?"

"Help yourself, son." She is nearly where she

wants to be. The clock ticks, the second hand jerks, and each time it jerks she knows who she is a little bit more. Lenny sits with his hands in his lap.

"I said help yourself, son." He starts to cry, puts his hands to the top of his head and rubs his eyes.

"You'll get beans in your hair. What is it? What's wrong?" He turns from her. "I can't help you if you won't say." He points to the stove.

"Oh damn, bloody hell." She goes to him, puts her arms around him.

"I'm sorry, I'm sorry. No, you can't go near the stove. What a silly Mummy. I'll do it for you. Here, let's have your plate." She never forgets, but today she does.

She shovels out more beans, the sauce now congealed. Lenny doesn't care. He'll eat them as they are. Jack was a fussy eater, even when he ate alone. He was a fussy kid from the start. When he was tiny he couldn't keep things down. She didn't say anything to Harold. He couldn't take things like that. Not Harold. Not bloody Harold, oh no. Jack's mouth was small, a tiny sucking orifice not made for mastication. She cut everything up. She sliced the meat into tiny pieces, the potatoes into small cubes. She would have blended it if she'd had a blender. When he'd finished, when she picked up his plate and took it back to the kitchen, she examined it for evidence. Evidence of what? She didn't know, didn't know in the kitchen under the high ceiling. But it didn't matter, it was the looking that counted.

She took Jack to the doctor. After the examination she told him to go outside while she talked to the man. She was ashamed to speak her fears. But what are you scared of? he said. What can possibly be wrong? How could she tell him what she thought, the picture she had in her head of her son's twisted organs, such a reproach to her. Is he all right? she said. Why doesn't he eat? She sat in front of the doctor's desk with its wooden penholder, a brass thingamy, a black book, saw the doctor's fingers intertwined to show tolerance. To the best of my knowledge, he said, there is nothing wrong with your son. I will examine him again. Is that what you get? Is that what you have to put up with? *To the best of my knowledge?*

He never ate with her again. That was the hole in her life.

Lenny shovels the beans in with his fingers. Let him get on with it. Today is different. He smiles at her. She is approaching her moment.

25.

"I'm going out," he says. The car's outside, his red car, rain splashing on it all over but it's all right. It shines under the light. It's getting dark now.

"You stay here," Mum says. "There's no need to go out tonight."

"I want to drive the car, I want to motor. On the ring road. Nowhere else, Mum."

"I don't like you going out there. There's too much traffic."

"Jimmy likes it on the ring road. He says it's the only place you can motor."

"Lenny, don't believe what Jimmy says. He doesn't give a damn about you."

"Jimmy's my friend."

He walks to the window to look at his car. If he were in the car he'd press his foot down and he'd motor, really motor. He'd fetch Jimmy and they'd go together. Jimmy likes going out with him sometimes. They go to some good places. Jimmy says things about Mr. Wyatt and Mrs. Wyatt but they're not true. Jimmy says they can go away together and never come back. Jimmy says it doesn't matter about that ugly fucking scar on his head, it doesn't matter about him being a fucking imbecile. They can go and drive on big freeways in the States, that's motorways in America, and pick up women. He says he'd have to come back to see Mum. Jimmy says he's too old for crap like that. He says yes, he's too old for crap like that.

"Can I go for a walk, Mum?"

"Where would you go for a walk in weather like this? What are you up to, Lenny?"

"I'm a good boy."

"You stay here with Mum. We've got things to do."

"Can I go to the farm tomorrow? I want to stomp the crates."

"We'll see, son. Let's wait for tomorrow to come."

"Can I go out?"

"Didn't you hear me?"

"Can I go out, Mum?"

"No, not this evening. No, you can't. Don't keep on. You're getting to me."

Mum's cleaning up. She's cleaning the pan she put the beans in. He knows she'll clean it again and again. She'll change the water and clean it. She'll change the water and do the plates again. She won't let him help. He could do it easily. Washing up is a piece of piss. She's scrubbing as hard as she can. He can scrub harder. He's a good boy. He walks to the door.

"Where are you going?"

"I'm going to the lav."

"I'm watching you, my boy."

He takes down his trousers and sits on the seat. He likes standing up and sitting down. Sometimes when Jimmy's peeing into a hedge he goes and pees with him. He likes that, both of them holding their willies. Once he asked to hold Jimmy's willy to see what it was like and Jimmy shouted at him and called him queer, bum boy. He isn't though. He only wanted to touch it. But really Jimmy likes him. Both of them peeing into the hedge, it was good, the noise it made.

He stands up and does up his trousers. He can wear a belt now. He used to have to wear braces because Mum said so, but he's a big boy now. Sometimes when you stand you splash. That's why he sits down. He never poos at the farm. He waits until he gets home. He only likes pooing in the bathroom. When they took him to the town he didn't poo all the time he was there. He tricked them. He didn't pee, either.

He told that to Jimmy. Jimmy didn't say anything. That was because he was thinking. Jimmy thinks sometimes and won't talk to him. He asks him what he thinks because he wants to think too but Jimmy won't tell him. He says he can't think, it'll hurt him. Mongols don't think.

He doesn't do anything in the lav. It's a trick. He only sits there and stands up and sits there again. He can do that. Sometimes he does tricks. Like they went to town, Jimmy and him, because Jimmy wanted to see a tart. He said he could watch if he wanted. Watch what? He stayed in the car but next time he'll watch. Jimmy says the bitch likes his mighty sword but he smiles when he says it. He wishes he could smile when he talks. Will she like Lenny's mighty sword?

He didn't do anything in the lav. It was a trick. He closes the door so you can't hear it and goes out the back door. He bends down under the window and out onto the road. It's a trick.

Careful! Watch the traffic. Down the road under the trees. Down the road to Maudie's house. He laughs because it's a big trick. Mum will laugh, too. He didn't hurt the policeman when he hit him. It doesn't hurt. He's asleep now because he's tired. He'll wake up in the morning.

He opens Maudie's gate, walks up the path and rings the bell. He likes the sound of it. Shiny things all around in the air. *La, la, la. La, la.* The button has a light in it. He rings it again and again. *La, la, la. La, la. La, la, la. La, la.* It's a trick on Maudie.

She shouts before she opens the door.

"You little sod," she says. He does it again because it's a trick.

"You little sod. You come in here and I'll tan your hide." She won't, not really. She likes it when he rings the bell.

"Come in, sailor," she says. "You're soaked. Don't you know it's raining? It's raining cats and dogs. Fancy, out on a night like this."

"No it's not, Maudie," he says. "How can it rain cats and dogs? How can it, Maudie?"

"Take off your jacket. We'll have to dry it before you go home. Otherwise your Mum'll be mad with me."

"You swore, Maudie," he says. "You said sod."

"Did I?" she says. "I'm sorry, Lenny."

"It's a trick," he says.

"What trick, Lenny?"

"The trick," he says. "I didn't go to the lav. Yes, I did. I went to the lav but I didn't go. Do you get it?" He laughs. He wants Maudie to laugh with him. She doesn't laugh. He's a good boy. Careful!

"I didn't go to the lav, Maudie. It's trick. I didn't go." He laughs so hard it tickles his belly.

"Sit down," Maudie says. He sits in the big old chair. He likes the big chair. You go right down in it.

"Don't get too comfortable," Maudie says. "I don't think you should stay. What are you doing out?"

"I don't have to say," he says. "I don't have to say. I don't have to say if I don't want to."

"Like that, is it?" she says. "I'll lend you my umbrella. That'll keep you dry."

"Mum will laugh," he says. "Won't she, Maudie? She'll laugh, all right."

"What about, Lenny?"

"I'm a good boy."

"What will she laugh about, Lenny?"

"She'll laugh about my trick. I didn't say anything. I didn't say anything, Maudie. I didn't, did I?"

His eyes are hot. He doesn't want them to be hot. It's because he's crying. Jimmy laughs at him when he cries. It's not fair.

"It's not fair," he says. "I didn't say anything. And I didn't wear the helmet. I'm a good boy. I am a good boy, Maudie."

"You're a good boy. What are you crying about? Tell Maudie."

"I'm not allowed. I'm not allowed, ever. I can't drive the car tonight."

"Why can't you drive the car, Lenny?"

"I'm not allowed. It's raining, Maudie."

"Yes, it is, Lenny."

"I don't have to say," he says. "Careful!"

"Give me your hand, Lenny," she says. She touches his hand.

"It tickles," he says.

"Don't be silly." She strokes the center of his hand with the ends of her fingers.

"You're a mystery to me," she says.

"A mystery," he says.

"It shouldn't be like this," she says. He strokes her arm. He likes to stroke her. If he had a dog he'd stroke it. Pat the dog, pat the dog.

"You're a lovely, kind boy," she says.

"Kind boy," he says.

"You must go home," she says. "It's time to go home."

"Want to stay here," he says. "Want to stay here."

"You have to go," she says. "Your mother will be worried." He laughs.

"Mother worried," he says.

"It's nothing to laugh about," she says. "She may not know where you are."

"It's a trick," he said. "I didn't want to go to the lav. It was a trick." He feels it now. He has to go to the lav.

"I've got to go home," he says. "I've got to go home now." She pushes her finger on his hand.

"You're a mystery," she says.

"A mystery," he says. He stands up and pulls his hand away. "I've got to go home. I've got to go."

"It's all right, Lenny," she says. She takes him to the front door.

"You could have the umbrella," she says. "But it's too windy. It'll blow inside out. Have this raincoat instead." She puts it on him. He bends down when she does it. That's helping her.

"Instead," he says. She puts her arm around him.

"Don't worry," she says.

"Worry," he says. He has to go to the lav.

"Don't dawdle. Go straight home. You'll get soaked and your mother will blame me."

"Cats and dogs," he says.

26.

She picks up the plate from the hot water and strokes its surface. It is so smooth, but if she were to look close enough she could see that it is pitted, marred, mis-shapen, like everything else. You have to believe in the perfectibility of things. That's what gets you through. Light at the end of the tunnel. She's not a believer. She's scared of belief, and also the absence of it, for what isn't there. But clean crockery is a start. At least it's something.

She is washing all the crockery again. She loves to feel something that is clean, and clean china is best. Having a clean plate is like having belief. It speaks for itself. It's good enough, for the time being. She puts the plate onto the rack on the draining board and washes another. Belief is like an engine that will purr, powering you through life.

She takes the plate out of the water and puts it against her cheek. The warmth of it is comforting. She likes the smell, the bubbles. She likes lifting it from the water and placing it on the rack. She would hate a machine that washed up. It's much too intimate an act for one of those.

Careful!

"Lenny," she calls. "You're a long time in the lav. What are you doing there?" She cannot lose him today. She slots in another plate on the rack. She likes the glistening line of them. Harold never washed up, not in all the time she was with him. Funny that. She wouldn't have thought any the less of him for doing it. Harold didn't know what she thought. He didn't seem to think it mattered what was thought. Perhaps he was scared to know. He could go for days without talking. Didn't he know that talking keeps you alive? Lenny Bruce had to talk to stay alive.

"Lenny," she calls. "Where the hell are you? Lenny, come here, please." She puts down a plate and wipes her hands on the towel. Goes into the corridor to the toilet.

"What are you doing in there all this time?" she says. She knocks on the door. "Come on, Lenny. I'm going to open the door." Curious for someone who is so unselfconscious, how much Lenny likes his privacy. Thank God she doesn't have to inspect his ass anymore. She knocks again.

"Lenny, please answer." She tries the door and opens it. A gurgle of water. The seat down. She runs to the kitchen and out to the stairs. She shouts.

"Where are you? Where are you? Lenny, Lenny." She runs upstairs to the bathroom, to the bedrooms, up to the top floor. She listens at the door. She opens the door an inch, peeps in, opens it wider to cover the whole of the room. Jack lifts his head, opens his eyes. He can see her. Damn, she didn't want it like this.

She goes down to the kitchen and out through the back door into the rain. She slips on the paving stones and sprawls on the wet ground. She feels her leg, knows that it's bleeding but she will not look at it now. She runs to the barn. She climbs up the ladder onto the rotting floorboards. She tells him to keep away from this, forbids him to climb the ladder, but she knows that still he comes here. She expects to see him huddled in the corner. She treads cautiously into the dark spaces but he is in none of them. She climbs back down the ladder and out into the rain. He has to be somewhere around. He has to be.

She runs out to the road. A car drives around her, sounds its horn. She shouts at it but her voice is lost in the rain. She runs down the road. Sees him coming up to meet her, a stupid raincoat draped over his shoulders, a stupid grin on his face. She can imagine Maude Edgecombe placing the coat over him, adjusting it with just her one arm, all that stupid display of care. She can see her opening the door for him, ushering him out into the rain.

She grabs hold of his arm, then hits him as hard as she can across the face.

"I told you not to go out," she shouts. "And what did you bloody do? You stupid fool. I told you not to." She slaps him again. He puts his hand up to his face.

"I'm a good boy," he says.

Careful!

"You're a naughty boy. I told you to stay home. What the hell have you been saying to that woman?"

"Cats and dogs," he says.

"Bloody come back with me," she says. "And what's this you've got on your shoulders?"

She walks behind him up the road. He stops to kick at a small branch that has fallen in the road. She walks behind him into the drive and into the kitchen. She sits him at the table and lights a cigarette. She sits beside him, sucking in smoke. She cannot suck fast enough.

"You have to understand what's going on," she says. "Nobody must find out." He's picking at a rip in the sleeve of the raincoat.

"Leave that alone and listen to me. You have to listen to me, Lenny." He smiles at her.

"Don't do that. This is serious. It's more serious than anything else in our lives." He smiles again. She takes hold of his wrist.

"Don't smile," she says. "Don't smile, Lenny." He keeps on smiling.

"Careful!" she says.

"No," he says. "No, Mum."

"Careful!" she says. "This is serious, Lenny. You don't know how serious."

"I'm a good boy, Mum. Honest I am. I didn't do nothing. I just went down the road."

"Who did you see, Lenny?"

"I didn't see anyone. I didn't."

"Lenny, who did you see? That's two Carefuls!"

"I saw Maudie. It was all right."

"She's *Maude* to you. What did you tell her? What did you say?"

"I didn't say anything."

"Careful! Lenny."

"I didn't say anything, honest, Mum. Honest, I didn't." He is crying now.

"Three Carefuls! Lenny." She catches hold of his wrist.

"No, Mum," he cries. She pushes the tip of the cigarette into the back of his hand. He screams. She holds on, lets the cigarette do its job.

"It's that bloody serious," she says. "Do you understand me? And stop that screaming." He licks his hand, his big tongue out, licking hard.

"I'm a good boy, a good boy."

"Come here," she says.

"No, won't," he says.

"I won't hurt you."

"I'm a good boy," he says.

"We have to do this for your own good," she says. "I don't want you wandering off." She catches hold of his arm.

"Lenny," she says. "Stop crying. Take off this stupid raincoat. Look at you, you're soaking. I'm going to put you in the cupboard. I need to wash. Then I'll deal with you."

She pulls him out to the hallway and down to the cupboard under the stairs. He's shaking, his whole body shaking with his sobbing.

"I want to go to town," he says. "I want to stay with the woman and the man."

"You don't," she says. "Oh, no, you don't." He is still licking the back of his hand, each lick a reprimand to her.

"Leave it alone," she says. "We'll do something about it later. You were a naughty boy."

She shoves him into the cupboard and slams the door. As soon as she turns the key in the lock he starts to scream.

"That won't do you any good," she shouts. "You're staying in there until I'm good and ready."

In the kitchen she empties the washing-up bowl and refills it with steaming water from the small heater over the sink. She could do this in the bathroom but she likes to do it here. She will bathe the blood off her leg to start with.

This is the way it started. Sitting in the kitchen waiting for the phone to ring. She knew it was wrong to leave Lenny at the hospital when it happened but the doctor said she needed the rest and anyway what about Jack? She'd brought him home. Her skin was smarting, the whole of her body, like she needed to be clean. Jack was sitting at his table in the other room. Her skin was sore. She filled the washing-up bowl with hot water,

water that was too hot to touch and she pushed her hand down into it, and then scrubbed herself, her skin burning with the heat and the scrubbing, her arms and her legs and her neck, under her arms and between her legs and there were red marks, shapes that she would endow with meaning, all over her body, and they are still there now. She threw the water away and filled it again. Used washing-up liquid and a metal scrubbing pad because her body itched so much.

The scrubbing was the center of it, not the water, not the heat, not the dipping of her hand into the bowl.

This is the way she does it now. Takes her time to remove her clothes. She fills the bowl with hot, steaming water and she places it on the floor by the end of the table. She takes a white flannel from the cupboard by the sink and a bar of green household soap. She dips the flannel into the hot water and wrings it out. The water is stinging hot, the way she wants it. She cleans off the blood on her leg, lets it smart, and rubs the flannel on the back of her neck, no soap yet, perhaps no soap at all. It is the rubbing that cleans, not the soap. She drops the flannel into the water and picks it out, the water so hot that sometimes she thinks she will finally see that there is nothing in this worth doing. She wrings out the flannel and places it stinging hot onto her breast. She used to wish that Harold had a fetish, some deviant thing that would drive him to do such things. Maybe something with her breasts, perhaps. No such luck.

Careful!

She hears Lenny shouting, his shouts changing into screams. She plunges her hand into the water so that all she can hear is the noise of the heat in her head. She decides she needs soap. She rubs the flannel hard on the soap to work up a lather. It takes time to do this the way she wants it with the lather creamy thick. She works at it, from time to time putting her hand back into the hot water to remind herself of what she does. Lenny stops for a moment and she thinks that she will refill the bowl. The water has lost some of its sting. There was a time when she mixed the hot with cold but that was a lapse that did not last long.

Later she will bathe the back of Lenny's hand. It will not lack love, it will not be in haste. He will take as much from it as she does. Later, but she is not ready yet. He is screaming again. She refills the bowl. Lenny is screaming as she pushes the flannel between her legs, as she feels its steaming heat. She pushes the flannel down her thighs, stands with her legs apart. She looks toward the window, the rain hitting it hard, the dark red brick wall of the barn. This is the time she feels most vulnerable, when the stinging pain does its work. Funny, she thinks. This is the time when she should feel strong.

She rinses the flannel and wrings it out, places it flat steaming between her legs and lets it stay, the pain seeping both ways, inward and outward. There is no difference, it is all the one thing. One thing becomes another. Lenny knows this. He has lived with her long enough to appreciate it for what it is. She lets the flannel stay, the pain taking what it has to take, standing with her legs together, holding the thing in place. This is what she has to do.

Lenny is screaming. He knows what he does. She knows what he does. They know it together. She drops the flannel into the bowl and takes the bowl back to the sink. She needs one last bowl of water. Two bowls are never enough. There are patches of pain on her body now, patches that tell her who she is. Lenny screams louder. He knows how long he must do this. She listens to him as she fills the bowl. This is the last bowl. This is the end for now. Lenny screams. He knows. Careful!

27.

It won't end, it won't. It goes on and it goes on. The white space is sticking to the back of his hand now. White space around it, too, around his hand and his arm, sticking, all shapes, going on and on, going on. It won't go away. Leaking. Dripping.

He hates the cupboard. He knows about the things in it. There *are* things in it. It's true. Spiders. He told Mum. She doesn't care. She hates him.

The white space sticks all over him. Go away. His hand hurts. He wants to look out through the window at the top of the cupboard but he can't reach it, it's too high. There's nothing to stand on, not in here. It's dark. If he could see through the window it would be good. The things outside would be good and he would be good. They would be good together. Just to see. It's not dark outside like it's dark in the cupboard. It's dark everywhere else but not out there, not through the window. The dark's like that. It fills up some things but not the others. Like it fills up the space at the bottom of walls. And in the barn. Under hedges. The park. They don't go in the park. They don't.

There's things in the cupboard that aren't nice.

Richard Madelin

There's things everywhere that aren't nice. Mum put the cigarette on his hand but it's his own fault. Naughty boy. There's crawly things that aren't nice. He screams when there are horrible things. Horrible things in here will do nasty things to him unless he shouts loud to keep them away. They'll creep up his trousers. They're nasty. He hates Mum.

He shouts. The noise doesn't go far. It doesn't fill up the cupboard and push out the white space. He shouts again, as loud as he can until it hurts his throat.

Mum hurts him because he's a naughty boy. She has to. She does. It's for his own good. He'll have to stay in here for a long time and he doesn't like that, but he has to. If he shouts she'll hear him. He knows she'll hear him. He's a good boy. Mum, I'm a good boy. Jimmy says his Mum is still a looker. Although she's really old Jimmy wouldn't kick her out of bed. He told Jimmy he can't go into her bed because he's not allowed and it's his Mum. Jimmy said he didn't give a fuck. He didn't tell her because she gets mad when he tells her what Jimmy says.

He kicks the wall as hard as he can. That'll keep the things away. He shouts, Mum, there are things in here. You didn't hurt me, see, it doesn't hurt at all. It's all right. Can I come out now? He scratches the back of his hand. It doesn't hurt, Mum. I'm a good boy. Let me out.

Tomorrow he'll stomp on the crates and burn them in the furnace. He has to. They burn great, they can burn up the white space, make his face hot, make his eyes sting. It's good. Mr. Wyatt wants it done. You can't leave them about. They get in the way. Mr. Wyatt likes it when he tidies up. He has to go. He has to go up the farm for the crates. It doesn't matter. It doesn't hurt.

Driving the car, the sacks are on the backseat. It's all right, it's only sacks. He has to get them up to the top field. Mr. Wyatt wants him to do it. Use your initiative, he says. What's initiative, Mum?

Mum, it hurts. No, it doesn't. Let me out of here. . . . Mum. It doesn't hurt at all. No, it doesn't. Honest.

28.

This is the best part, concentrating on the stinging in her body as she puts her clothes back on. She doesn't have to think about anything else. Enough to think about the pain. Pain fills in the spaces. It is the moment, the joining of this to that, so it can be what it is.

She'll not let him out, not yet. She'll sit and smoke a cigarette. She doesn't want to spoil it for the sake of a moment or two. She thinks of Jack in the lane, on the ground, Lenny's shadow as he stands over him. But there were no shadows. It has rained all day. It doesn't matter. How you see it is what matters, what you make of it. Jack on the ground. The blood, bruises, a broken tooth. It's all her doing. It's like the stinging of her skin. It's there and you don't want it, but you do. It's the two things together. And you don't know how it got like that.

She stands outside the cupboard listening for Lenny's breathing. She hears a sob, a knocking. She has to open the door.

"Mum, Mum," he says. "I'm a good boy."

"You're a good boy, son. Let me look at your hand." She takes him into the kitchen. He whimpers as she holds his hand.

"Don't be silly," she says. "Sit down."

"It hurts," he says.

"It doesn't hurt. You're a big boy now."

"I'm a good boy," he says.

"I'll bathe it and make it all right." He starts to cry. "Lenny," she says. "Don't cry. I can't bear it when you cry."

"It's dark in the cupboard. There's lots of things."

"There's nothing in there that'll hurt you. Believe me, son." She fetches cotton wool and puts hot water into a small porcelain bowl. He'll like this bit.

"There's monsters," he says.

"Lenny," she says. "There's nothing that'll hurt you in that cupboard. Nothing at all."

"You shouldn't put me in there. It's bad. You shouldn't."

"What do you mean, it's bad? What does that mean? What does bad mean, Lenny?" She dips the cotton wool in the hot water, squeezes it out, and puts it on the burn. "What do you mean?" she says.

"Bad," he says. "It hurts, Mum. Don't do it like that. It's bad when you do it."

"It's not bad. It's not bad that I do it. You've never said that before. What do you mean? Come on, what do you mean?"

"Don't do it like that. I'm a good boy."

"If I put you into the cupboard and lock it then you need it. There's nothing bad about that. Who said it was bad? Who said it, son? Come on, tell me."

"When I stand in the corner then they can't get me, but they try," he says. She pushes the hair out of his eyes. She bathes the wound. He winces.

"Don't you see?" she says. "Don't you see? I do this for your own good. Who else would do it?"

"My own good," he says, smiling.

"It's nothing to smile at, you silly fool. That woman down the road doesn't know a damn thing. Not what it means day after day. It's all right to care ten minutes here and ten minutes there, but it's a hell of a different thing to do it all the time."

"Maudie," he says.

"Maude Edgecombe," she says. "She knows nothing about what it's like."

"Maudie," he says.

"Shut up. I told you that you aren't to go down there. I mean it, Lenny. Do you hear me?" He lifts his hand and sniffs it. "There's no smell. I like it when you make it smell."

"Listen to me. We have to be careful now. I don't want you talking to anybody. It's important. What did I say?"

"It's important."

"What's important?"

"Not talking. They mustn't know. I've got to stomp on the crates tomorrow, Mum. Mr. Wyatt wants me to."

"I don't think it's a good idea for you to go to work,

son. Not for a few days."

Lenny stands up. "I've got to go. I've got to stomp on crates. Mr. Wyatt wants me to go." He is short of breath now, his face flaming red.

"Sit down, Lenny. Perhaps you can go."

"I've got to go. Mr. Wyatt says so."

"Forget Mr. Wyatt. There are more important things to think about." She goes to the drawer and takes out the tin of plasters. "Forget about Mr. Wyatt," she says. "Come on, choose your plaster."

"Any one?" he says. "The big one?" She nods.

"Let me do it for you. But the cream first." She opens the tube and holds it out to him. "Smell it, Lenny."

"It's the right one, the cream, the smell," he says. She strokes it onto the burn. He pulls his hand away.

"I have to do this, son." She peels the backing off the plaster and holds it over the wound. It's nothing to worry about. It's dark in the cupboard. A cigarette burns. That's the point. All these things. Does no one understand?

"Did you go down to see Maude Edgecombe, Lenny? Is that where you were?" He touches the plaster. "Don't do that. It'll come off. Did you go and see her?"

"I've got to stomp crates tomorrow, Mum. In my boots. They're good for that. Jimmy says so. Jimmy's got cowboy boots. He doesn't stomp crates with them. He lets me do it."

"Did you tell Maude, Lenny? Come on, tell me.

You did. I know you did."

"It's dark in the cupboard." He starts to cry.

"Don't do that. I don't want you to do that. It's not fair, son. I don't care if it is dark in the cupboard. You deserve it. You're a bad boy." As he cries she sees his belly go in and out.

"Don't do it," she says. "Don't do it. Stop crying or I'll burn you again."

"No," he says. "Please, Mummy."

"Tell me," she says. "Did you talk about this to Maude Edgecombe?"

"Don't burn me, Mummy. Don't."

"I'm not going to do it, you stupid fool. You know I'm not going to do it. Tell me."

"It's dark in the cupboard."

"Shut up about the bloody cupboard. Did you tell Maude?"

"Don't put me in the cupboard. There are things in there."

"I said, I won't put you in the cupboard. Now tell me. Did you tell Maude?"

"Can I go to the farm tomorrow? Can I stomp on the crates?"

"Did you tell Maude? I need to know."

"It's bad to put me in the cupboard. It's a very bad thing to do."

"Who said that? Tell me who said that. I'll kill them."

"It's bad," he says.

"It's not bad," she says. "You need it sometimes."

"I need it," he says. "My hand hurts. I want more smelly stuff."

"If I put some more on will you tell me who said it was bad? Anyway, it's no secret. I know who said it." She unscrews the top of the tube. "Let me take the plaster off, son. We'll have to be careful, so that it sticks back on."

"Sticks back on," he says. He holds his hand up.

"You can put it on the table," she says. He whimpers. He wants to hold it where it is.

"It's easier on the table," she says. He keeps it suspended, stupidly in the air. She peels off the plaster.

"Mum," he says. "The smelly stuff."

"Yes, son," she says. "I love you, Lenny. You and me together, son." She kisses him on the forehead. Keeps her lips there. He starts to cry.

"It's bad, Mummy," he says. She drops his hand.

"Bloody hell," she says. "You don't let up, do you. I could lock you in there again." He's crying hard now, his big belly shaking. "You're too fat by far," she says. "I'm putting you on a diet."

"The smelly stuff," he says. "You said."

"Here," she says. "Do it yourself. Or get Maude Edgecombe to do it for you. It's easy if you only have to see someone now and then."

"Now and then," he says.

"But it's not easy to do it all the time. You tell her

that."

"You put it on, Mum. I like it when you put it on."

"Listen, son. I do what I do to you for your own good. Do you understand that?"

"For your own good."

"For your own good."

"You put it on," he says. "I like you to put it on."

"Here," she says. "You dopey sod." She smears the cream on. He winces.

"Dopey sod," he says. She puts her hand on his stomach.

"Look at you," she says. "That's blubber."

"Blubber," he says.

"You're going on a diet, my friend. We'll watch what you eat."

"Plaster," he says.

"Right," she says. She presses the plaster back on.

"Ow," he says. It doesn't look like it will stay.

"Let's see how that goes," she says. He lifts his hand to sniff at it.

"Now what?" she says.

"It's not the smelly stuff," he says. "It's different."

"God help me," she says. "It's the same. The stuff you like. I'll put you in that cupboard for sure."

"It was a trick," he says.

"I'll trick you," she says.

She looks past him out through the front window. Susan Edgecombe is running by, under the street lamp, through the patch of light on the road, her body hunched under her load. Another run. That girl has something hounding her.

29.

He licks the plaster on the back of his hand. It's smooth. He licks it again. He can't taste it. He licks the skin on the back of his hand. He can taste that. There's a white space around his head with shapes like dogs with teeth. They're barking. Go away. It hasn't had dogs before. In a minute the white space will be on his face and in his head. He doesn't like the cupboard. There are things in it.

The white space comes at work, it comes everywhere. He doesn't tell Jimmy. Jimmy would laugh. He doesn't tell Mr. Wyatt. He likes working at the farm. He doesn't tell Mum about the white space. She'd get angry. The white space comes when he doesn't know it's going to come. It comes sideways when he can't see it. When he's bending, picking up stones in the field. It comes when he stands up to look at the hedge at the top of the field because he hasn't been waiting for it. Sometimes the birds bring it. They come out from a bush and it's all bones and dust, and feathers, stinky feathers and dust. Birds in the white space, the sun, the field, the hedge, a stone in his hand. Brown and white and blue. It hurts, but it doesn't hurt sometimes. It growls in his head like a dog.

Careful!

No, he doesn't tell Mum. He tells Maudie. Hello, sailor, she says. I'm not a sailor, Maudie. You are to me, my dear, a sailor out on the big, wide ocean. He tells her about the white space because she can hear. You go on, sailor, she says. You tell me whatever you like. He tells her how it hurts and she says not to worry or fret. There's too much to worry about, she says. She says it will go if he doesn't worry, and it does. She lifts her hand, her bad hand with her other hand, up to his face and things come, some like they're soft, things come and the white space goes, things come like the nice smells he likes, things come like the soft things he likes, things come he likes. Maudie will let him fuck her.

He doesn't tell Susan. She laughs sometimes but sometimes she doesn't. She doesn't call him sailor. She's in a hurry. She has a pack on her back. She sweats. She wears shorts and trainers that are green and white and big. They're light, though. Good for running up the road. She runs all the time. She doesn't go in for races. She runs because she's getting ready. Maudie says Susan doesn't know what day of the week it is. It's Thursday, Maudie, silly. Thursday all day.

The white space is growling, the dogs are howling, high whines and howls like the big, old radio, when it doesn't go right. Stop playing with the radio, Lenny. I'm not, Mum. It doesn't work.

When he's bigger it'll be different. Mum said that. It'll be different. Mum isn't going to die. Mrs. Wyatt will die soon. Jimmy says so. She'll rot in the ground. They'll bury her. Her flesh will rot. That's what happens. It will go green and then black. Greeny slime and then black. And her hair will rot and her teeth and her bones and she'll smell. Sometimes they burn people.

Mum isn't going to die. She's not, is she, Maudie? She isn't going to rot. Listen to me, Lenny, listen to me, sailor. She isn't, is she? The white space is hurting him now. He lies down, gets under the white, down on the ground. It can't get down here, can it? It can't. It hurts, Maudie. Listen to me, sailor.

30.

She stands outside the room to listen. Nothing. She wants to hear something. It's good to hear something, anything, when you're waiting. Lenny is shouting downstairs. She has to do it, like she has to wash in the kitchen, like she has to shout at Lenny, like she has to clean the room, like she has to get the table right. She has to do it because it hurts.

She opens the door. His eyes are shut. Damn him, doesn't he want to try? He opens them as she goes in. She has waited too long for any fancy bollocks. Too long for this.

"Listen to me," she says. "All I can think is that you didn't give a damn. That's why you went away. That's why you didn't come back. Why else? I've become an old and lonely woman. I know it. I'm full of spite and hate. I know it. I hate you. I hate your brother. I hate you both for what you are and what you've done to me. I hate you both because you have made me what I am. I hate your father for what he was, and what he was lives with me still.

"Do you know what I did today? Of course you don't. I stubbed a cigarette out on the back of Lenny's hand. That's a despicable thing to do. I can't think of much worse. And I'll tell you something else. I often do it. And do you know what I did then? I locked him in the cupboard under the stairs. He hates it there. It terrifies him. I know that and yet I do it. And after that I had the nerve to think that I could bathe his hand and get back into his good books, make retribution. I cheated him. I made him think it happened in some way that was not my doing. But he wasn't fooled. He knows. He gives me the benefit of the doubt. He wanted to forget it, to put it out of the way. He's quite good at doing that but it doesn't always work. He bloody knows. And what's more, I don't want him to forget."

Jack moves his head but it doesn't fool her. He's not about to talk, not if she takes the scarf out of his mouth. He hasn't talked in ten years. Why should he talk now?

"Sometimes I look at Lenny and I want to hug him to death. I love him so much. Like he might be driving and he changes gear, and I see that intense look he gets, watching the road. I love him for it. I want more of him, I want him to be who he really can be. And I still think it will happen. I do. The light will shine.

"I kept thinking you'd come back. I wanted to see you and ask you why. I knew what you'd say. That it wasn't what you wanted here. Let me tell you it wasn't what anybody wanted. It was the best we had. It was us, the three of us. I thought that you knew that. You didn't tell me anything. You left no message. You gave me no hope at all. I can understand a kid of eight doing that but I can't understand how you could keep it up until you were sixteen and leaving.

"And it's no good blaming Lenny. He wasn't a party to any of this, if being a party to it is knowing what you're doing. You can't blame him. You hear me? I don't want you blaming him. It's all right. I know you wouldn't blame him. I know.

"I keep finding things in the house, still. You remember how we found those knickknacks, the cups and saucers, the tins, the coins? How we wondered who the people were who lived here? I found a cocoa tin lodged in a crack inside the barn just the other day. There was nothing in it.

"It's like we're newcomers, still. We can't be anything else. With everything that's happened, we're still strangers in the village. You know I don't mind that too much. Not if I can share it. But I can't. Who can I share it with?

"I know you must be hungry. Well, that's your own fault. You shouldn't have left like you did. I feel it's as if you've been hungry for all that time. And I'll tell you something else. If you're going to leave, you should really leave. You shouldn't come back so near. It's obvious you wanted me to find you. I know that. You can't deny it. It's all your doing.

"Tell me this, son, go on. Why did you eat alone

for all that time? I want you to tell me. I need to know. How could you be so willful? Was it because of what happened?

"It isn't the first time I've hurt him. I make quite a regular feature of it. I'm ashamed. I'm not hardened to it. But it works, darling. Can you imagine how that makes me feel? Can you imagine how it makes him feel? What do I do? I don't know what else to do. There's no one bloody here to help me out. There's no one here to talk it through. Just think what it could have been like if you'd kept in touch. It would have made all the difference. I could have rung you, even if you couldn't get here. I could have said I'm at my wits' end, what do I do? And you could have helped me just by talking. Or you could have said, it's my turn to have him for a bit, Mum. Like brothers do. You need the rest. You take some time off. But you didn't do a sodding thing because at the first chance you fucked off out of it. You couldn't give a damn.

"You think I'm lonely? Well don't fool yourself. I find things to do. Maybe I could sell up, like my mother who never knew any better, and go and live where the sun shines all day. Dig my toes into the warm sand, paddle in a warm sea. Do I need the cold and the rain? The gossip? The hateful people in a small village? A job that pays next to nothing? Do I need it? It's not just being stuck with Lenny. It's being stuck *here* with him. But I can't move because Lenny's here. It has to happen here.

"You know what I do? I'll tell you this and I've told

nobody else, and who would I tell? You don't want to hear it, I know. A mother doesn't tell it to a son. I don't have sex. I don't think I want it. Although I'm not so sure. I wash myself in the kitchen. Strip off without drawing the curtains and I wash myself from tip to toe. I don't do it for people to see me, nobody can, I do it because I want to do it and don't bloody care. I never did things like that before. I had my worries and the things that had to get done or life wouldn't go on, but now it's all different. I have fetishes. I clean, I put things in order. And you know why? Because I'm scared. I'm scared that if I don't do them then life will change for the worse, that things will get so much worse. It happened before and I don't want it to happen again. They multiply. More and more things I have to do.

"I scrub myself between my legs, work up a lather and rub, it shames me to say, I rub until it hurts. You know, I've never enjoyed sex in my life. I don't think it's a thing that women enjoy. Young women, they say they enjoy it, but I'm not so sure. They sound desperately unsure to me. They want to enjoy it, bless them. Your father wasn't a man to enjoy it with. I wanted to enjoy it. I encouraged him but it didn't ever work like that. There, I've told you. Now you have to tell me something. But not yet. I'm not ready to take out that scarf. You'll have to wait.

"I want to hit you again. Just fucking because. I want to tell you things. Just because. I can't trust you.

How could I trust you? After what you've done? I want to hit you. I won't. After you'd gone I was lonely. Did you think of that? How could you run out on me? All I wanted was for you to be close. We were so close, son."

She puts her head against his.

"You're still my son. There's nothing you can do about that." The way she would put her arms around him to keep him close. The way she wrapped him up, all of him, the bundle of him, the boy that he was.

She puts her arms around him.

"It's all right," she says. "It's all right. You've been through a lot. I know that. It'll take some time to get over it, but I'm here for you, darling, and I'm going to be here for you. Don't you ever forget that."

31.

The bitch. She's on her knees, her ass is bare, in the air. She doesn't care that anybody can see her. You can see her thing and she doesn't mind. She's naked with nothing on. The man is on his knees kneeling behind her. He has a big thing, much bigger than Jimmy's. He catches hold of her. He's angry. He wants to hurt her. The woman's laughing, turning her head to look at the man. He puts his willy in the woman's thing. She moves her bum. Why does she move her bum like that? Stop it. How can we get on if you're going to do that?

The woman opens her mouth wide. The man's very angry now. He catches hold of the woman's hair and pulls her head back. He's jerking his body, putting his thing in and out like he can't make up his mind. He's gritting his teeth. Why is the man holding the woman's hair like that? Why is he doing that to her? Why isn't he nice to her? She's a bitch. That's why. Everybody knows.

He likes the music on the vids because it goes on and on. It doesn't stop and start again, it just goes on and on. He could play this music in the car if he had the tape. Maybe Jimmy has it. The music doesn't hurt.

If he had a woman with nothing on he wouldn't

mind. He wouldn't tell her to put her clothes back on because it was naughty. He'd say nothing because she's a bitch. She would be naked, that's with nothing on. He would give it to her good, bitch. He wouldn't take his clothes off. She would see him if he did that and she would tell. He'd cover his willy if he did. She wouldn't see it then. He'd say turn around bitch.

Jimmy gets girls to take all their clothes off in front of him. So they're in the nude, with nothing on. They don't mind. Jimmy takes his clothes off too but sometimes he leaves his cowboy boots on. Which is a lie because he has to take them off to take off his trousers. Maybe he puts them back on. It's such a lot of trouble. Bitch. You've got it coming.

He wants to try it with the vid and do it. He takes his willy out. It feels funny. He strokes it. He likes it when he does that. The man's going in and out, pushing, faster now. The woman's shouting and when she stops shouting she keeps her mouth open. Bitch. She doesn't like what the man's doing but he's doing it and he won't stop. She screams and the man laughs and grabs her hair again.

Another woman comes into the room. She is ever so surprised to see the man and the woman. She didn't know they were there. Oh dear, oh dear. Perhaps she thought they'd gone for a walk. She's angry because they didn't tell her. She's got on a short skirt and a T-shirt. You can nearly see her knickers. She takes her clothes off. It doesn't take long. But she leaves on her shoes, which are high heels. She can do that. It's not like trousers. Why does she do it? Does she forget to take her shoes off? They might make her slip or they might get in the way. It's silly. Perhaps the man or the other woman will tell her not to be silly and take them off. They don't.

He wanks his willy faster. It won't go hard. He wants to cry. Why won't it go hard? Bitch, bitch, bitch.

He doesn't tell Mum. Once when he stroked it hard, when he stroked it a long time, when the video was finished, once, stuff came out the end. It did. But it didn't hurt. It was all right. Jimmy says it's called come. But how could it be called come because it doesn't mean that? You say, will you come with me, please. They wouldn't know what you meant. And they would be wrong and it would be a trick.

He strokes faster. It doesn't work. Bitch. The woman is a fucking bitch. Both the women are bitches. Jimmy says if you do it too much you go blind. He doesn't want to go blind. He'd hate that. Being blind, you couldn't drive a car.

The other woman is lying on her back with her legs apart. She doesn't mind. The man is putting his willy into the hole between her legs. All women have holes between their legs. He knows. It's where they wee. The other woman is licking the man now, licking his bum. He wouldn't let a woman do that. It would tickle. He bets Jimmy doesn't let the women do that. It's a funny thing to do. Why is the woman doing that? It would taste on her tongue. Doesn't she mind? He's still got the taste of the sacks at the back of his throat and sometimes on his tongue.

The woman lets her skirt drop onto the floor. And her T-shirt. She doesn't fold them up. He rubs harder, up the top where it's best, that's what Jimmy says. And all the way down. But it won't go hard. The other woman has her mouth open. She has her eyes closed and now she's opening them wide. She wants the man to stop because she has to go somewhere. She'll be late. If the man doesn't stop she'll get into trouble. Why doesn't she tell him? She doesn't tell him because the man's angry. That's why he's doing this to her. Bitch. Perhaps she has to go to the shops. Perhaps she has to get the shopping.

Mum doesn't know. He wouldn't want her to know. He rubs faster, ever so fast. It hurts. It doesn't work. He doesn't tell Jimmy. Perhaps his willy is wrong. The man stands up and goes to the other woman who is standing with her leg on the bed. Why is she standing like that? Get your leg down. You might fall over. And where would you be then, my girl? The man puts his willy into her. She's going to fall over onto the bed but he holds her up. The other woman's watching them. Why doesn't she do her shopping? It might be getting late. The shops could be shut. She could go now and the man wouldn't mind. He's busy with the other woman. He's angry. He has a tattoo on his arm.

He wants a tattoo but Mum won't let him. He

doesn't tell that to Jimmy. One day he and Jimmy are going into town to get tattoos. He won't tell Mum. She won't know. He doesn't know what to get yet but Jimmy says the man has pictures in books. You choose one and he does it exactly the same. He copies it. He can do that. It doesn't hurt much. Not at all. He does it with a needle with a point that goes into your skin. Then ink goes in. It won't come off, not even if you scrub it when you wash it. Not even if you scrub it as hard as you can. That's what a tattoo is. The picture stays forever. You can scrub and scrub.

He feels it in the end of his willy. Jimmy calls it a prick. He's going to do it. He will come. But it won't. Jimmy did it once for him just to see. It got bigger and white stuff spurted out. The man's doing something to the woman. Mum won't know, not if he comes. The woman has her mouth open and the man is putting his thing in it. Why does the man do that? It might hurt. The woman might bite.

Bitch. The man gives it to her good. The other woman can do her shopping now if she hurries. She'll get home in time for tea. She won't say where she's been. She's a girl, really, not a woman. So is the other woman. The girl is shopping for her mum. Her mum will be angry if she doesn't get back in time. Naughty girl, where have you been all this time? Get into that room, my girl. I will hurt you. I will burn you. Get in that room. I'm sorry, I'm sorry. I didn't mean it. You made me do it. Wipe it off.

Make it nice and clean. We don't want any dirt in this house, thank you very much.

Jimmy lets him have the vids for nothing as long as he gives them back because he gets them off the back of a lorry. The lorry stops in town. They fall off the back of it. Jimmy knows where they fall off. Why doesn't the lorry driver tie them on? Because, kid, Jimmy says. He likes it when Jimmy says *kid*. They're good friends, him and Jimmy. He says Jimmy can I go in with you and see the vids fall off the back of the lorry? Jimmy says no, he has to do it by himself. He waits on a corner for the lorry to come by. They fall off at the corner. Which corner? Shut up, kid. Which corner, Jimmy? Shut up, we don't want the whole world to know, do we? No, Jimmy. It's a secret. I won't tell, Jimmy. Honest. Wipe it all off.

The television goes to a little white dot when he switches it off. Where does it go then? He's going to have a tattoo. He doesn't know what it will be. They have them in a book. It won't come off. Ever. That's why you have them.

32.

She runs hot water into the bowl but empties it immediately. Steam rises from the sink. He's going to be hungry. He will talk, he will have to talk. She has to give him food. This is the beginning of the end. Each little thing is so important now.

She takes out a plate and a knife to go with it. He can have bread and cheese. That's simple but it's nourishing. She'll feed it to him. She won't untie his hands or his legs. Not yet.

She polishes the plate with the tea towel. The white plate with the yellow border. A good one. Every little thing counts. She fetches the bread, takes care in cutting two slices, not too thin, not too thick. Too thin and it looks like it's for sandwiches. Too thick and it's too much to eat. She throws the first slice into the bin. Too thin. Takes her time. Cuts another. That will do. It's all right.

She goes to the cupboard for the cheese. She cuts a piece of cheese. It crumbles. She doesn't want that. She can't feed it to him if it's like that. She cuts a larger piece. Perhaps she should make sandwiches. No, just keep it as it is. He likes bread and cheese. Well, he used to like bread and cheese, but tastes change. He could like anything now. He could have a different palate, shaped by a busy wife who doesn't have time to look after him. It's all right. It has to be.

She switches on the kettle. He'll have to drink something. Something cold would be safer and easier. But he likes his cup of tea. She pours milk into a cup, scoops three teaspoons of tea leaves into the pot as she waits for the kettle. She could give him water. Just bread and water. That would be a start.

She pours the boiling water into the pot. Harold wouldn't drink tea, only coffee. He said he didn't like tea. She thought it an affectation. He told her once that none of his family ever drinks tea. She thought, everybody drinks tea.

She hears a tap at the window. Bloody Maude Edgecombe with a raincoat over her head, snooping as usual. Maude's face close up to the window. Alice can leave nothing to chance. She has to deal with this now. She goes to the back door.

"Come in, Maude," she says. Maude stomps her feet when she gets inside. She takes the raincoat off and drops it onto the floor.

"There's no need for that," Alice says, picking it up. "I'll hang it up. There's a peg along here. You know that, Maude."

"It's not worth bothering with." Maude wipes her face with her fingers.

"Here," Alice says. "Let me give you a towel."

"It's all right. Please don't fuss. I won't stay long. I just had to come up." Alice follows her into the kitchen. Maude looks at the table.

"Are you having a snack?" she says.

"Just a bite," Alice says. "Like some too?"

"I'm not staying."

"You can have some, it's no trouble."

"I've just eaten. I want to talk about Lenny."

"What about him?"

"Is he OK?"

"Of course. Why shouldn't he be?"

"He came to see me. He seemed agitated. I hope there's nothing worrying him."

"It's the weather. He's always affected by the weather. It's like the cat. The cat gets skittish when it's windy and raining. Lenny's the same."

"So he's OK, then?"

"Of course he is. Why shouldn't he be?" Alice asks. Maude shrugs. "Why shouldn't he be, Maude? What could be wrong?"

"I'm sure there's nothing wrong. I was just worried."

"Don't. I'll do the worrying."

"It's just that I get an itch, a funny feeling that he's not quite right."

"He's doing the best he can. We're doing the best we can. We'll be all right."

"I get feelings. I get something, I don't know what.

He said something about a helmet. Do you know what he means?"

"He's obsessed with the police. He wants to join the force. I tell him he can't. I'll have to buy him a helmet, I suppose. That'll stop him keeping on. Don't let it upset you."

"It's not like it upsets me. It's just a funny feeling. I can't explain it. I'm sorry. I'm being no help at all. I'll go."

"You don't have to help me, Maude. I don't need help. We're doing the best we can."

"But it must be hard."

"We just keep going. That's good enough."

"Sometimes you get desperate enough to think you might do something, don't you? I know I do." The cat curls itself against Alice's leg.

"Get out, cat," she says. "No, Maude. I don't get desperate. Never do I get like that."

"But nobody could blame you if you did," Maude says. "Living on your own can give you some quite peculiar thoughts."

The door opens and Lenny comes in. He holds his hand up to Maude.

"Look, Maudie," he says.

"Don't call her that," Alice says.

"I don't mind," Maude says.

"But I damn well do," Alice says. "He can learn your name like everybody else does."

"Look," Lenny says.

"Lenny, go to your room," Alice shouts.

"Look, Maudie," Lenny says. He goes to her, puts his hand up to her face.

"Lenny," Alice shouts. "I said go to your room. I meant it." Maude puts her hand on Lenny's arm.

"You have to do what your mother says, sailor," she says. Lenny rubs the back of his hand. "Do what your mother says, Lenny."

"It hurts, Maudie."

"It doesn't hurt at all," Alice says. "It's just a slight burn. He just likes to make a fuss."

"It's a big burn, Maudie."

"Lenny," Alice shouts. "Go to your room. Go on, get out of here."

"Mum put on a plaster. She cried. I didn't cry."

"That's not true. Go to your room." She grabs his arm.

"Ow, that hurts."

"It doesn't hurt at all," Alice says. "Come on with me. You're going to your room."

"Don't want to go. Don't want to go," he says. "It hurts, Maudie."

"It doesn't hurt," Alice says. She gets him to the door.

"Can't go yet," he says, using his weight to stop her.

"Why not?"

"I want to say good-bye to Maudie."

"Say it, then."

"Not here. Have to say it over there."

"No, you'll say it here."

"Over there."

"It's all right, Lenny," Maude says. "Say it to me from there." Lenny waves.

"My hand," he says.

"Your hand," Maude says. Alice drags him out of the room.

"Bastard," she says to him as they are walking up the stairs.

"Bastard," Lenny says.

"Shut up," she says.

"Bastard," Lenny says. "Bastard, bastard."

"Go into your room," she says.

"Won't," he says.

"Don't be a bad boy."

"Careful!" he says.

"Shut up, Lenny. Now get in there. Go on."

Inside the room, with the door closed, she takes hold of his hand and snatches off the plaster.

"Ow," he says. "That hurt. That hurt, Mum."

"Good," she says. "That's what I wanted it to do. You can cry as much as you like but you're staying here and you're going to cry quietly. I don't want to hear another squeak from you. I'll burn you again, son. I promise it. I'll burn you more next time."

"Good boy," he says.

"I'll do it, Lenny. I'll really hurt you. I promise it. You mustn't say things to Maude. You mustn't say things to anybody. And you mustn't talk about what happened today. You promised it. And don't mention the bloody helmet. Shut up about it. If you don't you'll have to go back to the woman in town. It'll come to that. You don't want that, do you?" He starts to cry. Puts his head against her shoulder. She pushes him away.

"I won't be nice to you unless you promise to be good. Do you promise?" He nods. "Say it, Lenny."

"Promise."

"What do you promise?"

"Promise to be a good boy. Careful!"

"Does your hand hurt, son?" He nods.

"It'll hurt worse, much worse, next time. Don't say anything." He sits on the bed. He holds up his hand.

"I'll come back up and put on a plaster when Maude has gone."

"Good boy," he says.

She goes downstairs. Maude is sitting at the table.

"Sorry," Alice says. "He gets a bit out of control if he doesn't get his way. I have to be strict."

"He's a handful. It must be a strain to have to deal with him all the time. Susan's a handful, a stupid girl. She doesn't know what the real world is about, but she can be left to herself. You get no rest. You know I can take him off your hands, if you like, from time to time. I've told you that before and the offer still stands."

"I find it difficult to let go. I know what he needs."

"Do it," Maude says. "Let him come down a bit more. It'll give you a break."

"I can't," Alice says. "Maude, do you think you could leave now?" Maude stands up. She smiles.

"It's still raining," Alice says. "You'll get wet."

"I'll be all right," Maude says. "I've got my raincoat."

"Maude," Alice says. "I'm all right. Everything's all right. Honest." Maude struggles to put her raincoat over her head. She pulls it straight with her good hand.

"You do what you have to do," Maude says as she goes out the door.

33.

He licks his fingers. They taste sweet, but not sweet as well. You can have that, two things together. He looks at the picture of the woman on the video box. She pokes her ass out, in front of him, turned round, like she's in the room. She's wearing knickers. Nothing on her top, anybody can see. Her back is nude. He strokes the picture. It makes him feel funny. She doesn't mind. She says you're a funny boy, Lenny. He says it's all right. I'm a good boy. She says you're a good boy, Lenny.

The girl opens her eyes wide, as wide as she can, like it's a thing to do. You can do it to me, she says. Just like Jimmy, he says. Yes, she says. He says, you're Jimmy's friend. He says do you know about the lorry with the vids? She says yes, of course, Lenny. He says will you show me? She says yes. She holds his hand in town and when people ask he says she's his girlfriend. He takes her to the pictures to see a film. She gets scared but he doesn't. He puts his arm around her. Chicks like that. He goes to the toilet before they go in so that he doesn't have to go again. Do you want to go to the toilet, he says to her when they're watching the film, because he doesn't want to, not at all, and she says no, and he says, neither do I.

Well, that's all right, then.

And after the film they stand on the corner and wait for the lorry and it comes and it drops the vids and she waves at the driver and he waves too and the driver says hello, I know you, both of you. You're Lenny, Jimmy's friend. The girl doesn't have a name. Sometimes they don't. She says to the driver this is my new boyfriend. We went to the pictures. We didn't go to the toilet, not once. Not when it had started.

He strokes the picture and puts his face as close to it as he can and still see her. She's wearing knickers but you can see through them. You can see her ass. Why doesn't she wear proper knickers? When she's his girlfriend he'll say you have to wear proper knickers, my girl. Don't you cheek me. I'll deal with you for my pains. But not all the time.

He touches his hand. It hurts. Mum shouldn't do that. It's naughty to do that. Maudie says it's naughty. She would say it if he told her. Maudie wouldn't wear knickers you can see through. But she will let him fuck her. Maudie has a bad hand and a bad arm. Mum says she doesn't really. But she does. He asked Maudie and it's true. If you burned the back of her hand with a cigarette it wouldn't hurt her because she couldn't feel it. Maudie told him that. He wouldn't burn her hand. He's a good boy. Careful!

He goes to the window. It's dark and it's still raining. He could be in the car now out on the ring road, gunning it, gunning the motor down the ring road, doing it hard. He wouldn't take Jimmy. He's not allowed. Sometimes though he takes him. Jimmy's his best friend.

He looks through the window. Rain shines, silver patches on the road like mirrors you can look in. He sees Susan running in the rain. He waves. She doesn't see him. He knocks the window and waves some more. Susan, it's me up here. Look. She's busy running. He taps the window, hits it as hard as he can. If he had a hand like Maude he could hit anything with it and it wouldn't hurt. He'd surprise people. Hurt my hand, go on, but they couldn't. He'd laugh then. It's a trick, he'd say.

Susan stops opposite the house under the light to bend and get her breath. She stands up straight and sees him and waves. He waves back. It's me, Susan, he says. She waves again. Come up here, he says. She puts her hand up to her ear. Sometimes Susan talks to him but she doesn't know many things, not like Maudie. Don't go, Susan. I want to talk to you. I can tell you things if you like. She told him the village is different from other places a long, long way away. She says people in the village are stupid. Sometimes she goes away for a long time, on a plane and a boat and a car and a coach, which is like a bus. You get off one and get on another. You can do that if you like. They have tickets.

Susan writes things down on pieces of paper and hands them to people. Sometimes they don't like what she writes. Susan says they're stupid, they don't know any better. Sometimes they do. She's a good girl, really. She doesn't wear see-through knickers. Sometimes she says he's stupid. He doesn't like her then. She says it with her mouth funny. If the wind changes you'll get stuck like that, Susan.

He likes the woman on the vid. She wears red see-through knickers. What color knickers does Susan wear? Once Susan handed out pieces of paper in town. He wanted to go with her but Mum wouldn't let him. Susan didn't care. He would have handed out the pieces of paper, just like Susan, as many as Susan. He could do it. She said she didn't care if he did it or not.

Susan says men are a waste of space. She says things have got to change. She says rich people run the world. They've got lots of money. He says he wants money. She says you don't know what you're bloody talking about. She swears. What do you want money for, Lenny? What would you spend it on? She says he doesn't need it. He says he'd get some boots like Jimmy's. She says he's just got some new boots. She says he paid for them out of his own labor and that's the best thing of all. He says he could wear his new boots one day and then the boots like Jimmy's another day. There's nothing wrong with that. She says he thinks he wants to do this but he doesn't really want to. He says he wants boots like Jimmy's. She says, no, he doesn't, not really. He says, yes, he does. Jimmy's boots are great. She says he'll find out in the end that he doesn't want them. But he does.

Careful!

Don't go, Susan. She's walking up the road. Soon she'll be running. She has to be fit. She says she wants to change things. He said he changed his car. But he didn't tell her why. He pushes his head against the window to watch her, straining to see her as she starts to run but she's gone. Susan, don't go. I want to talk to you. There are things I want to tell you. It's a secret, Mum said. I want to tell you. I could, if you wanted.

34.

She switches on the light and walks slowly up the stairs. She doesn't want to do this but there's no other way. The stairs are steeper than they should be. The ceilings are high. She wouldn't live in a house like this, not if she had the choice. And there's no need to live in it now. But things aren't like they should be. Should be is full of traps.

She stands outside the door. She has no plan. She believes in spontaneity, just like Lenny. But who the hell is she kidding? She agonizes over how she lays the table, over the color of the plates, over the next move. She couldn't play chess, and Harold loved to, couldn't play it because she was paralyzed by the possibilities in it, the moves, frozen by choice. Harold sneered at her.

The chessboard and pieces are stored in a drawer in Lenny's room. Sometimes Lenny takes them out and plays with them. He calls them soldiers. He lays the pieces on the board where he likes. Not frozen by choice, he can place them straddling the squares. He asks her to play his own silly version of the game but even then she is intimidated by the possibilities.

She stands outside the door. The worst thing

would be to think that this was a mistake. There is no going back. All she has to do is to claim her son. She wants him to invite her in. She can hear rain on the window and on the roof. Sometimes the roof leaks in this room. She does nothing about it. Some parts of her life are beyond her control. She can acknowledge that. Sometimes, just sometimes, when desperate enough, she can draw the line.

She does her best. She serves in the bookshop. She makes meals. But Jack is always there, when she's washing up, when the soap lathers, when her hands are raw.

She steps into the room, switches on the light by the door.

"Jack," she says. She has to tell him, get it over with. "I've wanted to talk to you for ten years. Will you talk to me now? Please open your eyes. I made you some tea but it got cold. The bloody woman from down the road called in. I've got some bread and cheese. I know you like that. I'll get it in a minute. You must be hungry. Maude Edgecombe is a pest. She won't leave me alone. She wants to know what's going on but I can't tell her about this. How could I? I was just coming up when she tapped on the window. Do you remember when you played out the back? I would always watch you from the window, keep one eye on you, to make sure you were all right. Of course I looked out for Lenny as well. He was younger than you. It's nothing to get worked up about. It's nothing to feel jealous about. I think I'll have to get that bread and cheese. You must be starving.

"You could have told me you were going. It might have been difficult but I wouldn't have stopped you. I wanted the best for you. You could have discussed it with me. After all, we were close. We were close, weren't we? I know there was that business about eating but that was something that all kids do. I didn't mind that. I let you get on with it. I didn't say you had to eat with us. What was that all about? Tell me.

"Perhaps the bread's a bit stale by now. I didn't cover it. I should have. That was a silly thing to do. Shall I go and get it? Are you hungry? It's raining cats and dogs. Do you hear it? Remember when we used to play up here, you and me? You were frightened at first but you got used to it. We never told Daddy, did we? Do you think he ever wondered where we were? I didn't care what the place was like then. It could have fallen down, for all I gave a damn.

"Daddy didn't like having kids. It worried him too much. That was why he did what he did. There was always something to worry about with kids, like you getting hurt or upset, or not having the money for food or clothes, or when you want a pet and you can't have one because a pet is too much of a responsibility, and clothes that have to be bought and there's so much that can go wrong with clothes. You know that, don't you? But you don't know what a worry it can be. Well maybe you do. It hurt your dad. He couldn't take it.

Careful!

"But I don't have piddling worries like that, not now. I've not worried these past ten years over things like that. I have bigger worries about destiny and fulfillment, about lives that are lived. I want to contain it all. You do see that, don't you? I want to put my arms around it, around you all, around the house and everything in it, however much it isn't what I really wanted it to be. Because I'm holding on. I can't let go. It isn't the plates with the yellow borders, or the way the knives and forks are laid out, or the washing up. It isn't that. It's bigger than that.

"You do see that my worries were not like your father's? What worries I had were about the sort of life that has to be led to go beyond what it is. I know a light can shine and that everything can change. I know that. You look at Lenny's face. That's what it's about. There's something there. I can see it. You will, too.

"No, Daddy didn't want kids. It scared him so much it made him do what he did. He was a selfish and cruel man. And to do it like he did. Just think. It could have been you who found him in the bathroom. That could have happened so easily. What the hell did he think he was doing? He could have done it at a time when you were not here. Lenny was too young to open the bathroom door. You were the one in danger.

"You must be hungry. I think I'll get the bread and cheese. I'll cut some more bread. I like freshly cut bread, don't you? But perhaps you don't. How do I know what you like now? You're married, I suppose, with a wife, a nice wife, who cooks for you. Kids, maybe. Yes, kids. I can see you with kids. There's nothing wrong with bread and cheese.

"Before I fetch it I've got a question. What made you join the police? I've nothing against them but it just seems so unlikely. But I do know why you came back here. No questions about that.

"That gag must hurt. I'm sorry, darling. But I have to keep it there. I'll take it off when I've got the bread and cheese. I'm so glad that you're not struggling."

35.

He stands with his cheek pressed against the window. The glass is cold. He licks his fingers. It's a different taste to other ones. He might lick the car in a minute. If he wants to. He talked to Susan through the window. She heard him. She is gone now. His hand hurts. He would have told her his hand hurts but she wouldn't have touched it. No, she wouldn't. Not like Maudie would. Susan doesn't do things like that. Her face is different from Maudie's. Her eyes are different. Susan doesn't talk much to him. She never touches him.

Sometimes Maudie touches his head, touches his scar. He doesn't touch it. It just came. That's what Mum says. It's funny when Maudie does it. She stands behind him and he feels her hand, her fingers, the end of her fingers, on his hair. It tickles. He doesn't mind. It's only Maudie. Maudie's going to let him fuck her. She is. She said.

Susan never comes into their house. She won't. She says there isn't time. Mum wouldn't care about a thing like that. But Mum doesn't like him talking to anyone else. He knows she likes it when he cries. Sometimes he likes it too. Tears are warm. He likes it when they play

Careful! But not all the time.

Sometimes Mum doesn't burn him. She hits him. It's only a game. You're in a toy shop, Lenny. What do you do when you see something you like? I get it. Careful! I get it and keep quiet. Careful! I stroke it, it feels nice, but I don't pick it up. It feels nice, Mummy. Careful! Only three Carefuls! Lenny. You've lost the game. You don't get the chocolate. That's not fair, Mummy. I want more than three. Naughty boy. I'm not a naughty boy, Mummy.

All right, one last chance, son. What do you do in the toy shop? I don't know. You don't touch. I know that, Mummy. It was a trick, honest. Oh, you naughty boy, here's the chocolate. And she gives it to him. He knew she would. He likes it because it tastes so good it stings the top of his mouth. He takes it to his bedroom to eat sitting on his bed. Mum lets him do that. He looks at the cover of the video. That bitch. She would want his chocolate. She can't have it. It's his.

He licks the window. It tastes funny but he likes it. He can't see Susan. Perhaps she'll come back down the road and he'll wait and call to her. He doesn't like her, but he does, both at the same time, like sweet and not sweet. He wants her to come in, up to his bedroom. That would be good. Susan would sit on the bed. Does she wear knickers under her shiny shorts? He thinks she wears knickers under them. She'll tell him when he asks. She'll show him too.

Careful!

He wanted to wear the helmet. He drove the car. It's not fair. He was going to wear the helmet because the policeman said he could. The policeman had a radio in the car. It talked to the other policeman. He could talk to it if he wanted. It's CB. You have to talk and then you say "Over," and then they talk back. "Roger, Roger." I want to wear the helmet, Mum. Careful! You naughty boy. You naughty, naughty boy. I'll burn you. "Roger, Roger. Over and out."

He doesn't like cigarettes. They make him feel like puking when he smokes one. He's old enough. It looks good. He wants to smoke. Jimmy smokes. Jimmy rolls his own. Jimmy lets him do it sometimes, but it's hard. Jimmy doesn't smoke the ones he makes. He tried once and it fell apart. Jimmy laughed, so it was all right. They both laughed. Jimmy said he was a ratbag. He liked it when he called him a ratbag.

He tried to roll one once when Jimmy wasn't there, when he'd left his tin. It got all over the floor. Jimmy didn't laugh. He called him a cunt. He didn't mean it. He didn't mean to spill it. It was a trick. He isn't a cunt.

He pushes his forehead against the window. It's cold. His hand hurts. He goes to the door and opens it, looks along the landing. Don't leave your room, Lenny. You're a naughty boy. But he's not. He knows the policeman is up the stairs. He's sitting on a chair. His hands are tied because he's naughty. That's what you do to naughty boys. He has a scarf in his mouth. He isn't cold. Mum put it there.

The light is on now, pushing out the dark into the shadows. He walks up the stairs to the top room. It's a good job he isn't wearing his boots because someone would hear him. He gets to the door. It's closed. The policeman will tell him where the helmet is. It's only a game. It's a trick. Careful! Mum says it's a game the policeman wants to play. I want to play, Mum. You can drive the car. Can I wear his helmet? No, you drive the car and do as I say. It's not fair. You drive the car, Lenny.

He is only an outline now. He is like Maudie says. You fill it in later. There's nothing inside. You draw the outline, sailor. The rest will follow. The rest is special. Maudie says he has to do this with her because it's good for him. He says it's only a game. She says, yes it's only a game, but do it. He fills in the outline with paint but only after he's finished and says he's finished. Are you sure? Are you sure? Start again.

Maudie says it's easy to think that you know what you see. He says he sees it. She says he's right but he has to keep doing it to make sure. I don't bloody want to do this anymore, Maudie. It's boring. You finish it now that you've started. He doesn't take the paintings home.

When he did the first one Maudie said take it home to show your Mum. Mum said what the hell are you doing in her house and what's this? She's getting you to do this to find out about us. That interfering bitch. She wants you to paint us so she knows. Nobody paints us and gets away with it. He didn't tell her after that. Careful!

He's at the door now. The policeman won't mind. He opens the door. It squeaks. It's dark inside but he knows where the light switch is. He does it and then it's light. The policeman looks at him. He looks back at the policeman. This is part of the game. He's not to say anything. He didn't say anything in the car. The policeman's hands are tied. The scarf is in his mouth, tied tight around the back of his head. Perhaps he doesn't like this part of the game. Perhaps he wants to blow his nose or scratch himself. He can't do it because his hands are tied in the game.

The outline he doesn't like, the one he won't paint, the one he won't tell Maudie, is the one in the park with the swings. He doesn't go on swings. He could if he wanted, but he doesn't. Inside the outline there is white. There's nothing there and nothing will go. It makes him sick. It makes him puke his guts up. Like he's been smoking, which he hasn't. No, he hasn't. He could if he wanted. He could roll one.

Sometimes something is there. He doesn't tell Mum. He told her once. He told her but she cried. Listen, Mum, listen. Don't cry. Listen, I'm talking to you, Mum. What's in the space, Mum? I don't mind. It doesn't hurt. Oh, that woman, that bloody, bloody woman.

"You said I could wear your helmet. I heard you. I

can wear your helmet if I want to, can't I? You'll let me. Mum says I can't." The policeman nods his head. He can't talk because there's a scarf in his mouth. He could talk if he took it out.

"Careful! I'm not allowed. I mustn't talk to you. I've got to stay in my bedroom. It's not allowed. But it's a trick. Mum doesn't know I'm here. You won't tell her. I can get mad. I've got a temper. I killed a rabbit once without my Belter. I picked it up and squeezed it. I throttled it. I've got muscles. Look." He rolls up his sleeve and shows the policeman the muscles in his arm. The policeman nods.

"You aren't allowed to talk. You've got a scarf in your mouth. I saw you eating sandwiches in your car. My car's outside. I'll show it to you. But you can't see it now. Hah, that's a trick. It's a trick because I took you in my car. You saw it. I don't like the dark. Mum says I mustn't talk to you." The policeman nods.

"I can wear your helmet, can't I? You said I could." The policeman nods. "You tell me. I don't know where it is. Is it here? It's all right. I won't hurt you. I could hurt you a lot, enough to make you cry. I did that to Jimmy once. He was teasing me. He took the car keys, the Metro, not the BMW. He wouldn't give them to me and I had to go home. He kept them behind his back. I squeezed him. It wasn't as hard as I could. He dropped them. He swore then and he was crying. I saw him crying. He said it was something in his eye but he was crying. I could have told him he was a crybaby. I was going to see Maudie. He shouldn't do that. I can wear your helmet, can't I? Where is it?" The policeman moves his feet. He's wearing black boots.

"I got boots. I got them in town with Mum. Vids fall off a lorry there. I want some cowboy boots now. Mum says I can't but I don't see why I can't. Two pairs of boots. It's my money. You can have two pairs of boots. She says I don't need them. I do. Jimmy's got cowboy boots. They've got pointy toes but they don't screw your toes up. Mine are Doc Martens. Yours are too. I bet they're Doc Martens. You can tell easy." He steps closer to the policeman. He can see the bruise on his neck now.

"Look at this burn on my hand. It hurts. It hurts more than your bruise. Mum did it. I didn't do it." He walks over to the window. He can't see much on tiptoe looking out. The window slopes back at him. He looks up and sees himself, like in a mirror, only it isn't.

"Susan runs up the road. D'you know Susan? She lives with her mum down the road. Her name's Maudie. I like Maudie. Mum says I mustn't. But I do. It's all right. I can do what I like." He goes back to the policeman. "You've got a bruise on your neck. You're a naughty boy. You'll get into trouble. I could hurt you if I wanted to. I'm strong. I've got muscles.

"Where's the helmet? You said I could wear it. Mum says I can't go to work tomorrow but I can go if I want to. I've got to stomp on the crates. I burn them. I stomp on the crates in my boots. I bought them in town. Where do you live? Do you live near here? Do you go home in the police car? How fast does it go? Does it do a ton? Does it do a ten twenty? I could take the scarf out if you wanted me to but only if you tell me where the helmet is.

"I've got to go now. I need a pee."

36.

His head hurts like hell. His tooth hurts. Damn Lenny, hitting him like that. And it was only three hours until the end of the shift. And then he was off with Nancy for a week in Madeira. This time of the year is best but it costs. Still, it isn't the cost, not when you're working things out.

His neck hurts like hell, his head worse, and his tooth must still be bleeding. The kid doesn't know, and just as well. But he'll have to know sometime if this is to end. Damn him. And him not knowing is no compensation at all. Three more hours and he was out of it. She'll be cursing. Typical. How could this be typical? How could it?

The gag's too tight. Come on, Lenny, take it out. He can't breathe, not with his sinuses like they are. At least he can see now that Lenny left the light on. He won't eat, not even if she does take out the gag. He's eaten his last meal here, ever!

Remember his training. What fucking training? Besides this isn't your typical hostage situation, is it? Who the hell knows? Who would bother to tell a copper on the beat? He's compromised all the way down the line. But the sergeant won't see it like that. Nor will any of the others. They've got no imagination. That's what stops his promotion, his bloody imagination because he knows there are always other ways of doing things. Always something else. That's the trick. That's what they don't see. He'll never get anywhere. Mother hates him. You don't run out on your mother. The first law of life.

Imagination. His imagination was kicked into life the day he opened the door. Went to the bloody bathroom for a pee. Why didn't he pee in the toilet downstairs? Why did he have to come all the way upstairs? What for? Why did he open the door? He could have peed against the wall of the barn. He often did that. It wasn't dark. There was no reason not to go outside. He liked peeing outside. Why did he go all the way upstairs?

He was inside the bathroom, desperate for a pee, before he saw him. The door was closed, and he'd locked it as well. Why did he do that? He couldn't open it again. Dad was in the bath, his head down on his chest. Dad, look at me, talk to me, Dad. I can't open the door. Help me, please. Why was the bathroom so tall? Why was it so narrow? Why did it make such a noise? Dad, don't do this.

The soap was on the end of the bath. Dad had folded himself into the water. He didn't take up much space at all. Dad, the soap is on the end of the bath, if you want it. His skin was white, whiter than the bath. Can't you find the soap? You want it, Dad, don't you? You do want it, Dad. Dad, you want the soap. I'll hand it to you.

Careful!

It'll be all right, then.

Please, Dad, I can't get out. I can't open the door. I need Mum, to tell her something. I can't open it. Why are you there, Dad? The soap's there. I can't open the door. I can't look, Dad. I can't turn around. He was turning the knob and pulling but the door wouldn't open. I'll tell Mum. She'll open it. You don't want that, Dad.

Why was there so much noise? What was wrong with the door?

The water was red. Water isn't red. It wasn't like water at all. It was like soup. Was it hot? Was it cold? He wouldn't turn around. He couldn't. He wanted to open the door. Dad, I'll tell Mum.

He didn't. The door opened easily. He didn't tell Mum. He went to his room and sat on his bed. He was cold. He still wanted to pee. His father was in the bath. He didn't tell Mum because that would make it more than it was. It was nothing. All Dad had to do was to pick up the soap. It'll be all right, Dad.

He sat on the bed. He felt sick. He waited for a long time. He heard his mother climb the stairs, walk along the landing. He heard her open the door, go into the bathroom but that was all he heard. She made no other sound. She didn't shout, she didn't scream. But was that because he didn't hear it? Did Dad pick up the soap? Was Dad scared to pick up the soap?

He waited. It was like one of those days where you sit and look at your feet, when the sun shines and dust motes drift, and there are pains in your body, in your arms and legs, and in your tummy. It was like days where there is nothing to do at all. But it wasn't like that really because there was a stillness that was a taste in his mouth.

He sat on the bed but she didn't come. He sat on the bed and waited for people to come, all sorts of people who would talk and talk and it wouldn't matter. He sat and waited but she didn't come. What was she doing?

Later his mother tried to talk to him but he knew what she wanted to say and he wouldn't listen. She wouldn't tell him what he wanted to know. Besides, he couldn't hear her. He heard water running in the pipes, he heard the creak of the walls, he heard water in the bath but one thing would not connect to another. She wanted to talk but there was nowhere in the house he wanted to be with her. He wanted to pee but he couldn't however much he strained, straining under the trees and up against the wall of the barn and in the toilet downstairs.

No policeman uses imagination. Don't believe what they say. They wouldn't use their imagination, even if they could, not when there are rules and regulations to cover whatever it is. That's what's important. It isn't like they say it is on telly. It doesn't go with the job. No detective ever uses imagination. He uses contacts if he's got any. Imagination gets in the way. When I want imagination sonny, I'll ask for it. Yes, Sarge. When I want imagination I'll ask for it but I won't ask you. Yes, Sarge. The day I ask you for imagination will be the day I fucking leave the police. You got that, sonny? Yes, Sarge.

He won't talk to her. What could he say, what could make a difference? Nothing makes a difference. Ten years makes the difference.

Damn, his head hurts like hell. Nancy will be waiting. It only goes to show, that's what she'll say. I knew it. I knew it. It only goes to show. It's late. She'll be in the kitchen, leaning against the draining board, smoking and scratching her arm. A week in Madeira costs a bomb, especially at this time of the year. A week to sort it out, between them. How do you sort out five years in a week? He won't talk to her. Not when she takes out the gag. He won't say a word.

There was a cutthroat razor by the soap, one he'd never seen before. An old razor with a shiny blade spattered with rust, a smooth black handle. Dad must have cleaned it up. Where did he get it? Would it have happened if he hadn't found it? Did he come across it? Is that how you get the idea? Does the idea form if the impetus is not there? Or did he make up his mind and then go looking?

She's coming up the stairs. He won't talk to her. There's nothing to say. The door opens. It's Lenny. He's back.

37.

The policeman moves his feet. "I can, if I want to. I can. I can go to work tomorrow. Mum says she won't let me." The policeman nods. "Have you got a pain? Does it hurt?" The policeman nods. Lenny lifts his hand.

"Look at my hand. Mum burned it. She told me not to tell. You won't tell, will you?" He walks to the window. It's still raining. Tomorrow, if he doesn't go to work, he'll go to Maudie's to paint. Susan will be there. He has things he wants to ask her but he can't remember.

"My hand hurts," he says. "It does. It's true." He can't see anything out the window. It's dark now but rain still goes on the glass. He touches the glass. It's funny you can see through glass but you can't feel through it. If you can see through it you ought to feel through it.

"Mum said I had to do it," he says. "But it was a trick. I had beans and mashed potatoes for tea. I hate chips. Careful! I'm a good boy. Mum says I'm a good boy." The policeman nods.

"You'll let me wear your helmet. You said so." The policeman nods again.

"Does your head hurt? It'll be all right. You mustn't play with it. I don't play with my hand. It'll be better

soon. Maudie told me that. It isn't a trick." The policeman stretches his legs. He knocks his shoes, the heels of
them, on the floor.

"Doc Martens," Lenny says. The policeman tries
to bend forward but his hands are tied to the back of the
chair.

"You can't do that," Lenny says. "It's not allowed.
It's naughty. You're tied up. It's not a granny knot." He
walks over to him.

"Why is it a granny knot? Have you got a granny?
That's a joke Mum said. I have a granny but I don't see
mine. She lives a long way away. Does your mum hurt
you? Does she make you sit up straight? Does she?" The
policeman shakes his head. Lenny laughs.

"You can't talk. You've got a scarf in your mouth.
Shall I take it out? Does she make you use a knife and
fork? Does she say you can't go out? Does she say you
can't go to work? My mum hurts me." The policeman has
short hair. Perhaps he has to have short hair to wear a
helmet. Perhaps the helmet doesn't stay on with long
hair. He's got short hair. Lenny wants his hair really,
really short, like Jimmy. And an earring.

"Short back and sides, please. That's what I say.
But I'm going to have a crew cut. Mum said so. I'm going
to have a number two. Jimmy's got a number one. Mum
said I could, then she said I couldn't. She lied. Does your
mum lie? Where do you live? Have you got a girlfriend?"
The policeman knocks his shoes on the floor.

"Keep quiet. Don't do that. It's not allowed. Jimmy hasn't got a mum, not anymore. She died. Mum said he never had a mother. That isn't true because I asked him. He told me. Is your mum dead? I'd cry if my mum died but she's not going to die. She won't die, will she?" The policeman has big feet.

"I take size ten. That's quite big but Mum says I have small feet for my size. Do you have big feet? They look big. Do you think I could wear your shoes?" The policeman nods.

"Can I have a go?" The policeman nods again.

"No, I can't because Mum's coming. She said I wasn't to come in here. Do you live in a house? Would you like to live here? You could. We could go out in the car together. I could let you drive. We could be friends. Jimmy wouldn't mind." The policeman shakes his head.

"Why?" Lenny says. "What's wrong with that? This house is good. It's convenient. Mrs. Wyatt says I live convenient. Do you live convenient? I bet you don't. Jimmy does. He's my best friend. You're not. You could be."

Lenny walks to the back of the room. There are dark corners there. He hates them. The other room, the cupboard, that Mum locks him in is the same. From the top to the bottom. He stands behind the policeman and sees the bruise on the back of his neck. He moves around to face him.

"I could take the scarf out of your mouth if I wanted to. I could untie you. You could come down to my room. I live here. It's all right. Would you like to live here? You could come down to my room and watch a vid. If you lived here we could be friends. I could show you all the places. I expect you could work on the farm. I could talk to Mr. Wyatt. There's lots of bedrooms here. You could sleep in one. We could be mates. We could play together. I could take you out in my car." Lenny walks to the door, puts his hand on the knob.

"If you lived here you could drive my car," he whispers. "I'd let you drive it. Down to the shops or to the town or anywhere. But I'd have to drive it most of the time because it's my car. They won't make me go to the town to live again. I'm a good boy. They can't make me."

The policeman groans.

"Don't do that. Mum'll come. She'll be angry. You don't want Mum to be angry with you."

The policeman groans again, knocks his heels on the floor.

"What do you want?" Lenny says. "Are you hungry? I can get you some food. What do you want? Why do you have to be such a trouble?" The policeman is looking at him. He won't stop looking at him. He closes the door. He has to get away. He could have reached up and drawn on the window with his finger, but he didn't.

38.

"Did I leave the light on?" she says. "I was thinking of you, I expect. I'm sorry I was so long. I got caught up with things. You know how it is." She puts the plate down, crosses to the window, and stands there.

"There are no curtains up here, but it doesn't matter. No one can see us. You'd like that, wouldn't you? They're looking for you, you'll be pleased to know. I can't see how they'll ever find you. Not unless they know who I am, where we live. But I don't think you've said anything about that. Not on the forms, not on the interviews. I guess you wiped out this life. I'm right, aren't I?"

He won't move his head, he won't indicate. But she can wait. It's not as if there's anything urgent that needs doing. He doesn't look any different. But how would she know? He looks like he looks. He looks like his father's son, that hunted demeanor, that keep away, I don't need you expression. Well, he won't get away with it now.

"How do I look?" she says. "Do you think I look that much older? Have I kept what I had?" She stands closer to him.

"You bailed out. You wiped it all away. You wanted a clean slate. Fucking hell, don't we all?" She wants to touch him but she can't do it, not yet.

"I suppose I have to take the gag out, if you're going to eat. No one will hear you if you shout. But you know that. Lenny doesn't know you. He doesn't remember. What do you think about that? I suppose that's how you want it. I suppose you believe that going away allows you to forget. Well, you're going to remember it all. You're going to talk to Lenny. You're going to be the brother he doesn't know he has.

"Who the hell did you think you were to run out on us like that? Without a word. Don't you think it hurt me? What about all those years I spent bringing you up? I don't want this to sound like recrimination but you weren't there. I don't know how else to put it. I loved you. Did I love you more than Lenny? How the hell do I know? It's a question. I bet it's a question you asked yourself. Well the honest answer is I don't know.

"I missed you. I missed you so much when you'd gone. I thought we were friends. I know there was the eating apart, and the spats, the arguments, but beneath it all I thought we were real friends. And I thought that was more important than love. I didn't have to put my arms around you and tell you I loved you. Anybody can do that."

She points at the plate of bread and cheese on the floor.

"If you're going to eat this then I have to take off

the gag." She walks around behind him. Stops. Touches the bruise on his neck.

"I'm sorry," she says. "Lenny doesn't know his own strength. I'll bathe it later." He shakes his head.

"Don't be like that. I won't take off the gag if you're going to be like that." She could put her arms around him, push her head into his hair, smell him now. Maybe it would make up for everything. She could kiss him on the top of his head like she used to. He bends forward.

"You must be stiff. You must want to stand up and walk around. I'm sorry, I can't let you do it, not yet. I hope that I'll be able to, son. I really do." She goes over to the window. On tiptoe she can just see the streetlamp shining on the wet road.

"I missed you," she says. "And it didn't get easier. I needed someone to talk to, to share it. Where were you? I wanted a friend. You know I don't make friends. Who was there to help me think what I think? Lenny couldn't help, bless him. I couldn't live without him but he wasn't what I needed, not living here. I wanted someone to share it with. I hated it here, I still do. But once you'd gone I was frozen. I couldn't move. I couldn't make a single decision. I should have sold up and gone but I couldn't. I worried that you wouldn't know where I was if I left. I know you can leave forwarding addresses but it wasn't enough. You see, I didn't give up. I couldn't. You're part of me and I'm part of you.

"Am I any different? Would any mother do that? I

think so. I know I embarrassed you. I know you hated the house. But that wasn't my fault. It was your father's doing. He didn't know what it was going to be like to live in a place like this. That's why he killed himself. That's what I think and I'm sure of it. It was too much for him. His trouble was he settled for too little. He didn't want to try. He was intimidated by everything. That's the last thing I wanted.

"One other thing. You're going to have to decide about Lenny. About what you want to tell him. You're the one who has to live with it."

She lifts her arms, starts to try to loosen the knot.

"I'm not sure about this," she says.

39.

You tell a cowboy by his gloves. Ken Kesey told him that at his ranch in Oregon. He helped him rope a steer, hold it down to inject it. He visited him the year after he left home. Went from one coast to the other. You don't tell a cowboy by his boots. Nor his gun. You tell him by his gloves. How do you tell a policeman? How the hell would he know? He's not a good policeman. It's just a job, something he fell into.

And Nancy. She was accommodating. He wasn't used to that. He was used to demands. She wanted an easy life. But she changed. Was it something he had done? Now she wanted him to live for her. Didn't want to go out. Left her job in the library, too scared to issue books. Too much at stake in the stamping of a book. Too much at stake in leaving the house.

He applied for the force. The money was good. He could have stayed working in the parks. It was good enough. But she said he was capable of more. She liked to see him in his uniform. Said it made her feel safe. She said there was too much fear in the world. She said he was there to put that right. Sometimes her hands shook when she talked. They still do.

Careful!

He does not tell her that he stays away from things that scare him. That he knows when to be deaf, dumb or just plain stupid. When not to hear a message. When to be somewhere else. When to park in a lane for his own good. Most policemen are like that. He has learned these things. No, he does not tell her.

She clings closely to him at night, not for sex, but for warmth, security, the smell of him. That's what she says. She doesn't like sex. It's too much of the moment, too much of being who she is. Each moment weighs heavily on her. It can go any way it wants to, it can explode. There is too much at stake. Sometimes in the daytime she takes off her glasses to talk to him. He asks her to put them back on. He doesn't like to see her vulnerable, to see her squint. But you like me without my glasses, she says. Put them back on. Please.

His mother stands behind him. She wants to take off the gag but she can't do it, not yet. He doesn't want her to do it. There's too much to decide when she does.

You tell a cowboy by his gloves. You tell a policeman by what he doesn't do.

40.

It's late but he doesn't want to stay in, not now that the rain has stopped. He won't drive. Mum'll hear the car. He'll walk down the road again. He knows it in the dark. He's not scared. He's a big boy now. He could fight anyone. Even in the dark. There's nothing there to scare you. No, there's not. He could walk anywhere. He could walk and walk and walk.

Susan lives down the road. She doesn't talk much. He might tell her what Mum did to him. He could if he wanted. But he doesn't like her. Once Susan said everyone had a right to work. Maudie told her to shut up. He told her he works on the farm. Susan said she knew that. She asked him how much he was paid. He didn't know because it comes in an envelope. Mum doesn't take it. He gives it to her and she opens it and gives it back. He said it was in an envelope. Susan laughed. Maudie told her to shut up. He works hard. He gets paid. He doesn't give it to Mum. He gives her the envelope and she gives it back. Everyone does that.

He asked Susan what she did. She said she was working to stop people starving. She said she was working to stop greedy people getting lots of money. He said he wanted to do that. She said it was hard work. He said he could do that. He could lift heavy weights. He could lift sacks of fertilizers. He didn't tell her about the stuff in the car but she made a face. It looked like there was a funny taste in her mouth.

He walks down the road even though it's late. When he walks in the puddles he splashes. His feet don't get wet. They're good boots. When he walks on the verge at the side of the road in the long grass his feet don't get wet but his trousers do. It doesn't matter. Mum doesn't know. He won't tell her. It's a trick. Sometimes Mum cries, but she won't die.

Down the road past the gate where the cows are. They're not there now. Cows will chase you. He's not scared. Mr. Wyatt's cows are all right, but he doesn't get them in for milking. Mr. Wyatt does that. Once he did. They didn't chase him. Mrs. Wyatt was there. He helped her. The cows aren't in the field. They've left. He crosses the road at the gate. The light shines on the road on the other side. The light shines most in the puddles. It isn't raining now.

He doesn't mind getting wet. Sissies are people who mind getting wet. He can get wet. Sometimes Mum tells him not to get wet. He doesn't care. He does what he wants. He's not a sissy. Sissies cry. Maudie says that men cry but he doesn't think so, not really, not like women. Once Jimmy got his finger caught in the door of Mr. Wyatt's truck. He didn't cry, he could see he didn't.

Jimmy's a man and Lenny's a man as well.

Mum cries because she's a woman. He looks after her. Don't cry, Mum. She doesn't have a husband. He died. That was his father. He died in the house. He doesn't remember. He wasn't alive. It was before that. Sometimes he remembers things. Mum won't die.

Down the road past the two houses together where the big dog lives. He crosses over. He's not scared of dogs but he doesn't want them to bark. Down past the tall hedge. You could live in a hedge. He saw a man in a hedge on the farm once. He crawled out and walked across the field. He had a bag in his hand. He told Mr. Wyatt. Mr. Wyatt said where, show me. He showed him. Mr. Wyatt said it was always something, somebody, why didn't they leave him alone? The man wasn't there but there was a space in the hedge where you could live. It would keep you dry. If he didn't live in the house he could live in the hedge. Mum won't die. He could live in the hedge if he wanted. Mr. Wyatt wouldn't mind. It'd be dry there. When it rained. No dogs could get him and no cows. But he doesn't mind them, the dogs and the cows.

Down to Susan and Maudie's house. Susan is Maudie's daughter but Maudie doesn't talk to her like she's her mum. Susan doesn't talk to Maudie like she's her daughter. They argue but it's all right. They shout at each other but it's all right. Maudie doesn't hurt Susan because, my boy, there's no need for it, so that's all right. Put that in your pipe and smoke it. I don't smoke,

Careful!

Maudie. Jimmy does. Sometimes I roll his cigarettes.

He opens the gate. He might play a trick but it's dark. It's late. He's glad there's a light over the door. He could ring the bell and run away and they wouldn't know who did it. They might be scared. But he won't do it. They might be scared.

Maudie opens the door. Her bad arm is crossed over her waist. He wants it to be all right. If she touches him he won't mind.

"Lenny," she says. "You again. It's late. Come on in." Susan's sitting at the table playing with a computer. She's doing things.

"What are you playing?" he says. "I know about computers. I learnt it at college. I went to college. I can play games."

"No, I'm not playing a game. I'm writing a letter."

"Why are you writing a letter? Games are better."

"There are some people who want to make too much money. They don't mind what they do to get it. They're going to knock an old building down. I'm trying to stop them."

"Shut up, Susan," Maudie says.

"I don't write letters," Lenny says.

"Not many people do, these days," Susan says. "But it's a good way of proving you've said something. If you don't, they deny they've heard what you said."

"I could say it," Lenny says. He knows Susan has a nasty taste in her mouth. He'll bring her some mints.

"Lenny," Maudie says. "What are you doing down here? You know your mother doesn't want you down here and it's very late."

"Mum," says Susan. "It's his life."

"I like it down here," he says. He likes the computer. You can play games. This one's got writing on it but it doesn't matter because you can change it. He knows that. You press a button.

"Don't touch," Susan says. "I haven't finished yet."

"Careful!" he says.

"What's wrong with your hand?"

"Careful!"

"Lenny," Maudie says. "You have to go home. Your mum doesn't want you down here."

"She's my mum. I want to stay. My hand hurts."

"What's wrong with your hand, Lenny?" Susan asks. "What happened to it?"

"Leave him alone," Maudie says.

"It hurts," he says. "It does."

"Lenny," Maudie says. "Don't keep on. You're all right."

"How did it happen?" Susan says. "It looks bad."

"Susan," Maudie says. "Shut up. It's Lenny's secret. It's a secret, Lenny, isn't it?"

"It's a secret," he says. "It's a trick. Tricks are good. Tricks are good fun. Mum doesn't like tricks."

"Lenny," says Maudie. "You know we like you, don't you?"

"I like tricks best," he says. "Susan, have you seen my boots?" He wants to tell Susan about the video, he wants to tell her about work. He wants to tell her about the policeman. But he knows that he can't. Why can't he? What's wrong with that?

"Lenny," says Maudie. "You have to go home. Come on."

"He doesn't have to if he doesn't want to," Susan says. "He can stay here as long as he likes."

"You don't give a damn," Maudie says. "You think you do, but you don't."

"I know enough to want to help him, don't I, Lenny?" He nods. Sometimes he likes Susan. She talks to him. He'll take her in his car. She'll wear her shorts in his car then he can see her legs all the way up to her ass. She would point her ass at him and pull down her shorts, if he asked her, so he could see her knickers. Women are like that. They don't do it if they aren't asked, Jimmy says.

"When have you ever wanted to help him? You don't want to help him," says Maudie. "You want to help causes, not people, not real flesh and blood people. You're scared of them. Leave him alone. That's how you can help him."

"That's nasty, Mother. Come on, Lenny, I'll walk you back up the road. Let me save this first." She presses a button on the computer. It makes a beep. Careful! She presses another button. "That's it," she says.

"Leave him alone," Maudie says. "Stay away from him."

"Come on, Lenny," Susan says. "Don't hang about." She switches off her computer. It beeps again.

Maudie touches his arm as he passes her. He wants to stay. It feels warm when she touches his arm. It goes all the way up to his shoulder. Maudie is going to let him fuck her. When Susan goes away.

"Take care, Lenny," Maudie says. "You take care. We'll do some drawing tomorrow, or the next day."

"I'm staying home tomorrow," he says. "I can't go to work. I'm not allowed."

"Why's that?" Susan says.

"Susan, shut up," Maudie says. "You don't know when to shut up, do you?"

"All right, all right," Susan says.

"Paint, not draw," he says. "I want to paint."

"You come down when you can," Maudie says. "But not if your mum tells you to stay at home. I won't have that, Lenny."

"Come on," says Susan. "Let's get out of here." She pushes him in the back. It doesn't hurt.

"Take care, Lenny," Maudie says.

"I'll take care," he shouts. "I will, I will. I'll take care, Maudie. I'll take care. I will."

"Come here, Susan," Maudie says. She whispers in her ear. Susan shakes her head.

They walk up the road together. Susan walks fast. She could be his girlfriend if she wanted. He would let her. He likes her. Sometimes he doesn't like her.

Careful!

Sometimes he does. They don't do it if they aren't asked.

"Don't be afraid," Susan says to him under the light. "There's nothing to be afraid of." He's not afraid. The puddles shine. He can walk through them if he likes. His feet won't get wet. Past the house with the dog.

"I'm not afraid," he says. "I'm not afraid of the dark. But I don't like the dark in the cupboard, in the corners, not when I'm in there. But I'm not afraid, Susan."

"What cupboard?" she says.

"I'm a good boy," he says. "Careful!"

"What cupboard, Lenny?"

"I'm a good boy, Susan. I won't hurt you. I could hurt you but I won't. I killed a rabbit. You're not supposed to hurt women."

"What cupboard, Lenny? Does she lock you in a cupboard?" They're standing in the road outside the house. He stomps his feet.

"My feet don't get wet," he says. "Not in the puddles. It's my boots. Look."

"That light up there," she says. "The one at the top of the house. I've never seen it on before. What's that, Lenny? It must be the attic."

"I'm a good boy."

"You're a good boy. Why is the light on?"

"Careful!"

"Why is the light on, Lenny?"

"I can walk in any puddle I like. My feet don't get wet. My mum doesn't mind." He likes the puddles shining when he's standing with Susan. He likes it better than when he's on his own.

"Susan," he says. "You can be my girlfriend. I won't hurt you. You can wear lipstick. I like lipstick when it shines."

"Thank you, Lenny. But I don't want to be anybody's girlfriend. Boyfriends and girlfriends are not where it's at. It's nice of you to ask."

"Don't you want a boyfriend? Lezzies don't have boyfriends. They have girlfriends. That's what Jimmy says. Are you a lezzie?"

"You tell Jimmy, whoever he is, to come and speak to me. I want a word with him."

"Jimmy's my best friend. He's got cowboy boots. He's got two pairs of boots."

"Why's that light on, Lenny? It's never on."

"You can wear your shorts in my car. I'll take you for a drive. I like your legs. Do your legs go up to your ass, Susan? You can wear lipstick, shiny lipstick."

"I never wear makeup, Lenny. I don't like it. I won't wear it. It's degrading. What's that noise, Lenny? What's that noise?"

"Careful!" he says. "Look at me, Susan, I'm stomping in the puddle."

"What's that noise, Lenny? Who's that shouting? Who is it? Who is it? What's that noise?"

"Watch me stomp, Susan. Watch me stomp. Watch me. Watch me."

41.

She won't take off the gag. It isn't right to do it yet. She walks around to face him.

"I can't take it off. Don't look at me like that. I'm not doing this to hurt you. It's your fault it has to be like this. You could have told me what you were doing." She thinks he is thinner than she remembers. There is no need for him to be so thin. If he'd stayed it would have been different.

"Look at you," she says. "I want you to be all right. That's all that matters to me. And Lenny to be all right, of course.

"Look at me. I'm not going to hurt you." If only she could place her hand on his arm.

"I used to watch you playing out back. I wanted you to do whatever you wanted to do, but I had to make sure you were safe. It's where to draw the line. I wanted to be hip and let you run wild. I tried it. I had friends in the old days, your father didn't want to know them. Their kids were the same age as you. Those were the friends who said you were either on the bus or off it, you know, what Kesey said. I tried it. I remember you naked, dirty as hell, not washed for a month, scabs on your knees, your elbows, and worst of all scabs on your face that wouldn't go away. But I knew you weren't happy. I knew none of the kids were happy, nor their parents. They wanted to be free but it hurt them. I remember their faces. They thought they were in a state of bliss, the parents, something that went beyond happiness, when all it really was, and anybody with an ounce of sense could have told them, they were in pain. Their bodies were stiff with pain. They mistook it for pleasure. It's an easy thing to do.

"I cared for you. Can't you see that? Everything I did, I did it for you. I know you wanted a life of your own. But you were so young to want it. Say something. It's been a long time."

She begins to untie the scarf. It has to be a significant gesture, but now it's taking too long. She pulls at the knot. It won't undo.

"I can't do it," she says. "I'll have to get the scissors." She knows she is crying. "No, I won't. I'll do it. You'll see. I'll do it. It's not as if I'm helpless. That's what you always thought, but I'm not." She pulls at the knot, she pushes, she digs in her fingernails. She pulls and yanks his head back. She walks around again to face him.

"Your poor face. I'm sorry. They're looking for you. I'm not going to hurt you. I love you. You know that." She pulls at the knot. It seems so solid. She is sure she didn't tie it like that. The bruise on his neck looks pretty sore. His teeth must be a mess. Lenny didn't know what he was doing. How could she ask him to do that?

"It's coming. I've loosened it." And then it's easy. She's separated the two ends but still she won't let go. He is bridled like a horse. She holds them there, not telling him.

"It's nearly done. I'll soon have it." She pulls back, gagging him.

"Nearly there, Jack." She holds on.

He is a small, smart kid. She is at the window watching him play. She is bathing him. She is setting a plate in front of him. She is holding him in her arms, nuzzling him, smelling him, sun on his skin, the warmth of the small boy. She is squeezing him hard, until he cries. She is holding him, holding him.

"There," she says. "It's done." The ends of the scarf pull apart. He takes a loud, deep breath, releases it. She walks round to face him.

"Before you say anything," she says, "I did this because I missed you. I missed you like I was crazy. That's all. When I saw you I had to do it. I'm your mother, you can't get rid of that. I'm sorry about the bruise, I'm sorry about your face. Lenny doesn't know his own strength. Don't be angry with him. Or with me. We love you."

She lifts her hand to stroke his cheek. He jerks his head back.

"Don't be like that, Jack. Talk to me. I'll untie your hands and feet. Just talk to me first."

He looks down, looking anywhere but at her. He used to do that as a kid. Always looking down.

"Come on, say something. I'm your mother. It's been ten years. You must have something to say. What did you think when Lenny walked up to the car? Did you recognize him? Did you know it was your brother? Did he speak to you? Come on, say something, anything, please."

He sighs. He did that when he was a kid. He shouldn't have done it then, he shouldn't do it now.

"Don't do that, Jack. Talk to me. There's a lot to say. You can tell me. Come on. It's exciting. You know it is."

She pulls his chair around to face the bed. It takes a lot of pulling and a lot of scraping the floor.

"It's all right," she says. "I can do it. You're light as a feather. What does that wife of yours feed you?" She sits on the bed.

"We've got time, son. They'll never find you here. Isn't that great? Talk to me. Tell me how you feel. After all this time."

He closes his eyes.

"Look at me. Don't ignore me. I'm not going away. There's a lot that needs saying." She leans over, puts her hand flat on his chest. "The uniform suits you." But then she has to stand.

"My god," she says. She is crying hard now. "My god."

Careful!

She goes out, closes the door, stands on the landing in the dark. She doesn't want to cry. She wasn't going to. She was going to talk, smooth it all out, turn things around. After all, this is what she has waited for.

In the moment, in the heart of Lenny's moment, right in the center where it happens, you stay there and it comes right. You don't want to let go but you have to because there is a letting go in all the best moments. But you don't let go so that you lose the moment, you let go enough to make it happen.

She stands on the landing and waits for something to happen. What can happen? She doesn't know. It's good to wait. She listens. She thinks he is angry. He had enough anger as a kid, he must be angry at her now. For everything and everything and everything.

"I'm coming back in," she shouts. "I want you to talk to me. That's not bloody well too much to ask." She opens the door.

"Maybe we can talk if I don't face you," she says. "It might work that way. That's what I've been doing for the last ten years." She picks up the plate.

"Here," she says. "Have some of this. I won't untie you, not yet. I'll feed it to you." She takes a piece of bread and squeezes it. Breaks off a piece of cheese.

"It's good bread. None of that pap. Good cheese, too, mature cheddar. You like that." She lifts it to his mouth. He presses his lips together.

"Jack," she says. "You have to eat. You haven't

eaten for hours. You must have this. Go on, take it. I'm your mother." She pushes the bread against his lips.

"Just like you. That's what you were always like. You haven't changed. I was hoping you'd have grown up a bit. I was hoping we could get things sorted. Eat it, go on. Eat it." She puts down the bread and picks up the cheese.

"Try the cheese if you don't want the bread. It's good cheese. I got it in the village shop. You remember? Come on, eat it."

When he was a kid and first decided not to eat she pressed the food on him. It didn't work. He was as stubborn as she was. They fought over it until she reached a point where she was so worried she capitulated. She never did that with Lenny. Poor old Lenny. He got the brunt of it then and he gets the brunt of it now.

He won't eat. She isn't going to let it get to her. There are other ways. It isn't the only thing.

"All right," she says. "If you won't eat then at least we can talk." She sits on the bed, her knees close to his.

"I missed you every day . . . every day, right up to now. Do you hear me? I expected you to return. I thought you wouldn't be able to make it on your own. I waited at the back door, at the end of the drive, in the village, expecting to see you. I knew you had to come. You needed me. You would miss me and you would miss Lenny. It was too strong a pull. That's what families are about, aren't they? And you were only sixteen. How could you cope on your own? And why did you bloody do it?"

He turns his head. She knows he has so much to say.

"Your neck, your teeth," she says. She shakes her head. He moves his shoulders. "I can't take the rope off. Not yet, you know that. Not just yet. Talk to me." She knows what's going on in his mind. It's so obvious. It's so easy for a mother to see.

She remembers him on a beach, then in the water up to his knees. She remembers how he waded in deeper, not disturbed to be lifted by the water. She remembers how she waded in herself and picked him up, his body small in her arms, much too small for so big a sea. She remembers how she deposited him back on the beach, how she screamed at him then. She remembers how Harold looked the other way and how it was the people on the beach who looked at her. She remembers his tiny body, how he shivered, how he cried.

She remembers how she wanted him to tell her what he was doing but how he wouldn't say a word. What the hell, she said, and there was nothing more to say. She rubbed him as hard as she could with a big beach towel, buried his body in it, but there was nothing that would rub away her anger. He pushed his head out of the towel to stare at the sea.

She wasn't a bad mother. She wasn't uncaring or insensitive. It was quite the opposite. She put him down then and screamed because there was no way out of this thing. Harold said nothing and did nothing and she had only contempt for him. He sat on the blanket, staring at the sea. Jack stood shivering in the towel where she had placed him.

She walked up the steps to the esplanade, her voice screaming inside her head. It was like the sea, what had happened. It was too much, too big to know.

"Talk to me, say something," she shouts. "Who the hell do you think you are? I'm your mother. You're no better than us. You have to say something."

"I said who the hell do you think you are? Who the fucking hell?" She picks up the plate with the bread and the cheese and throws it at the wall. The plate clatters to the floor, the bread and cheese fall softly.

"I'm your mother," she screams. "You're part of me. Doesn't that mean something? Talk to me. Go on, talk to me. Who do you think you are?"

42.

Susan looks up. It's starting to rain.

"What's going on?" she says. "Did you hear that?" Lenny sees the light shining on her face.

"It's raining," he says. "We're getting wet. Come in, Susan." He walks around to the back of the house, turns to see if she's following. "Come on, Susan. Come in now. Don't hang about." He stops under the light over the back door. He'll tell her.

"I like you, Susan," he says.

"Don't be stupid," she says. "Get inside." She pushes him. "What's that shouting?"

"I like you, Susan. I like your legs."

"Get inside. Go on."

"I'm not going to work tomorrow. It's a secret."

"Go inside."

"I like you, Susan. I do, I like you. I've got a new car."

"Get out of the rain."

"I'm a good boy. I am a good boy, aren't I, Susan?"

"How the hell would I know? Go on, go inside." She pushes him. She shouldn't do that. He wants her to put her hand on his arm so that it feels warm, all the way up to the shoulder.

"I like you, Susan." She pushes him again.

"Don't hurt me, Susan. You won't hurt me, will you? My hand hurts. It was burnt. Look."

"Let's get inside."

"It's not allowed."

"What do you mean, it's not allowed? Why isn't it allowed?"

"I'm not allowed for you to come. Ever. I was going to stomp the crates tomorrow in my boots, Susan. I'm not allowed. Mr. Wyatt wants me to stomp the crates. We burn them. I'm not allowed." He stomps his feet on the path. "My feet don't get wet. Look. I can stomp good."

"Stop this. You've got to go inside. I heard shouting and screaming. What's going on?"

"I'm not allowed." She opens the door. He can see the white space now. It's sticky. It wants to swallow him. It's a trick. Careful! He can't drive the car. He can't go to work. He did what Mum said. He brought the policeman to the house. He hit him like she said. What's wrong? He's a good boy. He wants to lick his fingers, lick the stuff off. Susan's by the door.

"You're not allowed. Mum'll be angry. She said it because of the man."

"What man? What's going on?" Susan pulls him along the hallway. He can't walk.

"What's wrong with your leg?"

"My foot hurts. It's not a trick."

Careful!

"I know about you and your tricks. I've heard about you. I've no time for this. They sent you away, Lenny, didn't they? Come on." She opens the door to the kitchen.

"Hello," she calls. "It's only us. It's Lenny and me." There's a smile in her voice now. People can change their voices if they want to. He listens. He can hear nothing now. It's a good sign. Red sky at night, shepherd's delight.

"We can go to my room," he says. "We can watch a vid. It doesn't matter. She won't know."

"Hello," Susan shouts. When she shouts she lifts her head. He can see her throat. He could stroke her throat. He'd like to do that to see if it's soft. Sometimes he strokes Pat's throat. It's soft, but not as soft as Pat's ears. Pat the dog, pat the dog. Get it? Susan's ears aren't soft.

"Hello," Susan calls. It's not his fault. He's hasn't done anything. He didn't say. Susan goes out of the door to the front hall and calls up the stairs.

"Hello," she says. "It's only us. Are you all right?" She's still got a smile in her voice. Why does she have that? He kicks the table leg. It doesn't hurt. Not in his boots.

"Susan," he says. "Come here. I won't hurt you." She won't move from the stairs.

"Susan," he says. He wants to touch her face. If he touches her face it'll be all right. He's not going back to town.

"Susan, come back in here."

He can't see her now. He hears her going up the stairs.

"Susan, that's naughty. You can't go up there. Mum's up there. Do you want to see a vid? Susan, come up and see my vids. Susan, don't go up there." He's crying now and it's her fault. It isn't his fault. He drove the policeman. He didn't stop at the horse. He went to his room. He didn't say. It's not his fault. Sticky white space. A taste. The stuff in the bags. His fingers.

He walks out to the stairs. Susan is on the landing. Why is she standing up there? What is she doing?

"What are you doing, Susan?" She puts her finger to her lips. What are you doing, Susan? He says it again but he doesn't say it out loud, he says it to himself. Maudie told him that. Say it to yourself, Lenny. Don't talk. It's a good thing to do sometimes. Why are you standing there, Susan? What are you doing? He doesn't talk but he says it. He's a good boy. Careful! How long will she stand there like that? The big white space around him. It's sticky. It doesn't scare him. He's a big boy.

43.

"I didn't want to go," Jack says. "I had to."

"*It talks,*" she says.

"Shut up. You don't know what it was like." She bends and kisses him.

"I'm sorry," she says. "I love you, son." She puts her hand on his shoulder. "I'm pleased you came back."

"I didn't *come* back. You brought me."

"It seems like you came back. Anyway that's only a detail. What's important is that you're back."

"No. What's important is that you brought me here."

"You've changed. It must be the policeman in you."

"I'm not that different. But you think I'm still sixteen."

"It doesn't matter. What's important is that you're back. It can all change now. It's all for the good."

"You shouldn't have done it. It won't change anything."

"Oh, yes, that's it, go on, spoil it."

"Spoil what? Is this a bloody party or something?"

"You know, it's so good to hear your voice, son."

"Listen to me."

"Go on. I love to hear your voice."

"Mum, listen to me. You shouldn't have done what you did."

"But I didn't do anything."

"You commissioned a crime. You're responsible. It's not something you can ignore. I can't explain it away."

"Don't be so dramatic. You're my son. It's not as if they'll bother."

"I can't believe this. Be honest. They're looking for me. You don't just kidnap a policeman and shrug your shoulders and say it doesn't matter."

"But you're my son. I haven't seen you in ten years. That's what's important."

"Mum, you know what I'm talking about but you refuse to listen."

"Let me kiss you."

"Keep your hands off me. Listen."

"I want to touch you. I've dreamt about this for ten years. Let me stroke your face."

"Keep your hands off."

"You always did have a temper. Not like your father. You knew what you wanted. I like that."

"Keep Dad out of it. Don't drag him into this."

"You're right. That bastard. I don't want to talk about him."

"Untie me now. If you do that maybe we can make

this all right. I'll say I had an accident or something. We'll find a way."

He thinks of Nancy in the kitchen, smoking, scratching her arm, scuttling down the street to the off license for cigarettes. He thinks of the holiday they will now not have. He thinks of a blue sky. He thinks of how close you can be and not realize it.

"I will untie you, but not yet. I want to talk some more. It's not a crime, I hope, for a mother to want to talk to her son."

"Listen to yourself, to what you're saying. Get this into perspective. It isn't just a mother and son thing. It's gone beyond that. Unless you untie me now this will be serious."

"I can't forget you shivering on a beach. The sun shining, the smell of the sand and sun lotion, the smell of the sandwiches, but most of all the smell of you. You in my arms, me with my chin on the top of your head. I'm standing there. I'm standing there forever. That's where I am."

"Forget it, for Christ's sake. Think about Lenny. What'll happen to him? He's your son as much as I am."

"He's your brother. He needs you."

"He doesn't know I exist. He forgot me years ago."

"He didn't forget. It was knocked out of him. I won't untie you until you think differently. He's your brother. You can change his life. You can make him realize who he is. You can sit there, tied up like that, and see how you think after a few days."

"Lenny knows who he is. There's nobody going to add to that. Untie me."

"I'll untie you when you see sense. Ten years haven't done much for you."

"That's what you know of it."

"Why did you go, son?"

"It's obvious. Nothing's changed. You were too bloody difficult to live with. You wouldn't let me forget. You couldn't get over it. You blamed yourself, you blamed me. I was sick of it. I couldn't cope. I was too young."

"So you ran out on us?"

"It wasn't running out, it was running away. I was too young to run out. I wasn't too young to run away."

"Do you know there's a light that shines on everything, that seals it, and makes it what it is? That's what I've come to understand."

"Gone religious, have you? When did this happen? I always thought there was a chance."

"No, I don't see it as religious. It's something to do with Lenny and what he is, what I am with him. I'm cruel to him, I know that."

"What is it you want? My forgiveness?"

"I just want you to know. I want Lenny to be what he can be."

"You think that he can be shocked into being himself. You think there's another Lenny, don't you, the one that you first knew, the one he was going to be? There isn't. He is what he is. There's no other Lenny."

"You don't know anything. You don't know what it's been like. You ran out on us. You ratted on us."

"Mother, I feel sorry for you. I'm glad I got away."

"So, why did you come back? Why move back to town? You could have stayed right away. There was something that was calling you."

"I saw an ad. They wanted police in this county. I didn't think it would mean moving back so close. In a year or two I could have moved on."

"No, it's not that. You say it is, but it isn't. Something inside you brought you back. You went out of your way to get back."

"You don't know the half of it."

"Well, tell me."

"There are other people in the world besides you and Lenny."

She hits him, hard on the cheek.

"Christ, what's happened to you?" she says.

44.

Susan runs up the stairs, away from him. She has long legs.

"Stop it, Susan. Don't go up there. It's not allowed. It's naughty. Come down here."

He follows her. She's going up the top stairs now.

"Stop it, Susan. You're not allowed." She opens the door. She doesn't care what she does. She writes letters.

"Susan, you mustn't go in." She opens the door. It isn't allowed. He stands outside. He won't look. He's a good boy.

"What's going on?" Susan shouts and then she laughs, but it's not a nice laugh, not with a smile.

"Susan, why are you laughing?" he says. "Stop it." He catches hold of her arm and pulls her. She's strong. She gets away and goes into the room. He follows. She has to behave herself. Behave, my girl.

"Bloody hell," she says. "What's all this?"

"Get out of here," Mum shouts.

"It's a bit late for that," the policeman says. He can talk now. There's blood on his face. It hasn't gone away. It might have. It won't stay. He'll wash it.

"Shut up," Mum shouts. Don't shout, Mum.

"Kidnapping a policeman," Susan says. "That's great. What are your demands?"

"Susan, you're a naughty girl," Lenny says. "Come out here, straightaway."

"It's all right, Lenny," the policeman says. The policeman knows his name. He will probably let him wear his helmet. Probably is a funny word to say.

"It isn't all right," Mum says. "I decide what's all right and what's not all right here."

"This is great," Susan says. "I'd never have the nerve. But why? What do you want? What's the cause?"

"Get out of here," Mum says. She's angry. Her face is red. Don't be angry, Mum.

"You can't send her away," the policeman says. "Not now. Not now that she knows."

"Whose side are you on?" says Mum. "Is this what they trained you to do?"

"I just want what's for the best. Untie me and stop all this rubbish."

"What's he mean?" says Susan.

"You wouldn't understand," Mum says. "It's too complicated. Please go away."

"Naughty," Lenny says.

"It's all right, Lenny," the policeman says. "Don't worry." But he does worry. His hand hurts. Look, he wants to say to the policeman. Look at the burn on the back of my hand. Careful! Sticky white spaces.

"Go away, Susan," Mum says. "Take Lenny with

you."

"You can't let her go," the policeman says. "Think about it."

"I'll do the thinking," Mum says.

"Is this to do with the bypass?" Susan says. "But that's hardly a local issue. It's miles from here. It must be thirty miles. Why did no one think of it before? You can say what you want. They have to listen. Kidnapping a policeman. I like it. It's like Colombia."

"It's nothing to do with that," Mum says. "You don't understand."

"Well, fill me in."

"I haven't got time," Mum says.

"She's involved now, whether you want it or not, whoever she is," the policeman says.

"Great," Susan says.

"You stupid, stupid girl," Mum says. She turns to Jack. "This is Maude Edgecombe's daughter. The woman who lives down the road. They moved in after you'd left."

"Mum," the policeman says. "Let her go."

"Mum," Lenny says.

"Mum," the policeman says again.

"My mum," Lenny says.

"Look," Mum says. "You're confusing him."

"Oh, I see," Susan says. "I see what this is."

"You don't see at all," says Mum. "You don't see anything. Just shut up."

"This is a family affair," says Susan. "How disappointing. How fucking unpolitical, how fucking trivial."

"Just shut up," says Mum.

"It's so contained, so bottled up. You people need to get out more. It's so fucking rural," Susan says.

"Don't swear, Susan," Lenny says.

"There are no wider repercussions," Susan says. "It's decadent. It's downright selfish if you ask me. You might as well sit on your asses and meditate, for all the good it will do."

"Shut up," Mum says.

"I'm not interested in this," Susan says. "Local issues are important. They reflect what's going on in the outside world, but this reflects nothing. It's boring."

She turns to Mum and points her finger. She has a good finger for pointing. Don't do that, Susan. He has the white space around him, thick now. It won't go away. It's sticky.

"It might be boring to you, you spoiled brat," Mum says to Susan. "But it's important to us."

"It's important to you. Don't speak for me," the policeman says.

"Don't give me that," Mum says. "You selfish bugger. It has to be important to you. Think of Lenny."

"Mum," Lenny says. Why won't the white space go away? Why is it around his head?

"It's all right, Lenny," the policeman says.

"It's all right, Lenny," Mum says.

"This is pathetic. I'm going," Susan says.

"Stop her, Lenny," Mum says.

"Let her go," the policeman says.

Lenny catches hold of Susan's hand. She pushes him away.

"Keep off me, you idiot," she says. His face hurts. The white space is on it, sticking to it now. "I'm going."

"You're not going anywhere," Mum says. "Lenny, don't let her go."

Lenny catches hold of Susan's arm. She tries to pull away. Lenny holds on. He's crying again. His cheeks are hot. The white space is hot and sticky and covers his eyes. He likes her legs.

"Let her go, Lenny," the policeman says.

"Mum," Lenny says. "I'm a good boy, Mum. I'm a good boy, Susan."

"You're a bloody idiot," Susan says. "They'll send you away, back to town."

"Mum," he says. "They won't send me, will they? They won't."

"They won't, Lenny," Mum says. "You keep hold of her. It's all right."

45.

He isn't a policeman. Not like policemen are supposed to be. He doesn't even like the uniform. Besides, he wants to think for himself. He wants to think of the wider implications, more than just what the job entails. Like if he's policing a bypass protest, like the girl said. Why should he be doing that? A policeman is expected to uphold the law. But what does the law mean? You take a county sheriff, the one they had to deal with. What a bastard, what a pompous, self-centered, self-serving, ignorant bastard. He doesn't want to uphold laws in that man's interests. If the truth were known he wants to think more like Susan, the bitch. But not in her half-assed way. It has to be more than that.

She's right, of course. This is only a family affair. He can go beyond it now. Nancy thinks like his mother. He left home to get away from that. He doesn't want to bother with family affairs.

He needs to get his hands free. Not that he wants to do anything yet, not necessarily. It's just he can think better that way. This is nothing to do with him. His mother wanted to live her life through Lenny. She still wants to do that and she still thinks there's a chance of redemption for herself and revelation for Lenny. When will the light shine, Mum? When will the change come?

All of Lenny's life she has been looking for a revelation. Believes it will come if she works hard enough at it. It takes application. Lenny will be cured only through effort. Lenny will be cured only through her grit and determination. That's when the light will finally shine. That will be the reward. But it doesn't happen like that. There is no light, Mum. And if there is, it won't happen the way you think it will.

Nancy never thinks about the light that shines, or redemption, or alternative lives, or politics, or anything else. That was why, at the beginning, he liked her so much. And the sex, of course. But both of these things have had their day. He wants her to think. To be what he wants her to be. But that's unfair. She wants him to be a policeman. She loves it. He just wants a job.

Dad got through, just about got through. He remembers Dad in his gray suit on the beach, hands in his pockets, hands out, patting his pockets, looking for something, but he doesn't know what, patting just to make sure, just to know, just in case. So far, so good, so far, so good. Dad looking out to sea. What's out there, Dad? Nothing, son. He didn't want a light to shine, he didn't want revelation. That was too much to bear. But why did he end up in the bath, in the red, red water? Why wasn't it Mum in the bath? She was the more likely candidate.

Careful!

Dad walking down the lane, stopping for no reason. Why stop, Dad? He just wanted to touch something, something in his pocket, or one hand on the other. The feel of his skin, skin against skin. He didn't mean anything by it, any of it. You could put that on Dad's grave. *He didn't mean anything by it. R.I.P.* And Mum all the time itching, digging, scratching to know what was there.

He isn't really a policeman. The sergeant doesn't think he is. Nancy doesn't think he is really, not how she wants him to be. After this he won't be a policeman for much longer. What would Lenny Bruce or dear old Jack Kerouac think about that, Mum?

46.

He likes Susan, sometimes he does. He likes Mummy. He likes Maudie. He doesn't know if he likes the policeman. He likes his helmet. Why is the policeman tied up? The white space is all over his face and all over his head, sticking to him. There's a taste on his tongue. He wants to lick his fingers.

"Let her go," the policeman says.

"Don't listen to him, Lenny," Mum says. "You do what I say." The white space won't go away, it never does, only sometimes. It's like the spaces when he draws. Sometimes it hurts to fill up the shapes. Never mind, sailor, Maudie says. You don't have to do it.

The doctor asked him about the space. Silly doctor. It's a trick. It doesn't hurt. He's good at drawing. He can draw a dog and a house. A dog and a house together on the same paper. They could have a dog if Mum would let them. Mum says he's kind. He strokes dogs but not if they growl. The dog would sleep in his room on his bed. He'd let him. Come up here, Pat. Like Mr. Wyatt's dog. That's a good name for a dog. Pat's a boy or a girl's name. Mr. Wyatt told him. His dog's a girl. He doesn't mind whether the dog would be a boy or a girl. A girl is a bitch.

Up on the bed, Pat. Good boy. Mr. Wyatt says it's soon the end of the road for Pat. What road, Mr. Wyatt? Pat the dog, pat the dog. Get it?

The white space mixes up the other things, the drawing and the dogs and the spaces to be filled. Mum, stroke my arm, please, Mum. Mum, I won't go there. They can't make me, can they? It hurts.

"Don't let her go, Lenny," Mum says.

"Let her go, Lenny," the policeman says. Susan's pushing him. Sometimes he doesn't like Susan. He likes Maudie. He's going to fuck her. She said so. Hello, sailor. He holds Susan tight.

"Let me go, Lenny," Susan says. The white space is singing. He doesn't like it when it sings, not in a high voice. Dogs can hear high voices, high whistles, even. Pat can. Mr. Wyatt's got a whistle that Pat can hear. Lenny can hear it. It's high. No one else can hear it. Can you hear it? Stroke my arm, Mum.

"Don't hurt her, Lenny," Mum says. He holds tight to Susan's arm. She pulls at him. Her arm is thin. She doesn't have muscles. Not like his muscles. Jimmy says he has muscles. He bends his arm to show him. He keeps a packet of cigarettes in his rolled-up sleeve. That isn't a muscle, Jimmy. He flexes his muscles, that's what he says, flexes, that means makes them bigger, but Jimmy doesn't have muscles, not really. He doesn't tell him. Look at my muscles, Jimmy. Jimmy doesn't really look. He won't look. Feel that, Jimmy. All right, kid.

Jimmy says you don't let any woman step out of line. His head hurts. The white's sticky from the sacks. There's a taste in his mouth.

"Come on, Lenny," Susan says. "Don't hurt me. Let me go."

"There is no light, Mum," the policeman says. "Don't you see that? You can't make it happen."

Mum stands by the policeman's side. Suddenly she hits him on the face, where the blood is.

"You see?" she says.

"I'm a good boy, Mum," Lenny says.

"You see?" Mum says. She says it to the policeman. Talk to me, Mummy.

"That won't change it," the policeman says.

"Change what, Mum?"

"Let me go, Lenny," Susan says.

"Change what, Mum? Tell me, tell me. Change what? I'm not going to town. I'm not, Mum. They can't make me. They can't. What change?"

"It's all right, Lenny," Mum says. But it isn't all right because the white space hurts.

"He is what he is," the policeman says. "You can love him for that, can't you? If you don't, if you want him to change, then doesn't it mean you don't really love him as he is?"

"Don't hurt me, Lenny," Susan says. The smile isn't in her voice. It's something else now.

"Don't let her go, Lenny," Mum says.

Careful!

He squeezes Susan's arm. Don't let go. Hello, sailor. A bitch is a dog.

"Let go, Lenny," the policeman says. Susan's crying. He's not hurting her. She's a bitch. He squeezes her arm. Susan hits him in the face.

"Bitch," he says.

"Lenny," Mum says. The white space is sticky.

"I'm a good boy, Mum," he says. He holds onto Susan good.

"Let her go, Lenny," the policeman says.

"Good boy, Lenny," Mum says. He won't let go. Careful! Susan bites his hand.

"Bitch."

"Let her go, Lenny," the policeman says. She bit him. Jimmy says don't let women step out of line. Susan bites him again. It hurts.

"Let her go, Lenny," the policeman shouts. But Lenny hits Susan, slaps her in the face. He slaps her good. She deserves it.

"Bastard," she shouts. "You're going away. You're going away for good, you stupid fool."

"Let her go," the policeman shouts.

"Don't let her go, Lenny," Mum says. He's not stupid. He's not. It's a trick. Careful!

47.

"Lenny," he shouts. The girl screams, Lenny hits her, again and again. The more she screams the harder he hits her, his face red, drooling like an idiot.

"Stop it, Lenny," he shouts but Lenny isn't going to listen to him. "Untie me," he says. "Let me go. I'll stop him." Mum looks at Lenny; she won't look at him.

"Stop it," the girl screams. "What the hell d'you think you're doing? Let go. You're really in for it now, you sod. They'll come and take you and you'll never come back."

"It's all right, Lenny," he shouts. "Untie me, Mum, for fuck's sake." But his mother won't look at him.

"LENNY," he shouts. "LENNY, IT ISN'T A TRICK. IT ISN'T A TRICK, LENNY."

Lenny is on the swings. He's shouting and screaming and Mum is at the other end of the park, smoking and dreaming and looking far, far away. Lenny's screaming, but that's all right. It's what he always does. It won't hurt you Lenny, it's a trick. It doesn't hurt. It's a trick. Let go, Lenny. It's all right, you don't have to hold on. The swing's going higher and higher, he's pushing it as hard as he can, it's swinging its

way up, up into the blue, blue sky. Higher and higher.
It's all right, Lenny. It's only a trick. Mum's smoking and
dreaming, looking into the blue, blue sky. The chains
creak, Lenny screams, and he pushes the swing as hard
as he can. The chains creak, the seat comes back to him,
Lenny's small body coming to him, and he catches hold
of Lenny's shoulders and pulls the swing down and the
swing lifts him off his feet as it comes, a pendulum, back
up then to the top of its journey, a lull, and the sky is a
deep, deep blue, the swing holding its position, high up,
as the sun smiles down on them, and then the swing tilts,
gives a sigh, and begins its course, down to earth, and
up again, Lenny screaming, gripping the chains, want-
ing to get off but there is no way that he can do this, the
swing moves too fast and too high, the momentum too
much, the sun shines too bright, the air is too hot in the
park, Mum standing by the hedge, dreaming, too much
for Mum to think about, far too much, it's a trick, Lenny,
don't cry, you're all right, crybaby, what have you got to
cry about, don't hold on, you don't need to hold on, don't
hold on, Lenny, let go, Lenny, I tell you let go, you must
let go or Mum won't buy you ice cream, Lenny, you'll
have to sleep in the barn, Mum will shout at you, you
have to let go, you sod, let go, Lenny, let go, it's a trick,
it's a trick, it's all right. Let go, Lenny.

And Lenny lets go because he does everything his
big brother tells him, his big brother, and he is short of
breath now as he heaves at the swing to pull it down and

push it higher, higher up into the blue, blue sky, the sun bright, the chains creaking, it's a trick, Lenny, it won't hurt you, and Lenny is sitting with his hands grasping at the shining, shiny air and at the top of the pendulum swing he tilts backward from the seat, his little brother, and slowly like a dream he drops off into the space between the earth and the blue sky and the sun shines down hard, smiling all the while, and Mum is smoking, dreaming. It's only a trick, Lenny, only a trick.

Lenny is on the ground and has stopped scream-ing. Mum smokes, looking down into the shadows of a hedge. He shouts into Lenny's ear, Lenny, Lenny, it was a trick. He sees blood trickling from Lenny's ear. Lenny, you can get up now. You can get up. Hurry up. Mum's coming. Except she isn't, she's looking into the hedge as if she sees something there that she has missed all of her life. Get up, Lenny, before Mum comes. It was only a trick, Lenny. Get up. But he doesn't get up. The blood trickling from his ear won't stop. Get up, Lenny. It was a trick. You have to get up now. It's not allowed to stay down there, Lenny. You're all right, really. Stop it.

Lenny doesn't get up. Mum stomps on her ciga-rette and turns, looks to see what is happening with her bloody kids. Starts to walk slowly across the field to where her sons are playing.

"IT ISN'T A TRICK, LENNY," he shouts. "IT ISN'T A TRICK." But Lenny won't let go. He has his hands around Susan's throat and is squeezing her as hard as he can.

"Mum, stop him," he shouts. Mum smiles, tears on her cheeks. She is looking at the window.

"Mum, don't you see what's happening? Mum, he'll kill her. Stop it." Susan's hands clench and unclench. Her eyes are open wide. Lenny's face is close to hers. She can't speak now. Mum is smiling, looking at the window.

"Untie me" he shouts. "You have to untie me. You can see what he's doing." Mum is shaking, her whole body shaking.

"Mum, there isn't another Lenny. There's only the one you've got. Stop him, stop him now! Mum! MUM!"

Lenny is squeezing, squeezing, squeezing.

Susan has stopped moving. Her hands are half-clenched, neither open nor closed.

"Where's my cigarettes?" Mum says. "I see now. You can't make it happen. Either it does or it doesn't. A moment comes when it comes." Lenny squeezes Susan.

"Mum, untie me. Tell Lenny to let her go."

Mum is fumbling at a pack of cigarettes, taking one out, putting it into her mouth. The end moves too much to light it. She holds the cigarette close to the end and puts the flame to it. She burns her finger.

"Damn," she says. Lenny is looking at Mum.

"Mum, tell Lenny to let go."

"Be quiet, I'm thinking. I need to think now."

"Untie me."

"Shut up. Shut up, will you? How can I think now,

with all this fuss? All this fuss. I NEED TO THINK!"

48.

Change what? Mum, change what? He wants to know what will change. They won't send him to town, they won't, they won't! Susan's naughty. She's a naughty girl. Tell her she's naughty, Mum. She says horrible things. He's squeezing her because of what she says. It's all right. He's a good boy.

He wants Mum to stroke his arm. It's all right, Mum. He won't let her go. She's a naughty girl. He's a good boy. He is, isn't he? Susan swears. She mustn't swear. The white space is sticking to his face. Stop it. Hello, sailor. Tell him what to do. Careful!

Susan shouted. She shouldn't shout. She's naughty. Sometimes in the white space there is something else. It isn't a trick, is it? Yes, it is a trick. Sometimes in the white space there is someone else. Sometimes in the white space he can hear someone else. It's only a trick. Susan said he'd have to go to town. He won't, will he? Mum? She can't make him. She's a bitch. He doesn't want to go to town. In town they made him sit on the bed and not come down. It was cold and he didn't like the room. There were things in the mirror. He hates chips. Honest. He hates them. He doesn't want any.

He's a good boy. In the mirror it goes up and down, and up again. There's a space that shines and shines. He won't look at it. They can't make him look at it. It hurts. In the mirror it grows when he looks at it and it grows when he doesn't look at it. He won't stay in the room. He shouts and screams but they make him stay. He sits on the bed and he doesn't look at the mirror but he knows about it. There's a big mattress up against the wall that will get him.

Susan should shut up. She ought to keep quiet if she knows what's good for her. He won't let go, Mum. He's a good boy.

The white space in the mirror is singing. He won't let go. She hasn't got muscles. She's weak. The bitch.

Mum hits the policeman on the face. Lenny wants Mum to stroke his arm. He won't let Susan go. He'll hold onto her, the bitch, she's got it coming. His head hurts. Change what, Mum? What will change? What light, Mum? His face hurts. She can't make him, she won't make him, he won't let her. He's squeezing, he has to. He's a good boy. She can't make him, she can't make him. Not ever.

Susan hit him, the bitch. Hit him hard. Take that, bitch. He hit her hard in the face. She's bleeding. Well it's her own fault, he told her but she wouldn't listen, she brought it on herself. Don't hit him, he'll hit her, take that, you bitch, shut up, you can't make him go to town. He warned her. It wasn't a trick.

Careful!

Now what has she done? What has she gone and done? See what she's done. He told her. What have you done, my girl?

He won't let go, Mum. He won't ever let go. There's a trick in the mirror. He won't look. There's a mattress on the wall and he can't breathe. He won't let go.

Change what, Mum? Change what?

The bitch, the bitch.

It is a trick.

It is.

It is.

Careful!

Careful! That's twice. Look out, Lenny. It's coming.

49.

Where the hell do you draw the line? She's trapped in the doing of it, has been for years. She's lost it. There is a moment. There was a moment but she is not sure when. Somewhere between the beginning and the end.

She puts her hand on Lenny's shoulder.

"It's all right, son," she says. "You can stop now." Lenny lets go, wipes his hands on his jeans. He smiles at her.

"It's all right, son," she says. But where is the moment? Where did it go?

"You'd better untie me," Jack says.

She doesn't know where to draw the line. She never did. That's what makes the difference.

"It's all right, son," she says. And she puts her arms around Lenny. He puts his head onto her shoulder. He's too big to cuddle, for a proper cuddle. She's never cuddled him like she should. What are the things that make a difference?

"Untie me," Jack says.

Drawing a line is the only thing you can do, the only thing that makes a difference; everything you want one side of the line, all the crap the other side. It's arbitrary, it's artificial, but so what? That's the point.

She puts her hand on Susan's forehead. She feels nothing. What did she expect to feel? She tries to take her pulse but she's not sure how to do it. She squeezes the girl's wrist between her thumb and forefinger. She feels nothing, but she never could do it anyway. Christ. How is she supposed to know?

She pushes Lenny away and folds Susan's arm against her side. Straightens her leg. Death is not what you think it is. It's far less. It's inconsequential. It happens before you know it. It isn't much. It's uneventful. Not enough that you should make a fuss. Not enough for a song and dance. Harold was the bloody same, his small body in the tub, in the red water. It was all over before she knew it. Then she had to deal with it and it wouldn't be dealt with. It ran away and came back when she didn't expect it. It's not what you think it is.

Lenny puts his arms around her.

"I'm a good boy, Mum. I'm, aren't I?"

"You're a good boy, Lenny."

Lenny starts to cry, big heaves of his chest.

"There's a taste, Mum," he says.

"It's all right, son," she says, patting his back.

Jack struggles with the rope around his wrists, kicks his legs. She puts her hands on Lenny's cheeks, pushes her face close to his. "Look at me, son, come on, look at me. Are you there, Lenny?" she says.

"I'm a good boy, Mum. Don't send me to town. I

won't go, Mum."

"I won't send you to town, Lenny. I promise you I won't."

She hugs Lenny. He's crying and she cries with him. She knows the sense in Lenny is in his body, the words don't count. She holds him as hard as she can. She looks at him, straight into his eyes. Squeezes and squeezes him, holds him as tight as she can.

"My boy, my boy, my Lenny," she says.

"I'm a good boy, Mum. Careful! I'm a good boy," Lenny says.

She hugs her son, squeezes him to her.

"Lenny," she says. "My Lenny."

50.

Maude walks up the dark road from her house, up under the trees. She walks for the sake of the walk. Susan's out late. But it's all right, she's old enough to know her own mind, she's always known her own mind.

She crosses the road under the big trees to avoid a puddle. It is, she thinks, what people decide, what happens in their lives, that makes them what they are. Sometimes she thought she knew what love was. Now she is not so sure. Perhaps love is wanting people to be all right in themselves, to let them be who they are, so that the insides match the outsides, the balance, the give and take. She listens to the squish of tires on the road, a car as it goes through the village.

She speeds up, walks faster up to the big house. She does not know why she does this. She turns into the drive. Lenny's car starts up behind the house and comes quickly around the corner toward her. She steps back to avoid it.

"Lenny," she calls. "Where are you going, sailor? What's wrong?" She sees the bright red of the brake lights as the car reaches the road, she hears the back wheels spin, she sees the car accelerate down the road.

She sees the headlights licking at the trees.

"Lenny," she calls.

She runs to the back door of the house. She opens it. Why is she here?

"Is anybody there?" she calls.

51.

He stands by the phone but he won't pick it up, not yet. He isn't a policeman, not like he's supposed to be. If he were a policeman he would do it straightaway. Being a policeman is being someone else, not being weak. He wants to think for himself. That's weak, isn't it, Sarge?

Nancy would tell him to ring, would expect him to. There is no light for Nancy, no light that illuminates one thing and then perhaps all things. There is only who she thinks she is, not what she can be. She wouldn't let him get away with it. Nancy is like Gran. Nancy would sit on the beach all day and dip her toes into the water. She doesn't want kids. She won't have them. She doesn't want to think about it. No Lenny or Jack around the house. She knows about making beds and lying in them.

Christ his teeth hurt, and his neck too. Funny, the way his mother untied him, like it was such a small thing, like she really didn't want to bother at all.

He touches the phone, just to reassure himself, a connection to the outside world. He doesn't know what to say. Anything he says will be compromised by the house, his mother, his brother, his father too, for God's sake. He wants it to be what it was before, when he was parked down the lane. He had no part to play in this at all. He wants to go back. There is no going back. Christ, he can see that, he can feel it. He could always see it.

He should be on the plane, halfway to Madeira, looking out the window at the blue, blue sea. Turning to say something to Nancy, but not knowing what to say, irritated at how she scratches her arm. Christ, why doesn't she go to the doctor to see, to find out what it is? She wants to smoke. This is a no smoking flight. All flights are no smoking. It wasn't my idea, Nancy. You know that. It's the policy of the airline. You'll have to wait. Don't bitch all the time. But he won't say that.

He touches the phone. He will pick it up. Who will answer? The sergeant, for sure. Don't get clever with me, sonny boy. Just get on with it. Where are you? Tell me what happened. How can he tell him? How can he say? He doesn't know where Lenny is. He doesn't know where Mum is. He certainly knows where the bloody girl is.

Perhaps he should ring Susan's mother. She should be the first to know. But what is the number? In what capacity does he tell her? As a policeman? As a brother to Lenny? As a son to his mother? What are the words, what are the feelings that go with the words? That's the trouble, isn't it? He doesn't know who he is. If he knew, the words would be there for him to say them. Nancy gets angry sometimes, calls him spineless. But it isn't like that. Christ his teeth hurt.

He has to do something, to get this thing started,

just to get it under way. They won't want him in the force, not after this. But what could he have done? They'll tell him, they'll fucking tell him, they always do. He picks up the phone, listens to the dial tone. It sounds a long, long way away.

52.

She sits on the swing in the park, feels it move slowly forward and then back, a lull, the space in between. She looks at the sky, just getting light now, clouds but no rain. She grips the chains hard enough to hurt. She wants a cigarette but she has none and it's only a whim and there are too many of those in life.

She knows that Lenny is out there somewhere in his car, driving as fast as he can because that's always what he wants to do and she can't stop him. She knows her son, who he is, what he wants to be. She knows it fills his head, just the one thing, one thing at a time.

She knows about the light now, the one thing she wanted. She saw it when Lenny had his hands around the girl's throat. She saw it and she knew it for what it was. There is no one light that shines, no one light that does what you want it to do. Rather, it is a light that shines through all things, through every single thing, every single moment. You can't pick and choose. It is there all the time and you see it or you don't and she didn't want to see it for what it was. Lenny has a light that shines, that makes him what he is. There is nothing she can do about that. She didn't see it but she sees it now.

Careful!

She kicks her heels to move the swing, to move it forward and then backward, and she starts to sing a song, the good ship sails on the ally, ally oh, the ally, ally oh. She hears footsteps on the grass, the oh, so sodden grass. She sees two of them. It is just getting light now, light on the wet grass, light tipping the top of the hedge. She feels hands on her, the two of them, hands on the swing. She does not want to let go.

"It's all right," somebody says. "You're going to be all right." She is, she knows she is. Lenny out there somewhere, out on the road in his car. I love you, Lenny, my son, I love you, my boy.

"It's all right. You have to come with us now," one of them says. She sings again as the swing rocks forward, rocks back, rocks and rocks. It is getting light. It will be all right. It will. Light on the grass, beads of light, white light, light on the tops of the trees.

"You'll be all right, Alice. You'll be all right, darling."

"I'm nobody's darling."

"You'll be all right, love."

"Have you got a cigarette? Just the one? And a light?" She sings, just because she wants to. The good ship sails on the ally ally oh, the ally, ally oh, the ally ally oh. Oh, yes it does.

53.

Careful! This car goes as smooth as hell. Fucking good car. If Jimmy could see him now. It's got the power. Grip the wheel. Grip it tight for the feel. Grip the power. Go faster. It's dark. Down through the tunnel of the lights. His lights are bright. Everyone can see him coming. Look out.

Good old Maudie. Can't talk to her now. Got to go. Careful! If only Jimmy could see him. Look, Jimmy, how fast this goes. It's never been so fast before. Where are the vids, Jimmy? But not now. He hasn't got the time. The taste in his throat hurts, he has to go fast to get away from it. Get away from the white. And he won't touch the back of his hand. It heals quicker that way. Don't touch.

He's not stupid. He's not dumb. He's not silly. He's a good boy. He does what Mum says. But he can do what he likes, too. He can drive far away if he wants. The pain in his guts is back. If he drives far away it will go, he can leave it behind. He won't lick his fingers. He will lick his fingers. He won't. He can drive as far as he wants. He can drive as fast as he wants. He can. It isn't a trick. No, it's not.

If he goes he may not come back. They won't see

Careful!

him crying. Men don't cry. Jimmy did. The policeman won't see him. He's not going to town. He's not going back. They can't make him. Mum says he's not going back. He's not. He doesn't like chips. He doesn't have to eat them. He likes mashed potatoes.

The white's come back, sticking to his face. It won't go away. He'll go faster to get away from it. He'll put his foot down, yes, he fucking will. Down through the lanes and out onto the big road where he can go as fast as he likes. Put his foot down hard. Put his boot, his good boot down, hard, push it to the floor.

Careful! This car goes as smooth as hell. Foot down to the floor. Headlights on the fields, the trees, the hedges. People can see him coming. Look out. Bright lights on the filling station, the bakery, the sign at the corner that says where things are. Past the supermarket and out onto the dual carriage way where the yellow lights shine. Past a lorry, past the cars. Through the green light and up the hill to the top. Faster. Faster. Faster. Faster. Faster. This car goes like hell.

It's not a trick. As fast as he can go. The white hurts his eyes. There's more white now, sticking. He can't see. Mum, he's a good boy. Yes he is. He could have cleaned the Metro. It wasn't his fault. He could have cleaned it proper. He likes the policeman. The policeman will let him wear his helmet if he asks him.

He's not stupid. Down the hill to where the road narrows, to where the dual carriageway disappears.

Richard Madelin

Down to where a line of lorries, a line of cars is going slow, too slow for him. Out of the way. He's going to overtake, he's going far away. Get out of the way, fast, faster than he's ever gone, he can do anything now, the white is all over him, in his eyes, it doesn't matter, he's going so fast, look at me Jimmy, this car is fast, it goes like hell. Fucking fast, look at me, look at me.

Faster. It's the whole white inside, filling him up, burning him. He can get past them, it's easy when you're going fast. Look at me, Jimmy. Look at me when I'm talking to you, son. The lights are there, the taste in his mouth, the pain in his guts, faster, Careful!, faster, Careful!, faster. Careful!